SEA OF GLASS

The world is fear.

The fear comes from the men in black. Daddy says it again and again: "Tommy,

"Never open a window.

"Never move the downstairs shades.

"Never talk, laugh, or cry loudly.

"Never answer the door.

"Never answer the telephone.

"Never, *never* go Outside.

"If anyone comes to the house, hide in your attic room and be very, *very* still. And you *must* obey this. If you disobey about this and give me that little smile and that twinkle in your eye, it won't be like when you should clean up your room.

"I won't get cross for a moment and then laugh.

"I will die.

"Your mommy will die.

"And the men in black will come and take you away forever."

I ask my daddy "Why?"

"Because. Just because."

Because must be a terrible monster. I imagine Because as it hovers over the world flapping its leathery wings, waiting with its great hooked beak and sharp talons to fall in swift horror upon those foolish children who venture Outside.

SEA OF GLASS

Barry B. Longyear

A Legend book
Published by Arrow Books Limited
62-65 Chandos Place, London WC2N 4NW

An imprint of Century Hutchinson Limited

London Melbourne Sydney Auckland
Johannesburg and agencies throughout
the world

First published 1987 by St. Martin's Press, USA
Legend edition 1988

Printed and bound in Great Britain by
Anchor Brendon Limited, Tiptree, Essex

ISBN 0 09 9589702

To Jean

Special Thanks
to
Tom Eastler,
Kathy Lynch, and
Sharon Webb

And I saw as it were a sea of glass mingled with fire, and those who had overcome the beast and its image and the number of its name, standing on the sea of glass, having the harps of God.

The Apocalypse 15,2

Wardate: 21:36-7AUG2033
Downlimit: 183962:59:07

100

My name is Tommy, and this is what I know:

Year is as long as it takes for Earth to travel around Sun. 365 days make up Year, except every fourth year when an extra day is added.

Day is sunrise to sunset. Night is sunset to sunrise. But Night is also a part of Day.

Day is divided into hours.

Hours are divided into minutes.

Minutes are divided into seconds.

Daddy says this. I try so hard to look like I understand but there is no Earth, there is no Sun. Because there is no Sun Mommy makes me take pills. But Daddy says there is Sun and it is Outside with Day, Night, and Moon.

Daddy says that this is the year Two Thousand and Twelve. I wonder why Year has that, or any, number.

Sun, Day, and Night are Outside with the men in black.

Hours, minutes, and seconds are kept in a box on the wall.

I must remember to ask again about Moon.

In the time called winter the world smells like burning wood. The world is both dark and light, full of love and fear.

The fear.

The windows are dark. Painted black and nailed shut. If they weren't, things from Outside might see us and get in. We must never let the Thing from Outside see in.

The light is the fireplace. It is red. And the light is the

electric lamp beside my bed, my mother's face, my father's arms. There, too, is the warmth and the love.

The world is the house.

Daddy says that the house is in a city called Peterborough, which is in a province called Ontario. Ontario belongs to a national district called Canada, which belongs to the Compact of Nations. They are curious words, but they are like Earth and Sun: only words.

I only see the house, so the house is the world.

Daddy says that Peterborough is also called Petertown, but not to call it Petertown because Mommy doesn't like the name.

" 'All the world will be your enemy, Prince with a Thousand Enemies, and whenever they catch you, they will kill you. But first they must catch you—' "

"Why?"

Mommy smiles as she looks up from the book and strokes my cheek. "Frith isn't mean. If he lets the rabbits multiply and eat up all of the food in the world, all of the other animals will starve. Frith must look out for all of the animals."

"Why?"

"Because. Just because."

"Is Frith God?"

"It's just a story, Tommy."

The world is fear.

The fear comes from the men in black. Daddy says it again and again: "Tommy,

"Never open a window.

"Never move the downstairs shades.

"Never talk, laugh, or cry loudly.

"Never answer the door.

"Never answer the telephone.

"Never, *never* go Outside.

"If anyone comes to the house, hide in your attic room and be very, *very* still. And you *must* obey this. If you disobey about this like you do sometimes when you should clean up your room, and give me that little smile and that twinkle in your eye, it won't be like when you should clean up your room.

"I won't get cross for a moment and then laugh.

"I will die.

"Your mommy will die.

"And the men in black will come and take you away forever."

I ask my daddy "Why?"

"Because. Just because."

Because must be a terrible monster. I imagine Because as it hovers over the world flapping its leathery wings, waiting with its great hooked beak and sharp talons to fall in swift horror upon those foolish children who venture Outside.

Sometimes when Daddy is watching I am allowed to use the telephone in the living room to call Mommy on the kitchen unit. The numbered buttons are black. To begin a call I must push the silver button. The black buttons are always cold, the silver button warm.

Wardate: 21:36-7AUG2033
Downlimit: 180288:01:35

99

The world is made of black marks on yellowing paper. The paper smells like dust and mildew.

It's a little girl in a red cloak being chased by a wolf.

It's a very special spider.

It's a wizard in an emerald city.

It's a circus that flies among the stars.

It's a boy and a black man drifting lazily down a river called the Mississippi. It's a knight who rescues a king. It's a lord who becomes a forest bandit.

It's a young sailor who is imprisoned. The sailor digs through the walls of his cell and finds a great teacher. The teacher gives the sailor knowledge, wealth, and freedom.

The books are Daddy's, and I am to take very good care of them. They cannot be replaced.

Daddy says he has a surprise for me. It will be here this afternoon. I love surprises, and I watch time in the box on the wall for when Daddy gets home.

Daddy teaches at a school. He teaches different things about theater. Theater is when some people get together to play pretend a story for others instead of for themselves. Daddy is just finishing up teaching History 227, which is about movies.

When I asked him what are movies, he said to wait for the surprise.

I wait.

* * *

There is a window to the universe. It is a glittering colored screen.

It calls itself the eye to the world. It calls itself the greatest communication medium that has ever existed. It calls itself mindless, a wasteland, corrupt, filthy, biased, immoral, and antigod. Once in a while it calls itself television.

Daddy is finished teaching his history, and the school doesn't want the television anymore because it's getting a new one. That's why it let Daddy buy this one.

It is wonderful.

We can make our own shows or bring in shows from Outside. I love movies. The stories, the worlds, the lives—the places I can go, the people I can be, the worlds I can see.

And I see trees, flowers, animals, and people. People. A world of people.

Children.

A world of children.

Boys and girls.

The children have other children to be with, to play with. They have friends. I want to know why I can have no friends.

"Maybe the television was a bad idea." Daddy's voice sounds very serious.

Mommy's voice sounds impatient. "You know he's different. You should have thought of that." She folds her arms. "Well? What do we tell him now?"

"I guess we tell him the truth."

The truth.

I can have no friends because the men in black will come and take me away.

"Why don't they come and take away the boys and girls on the television?"

"You'll understand when you get older. The things you see on the television aren't always true, Tommy. They're like the movies; not always true. Wait until you get older."

It doesn't seem fair, but I don't want them to take away the television because they think it upsets me so I nod. Still, it is unfair. Somehow I sense I can lay the blame at the feet of Because.

* * *

Outside.

There is the something they call Outside on the TV. They call it Outdoors, the Woods, Wilderness.

There is a part of Outside called the Grand Canyon. I would trade my life to stand on its rim for an hour.

I see a part of Outside called Space: there is Moon, Sun, Saturn, men in strange suits walking around on Mars, men in strange black crawling machines on Venus, and Stars.

Stars.

I would trade my life and a thousand Grand Canyons to go there. So would the men and women on the television. They don't think that humans can ever reach the stars. We can't travel fast enough. Our beginning, our ending, is here on Earth.

Just where *is* Outside? What is it? Is it even real?

Above Wilderness is something called Sky. Blue and red and black and orange and white and gray. Sometimes Sky will carry the huge, blinding ball called Sun.

Sky at Night carries Stars, and now I know about Moon.

They write of Sky in the books I read. It is like Heaven or Outside. It is nice to think about, but it is not something to want. If you want what cannot exist you become unhappy.

Sky is just a nice thought that an author or television person dreamed of, like the Mississippi, like Oz, like the *Enterprise*, like Wonderland.

I am grateful that there are men and women who dream up such thoughts for me to enjoy.

In the breaks between programs on the television, there is a number, and it is always the same:

21:36-7AUG2033

Sometimes when I see the news program at noon or in the early morning I see the same number. Mommy says she doesn't want to know what the number is for.

On the television they just call it "then" or "the date."

One documentary calls it the "optimum war probability projection date," and they talk about it like it was a fairy tale from ancient times.

Daddy says it's the Wardate. "It's when the war happens."

"Is it like the clock Marshal O'Niel looks at all the time in *Outlands* to see when the bad men arrive on the shuttle?"

"No. Marshal O'Niel's clock tells how much time is left. His clock is like a number called the Downlimit. The Wardate tells what time it will be. The Downlimit tells how much time is left, or something like that. And the Wardate is no movie. It's real."

"Marshal O'Niel is very real to me."

My daddy laughs and plays another movie for me. It is called *High Noon*. In it there is a Marshal Will Cain and a clock and a train full of bad men arriving at a particular time. Marshal O'Niel's story is an old one, set in a different time.

"Just because it is an old story," I ask Daddy, "does that mean that it isn't true?"

He thinks for a long time. Looking at me he says, "Being old makes it truer, but a different kind of truth. Many times we feel that to do right we must go against unfair odds, and we must fight the bad guys all by ourselves—all alone. The special kind of truth used by the two movies is that just about everyone would like to believe that, faced with the same challenge, they would do like Marshal O'Niel and Marshal Cain."

"Doesn't the world have any Marshal Cains in it, or any Marshal O'Niels?"

Daddy thinks again for a long time before answering. He gets to his feet. "Maybe. But I never met one."

Daddy says that he will get a copy of an even older story for me to see. It will have a different kind of character and a different kind of right. The character is a swordsman named Cyrano de Bergerac.

Daddy smiles and says maybe we would just like to believe that such characters can exist in the world. He says, "My daddy used to say that movies are mental chewing gum—a collection of impossibilities in a nonsense universe, massaging the eyeballs of malcontents. Does that make any sense to you?"

I shake my head.

Daddy makes a small laugh and he looks at the floor. "I guess it doesn't mean anything, except that my father disapproved of me watching movies."

He kneels in front of me and takes my shoulders in his hands. "But if we can't believe in the possible existence of a Marshal O'Niel, what happens to our desire to become better persons? If we can't believe in THX's escape, or Montag's defiance, or that we can someday reach Watership Down, what is the point to any of it?"

He studies my eyes. His eyes glisten. He laughs and shakes his head. "You don't have any idea what I'm saying, do you? Don't be frightened."

"I'm not frightened, but I don't understand. What's THX? Where is Watership Down? Do you mean the story that Mommy read to me?"

His lips repeat the question, where is Watership Down. "Where, indeed?"

He pulls me to him and holds me tight. "I love my father, Tommy. I really do. But he just won't listen. He just won't listen." He holds me out at arm's length.

"Tomorrow. Tomorrow when I come home we'll see if we can find Watership Down."

Wardate: 21:36-7AUG2033
Downlimit: 178872:21:50

98

"But after a time the rabbits wandered everywhere, multiplying, and eating as they went.

"And the Great Frith told the Prince of Rabbits, 'If you cannot control your people, I shall find ways to control them.'"

Daddy laughs and tells Mommy that Frith must think he's Aubry Cummings. Mommy gets up and goes into the kitchen.

The small rabbit, Fiver, sees a vision of the fields bathed in blood. It is coming, this horror, but only he can see it. He tries to warn the rest of the rabbits, but only a few listen. Those few leave the warren on a search for a safe place. It is a grassy hill from the top of which the rabbits can see the world. A hill is sometimes called a down, and this is Watership Down.

It's like the old book Mommy read to me at night. But this is an animated movie. Daddy is watching the story with a frown on his face. With each minute that passes, the creases on his forehead grow deeper.

I want to ask Daddy if he doesn't like the movie, but I don't ask right away. Soon I am caught up in the story, the adventures of Hazel, Bigwig, Fiver, and the rest as they find the down, get other rabbits to join them, and then fight to protect the down against the General and the bad rabbits.

After Hazel grows old, dies, and joins the Black Rabbit, I look again at Daddy. The screen is blank, yet it is as though he sees something there.

"It's over, Daddy."

He nods and repeats, "It's over." He pushes himself to his feet and removes the disc from the player. Placing it on the palm of his hand, he studies it. "Funny. Like seeing it for the first time. With a different set of eyes."

He puts the disc back into the player.

"*—the rabbits wandered everywhere, multiplying, and eating as they went.*

"*And the Great Frith told the Prince of Rabbits, 'If you cannot control your people, I shall find ways to control them.'*"

Daddy removes the disc, slowly shaking his head.

I don't know what's bothering Daddy. My head is filled with the images and ideas of the story. Frith. The Black Rabbit. The terror of the General. The bloody battle in the run, with Bigwig and the General fighting to the death.

In the dark in my bed, I think of the Great Frith, creator and god of the rabbits. The Wizard of Oz turned out to be only a man. The god of the tortured animal people on the Island of Lost Souls, the hand that struck the gong, was only a mad scientist.

But the old rabbit, Hazel, did die. And Hazel did see the Black Rabbit, and the Black Rabbit does the will of Frith. If Frith created all of the animals, then Frith created me.

Daddy climbs up the stairs and sits on the edge of my bed. I ask him, "Daddy, is Frith real?"

"What?"

"The god of the rabbits. Is the Great Frith real?"

"No, no, no." He shakes his head and smiles. "That's just a story. A cartoon."

He still looks sad. "Daddy, is everything all right?"

It is almost as though I can see the answers to my question being tested and discarded behind my father's eyes. At last he answers.

"Sure. Everything is fine. Go to sleep."

I know Daddy is lying. He is still thinking about his daddy. They hate each other. I think my daddy is trying to decide if he wants to change that.

I hope they become friends. It would be fun to know another human.

That night I hear Daddy tell Mommy about special TV discs for educating gifted children. Daddy would like to bring some for me. Mommy forbids him.

"It would be stupid! Do you think the police are stupid?"

I am not going to get the special discs.

Wardate: 21:36-7AUG2033
Downlimit: 178440:16:19

97

At last Daddy finds a copy of *THX 1138*.

On the screen is a bald man in white clothing. He is with another bald man, dressed the same, and they are running away from men with steel faces dressed in black.

"Daddy, are those the men in black?"

"No, they're only characters in a story. Not men at all, but robots. Which is not to say that the Compact Police are not robots." He laughs.

"David, you're confusing him." My mommy's voice sounds a little angry.

I watch this story. Daddy says it is forty-two years old. It is about a man who has a number instead of a name. He lives deep underground in a land without sunlight.

He has a wife that is bald and dresses the same as him. Except that she is not really a wife and is taken away, or she leaves. Another bald man, SEN, tries to take her place. Her name is LUH. THX works remote arms and takes a lot of drugs.

I don't understand almost any of it.

The only thing I understand about the story is THX 1138. He is confused. He feels lost, afraid, unbelonging, in black despair. His world has no Outside, no Sun, no purpose, no meaning.

He wants out. He wants out of everything. He wants to climb out of the dark into a sun he has never seen.

THX 1138 touches a very strange part of me, deep inside.

ugging, beeping sound. The creature's face
n expression of hope and joy as it looks toward

c, my boy!"
of a robot wheels up to the creature, its lights
hissing from a whistle on the top of its head.
s, its mouth-lights flashing, *"I have found the*

e places an arm around the machine and hugs
ould count on you, my boy. Tell me, Mac, how
the human race this time? Poison, flame,
ss lobectomy?"
face of the robot fills the screen. *"Father, ladies*
n, may I present the Twenty Thirteen model of the
d Plan. No one will ever be hungry again, and
ay have all the children it wishes! Watch." The
ds an appendage.
picks up to jingle tempo as the image changes to
of scantily-clad dancing girls, their faces painted
white, and wearing red noses, their black diamond
ng from beneath orange fright wigs.
clown chorus line dances and kicks to the superam-
usic it sings:

Burgers hit the spot,
big ounces, that's a lot.
es, fries and onions too,
y Burgers are the treat for you."

e jingle continues, the image switches to the mountain
l babies being fed by an endless belt into an enormous
r. The picture changes to show a belt lined with an
s parade of triple-decker burgers issuing from the same
ine.
n the screen appears a family of four, seated behind a
—a mother, a father, a boy and a girl—happily munch-
heir burgers, great gobs of red sauce oozing from between
patties, dribbling over their fingers onto the table and
n the fronts of their shirts.

On the box that the old movie came in is pasted an old printed opinion. The opinion says that the script is dull.

I am not sure why the opinion makes me angry.

The movies we see—the ones Daddy brings in—are all old. Many years older than I am. Some even older than Mommy and Daddy. Daddy says it's because the new movies are being fed to us by the machine. The old movies are entertainment.

I ask him what the machine is and he says to wait until I get older.

Daddy is alone in the living room watching the television. The man who talks the evening news is on the screen. He is talking about an Otherworld nation called the Soviet Union. There are pictures of long lines of grim men and women, sad hungry children.

I sit on the arm of Daddy's chair and see the tears running down into his beard.

"Daddy, why are you crying?"

"With God as my witness, I never thought it could happen. No one thought it could happen."

"What, Daddy?"

"The world. What it's become."

"What's wrong with the world, Daddy?"

Daddy hugs me, shakes his head, and cries. It frightens me to see Daddy cry. I hope he never does it again.

Wardate: 21:36-7AUG2033
Downlimit: 178272:26:33

96

My eyes open to the darkness of my attic room. There are voices and laughter from downstairs. Mommy and Daddy are watching the television. I remember Daddy talking to Mommy about the program when he came home this afternoon. Daddy doesn't watch the television programs much, only movies. But he wanted to watch tonight.

I climb out of my bed as ghostly music comes from below. Again Mommy and Daddy laugh. It sounds good. They never laugh much, and it sounds good. I want to share it.

Softly I creep down the attic stairs, feeling my way in the dark. When I come to the head of the stairs on the second floor the light from the living room below is red.

Music, laughter, a strange threatening voice. I inch my way down the steps and look at the screen through the turned posts supporting the banister.

With its left arm the horned creature on the screen lifts the struggling baby by its feet and grins at the viewers as the deafening music quiets to an ominous background roar.

The creature's right hand points a clawed finger at the viewers.

"*People of Earth.*" The clawed finger swings until it points at the child. "*Meet your enemy.*"

The baby's cries become hysterical, gasping screams. The creature cradles the baby in its left arm. "*Hush little baby, don't you cry.*" The claws of the creature's right hand dangle tantalizingly over the child's pulsating belly.

"*Aubry will love you 'til you die.*"

I gasp and hol
child's middle; a sc
dripping blood. I se
open to reveal a tin
Mommy holds her
"Isn't that a bit muc
"I just hope that ba
Daddy's voice is me
The creature's grinnin
friends. Imagine, if you w
resources your enemy emp
of muscle twitching."
The dead baby fills the s
The horned creature fling
motion the body tumbles in
upon a mountain of dead b
The heap of infant flesh q
I close my eyes. I think I an
"*What are we to do?*" The cr
are to do. I am about to go back
do.
But I don't. I open my eyes an
going to bed and watching this h
The creature's eyebrows go up i
patience. He holds out his clawed h
told you once, I've told you a thousa
much to go around. If we are to ha
pursuit of happiness, we must have
desolation! If we are ever to reach the s
our future!"
The clawed fingers come together, pa
creature prays reverently, "*I, Aubry The L*
have spoken."
The creature lifts its arms and shrugs. "*B*
babies, don't you?" It waves its arm at the
babies. "*Do you have any idea how many tur*
gave their lives to produce that?"
The creature lowers its arms in mock deject
am I to do with you people?"

The point of view lifts a little to show a young child seated and hidden between his parents. The child's eyes are wide and white with unspeakable terror.

The music suddenly stops. A voice says, "*Naughty, naughty! One child too many. Into the hopper with him!*"

The chorus line repeats, "*Into the hopper! Into the hopper!*"

The screaming child is torn from the arms of his screaming parents by brightly smiling, black-clad waitresses and tossed over a railing into the huge hopper.

There is a whine, the crunch of bones grinding. A *glup, glup* sound like when I flush the upstairs toilet.

The jingle resumes:

"Baby burgers hit the spot,
Six big ounces, that's a lot.
Pickles—"

"*Tommy!*"

I see Mommy standing, looking back at me. "You go back up to your bed this very instant!"

I run up to my attic room, jump into bed, and pull the covers over my head.

I can't see what Mommy is angry at. It's a dumb show anyway. Disgusting. Who would want to eat babies?

It's not like when they made crackers out of the dead in *Soylent Green*. Crackers aren't anything like people. Those burgers would squish when you bite them.

I don't think the show was funny, although the Devil was kind of neat. I wonder why the Devil called himself Aubry Cummings.

There is the smell of Mommy in the dark. I feel the covers being tucked in. She leans over and kisses my hair.

"Mommy, what was the show about?"

"It was a satire, honey."

"What's a satire?"

"We'll talk about it in the morning."

"Mommy, who is Aubry Cummings?"

"*Shhh.*"

"I want to know."

"He's an important man in the Compact government."

"What does he do?"

"He's the Secretary of Projections."

"But what does he *do?*"

Mommy is silent for a long time, standing there in the dark next to my bed. She bends over, kisses my hair again, and leaves the room, closing the door behind her.

Wardate: 21:36-7AUG2033
Downlimit: 178104:54:01

95

Daddy is away teaching movies, and Mommy is down trying to clean up the basement, sneezing at the dust, straggles of her long black hair dangling in her face.

The television is on, and there is a man with a very deep voice saying that Laura Wilson, you have been found guilty of violating the provisions of the 1998 Citizenship Act. Under the authority of the President-General of the Compact of Nations to carry out the orders of the Sixth Compact Canadian National District Court—

Oh, it sounds like the officer reading out the order to the soldier at the beginning of *The Dirty Dozen.*

"Private Arthur James Gardner, you've been found guilty as charged of the crime of murder. Your case has been appealed three times, has been reviewed three times, yet the verdict of each court-martial has been the same: guilty as charged. Do you have anything to say before sentence is carried out?"

Private Arthur James Gardner only said that he didn't mean it and that he was sorry.

Then the man in the white helmet pulled a handle, and Private Arthur James Gardner dropped through a hole in the floor and was stopped by a rope around his neck.

But Daddy said that was just a movie.

Mommy said not to watch movies like that, even if they are old. But how am I supposed to know that it is that kind of movie unless I watch it?

Now there is a woman sitting on a heavy white plastic throne. Tiny wires are connected to her legs, arms and head.

There are black plastic bands around her ankles and wrists and around her waist and chest. Her eyes are wide and frightened.

Sound. Her mouth opens and she calls out a name. She is calling her mother, saying, "*Please, please!*"

She screams and begins twitching, her face making funny looks. She sounds funny, too, and I laugh at her. Mommy turns off the television.

Mommy's face is very pale and her teeth nibble at her lower lip, her eyes wide and frightened like the woman in the chair.

"Mommy, what's wrong?"

"Why were you watching that?"

"It was just a show. What's wrong, Mommy?"

"Nothing. That's enough television for today, Tommy. Go play in your room."

That night I hear Mommy crying and Daddy trying to comfort her. I sit up in my bed and listen very hard. Mommy is frightened. It makes me feel frightened.

Wardate: 21:36-7AUG2033
Downlimit: 177984:02:02

94

It is the day before my birthday.

The wood stove downstairs washes my face with heat every time I pass near it. The heat moves up the stairs and gathers in my attic room. There are the smells of hot iron and smoke.

I don't find my usual comfort in the deep bed with the puffy quilt, or from the many drawings I made and pinned to the rough wooden walls. I can hardly breathe. I have seen all of the old movies a hundred times apiece.

Daddy will be home soon from work with two new movies. Mommy is downstairs cooking, adding more heat to the attic.

With my eyes closed I sit and rock on my bed, my camel lurching this way and that as Lawrence leads us across the Devil's Anvil to attack a place called Aqaba. The heat shimmers from the desert floor, washing my face, making me nod in my saddle—

It is so hot.

I get up and place my hands on one of the black-painted panes of my attic window to feel on my palms the cold from the other side.

I rest my forehead against the pane and feel the cold. I see a crack of light. It is no thicker than a hair, but there is light coming from beyond the black. I place my right eye very close to the crack in the paint.

There are shapes and blobs, foggy colors, on the other side. There is that blue color—the color of Sky.

I reach my right hand up, and with a fingernail I pick at the scratch. A piece of black paint the size of my thumbnail pops from the glass and falls to the floor.

In panic I drop to my knees and search for the piece of paint, to put it back. There are big cracks between the planks of the floor, and I resign myself to the fact that the piece of paint is gone forever.

I stand up, trying to think of something else with which to cover the hole in the paint. As I stand there, I place my right eye close to the hole.

Sky!

Endless stretches of clear blue Sky.

It is *true!*

I'm so excited, but there is a deep anger in my chest. I'm confused. I had talked to Daddy about Sky. And Mommy, too. The talk was always changed to something else.

My head comes up a little. Below Sky is Outside. Houses like on the television, broad snow-covered fields, trees, like on the television.

Very low there is a street, dirty snow heaped in ridges along its sides. Across the street is a white house with many windows. The snow and ice drip glittering jewels that sparkle in the great light.

Light such as I have never seen before. Light so bright that it hurts my eyes to look at it for long. Light like when THX 1138 climbed from the underground tunnel and was standing Outside.

I can't see the source of the light. I can't even imagine what the source would be. It could be Sun.

I move away from the hole and back up until I sit on my bed. I am stunned I am so angry. I'm trembling.

It has always been on the other side of the black paint.

Daddy and Mommy said so, didn't they?

Yes, but it was like it was something like I shouldn't *really* believe. It was—

I know I shouldn't feel this way but I can't talk myself out of my anger. Sky is *real.*

Sky.

Outside.

All of a sudden I hate my bed, my room with its wooden

walls and black-painted windows. And my parents, who withheld this great truth from me, this wonder.

Sky.

The room is even hotter. I return to the window and try to pull it open. It jiggles and I can see the heads of the nails move. The nails that are keeping me from Sky.

On the table at the foot of the bed are my birthday presents. The hammer is in the long red package. I know that. I felt the weight of the packages when no one was looking. I begged Daddy for one just like his. There it is.

I walk to the table and tear open the long red package. The hammer gleams at me, its head of burnished and black-painted steel, its tan handle of new wood. My name is burned into the handle. Thomas Windom.

I pick up the hammer, go to the window, and work the claw around one of the nail heads the way Daddy does. I pull down on the handle and the nail slips easily from its hole. I drop the curved nail to the floor and put the claw on the second nail. It, too, pulls from its hole.

I put the hammer down upon the floor, put my hands against the window, and push up. With a frightening slam it opens all of the way, icy air rushing over the sill into the room. The clean coldness of it startles me.

—Never open a window.

In panic I reach up, jump, trying to grab the bottom of the window to close it. I only meant to open it a crack. I swear if I can just get the window closed I will be good forever and will never break another rule.

I stop jumping when I realize that if I move the table over next to the window I can stand on it and reach. I start to turn, then I see that the door on the house across the street is opening.

I stop and look.

A figure appears in the doorway. It is a woman in a light brown cape and hood. She carries a bundle in her arms, and she pauses when she comes to the steps leading down from her porch. She is very old and has a kind face with wisps of white hair curling around the edge of her hood. Besides Mommy and Daddy she is the only real person I have ever seen.

Before she steps down she looks across the street. Her mouth opens slightly as she sees me. I smile and wave my hand. The woman nods her head just as Daddy comes riding up the street on his bicycle. Daddy looks at the woman for a moment and turns back to look up at me. There is a strange look on Daddy's face. He closes his eyes and hangs his head down inside the fur collar of his coat like when he pretends to be angry with me.

The woman keeps standing on her porch, looking up at my open window. Daddy gets off of his bicycle and takes a step toward the woman. She shrieks, drops her bundle, and runs into her house.

Why is she frightened of Daddy?

He pauses, turns about, and runs beneath the windowsill. He shout's Mommy's real name, Beth.

Loud talking, shouting, coming from downstairs.

I hear my name and I quickly go to the foot of my bed and pull the table over to the window. I climb up on the table and pull down the window, cutting off the bright light from the room. I turn and see Daddy standing in the doorway. He is puffing, the wild eyes and the fierce brown beard making him look like an angry bear.

"I'm sorry, Daddy. I'm *sorry*. It was only open for a very little while."

Daddy's face changes from being angry to being very sad. He is carrying a cardboard box in his left hand. "That doesn't matter now, Tommy. We have to go. Now."

"Go?"

Daddy tosses something small on my bed, opens a drawer, and begins stuffing clothes into the box. On the bed are two tiny golden discs. They contain the two movies Daddy brought home.

"Can we bring the television?"

"No."

I read them. The discs are *Moby Dick* and *On The Beach*. "Please, Daddy. Can we watch—"

"Come here." He finishes and hugs me with his right arm. "You can take a book and a toy, but hurry. Come downstairs as soon as you can. Hurry."

"What about my birthday presents?"

"Hurry!" Daddy rushes down the attic stairs without answering. More urgent words.

I look at my tiny collection of books. I want to take all of them. The voice comes from downstairs. "Hurry!"

I grab *Huckleberry Finn* and *Tom Sawyer*, wrap them in an old towel, and run for the stairs.

Mommy meets me on the stairs, picks me up, and bundles me in a blanket. Her face is so contorted I hardly recognize her. The blanket obscures my vision, and I feel myself jerked about as Mommy runs.

Her arm beneath my ribcage hurts. I cry out but Mommy isn't listening.

The door slams. Daddy's heavy footsteps running behind. I feel myself seated on Mommy's lap. Something crashes. Distant footsteps and another slam.

A whine, then I feel myself lurch back against Mommy's breast. I work a hand up and push a corner of the blanket away from my face. We are in a car, the scene outside swinging crazily around.

Outside. I have never been Outside.

The woman in the brown cape and hood is watching us through her front window.

"Can't you go any faster?"

"I'm going as fast—" Daddy's voice falls silent. The whine grows rapidly in pitch, then falls sharply, a lurch toward the door.

"Shit!"

The whine goes back up. There is an eerie, erratic whistle sound. Another lurch. Daddy's voice again, this time almost crying. "C'mon, dammit! Go, *go!*"

I hear Mommy gasp; feel her fingers digging into me.

The whine decreases slowly and I feel the car stop.

Again I push the blanket from my face. Through the window I see a black aircar with flashing blue lights on its roof. Two men are walking toward us. They wear black uniforms, caps and boots. The door opens and I feel myself torn from Mommy's arms, her screams hurting my ears.

The men in black have come to take me away.

Wardate: 21:36-7AUG2033
Downlimit: 177982:47:13

93

Shut my eyes, cover my ears, hold my breath, and the nightmare will go away. It always works.

"Don't piss on the seat back there, caster. You're only passing through; I live here."

The man in black who drives is grinning at me from the mirror. The man in black sitting on my right is a woman. "At least this one doesn't smell too bad." I look at her. She doesn't look mean. Her hair is short and blond, her eyes brown. All of a sudden she jumps at me and screams "Boo!"

I start screaming.

"Jesus Christ, McNally! Why'd you do that?"

"Aw, I was just fooling around." She pushes at my shoulder. "Shut up, kid." She punches me in the arm. "Knock it off, or I'll give you something to cry about." She slaps me in the face, but I cannot stop screaming. I am outside of my skin, off to one side urging myself to be quiet and to stay out of trouble, but she keeps on slapping and I keep on screaming. "Come on, kid! I was just making a joke—aw, shit! Fleury, pull over! He's pissing in his pants."

"Jesus, McNally, you got the brain of a fucking eggplant. Quit hitting him! If you want him to stop crying, quit hitting him." The man driving shakes his head. I watch as the woman in back slaps the little boy again, trying to get him to stop screaming. The little boy screams and cries and pisses in his pants some more.

"The brain of a fucking eggplant."

* * *

The world is a rapidly changing fog of images, angry voices, and strange faces. Some of the faces are kind, some cruel. Most are indifferent. Through the night it is a groggy, terrifying flight to a huge city. The next morning there is another screaming little boy clutching at my arm. It is a black mask that chokes me, fingers probing me, girls and boys with dazed eyes. Questions asked, buttons punched, machines buzzing, the sting of a thousand needles in my upper left arm leaving behind a string of black numbers oozing red.

13759995.

I think of a documentary I once saw about horrible things that happened to a lot of people before there was color. I remember this little girl pulling up the sleeve of her coat to show the number tattooed there. The bad men tortured and killed those people, and I remember the big machines that pushed all the bodies into big pits in the ground to bury them.

I have a tattooed number now, but I can't make room to wonder about it. The tattooing didn't sting all that much, and everywhere around me there are windows that are *clear.*

I can see endless Sky, and Sun.

And children. Whole rooms full of boys and girls of all ages.

Friends.

Now I can have friends.

Wardate:	21:36-7AUG2033
Downlimit:	177971:24:16

92

I am crammed into a highspeed that shrieks across a huge body of water, depositing many of us at a station in another city on the edge of the water. At the station we are moved into a trans. The trans is fast and quiet, the things outside that are far away still, the ones close moving so fast that I can't make out what they are. The trans speeds through countless towns and cities. The images flash by like the short cuts in the movies when the director is trying to confuse the audience on purpose. It is a drug to my vision, this gift of Outside.

In another city we get off the trans and stand waiting in another station. The two stations look the same. If it wasn't for the different views from the windows, I couldn't tell them apart.

While we wait I see a row of telephones next to me on the wall. I reach up. The black buttons are still cold, the silver buttons still warm. It is a link between me and home. I know the number to call to reach Mommy in the kitchen. Is she there? I still don't understand why Mommy and Daddy let the men in black take me.

"Get away from there, kid."

The man in black sounds irritated, but not angry. He nods with his head for me to go back with the other children. Moments later an airbus arrives and we are told to board it.

The bus moves along a huge highway crowded with other air vehicles and older wheeled vehicles. There is a girl sitting behind me with a bloody face. The girl sitting across the aisle from her is crying. She had gotten up to help the girl with the bloody face and had been slapped back into her place by the guard. The guard orders the girl with the bloody face not to bleed on the seats unless she wants a beating.

I hold my hands over my ears and look through my window at the passing scenery. There is nothing I can do about the girl with the bloody face, so I don't want to see her, I don't want to hear her. If I see her or hear her I will have to try and help her, and I can't do anything but get in trouble that way.

But she cries. So loud.

—I lift my arms, the folds of my black cape forming the wings of a huge bat.

"Cheeldren uff duh night," I cry, "Shut up."

We pass an illuminated sign with red letters and numbers on a black background:

21:36 7AUG2033.

Will Cain's clock tells what time it is; Marshal O'Niel's clock tells how much time is left; the Wardate tells what time it will be. Every town, every city we pass through has one of those numbers. I don't want to look stupid, or get beaten, so I don't ask why. Instead I look at people. Real people. More real people than I really believe exist.

The bus turns off the highway and takes a small road that twists and turns through stretches of farmland. The bus stops, the whine of its fans dies.

The door opens and a man in black climbs up the stairs. He stands at the front of the bus, his arms out to his sides, each hand gripping a seat. He has a pleasant face and a harsh, cold voice.

"Listen up. My name is Citizen Gammon. This is the New York Orphanage at Ossining. Outcasters Orphanage. Because of the 1998 Citizenship Act, you are outcasters." He nods toward the windows. "This all used to be homes and buildings here, and now it's reclaimed farmland, and that's what you do: you farm."

I remember a farm. When he was a boy, Superman lived on a farm. It was in a very flat land with a beautiful blue sky.

Planting and growing things'll be fun, but all of those animals! Lambs, cows, horses, a dog—

"Pay attention."

With his left hand Citizen Gammon points toward a building. "That is where you are going to live, and that is where you are going to die." He lowers his hand back to the seat. "Make things easy on yourself. If you can't remember anything else, remember this: Do what you are told when you are told to do it; keep your mouths shut unless you are asked a question; address all guards and wardens by the title 'Citizen.'" He nods his head toward the door and speaks to the second guard.

"Move them out."

Outcasters Orphanage.

I look through the window down at the hard black pavement and look up at the building. It is huge, gray, and dismal, surrounded by a high wire fence. The coils of barbed wire on top of the fence are ridged black laces against gray Sky. There is more fence, enclosing fields and woodland, and it extends from the building farther than I can see. There is a tight feeling in my chest. This doesn't look much like a farm. Instead, it looks like where all of those men, women, and children were gassed, burned, and buried before there was color.

The girl with the bloody face, still in the bus, cries as another girl tries to remove the glass splinters from her face.

"Why'd she do it?" asks the girl with the bloody face.

The bus had gone through the main right-of-way of a town before getting on the highway. A woman in a pretty violet suit and cape had thrown a rock at the airbus. After the glass had shattered, I saw her stoop to pick up another stone. The black-uniformed guards on the bus hurried the driver along.

"Why?" repeats the injured girl.

"Shut your face!" shouts the second guard. "If you knew why, what could you do about it?" The guard laughs and pulls the bleeding child up by her shoulder. It's like any place else in the world this man would be a human. Maybe even a father or older brother. Here he has to be something evil.

"Get on out of the bus. We got a doctor inside that'll take care of that." He looks at me. "Do you have the dumbs?"

I don't know. I don't know what he wants.

"Are you eating stupid pills? I said, *move!*"

I move, remembering Carl the floorwalker saying to Cool Hand Luke: *"I hope you ain't gonna be a hard case."*

Luke shook his head to say no, but he was laughing when he did it.

Luke turned out to be a hard case.

I'm not gonna be a hard case, like Luke, like the Birdman, Bob Stroud. He *was* taking stupid pills. *"You ain't got much, Stroud, but you keep subtracting from it."*

Stroud had the dumbs bad.

All I want to do is stay out of trouble and go home. I must learn to listen harder. Listen hard, understand quickly, and move.

The air is wet. The chilly wind picks up, carrying a light drizzle that makes me shiver. I hunch into my blanket and make certain that the drizzle doesn't get on my two books.

"Line it! Line it! Line it! Line it up and stand still, redshit, so I can get a count."

We stand in a line. It doesn't seem to make any difference what order we're in. The guard points at each of us as his lips move, and then he shouts at Citizen Gammon. "Fourteen in, fourteen out, fourteen on the asphalt."

Gammon hands a slip of paper to the bus guard. The bus guard takes the paper, climbs back on the bus, and flops into a front seat as the bus fans up and glides away.

Citizen Gammon looks at us for a long moment like he has a bad taste in his mouth. He shakes his head and speaks. "From now on when you line it, you line it right-to-left facing the guard in charge, tall to short. Keep your eyes to the front and your mouths shut. Understand?"

We mumble and nod.

"Now, I don't want you cupcakes to hurt your vocal cords or put a strain on my eardrums, but you are going to have to speak up just a bit. Now, do you understand what I told you just now?"

We mumble again.

"You are supposed to say, 'Yes, Citizen Gammon.' And you are supposed to say it loud enough for me to hear. So let's do it again."

Again.

Again.

"I can't hear you!"

"YES SIR!"

"The man in the moon can't hear you!"

"YES SIR!"

—Jack Webb, Don Dubbins, *The D.I.*, nineteen fifty-seven, I am so scared—

"Up the stairs, move! Up the stairs, move! Climb it, climb it, climb it!"

Gammon and another guard run us up a great set of concrete stairs, through the main doors of the gray building, into a large, wood-paneled hallway with a shiny concrete floor. The smell of polishing wax is heavy in the air.

He orders us to halt. Fourteen of us. Six boys and eight girls. The youngest is a little boy that looks to be three or four. The oldest is a girl that might be fifteen or sixteen. A woman in a black uniform meets us in the hallway. Her face is stern, her light brown hair cut short and brushed back.

"I am Citizen Sayther, second floor dorm warden. I am responsible for settling you in at Outcasters. Keep your mouths shut and do as you are told as quickly as possible. All of you, strip down to your skins."

We look around at each other, hesitantly fumbling with a button or zipper, no one wanting to be the first. I stand staring at one of the older girls. She is shaking her head.

Citizen Sayther walks over to the girl and calmly slaps the girl's face. "Skin down, redshit."

The girl continues to shake her head, tears streaking her cheeks. The warden slaps the girl, first with one hand, then the next, time and time again, until the girl begins to open her jumpsuit.

We all skin down.

As we stand on the cold concrete trying to hide our nakedness, a man in a white suit comes to each of us, enters our shoulder numbers into a tiny blue box, and looks into our mouths, ears, between our legs, shines a light in our eyes, and goes through our hair with his gloved fingers. He pokes around my scrotum, but it doesn't hurt the way the white suit did at the Toronto Processing Station.

He has a round bald spot on the back of his head. His white suit looks like THX's, but with big pockets.

As he comes to the girl with the bleeding face the man in the white coat stands and looks at Citizen Gammon. "What happened?"

"Civvie tossed a rock at the bus going through Kisco. Damn near got the bus guard."

The man in the white coat snickers, orders a kit from another guard, and quickly looks at the girl's cuts.

Citizen Sather orders us to gather up our things and to put them into a large paper barrel in the center of the hall. We try not to look at or to touch each other as we gather around the barrel, our arms full of clothing. I notice that all of the girls have small pink bandages just below their navals, and I wonder why as I put my clothing, blanket, and towel into the barrel.

"You!"

I freeze and stare at Citizen Sayther. She motions at me with her finger. I frown because I don't know what she wants.

"The books. In the barrel. Everything goes in the barrel." She turns toward one of the guards. "I don't know why they don't confiscate that junk at the processing station."

I look down at the two volumes beneath my left arm. Will I get them back? Daddy won't like me losing his books. I can't find my voice to ask the warden. She has that Carl-the-floorwalker,-am-I-gonna-be-a-hard-case look in her eye.

I put the two books in the barrel. They are quickly buried.

"At the window. Line it up."

As we line it and move toward the window, Citizen Sayther sees a little boy clutching a filthy rag doll to his chest. She takes it and throws it into the barrel, brushing her hands against her trousers as though to remove contamination from them.

The boy cries out, and one of the guards lays a short whip across his back so hard that the boy sinks to his knees on the floor, eyes wide, his mouth open. I quickly look away, afraid to attract attention to myself with either my looks or my thoughts. In line I keep my attention fixed on the back of the person in front of me. A tall girl. She has pimples on her back. Citizen Sayther pulls her out of line and moves her to the front.

The guard at the window gives each one of us a pile of things: underwear, red cloth shoes with rope soles, a bright red one-piece jumpsuit. No socks. The girl with the pimples starts putting her red uniform on, but the warden stops her.

"No dressing until after showers."

Lined up with our bundles we march out of the hall down a long, narrow flight of cold concrete stairs. At the bottom of the stairs we enter a low-ceilinged, unpainted, musty-smelling room, with shelves built along one side. Citizen Sayther's voice comes from right behind me.

"Put the gear on one of the shelves. Erase the old number on the edge of the shelf and mark down the last four digits of your number."

I stuff my things into one of the openings and rub the old number off of the shelf with my thumb. There is a marker hanging from a string to my left. I check the number on my shoulder again, remind myself that the sixes I see are upside down nines, and mark 9995 on the edge of my shelf.

The little boy who had been lashed puts his bundle on the shelf next to mine. The boy's eyes are cloudy, a confused look on his face. He isn't crying. I'm glad because crying makes the guard angry. I can't look at the horror of the boy's back. I don't want trouble. I just don't want any trouble.

I think on remembering my shelf number. Nine nine nine five. Do what I'm told; keep my mouth shut; don't give anyone a bad look; do what I'm told.

Citizen Gammon taps five of us on our shoulders with his short whip and points with it toward an opening in the wall. We hurry into a dark, damp room that smells of ancient sweat and mildew. Moments later icy needles of disinfectant shoot at us from every direction. The boy with the cut back screams and tries to get out, but the guard shoves him back.

"Pick up some soap and use it. Kill all them little buggies! Try and get it done before the war gets here!"

Citizen Sayther herds the next group into the shower, and my group rinses off and leaves. I am so cold I can't stop my teeth from chattering. The guard orders us to wipe off the water with our hands and to jump around to dry off. There are no towels. I wipe off what I can and stand there shivering, my arms wrapped around my chest.

I hear a sharp crack and something knocks me to the floor at the same time. Fire cuts a path across my back.

"Run, redshit, run!"

The guard stands over me, tapping me on the top of my head with his whip. I jump up and wave my arms about while running in place. I am so surprised at the pain in my back that I forget to cry.

As I get warmer I run my hands over my arms and legs. With everything dry but my hair, I turn to look for my shelf. One of the girls is standing still next to the shelves. She has little breasts and a tuft of blond hair just below her bandage. She is trying hard not to cry. The guard is touching her buttocks with his hand.

My red uniform fits very well, and as the others in the room get dressed, all of us in red, I feel closer to them and not quite so alone. The crying girl helps me to tie my shoes. Her name is Elana. She is pretty, except that her eyes are all red. When all of us are dressed, we line up and march outside into the gray, windy evening.

We go down some steps from the gray building, along a crunchy gravel path, to a long, white frame building with black smoke coming from a stack at one end. I smell food and remember I am very hungry.

Wardate: 21:36-7AUG2033
Downlimit: 177962:00:31

91

Inside the building we are in a huge dining hall, tables gleaming white, narrow, and placed in rows with benches only on one side of each table. I remember this dining hall. The Birdman ate in a dining hall like this when he was in the Leavenworth prison.

Other children in red uniforms and white aprons stand behind the serving line. I follow the file, pick up a battered metal tray, a spoon with a cutting edge on one side and blunt tines for stabbing at the tip of the bowl. The children behind the serving line fill the compartments of the tray. I recognize the peas. We sit at one of the tables, facing the front of the room.

"Sit straight, keep your hands in your laps and your mouths shut." Citizen Sayther stands in front of us with her arms folded. "You will be told when you may begin eating."

In Leavenworth's dining hall they had a band playing while the prisoners ate. Here there is no band, no music.

Hundreds of other boys and girls begin filing into the dining hall, all wearing red and guarded by men and women in black. The children move quickly through the serving line and to the tables. Not a word is spoken the entire time.

Citizen Sayther sits at a table at the front of the room, facing us, and as other groups come in more wardens join her. The guards stand at the back of the room.

When all the boys and girls have trays and are seated, the room becomes very quiet again. The six wardens look like a row of statues. One of the wardens nods and I see the others begin to eat. I dig in.

"Don' look back," whispers a voice behind me. "Make sure you eat everythin' on your tray. If you don', you get called out."

I start to turn around and catch a glimpse of a handsome boy with black hair and dark eyes. "You got the dumbs? Face front!" he whispers urgently. I look at my tray and concentrate on finishing my food, my face hot with embarrassment. Again the voice from behind me: "The terminal dumbs; you got it bad, chicky."

Another voice: "Chickchickchick!"

There are a few chuckles, then Citizen Sayther looks up from her dinner and deadly silence drops on the hall. She returns to her meal and I return to mine, not hungry at all.

Wardate: 21:36-7AUG2033
Downlimit: 177961:26:22

90

After the meal we form up and march back to the gray building. Once there we are assigned to dormkeepers. Citizen Sayther assigns me to an older girl wearing red. Her name is Helen. She is plain and hard around the mouth and eyes. Her brown hair is wrapped up in a tight bun, and she has a deep scar on her right cheek.

A little blond girl is also assigned to Helen. We follow Helen to the hallway window where we had earlier gotten our uniforms. The guard gives me another set of underwear, another red uniform, two sheets, a blanket, and a pillow case. He leans over the sill of the window and looks down at me. His hair is gray and cut very short. "You a pisser?"

I just look back. Not answering is bad, I can tell. But I am certain a wrong answer would be worse. Helen jabs my right arm. "Answer, redbird. Do you wet the bed at night?"

"No." I shake my head. No, I don't wet the bed. Not for a long time, and that means that I don't do it anymore—

The guard drops a thin mattress roll and pillow on top of the burden in my arms. Staggering beneath the load, I follow Helen and the little girl up the front staircase to "E" Dorm.

"E" Dorm is a long, high-ceilinged room with a row of wire-mesh-covered windows along the top of one of the pale green walls. A double row of light bars extends the length of the room, casting everything in a harsh, white glare. The room holds forty single cots, twenty on each side of the central aisle. Helen shows me to a cot along the solid wall opposite the windows.

"Leave the rack traps and stick the rest in your home." She nods her head toward a shelf—an open-ended box—hanging on the wall behind the cot.

I put my load on the cot frame. Leaving the mattress roll, pillow, and bedding behind, I put my uniform and underwear into the shelf at the head of my cot. My home. Helen takes my mattress roll to show me and the little girl how to make up racks. After making up mine, she shows me how to stow my stuff in my home with everything neatly stacked and folded to the exact width of two marks painted on the lower shelf.

Helen taps her finger against the marked shelf and looks at me. "This is your south wall." She points at the opposite shelf. "North." Right. "East." Left. "West."

"You." She points at the little girl. "Pay attention. If tomorrow when the blackshit shoots it to you, you act like you got handful of dumbs between your ears, you'll get called out." She glances at me and looks back at the girl. "You don't want to get called out."

Helen takes the little girl across the aisle and helps her to make up her rack and put her reds and whites home. I watch, standing by myself next to my rack, not knowing what to do with myself.

I see the handsome boy with the black hair, who said I had the dumbs back in the dining hall. He is on his rack, his hands behind his head, talking to another boy.

The door at the hall end of the dorm opens. Citizen Sayther leans in and nods at Helen. The dormkeeper walks quickly to the door and the two of them talk. The warden leaves and Helen faces the room, her face red.

"We got zipped at morning inspection for dirty floor. Because of the zip, lights out in five minutes. Hit the racks, and if you buy me a zip tomorrow, tomorrow night we're going to get down and tongue-polish us some concrete."

Helen walks up to me and the little girl and points to a door at the other end of the dorm.

"My room is right there, so no talking and no fooling around after lights out. Understand?"

We both nod.

After she leaves I begin undressing, nervous again about being naked in front of the others. Some of the boys and girls don't seem to mind. They simply skin down and climb under their rack traps. Some of the others in the dorm get under their traps first. The little girl and I climb under our covers to undress. Everyone folds their uniforms and underwear—reds and whites—and places them at the foot of their racks.

By the time everyone is quiet under their covers, Helen stands in the doorway to her room and looks around. Reaching to a switch beside her door, she turns off the lights.

I am on my back, the covers up to my chin, looking up into the blackness. It is dead quiet interrupted here by a cough, there by a squeak as someone rolls over.

Things emerge in the dark. Thoughts.

In the morning when they took me from Mommy and Daddy I was terrified, then miserably sad. Sick for my home. For my little dark room in the attic. My mind was soon filled, however, with the bustle of the Toronto Processing Station and the thrill of the highspeed across the lake to Buffalo, and then to the processing center in New York. All day I rushed from one station to another, getting papers initialed, getting shots, being poked and probed and told to sit and wait until I was told to rush someplace else, until I was finally herded onto the airbus for Outcasters.

New things, loud noises, people, people, and more people—I didn't have time to think. In the quiet and dark of "E" Dorm, the things the day had chased from my mind come back.

An eerie, blue luminescence fills the room, reflected off the night air from the security lights on the wire fence. There are light patterns on the ceiling. The racks on either side of me are empty, and loneliness knots my stomach. The rack sags uncomfortably.

At home I sleep on a bed. A real bed. It is thick and I sink into it when I go to sleep. Daddy carries me up to the attic and Mommy tucks me in and kisses me goodnight. She tells me stories. Sometimes she tells me the story of the bad little boy who liked to talk to strangers and all of the horrible things that happen to him.

I wasn't bad. I never talked to strangers. I never even saw any strangers. I never saw anyone except Mommy and Daddy. All of my playmates were on television.

All I did was to open the window.

I think of the hammer Daddy gave me for my birthday. I don't even know what my other presents are. Will Mommy and Daddy save my presents for me? Why don't they come for me? Where are Mommy and Daddy?

The sound of sniffling comes from the other side of the aisle. Crying. The little girl.

The light in Helen's room goes on, and I bury my face in my pillow to stifle my own sniffling. My back still hurts from the guard's little whip, and I remember the girl with the red welts all over her cheeks because she wouldn't skin down fast enough to suit Citizen Sayther. Helen told us not to make any noise. I only want to stay out of trouble.

But there is this thing eating away at my heart: a thing of horrible fear and abandonment. Alone.

Alone, alone, it just isn't fair. It isn't. I didn't *do* anything. I didn't *do* any—

Helen comes into the dorm without turning on the lights. She walks to the little girl's cot and bends over it. I hear her talking to the little girl but I can't understand anything she says. I curl up under my pillow and covers, but the sniffles grow into a flood.

Do Mommy and Dadddy know what's happened to me? Why don't they come for me? Why was Mommy screaming? When Daddy warns me about the men in black, he says he and Mommy will die if the men in black—

Like a scab: if I don't pick at it, it won't bleed. Like the paint blister: if I don't pick at it, it won't fall off. Like—

I wasn't bad.

"What's the matter?"

I feel someone sit on the edge of my cot. It's Helen. I bite my lip but I can't stop crying. Helen takes the pillow from my face and sits me up. The light from her room lets me see only a little of her face, and her hair is hanging loose. With a gentle touch she brushes the tears from my face. In the dark and with my eyes blurred by the tears, she looks like Mommy.

"Get some rest, little redbird."

"My name's Thomas."

"Go to sleep, Tommy. You're with us now. We're your family."

"I already have a family."

"We're your new family."

She leans over and kisses me on my cheek. I kiss her back and taste the salt of her tears. She is crying. I do not understand why.

She strokes my hair and face, humming softly. I close my eyes and listen to her soft voice, the touch of her hand warm and gentle.

I feel my head loll as my eyelids close.

I fight against the sleep. Helen will leave me alone if I fall asleep.

I can't stay awake.

I don't want to be alone, but I am seven years old today and very, very tired.

Wardate: 21:36-7AUG2033
Downlimit: 177951:21:51

89

•

"Out of those racks!"

A whistle screams and the dorm lights go on. The glare hurts my eyes and I squint against it. My hand shields my eyes from the lights as I look up at the row of windows. Outside it is still dark.

"You waiting on the war? Roll outta those racks! Let's go! Let's go! Let's go!"

The guard stands at the door until he sees us getting dressed under our traps. He leaves. More shouting as he reaches the next dorm down the hall.

The room is freezing cold. I put on my underpants under the covers, hop out of my rack, and slip on my red uniform and shoes. I look for someone to help me tie my shoes, but Helen is checking the dorm for inspection. The others are making up their racks, dressing or cleaning up. I sit on the edge of my cot and try tying them myself.

"Don't you even know how to tie your own shoes?"

The new girl stands in the aisle, hands on her hipless hips, looking at me with a stupid smirk on her face.

"Sure I do." I go back to making a mess of my laces, now a tangle of knots.

"Let me. You'll never get it right."

She kneels on the floor, pushes my hands away, and unknots the laces saying, "Tisk, tisk," her blond pigtails shaking back and forth. "There." She gets to her feet, and I look down at my neatly tied laces. My face feels a little hot.

"I could have done that."

She laughs.

"Anyway, thank you, I guess. I'm Thomas."

"I'm Ann. I'm seven years old."

"I'm seven too. My birthday was yesterday."

"I'm older than you are."

"So what?" Again she laughs at me. I decide that I don't like her very much.

"My birthday is in December, Tommy. I'm only three months older than you. Will you be my friend?" She smiles but her eyes pull at me as though she would cry if I said no.

"I never had a friend." I shrug and look down, embarrassed. "Sure." She laughs again and skips back to her rack to make it up.

I smooth the wrinkles out of my cot and wait for Helen to check it. On the way to the hall end of the dorm, Helen straightens a wrinkle here, points something out there, getting us all ready for inspection. As she passes by my cot she nods at me and walks on.

A boy stands at the foot of my cot. He is in his teens and his face looks very grim.

I frown back at him. The boy just keeps looking at me. "Do you want something?"

He glances down, nods toward the little girl who tied my shoelaces and looks back at me. "You don't want to make any friends here. Friends are expensive." He snorts out a laugh and shakes his head. "You aren't going to listen to me any more than I listened to them."

"Them?"

But the boy turns away, heading for the hall end of the dorm. Helen stands near the door.

"Line it up. Prepare for inspection."

The boys and girls form two rows down the center aisle close to the hall door. Helen pushes Ann and I into line and takes her place in front of the formation. I wonder if I should ask permission to go to the bathroom. I don't know how long the formation is going to take, and I am beginning to get uncomfortable.

We wait.

A moment after I hear footsteps coming down the hall, a guard slams through the door, heads for the first line, and begins inspecting us one by one with Helen following. I recognize the guard as the one who turned on the lights. He is a big man with a dark, scowling face. Instead of a whip he carries a long thin stick pointed at one end.

I am in the front row at the end, and as the guard comes closer, I am frightened. Towering over me, the guard looks down at me forever while I try desperately not to wet myself. I swear that the next time I will go to the bathroom before inspection. The guard nods, turns, steps around the end of my line, and comes to a halt in front of the person at the end of the second row.

"Dirty uniform."

I turn and see the guard standing in front of Ann, tapping her knees with his stick. There are faint smudges on the knees of her reds where she knelt to tie my laces.

"Have her fall out for punishment tonight."

"She just got here last night, Citizen Lathrup."

"That makes no difference, Helen. Have her fall out tonight after evening chow."

"Citizen Lathrup, she's only seven."

"Don't argue with me! You know damned well that she's old enough to keep her uniform clean."

"I just mean, be careful, Citizen Lathrup." Helen's voice sounds curiously calm.

"Careful?"

The big guard storms halfway to the door and rushes back, stopping with his face a short distance from Helen's.

"Careful? *Careful?* You little puddle of piss, just how much ass do you think you got to swing around here, Helen? Threaten me?"

"Of course not, Cit—"

"Damn!" The guard taps her sharply on the shoulder with his stick. "Damn you! Do you really think that I'm scared of your silly little girls club?"

"No, Citizen—"

"Shut your face!" He marches to the door, throws it open

and faces her. "I want that little piece of shit out for punishment tonight! You copy that?"

"Yes, Citizen Lathrup."

Turning his attention to the rest of the formation, his eyes search us out one at a time. "You little shits think you own this place." He holds up a hand and slowly closes it into a fist. "That's where I got you! Every last damned one of you! Right here!" Turning abruptly, he leaves, slamming the door behind him.

Helen looks at Ann for a moment and then faces the door. "March out!"

Wardate: 21:36-7AUG2033
Downlimit: 177950:51:13

88

Breakfast is a soup made from some kind of grain. As "E" Dorm takes its places, I glance at a little girl sitting at the table behind. I look away, shocked. She is so ugly I don't believe it. Just before I sit down I quickly peek again. Her eyes look crossed and as though they only open halfway. The space between her eyes is very wide and flat. Her whole face is lumpy and fat-looking, and her tongue looks like it's too big for her mouth. She looks so stupid I don't even think she understands what she sees.

I sit waiting for the signal to begin eating. I hear a splat and feel a gob of something hit the back of my neck. I reach back with my hand and wipe it off. Somebody threw some of the grain soup at me.

I turn around, very angry, and see the ugly girl grinning back at me just before I feel a sting in my arm. I yelp and look back. Citizen Sayther is standing over me holding a finger to her lips. She turns and continues walking down the rows of tables.

As I rub my arm I hear a voice from behind me. "Beauty is only skin deep, chickchick. The dumbs go all the way to the bone."

After morning chow, Ann and I are assigned to a detail with boys and girls from other dorms. We go to a large shed built into the side of the gray building, and there I am issued a leaf rake. The others are issued weed whips, rakes, and pitchforks.

The black-clad officer in the shed, each time he hands out a tool, says, "That's the way I want to see it when I get it back."

When we are told to, we pile onto a horse-drawn, flatbed wagon driven by an ancient guard, Citizen Brown. He snaps a switch on the horse's back and the wagon bumps and rumbles down a road that heads into some trees.

Riding in the feeble sunlight, the sky obscured by layers of thick haze, the brown fields and bare trees look gloomy. The wind picks up and a chill shakes me. I huddle against Ann in the center of the wagon bed, trying to keep warm.

In the trees the wagon turns left and comes out on the edge of an overgrown field lined on all four sides with tall evergreens. Citizen Brown stops the horse and tells the children to get off. We assemble next to the wagon, holding our tools.

"Any chicks—new kids—on this detail?"

Four of us raise our hands. "You new kids, get this. Don't get any smart ideas about running off. Fences all around here. Electrified fences. Touch one and it'll turn you into a piece of bacon. We can spot those reds, too, faster'n a turd in whipped cream." Citizen Brown pats a holstered pistol hanging from his belt. "Besides, there's no place to go. Not for you. Never for you."

The detail is supposed to gather up weeds and leaves for the compost pile. Ann whispers that compost is good to grow things, but I don't see what difference piling up the weeds made. I ask her why we don't just leave them on the ground. She tells me that her father is a farmer and that it's so.

"You two! Knock off the jaw music and bend your backs."

One of the older boys asks permission to talk to the guard and complains that the weed whips don't work. The winter has beaten down the weeds making it impossible for the whips to get a good swing at them. The guard tells me and another boy to put up our tools and to hold the weeds upright for the whips.

We cut and load weeds for hours, which keeps everything but our fingers warm. A stop for lunch. Citizen Brown takes sandwiches out of a pail and issues them to us. My sandwich is a piece of tough, synthetic meat on a dry roll. We have water to drink.

After lunch, it is back to the weeds.

Late in the afternoon I am so sore from lifting and hauling weeds that my feet keep stumbling. The guard calls us to bring in the last load. After throwing up our tools we climb up on the weed pile and jerk around as the wagon rumbles off.

The weeds smell wet and rotten. In the trees we take a new road and follow it until a huge, green-painted machine looms to the left. The wagon stops.

Without being told, the older boys and girls climb down and walk to a big spoked wheel set on a post in the concrete next to and below the machine. They each grab a spoke, strain against their arms, and begin pushing the wheel counterclockwise. As they go around, a whine deep within the machine gets louder and higher as the speed of the wheel increases.

The guard motions to the rest of us to get down and haul the weeds to the machine. When I get to the machine, both arms loaded, I stare into the hopper and see hundreds of blades flashing and spinning. I throw in my bundle and it instantly disappears. The spinning knives pull at me, drawing me toward the chute. I see a flash of the devil feeding all of the dead babies into the hopper. The boy behind me shoves me out of the way and throws in his own bundle.

At the wagon for another load, I listen as the boys and girls on the wheel begin keeping step with a low, mournful chant. The whine of the machine increases, and from the wagon I can see tiny flakes blowing out of an arm on top of the machine. The flakes fly to a black pile behind the machine. White wisps of steam come from the pile.

It's whining, it's roaring,
The blackshit is snoring.
He went to bed, we cut off his head,
Now, he won't get us in the morning—

I look at Ann watching them push the wheel. It goes around so fast the boys and girls almost run. Their eyes look strange, flashing with some loathsome desire. I feel my skin crawl.

It's whining, it's roaring,
The blackshit is snoring.

I reach out my hand, shake Ann's shoulder, and point at Citizen Brown. Both of us pick up more weeds from the wagon. Still holding the reins, the guard sits watching the children on the wheel. His face is pale and the reins in his hands shake.

He went to bed, we cut off his head,
Now, he won't get us in the morning—

Wardate: 21:36-7AUG2033
Downlimit: 177941:21:02

87

After evening chow, Helen takes Ann away.

We are dismissed and have the rest of the evening to ourselves. I sit alone on my rack and watch the others in the dorm talk or play games. The ones who had been working outside take off their reds and carry them into the hall. Some others clean the floors around their racks.

Carrying his reds, an older boy dressed only in his whites stops by my cot.

"Look at your reds."

I look down at the pants to my uniform. They are grass- and mud-stained. My stomach knots as I remember the almost invisible marks that got Ann called out for punishment. The boy is tall, slender, and has scars, pits, and little red marks all over his face.

"I'm Francis. What's your name, chick?"

"Thomas."

"Peel off those reds, Thomas, and zip 'em here. I'll do 'em along with mine."

I begin thanking him, but he snaps his fingers at me to hurry me up.

"Let's go. Don't want to get caught in the war." I hand Francis my reds.

"Do those shoes yourself, redbird, or you'll get zipped tomorrow."

As Francis goes out the hall door, I look at my mud-caked shoes. The mud is dry, and I break it off into a trash can. After beating and rubbing them, they don't look any worse than anyone else's. I place them on the floor beneath my rack.

Three girls wearing only their whites are playing jacks in the center aisle. The jacks are made out of little pieces of wood, and the ball is red plastic. The first girl asks me if I want to play. She talks funny. I try the game for a few minutes, but I'm not very good at it. The girls talk to each other with words I can't understand. They giggle at me a lot and I leave.

I walk past two of the older boys. They are sitting on their racks talking to each other. One of them is the handsome boy with the black hair.

"You're Tommy," he says to me.

"Yes."

"I'm Manuel." Manuel is very dark. He points to his left at his companion who is even darker. "This stupid here is Godfrey."

Godfrey grins at me and pulls me down until I am sitting on the bed next to him.

"Tommy, Manuel is a bit empty-headed. All redbirds have a duty to watch him all of the time to see he doesn't hurt himself."

Manuel makes a spitting sound with his mouth. "Don't listen, kid. The only one I'm going to hurt is that bushman that keeps flapping his lips."

"I am from Uganda, Tommy." Godfrey jabs himself with his thumb. "Do you know where Uganda is?"

I shake my head. "I'm from Peterborough."

"Is that in New York?" Godfrey looks slyly at the other boy and whispers, "Crazy Manuel is from New York."

"Peterborough is in Ontario." Godfrey is the darkest person I have ever seen.

"Are you from Africa, Godfrey?"

"See, Manuel!" Godfrey slaps the other boy hard on the arm.

"Ow!"

"See, I told you he would guess."

"Ahhh, he don't guess."

"He did. Tommy, you did say Africa?" I nod. "There, you see?"

"Dumb bushbunny. He supposed to say Uganda'n you told him that. Anybody can see you from Africa. You still got a bone in your nose."

Manuel laughs and Godfrey looks very offended. "Do not listen to the crazy boy, Tommy. My country is very civilized. We do not wear bones anymore."

He pinches my thigh, smacks his lips and rolls his eyes. "But roast babies. Now that is another matter!" He grins broadly at me and I laugh.

Manuel hits Godfrey on the head with his pillow.

"Cannibal! Cannibal! Run for your life, Tommy!"

Godfrey tickles me and soon I can hardly breathe from laughing. A guard looks in from the hall door and Manuel hisses, "Blackshit!"

We quiet down. The guard looks around the dorm and leaves. The dorm resumes its usual noise level.

I talk. "My father teaches about movies. What does your father do, Manuel?"

Manuel raises his heavy black brows and looks at Godfrey. Godfrey shakes his head. Manuel shrugs. "He's a handyman. You know, Tommy, he goes around fixing things." Manuel looks toward the wall.

"He's very good at it. Fixing things."

Godfrey puts his arm around my shoulder. "My father owns a department store, Tommy. The largest one in Kampala. What do you think of that?"

"I've never seen a department store, but I read about them."

"It's wonderful. Anything you want: boots, jumpsuits, perfume, flowers—"

"Missionary sauce," Manuel interrupts.

"Oh yes, and great black cooking pots!"

"Bone polish, spears, tooth files, fourth floor—"

The dorm becomes very quiet. Citizen Sayther stands in the open hall door.

"Where is Helen?"

A redbird close to Helen's room jumps up and pounds on the door until she opens it. Seeing the warden, Helen walks quickly to the hall end of the dorm.

I look at Manuel, but the boy only sits and watches. When

the warden leaves, Helen nods at Manuel. Manuel taps Godfrey's arm.

"Let's go, bushman." Godfrey and Manuel get up and I stand to go with them. Godfrey puts his hand on my shoulder.

"Stay here, Tommy."

"Why?"

Godfrey's face seems to harden. "Do as you're told. Stay alive and do as you're told."

The two boys go out the hall door after Helen, and I go back to my rack. My cleaned and ironed reds are neatly folded at the foot of my cot. I look for Francis, but can't find him. The boy who warned me about the expense of friends this morning is on his rack, still dressed, his hands clasped behind his head, his eyes staring at the ceiling. I decide that the boy doesn't look as though he is interested in talking.

Anyway, my muscles are sore from the detail and I am very tired. I climb under my covers and close my eyes against the dorm lights.

Wardate: 21:36-7AUG2033
Downlimit: 177937:13:51

86

Something wakes me. I open my eyes.

Except for the ghostly blue reflections of the fence lights, the dorm is dark. Silent.

I don't know why, but I am frightened.

Something—

I hear it. Crying. Painful sobs. Hoarse screams off in the distance. Too hoarse to be screams. Croaks and whimpers.

The sounds of slow footsteps come from the stairwell.

Heads rise and turn as the hall door opens, flooding the dorm with light from the hall.

Helen enters first and holds the door for Godfrey and Manuel. They carry Ann. Francis follows. Helen closes the door and turns to a boy near the door.

"Lie down and go back to sleep." She looks up. "All of you, go back to sleep."

Godfrey and Manuel carry Ann to her rack. Helen rushes in front of them to pull down Ann's covers. The boys stand the little girl up on her feet, supporting her by her arms, and take off her reds. Helen looks at Ann's back.

"My god."

"Francis," she whispers, "go to the crapper and get warm water and a clean cloth."

Francis hurries out into the hall as Helen puts a finger beneath the waistband of Ann's whites. Ann flinches and Helen removes her finger. Francis comes back carrying a basin. He holds it for Helen. She reaches in and takes out a dripping wet cloth.

With the cloth, Helen wets the back of Ann's underpants. After a few minutes, Helen puts her finger under Ann's waistband and gently pulls it out and down, taking them off. Helen moves Ann's legs apart and washes her crotch and the insides of her legs, only blotting the backs. Ann keeps making noises like a crying kitten.

Godfrey and Manuel lift Ann and place her facedown on her rack. Helen whispers to the little girl while Francis gathers up her reds and underwear and goes into the hallway.

Helen looks up and quietly says something to Godfrey. He nods, walks across the aisle, and leans over me.

"Tommy? Are you awake?"

"Yes."

"Unass the rack."

I throw my covers aside, put on my underpants, and walk across the icy floor to Ann's rack. Even with only the fence lights I can see the ugly, dark marks on the little girl's back from her knees to just above her waist. Helen stands and puts something into my hand.

"Here, she wants you to put on the ointment. Sit on the rack."

I sit next to Ann, and Helen opens the tube. "Squeeze some out and rub it between your fingers until it liquifies, then rub it on where you see the marks, understand?"

I look up at Helen and nod.

"Be very gentle. And don't ask her anything about what happened. Do you have that straight, Tommy?"

"Yes, Helen."

Helen and the two boys start heading toward the hall door, pausing first to get another little girl out of her rack. The four of them go out the hall door, closing it behind them.

The ointment is greasy and it smells bad as I rub it between my fingers. When it softens I touch the back of Ann's left knee. She whimpers and I pull back my hand.

"Ann, Helen says I have to put this stuff on."

"I know." Ann talks through her tears.

"Please cover me up, Tommy. Cover me. I'm cold and I don't want everybody to see."

I put the tube in my lap, and with my left hand I pull up her sheet and tent it over my shoulder, keeping it off her back and legs. Her left hand finds my leg and grips it with such strength that it startles me.

"Go on, Tommy. Put it on."

Even more gently than before, I rub on the ointment, doing the backs of her knees first, working up her horribly swollen legs. Her skin feels hot and tight. The marks are the worst on her tiny buttocks, and I feel the cuts. There are tears on my face, and I lean back to keep the salt from dripping into her cuts.

"I'm sorry. I'm so sorry, Ann, about tying my shoes."

Her hand is relaxed. She is asleep.

By the time I finish her back I feel like I am freezing to death. The girl is cold, too. The upper part of her back is bare, and except for the sheet tent, the rest of her is bare. She trembles in her sleep, and my teeth start chattering. I can't put the traps on her. They might hurt. Anyway, blood and ointment would get all over the sheet.

I look around for Helen and the others, but I'm all alone. The wind picks up outside and the room seems to get even colder. I take the sheet from my shoulder and bunch it up at the foot of Ann's rack. Running to my own rack, I pull the top sheet and blanket and run back.

Sitting next to the sleeping girl again, I pull both her blanket and sheet up and tent them over my shoulder. With my own traps, I protect her shoulders and my legs, forming the missing half of the tent. In a few minutes my teeth stop chattering.

For a long time I watch the door, waiting for the others to return. When I'm not looking at the door I watch the little girl's face. Her face is very beautiful. Peaceful.

The wind howls, rattling the mesh-covered windows. Things fly by the security lights, casting fleeting shadows on the ceiling.

Ann wakes up and begins crying. I take her hand and gently hold it. Soon she drops back to sleep.

I wait, my eyelids drooping.

* * *

Daddy lifts the hammer and swings it down, driving in the nail with one blow. The thin shaft of metal sinking into the wood fascinates me. Daddy hands me the hammer, but even with both hands I can't swing it properly. I take the hammer and hit another nail again and again until its head is flush with the wood. Daddy beams at me, gives me a big hug, but I want more nails. Daddy laughs—

—Awake.

My back hurts. The wind outside makes me shiver with its almost animal wails. I move to another position, easing the strain on my back.

Ann is still sleeping.

For a moment the windows stop rattling and I think I hear an almost familiar whine coming from a far distance. The wind shifts, shaking the windows in their frames, and I can no longer stand it. I ease my head back and close my eyes.

I try to think of movie titles in alphabetical order, *Across the Pacific, Bananas, The Caine Mutiny*—but I can't remember why Daddy said The Caine Mutiny is a "C" and not a "T"—

But I know another "C". One of my favorites, *Charly*—

—will we get to see movies here? I don't think I can bear it if we never get to see any movies—

—so tired.

—Running. They are after me. I'm naked, afraid and running. Behind a wall I crouch down, making myself small. It's dark and maybe they can't find me. My eyes open and see bright light. The wall—is gone! Black things—shapes—are moving toward me, but my feet won't move. A long black hand closes on my shoulder—

"Tommy—"

"—Tommy."

Helen shakes me awake and kisses me on my cheek. Lifting

the covers from my shoulder, she puts her hand under and feels Ann's skin.

"She's all right, Tommy. You can go back to bed."

I fight to stay awake long enough to drag my sheet and blanket back to my own rack. I throw the covers on the rack and climb under them.

I notice Manuel, Francis, and Godfrey getting into their racks. The boy who had warned me about expensive friends—his rack is empty. Stretching my aching muscles, I curl up, snuggle the covers around and over my head. Helen pulls them back a little and kisses me again.

"Goodnight, little redbird."

I am asleep before I can answer.

Wardate: 21:36-7AUG2033
Downlimit: 177931:04:22

85

Morning.

I keep my eyes closed against the dorm lights, letting the light through my eyelids fill my vision with red. I don't want to get out of bed. It's unfair—

The bed shakes, rocks, the foot going high in the air before it drops with a crash. I open my eyes and lift my head. Godfrey is grinning back. "On the floor, chicky mine. There is an excellent chance that the sun will come up this morning."

He continues down the aisle, pausing to wake another sleeping person.

I'm almost dressed by the time I realize that what Godfrey said was real dumb.

The last wrinkle is smoothed, the last smudge wiped, the last piece of dust gathered and dumped. We stand in formation for inspection. The guard is late. Ann looks stiff and sore, but with only a little help she stands with us. Her face looks awfully old. I tied my own shoes, deciding to worry about how to get the knots undone later. Helen looks us over and takes her place up front.

We wait.

After a long time, Citizen Sayther opens the hall door a crack and pokes in her head. She pulls back her head, closes the door, and I hear her talking to someone in the hall. After a few more moments, she again opens the door.

"Helen?"

"Yes, Citizen Sayther?"

"Has Lathrup been by this morning?"

"No, Citizen Sayther."

"Are you sure?"

"I'm sure, Citizen Sayther."

The warden goes back into the hall, closing the door behind her. More talking in the hall. Hurt and angry. Someone laughs and the warden shouts, "I won't! Bring them here first!"

Footsteps move off down the hall and the dorm door lock slams home. We wait some more. I feel my knees beginning to lock. The world seems to fill with the pain from my legs—

"Is this your soldier's code: murdering unarmed men?"

Colonel Saito looks from the doctor to Colonel . . . Colonel—Alec Guinness—the ranking British prisoner. Then the Japanese commandant looks up at the hot sun, glances at . . . Colonel What'shisname, turns and goes back into his quarters, leaving the British officers standing at attention in the heat.

Saito will let the sun do his murdering for him.

It is so hot, the chatter of the jungle insects very loud. We stand, and stand, and stand, the two enemy soldiers in the back of the truck studying us, ready to fire the machine gun—

Daddy said that the movie is called *The Bridge on the River Kwai*, or *I Kwaied a Wiver Over You*. He laughed then until he couldn't breathe. I don't always understand Daddy—

—Funny I can't remember the British colonel's name—

—*My legs hurt*—

"Stand still, Tommy."

"Yes, Helen. I'm sorry."

—*Time.*

We weave in the heat, feeling the sweat, the mosquitoes. Watching the native sitting on Saito's porch. The native pulls at a rope that moves a fan inside Saito's quarters that cools the commandant.

Heat.

One of the officers drops facedown in the compound. We keep standing. Waiting.

I'm so thirsty—

More footsteps and the door unlocks. Citizen Sayther walks in followed by two guards. The guards take up stations on either side of the door, smiling and smirking at the warden. She walks over to Helen and tells her to begin the inspection.

As they walk toward the first row, Citizen Sayther looks back to see if the guards are still there. They laugh out loud at her.

"You two button it up, or I'll number you straight down to extra duty!"

They stop laughing, but the smirks remain.

The warden almost runs down the first rank and up the second, hardly looking at any of us. She and Helen return to the front and the warden turns and faces the formation.

"Citizen Lathrup did not report in for work this morning. Do any of you know anything about it?"

She scans the double row of redbirds. "If you know something, tell me or it will go hard." She turns to Helen. "Did you or those kids see anything when you went to get that girl?"

"Citizen Lathrup was in his quarters when we left with the girl. Citizen Brown was there and saw us leave."

Citizen Sayther looks at someone standing behind me. "Louisa, did you see anything?"

"No. I cleaned up." A little girl's voice. She must be the one who snuck out last night with Godfrey and Manuel.

"What do you mean?"

"When everybody left, I stayed behind and cleaned up, Citizen Sayther. The Drum Room. There was a lot of blood and stuff—"

"Very well." She turns her head. "Did you boys see anything?" Godfrey and Francis shake their heads. Manuel raises his hand.

"Yes, Manuel?"

"Well, Citizen Sayther, I see the little girl in there. She's beat up pretty bad. And I see Citizen Lathrup zipping up his pants."

"Well?"

"Maybe they wouldn't be so much blood if they don't do that kind of stuff. Anyway, that's what I seen, Citizen Sayther."

"I do not approve of such things, Manuel, but what does this have to do with anything?"

Manuel shrugs. "Maybe he won't do that no more, Citizen Sayther."

The warden backs toward the door and checks again to see if the guards are at their posts. One of them smiles and waves at her. She looks back at Manuel, her face reddening.

"Manuel, is this some kind of threat? Or an admission? There hasn't been an incident here for years. What do you mean?"

Manuel holds up his hands, palms out. "Oh, no, no, no, Citizen Sayther. I don't mean nothing. Nothing at all. The little girl I think learned her lesson and will keep her reds real clean from now on. That's all." He looks at Ann. "Right, chicky?"

"Real clean," she replies.

Manuel gives the warden a sly grin. Citizen Sayther moves to the door, turns back, and faces the room.

"Helen, march them out for morning chow."

"Yes, Citizen Sayther."

The warden leaves, followed by the two guards shaking their heads and snickering. When the door closes, Helen turns back and faces the formation. Her gaze slowly moves over all of us, stopping on Manuel.

"Manuel, that was very stupid."

Manuel shrugs, smiles, and Helen smiles back at him. Behind me Ann giggles.

"March out!" We all turn right and walk in formation toward the door.

Nicholson.

That was the name of the British colonel. I don't want to forget these things about the movies.

Nicholson.

Wardate: 21:36-7AUG2033
Downlimit: 177929:14:09

84

After chow, Ann and I are detailed to pick up litter along the security fences by the gray building. The day is clear and the sun soon takes the chill out of my bones. Six redbirds are on the litter detail, picking up scraps and leaves from the large lawn, still brown and muddy from the spring melt.

Through the fence, toward the yellow haze above the city, I can just make out the glowing red sign by the road. It's the time it will be: 21:36 7AUG2033. 2033 is so far in the future, it is beyond the time where I can believe it will ever come.

I hear the guard bellow angrily at another redbird, and I quickly bend over and return to gathering up the trash.

I glance at Ann. There is something I don't understand. I had seen—had felt—her cuts and bruises. It must be painful for her to bend over but she just giggles. The guard is at the other end of the building supervising the other redbirds.

I move next to Ann. "What's so funny?" Ann just shakes her head, a smile still on her face.

"Tell me."

"I can't.

"You must."

"I can't."

"If you don't tell me I won't be your friend."

"I can't. Don't ask me."

She goes off to another part of the lawn, leaving me alone. I turn to pick up some mud-covered stuff near the fence, and through the fence I see three civvie kids gawking at me.

"Caster! Hey you, little redshit!"

"Isn't that what they call you? Redshit?"

They all laugh.

I turn my back on them and pick up some litter near a mud puddle. A small stone hits me on the back of my head. It stings. With tears in my eyes I turn and see the three civvies punching each other and laughing. I scoop up a double handful of mud, run to the fence and sling it at them, hitting one in the face and spattering the other two.

"Guard! Guard!"

The detail guard rushes from the other end of the building, stopping next to me. "What's the trouble, kids?"

"This caster threw mud at us."

"Yeah."

"Little snot."

"We can't go to school looking like this."

The guard looks down at me. "Is that true?"

"They threw a rock at me—" The guard slaps my face, knocking me down. Dizzy, my nose feels strange, and there is something loose in my mouth.

Then, the pain.

"You threw mud at these citizens?"

I am crying so hard I can't answer. The guard kicks me in my ribs and I scream. One of the civvies pokes the other two, and they all run off.

Grabbing me by my hair, the guard drags me to the side of the building near a pile of scrap lumber. I can't stop screaming long enough to take a breath.

Standing me up by holding my head fast by my hair, the guard slaps my face again and again until I am blind from tears and pain. I still can't breathe.

I feel myself falling, hitting the ground, a heavy weight falling on top of me. The guard pushes himself up off of me and I hear the guard and the redbirds shouting. By the time I clear my eyes, the guard is standing over Ann's body.

Her neck is crooked and her chest doesn't move.

The redbirds gather close to the guard.

"Blackshit."

A boy spits out the words. "You killed her, blackshit!"

On the ground behind the guard is a piece of lumber. The guard points back toward it.

"You all saw her! She attacked me. Get back to work, or I'll have you all called out for punishment. I promise you that!" He pulls his gun slowly from its holster.

I frown at Ann's still image. Dead? I never saw dead before. The guard was hurting me and Ann attacked him. Then he killed her.

Dead.

I look up at the guard's back.

"Blackshit. Blackshit. Blackshit."

The redbirds move closer.

The board. Ann's board.

In a daze, I get to my feet and pick up the board. It is heavy and has two long nails sticking out of one end. The lines of light and dark in the wood are very pretty.

I pull it back over my head and swing it with all of my strength toward the guard. It strikes the guard on the back of his head. I let go of the board but it sticks fast to the guard's head.

The nails have been driven into his brain.

The guard staggers around and looks down at me, a surprised look on his face. The gun falls from his hand.

It tumbles over and over, the guard swaying in the distance.

Slowly he sinks to the ground.

He bounces, and bounces again.

He is still.

It takes forever.

Everyone is frozen for an instant. I move in a fog to Ann's body while the others drag the guard's body off and hide it under the scrap lumber. I kneel down next to her as a girl runs into the gray building. I touch Ann's face. Her head flops down on one cheek facing me, her lips curled back in a snarl.

"Her neck's broken. Leave her be."

How can she be alive one instant and dead the next? And especially after what happened last night?

"Ann?"

One redbird tugs at my sleeve while two more try to pick up Ann.

I fall across her body, clinging tightly to her reds. "Ann? Ann? Open your eyes!"

I scream until I feel nothing.

Wardate: 21:36-7AUG2033
Downlimit: 177912:04:20

83

Here is a dark.

I can't see. It is endless dark. I do not think for the monsters of the night surround me, waiting, waiting for the flicker of an eyelid.

I am not bad. All I did was open a window, and I really didn't mean to do that.

The guard's face turns around, a surprised look—

—I didn't mean to do that. I really didn't mean—

—bed.

I am in a real bed. I look for the reflections of the lights from the fence on the ceiling. There are none.

My face hurts and I lift my hand and begin to explore the lumps and welts. My nose is swollen shut, my tongue finds a gap in my teeth and a thousand images streak through my mind.

—the gun tumbling slowly from his hand, he bounces—

"Tommy?"

Helen's voice. "Tommy, are you awake?"

My whimper sounds like that of a wounded, frightened baby animal. I sound like Ann. Dead Ann. The more awake I become, the more everything hurts. The more I remember. The more fear crushes my chest.

"You're in my room."

"You have a real bed. With a mattress."

"Because I'm a dormkeeper. My own room and a bed with a mattress are some of the privileges. That's why we call them feathers."

"Call what feathers?"

"Privileges. They're called feathers because of the mattresses." She pauses and smiles. "A long time ago they used to stuff mattresses with feathers."

"Oh."

Helen takes my hand and sits on the edge of the bed. Sitting up, I bury my face between her tiny breasts.

"Helen . . . Helen, I—"

"I know, Tommy. I know." She strokes my hair and rocks back and forth.

"I didn't mean to, Helen. I really didn't mean to. What'll they do to me? What'll they do to me? I didn't mean—"

"It's all right, Tommy. Everything is all right."

"But, but—"

"Listen."

I lift my head, stop sniffling and strain my ears, trying to hear past the beat of my heart.

The whine. The same whine I had heard for a moment standing watch over Ann. It is far away, but there is no wind to obscure it.

"They won't do anything to you, Tommy. No one will ever find him. Listen."

The whine—it is the compost shredder.

The Green Machine.

What was that movie where the angry man fed the bad person alive through a huge meat grinder? Mommy turned off the television and made me go to back to bed before I could really see anything.

As I try to sleep, that snarl on Ann's face is before my eyes.

Wardate: 21:36-7AUG2033
Downlimit: 177906:16:19

82

The mornings, the days, the nights. I am caught in a nightmare without feelings. The blood is before my eyes and now it covers my hands. The other redbirds act like nothing is happening. Manuel and Godfrey talk as they talk every night, the French girls play jacks, Francis does laundry, Helen lets me sleep with her.

The boy who thought friends were too expensive tried to escape Outcasters. The blackshit police on the road catch and return him half dead. The Outcaster guards take care of the other half. A gray van comes and takes away his body.

Daniel, I remind myself.

The dead boy's name is Daniel. Friends might be expensive, but Daniel showed me the price of being a loner. I am screaming inside. I cannot believe no one hears me.

A redbird called Hey You frightens me more than anything else. Hey You moves like a toy robot, and only when ordered. He does not speak at all, and his eyes are vacant. Godfrey says that Hey You came to Outcasters two years ago, when he was six, and that he became that way during a beating. Everyone had been there to witness the punishment. One second he was begging and screaming, the next second he was dead silent.

The other dorms have their own Hey Yous. Sometimes the redbirds play games trying to get Hey You to blink or flinch which he never does. Not unless he is ordered to blink or flinch.

I wonder if that could happen to me. Would I become another Hey You? An unfeeling object of cruel pranks?

This morning there is no inspection and all details are canceled. From the stairwell one of the redbirds sees several men and women in civvies going into the chief warden's office off the big hall downstairs.

They are there for three days asking questions. They take the older redbirds first. On the third day I am called in to the chief warden's office.

The woman in tan civvie slacks and white blouse is young. She is seated behind a machine in the chief warden's outer office. I have never been in there before. The walls are painted pale rose, the ceiling white. There is a painting of a sailboat on the wall across from the door. The woman's machine is facing away from the picture, and next to the machine is a table. On the table is a silver box connected to the machine. Citizen Gammon stands next to the table. He points at the floor in front of his feet. I walk to the place indicated and come to a halt.

The woman begins speaking in a bored monotone, not looking up from the machine. "Place your right hand palm down on the sensor plate and state your full name and registration number."

I frown at the silver box. Can it tell if I am lying? I look up at the guard. "Put your hand on the box and spit it out, redshit."

I place my hand on the box. The surface of the silver plate is very warm. The woman glances at me "Name?"

"Thomas Windom."

She hits six keys in rapid succession. "Spell the last."

I frown at the guard. "Spell your last name, idiot."

"W-i-n-d-o-m."

Her fingers clatter the keys. "Number?"

"1-3-7-5-9-9-9-5."

More clattering. I stand with my eyes shut, waiting for the accusation. "Can you read?"

I open my eyes and nod. The woman is holding out a small

white card. "Keep your right hand on the plate and read this out loud." She wiggles the card at me. "Take it."

I take the card with my left hand and begin reading to myself. *Molly prayed and Polly made a fallow folly—*

The guard grabs my shoulder. "Read it out loud and sound off, chicken. And if you stall around any more I'll have you called out for punishment. Copy?"

I nod, moisten my lips, and read the nonsense words, embarrassed because I stutter through the entire reading. When I am finished the woman takes back the card.

"That's all."

I turn and stumble as quickly as I can toward the door. Back in the dorm I ask the others, but no one seems to know what is going on in the chief warden's outer office.

Wardate: 21:36-7AUG2033
Downlimit: 177774:49:32

81

There are changes.

Each time we form up for mess there are guards along the entire route, and only one dorm at a time eats. There are more guards inside the dining room and they all carry guns.

I see the two guards that had laughed at Citizen Sayther the day before. They aren't laughing now. They look grim. Frightened.

Yes, frightened.

It makes me feel good, and I don't think that I should feel that way. The wardens no longer eat with us.

I am taken off lawn detail. Now I wax and polish the big hall downstairs.

The ugly girl no longer plays tricks on me. Her name is Doris and she lives in "G" Dorm.

On this night I wash and iron my own reds, clean my shoes and rack area, and spend the rest of the evening trying not to look at Ann's rack. It is empty; the bedding turned back into the supply room. Lying on my rack, I stare past the light bars at the blank ceiling.

Mommy and Daddy must not know where I am. If they knew they'd come and take me away from this place. How can I let them know where I am? Where are they? I can't think of them being anyplace but home.

"Come with me, Tommy."

I look down toward the foot of my bed. Helen stands there

and cocks her head toward the hall door. I get up and follow her into the hallway, past "F" and "G" Dorms, the crapper and laundry room, to the back stairwell.

It is enclosed, and Helen opens the heavy door and follows me onto the landing. The stairwell smells musty, and the only light comes from the small window in the door.

We feel our way down two short flights and come to the first floor landing. Through the dirty window in the door I can see the big hall.

"Where are we going, Helen?"

"Quiet."

Two more flights down and we come to a solid metal door. Helen opens it, and I enter a dimly lit passage with wires and thick pipes along the ceiling and walls.

The heat in the narrow corridor is oppressive.

We pass a room filled with coal, turn down another passage, and walk to its end. Helen opens another metal door and motions me to go inside.

The room is small with junk piled all around the walls. In the center is a large crate. Seated around the crate on smaller boxes are Manuel, Godfrey, Francis, and a little girl my age from "E" Dorm. The only light in the room comes from two small candles set in holders made from old cans at both ends of the crate.

Helen sits on an empty box and points to another box between her and Godfrey.

I sit on the box and place my hands in my lap.

Helen reaches across me and takes Godfrey's hand. The rest of them join hands around the crate and close their eyes. Helen speaks a single word.

"Redbirds."

"Redbirds," repeat the others. They hold their circle of hands for a moment, speaking in unison:

"Brenda, your redbirds gather here to keep the fight, hoping for blood if we cannot hope for right."

The circle breaks and Helen turns to me. "Do you know Godfrey and Manuel?"

"Yes, and Francis."

She nods toward the young girl. "This is Louisa." Helen looks around at the faces.

"I want to take Tommy into the girls club."

Godfrey frowns. "He's only been here for a few days, Helen."

"I know. I also think we all know he belongs with us."

"Tommy?"

I look at Godfrey.

"Do you know about the club?"

I shake my head.

Godfrey thinks for a moment and then sweeps his hand around the crate. "We are redbirds, Tommy. All redbirds are outcasters—illegal children. Do you know what that means?"

"No."

"It means the law says we aren't even supposed to be alive. Our parents broke the law by having us."

"My mommy and daddy wouldn't break the law—"

"They did. That's why you're here." Godfrey looks at the others and continues. "The law says we have no rights. The blackshit can do anything it wants to us. You've seen that."

I nod, my eyes glistening. I keep seeing Ann and that guard's body falling slowly to the ground. Helen places her hand on my shoulder.

"A long time ago the very first redbirds formed the girls club. The club protects redbirds by judging and punishing the blackshit that hurts us."

"How can you punish a guard? He'd just tell who did it—"

"We only have one punishment, Tommy. Death. Dead blackshit doesn't talk. We do it so nothing can be proved. But we let the blackshit know why it was done."

"Citizen Lathrup?"

"The club took care of him. His stick was dipped in his blood and left in the guards' quarters. We also let the blackshit know why McDermit was killed."

"McDermit?"

"The guard you killed, Tommy. You remember the guard you killed?"

"Yes." Dumb question. Do I remember the guard— I nod,

my eyes closed. I begin shaking my head. "I didn't know his name."

Tears. I mean the tears for the dead guard, not for me. Nameless, the dead guard is part of a faceless "them," a detachable memory. Named, the killing assumes horrible proportions. With a name he becomes a person. Maybe a family, people that he loved and that loved him. Maybe he even had a son—

I open my eyes and look at Helen. "What happened to Ann? How did you let them know?"

Helen takes her hand from my shoulder. "Ann was put on the steps to the guards' quarters. McDermit's papers were in her hand."

Godfrey leans toward me. "Will you join us, Tommy?" Ann's face, cold and snarling, is burning in my mind. I don't want to kill, but I don't want to die. And the blackshit should pay. And I have already killed. And the blackshit should pay. The blackshit should pay.

"Yes."

"Tommy."

"Yes, Manuel?"

"You are never to repeat anything you hear in this room. Understand?"

"I understand."

"Be sure you do. If you talk, one of us will kill you."

I look at all of their faces, shocked. They are serious. Manuel continues, "If one of us repeats something, Tommy, what will you do?"

I shake my head. I don't even want to think about it. Not even as a play-pretend joke.

"Say it, Tommy."

Godfrey grabs my arm. "What will you do?"

"Kill you."

Godfrey puts his arm around my shoulders and kisses me on my cheek. "I move that the membership be accepted."

Helen calls for the vote and everyone puts up a hand. Godfrey continues to hold me while Helen tells me about my parents, how they were executed for giving me life. It was done by what they call slow electrocution.

Televised. A monstrous ritual dreamed up in a huge computer in the government called MAC III.

—There was the horned creature named Aubry Cummings and his mechanized son Mac—

—I remember Laura Wilson, guilty of violating the provisions of the 1998 Citizenship Act. I remember her crying for her mother. I remember her twitching away her life. I remember laughing at Laura Wilson because I didn't know. I remember Mommy crying that night—

I learn about Brenda, the murdered founder of the girls club, who was the first redbird ever to execute a guard.

My world grows even smaller, darker, more fearsome.

There is something I had forgotten. In the mad rush to escape the men in black, there was something I didn't do. "I never said good-bye. My mommy and daddy. I never said good-bye."

Godfrey hugs me. "None of us did."

"I see."

Looking around the crate, I realize that none of us have parents. None of us. Outcast. A union of bastards. My new family.

"I see." Shrugging loose from Godfrey's arm, I sit straight on the box.

Helen takes her right thumb and draws it slowly down the line of her jaw. "This is the sign by which you will know members from other dorms and how you will identify yourself to them. We cooperate with the other clubs. Sometimes we swap hits—we kill some other dorm's and they kill ours. I command the "E" Dorm club, but we vote on the things we do. Understand, a vote is an order that must be obeyed at all costs."

"I understand."

Helen takes my left hand and Godfrey takes my right. Hands join until the ring is complete. They speak and I listen.

The blackshit took a great big ax
And gave a redbird forty whacks.
When Brenda saw what they had done
She gave the blackshit forty-one.

Wardate: 21:36-7AUG2033
Downlimit: 173358:53:59

80

For weeks the guards carry guns, but by the end of April the guns disappear, the sticks and whips come out, and inspections and details resume. Outcasters must support itself and we are late getting in the crops. The red sign beside the road still carries the same number: 21:36 7AUG2033.

The planting is hard work, but most of the time I am waxing the big hall floor. Every so often I am put on crop weeding, and once in June I am assigned to the detail that thins the lettuce field.

The guards treat the redbirds warily at first, but in July a boy is called out for punishment. The beatings resume. A redbird is found dead from a fall, and another is found drowned in a toilet. No one sees anything.

The "E" Dorm club meets to decide tactics. Afterward we all work and travel in groups of no less than three. If a guard singles one out, the others know who the guard is.

During the harvest three redbirds going back to their detail after noon chow meet two guards on the gravel path. Citizens Maison and Bond. Maison slaps one of the redbirds and accuses him of bumping into him. Sending the other two back to their details, the guards take the boy behind the dining hall, to their quarters.

The boy is found that evening sitting on a toilet in the first floor crapper with a large sharp stick shoved up his anus. The guards laughingly suggest that the boy must have been playing with himself.

The dead redbird is from "B" Dorm, downstairs. Within

two days the "B" Dorm girls club disposes of Citizen Maison. Two more days are let go by to allow Citizen Bond to think upon the missing Maison and spread tales among the other guards. Then "E" Dorm draws garbage detail for the week. Citizen Bond belongs to us.

It is my first job for the club.

It is late in the afternoon.

Single guards live at Outcasters in individual apartments with a central bath and washroom. Manuel follows Bond to the guards' quarters and waits until he sees Bond wrapped in a towel heading for the shower room. The rest of us wait around the corner of the dining hall, and when Manuel signals us we quickly follow him into the hallway of the guards' quarters to the shower room door.

Because redbirds are detailed to do the guards' housekeeping, their quarters are as familiar to us as "E" Dorm.

We know Bond is alone and will be alone for a long time. By an arrangement between all the clubs the other details will be slow to finish. Citizen Bond's detail, however, finished in record time. The other guard shift is in town.

Manuel carries a length of steel pipe. He opens the door and motions us to follow him. Helen moves, then Francis carrying a brown cloth bag, then Louisa and me.

The room is steaming and we can hear the shower running. Bond is whistling a happy tune. Moving past the sinks and crapper stalls, Manuel and I wait at the opening to the shower. Godfrey, Helen and Francis wait by the sinks, out of sight. Louisa watches the hall. Manuel presses himself against the wall to the left of the shower room door and I do the same on the right.

The shower's hiss stops and the slap of wet feet moves toward us. I step away from the wall into full view.

"Citizen Bond?"

The guard looks surprised as he moves toward me, his fist raised. "You little redshit, what'n the hell are you—"

Manuel brings down the pipe on the back of Bond's head, and the naked guard makes a noise like a slap as he hits the tiled floor, rolling there, moaning. Francis rushes up with his bag and hands Manuel a length of rope. While Manuel ties the guard's hands behind his back, Francis stuffs a cloth in the guard's mouth, gagging him.

Bond groans again and opens his eyes.

Francis shows the guard the sharp wooden stake, still blood-covered from the redbird it had killed.

Francis hisses, "Up your ass, blackshit. Up your ass."

The guard snarls and Godfrey sits on his back between his arms. Helen sits on one leg and Manuel sits on the other while Francis, kneeling between the guard's legs, inserts the sharp end of the stick into the guard's anus and shoves hard.

Bond struggles with frightening strength and Francis has to help Helen hold the guard down. As he gets a good grip on the guard's ankle, Francis nods toward the bag.

"Tommy. Get the mallet."

I reach into the bag and find a heavy wooden hammer. How many centuries ago was it that Daddy gave me a hammer for my birthday? Francis points at the stake. "Drive it in."

As the mallet strikes the stake I watch fascinated as Bond's entire skin begins glistening. As I hammer in the stake I try to keep my feet out of the widening pool of yellow gathering under the squirming guard's body. For a moment I stop to throw up. I continue.

—Van Helsing. That was the man's name who drove the stake into Dracula's heart. Van—

Oh, it takes a long time for Bond to die.

"—*You must make a friend of horror,*" said Colonel Kurtz. Yes, that's the one. Daddy said he was just a little boy my age when *Apocalypse Now* was released. I didn't understand anything about the film. Now I understand Kurtz. "*Horror and moral terror are your friends. If they are not, then they are enemies to be feared.*"

—When the mallet strikes the stake, the stake vibrates so that it hums—

It takes such a very long time.

Wardate: 21:36-7AUG2033
Downlimit: 173355:12:02

79

Bond is not an unusually large man and the older ones have little trouble hauling him outside. Louisa takes the stake, puts it on Bond's bed, and joins the rest of us waiting behind the dining hall. I go to the kitchen door, where a redbird on kitchen detail strokes his jaw and nods. I wave to Helen and Louisa, and the three of us move the two-wheeled garbage cart behind the dining hall.

After the boys load Bond into the cart, all of us cover the body with garbage. When it is well concealed, we push the cart back to the kitchen door and return to the dorm to wait.

I open my eyes and Ugly Doris is looking down at me. She has a box under her arm. "I want to play a game," she says to me. She holds out the box. "You will learn how to play chess."

I sit up on my rack and take the box. "I'm no good at games."

"Then you are dead, chicken." She sits at the other end of my rack, her stubby legs crossed beneath her, and begins setting up the board.

"See the colors, chicken?" The chess pieces are black and red.

I cannot think, I cannot see, I cannot feel. One set of pieces is black. One set of pieces is red. "So what?"

She shakes her head and laughs. "Chickchick. What a chickchick."

* * *

After the evening meal, and a few minutes after lights out, all of us return on regular detail to the dining hall and pick up the cart, topped now with garbage from evening chow. We push the cart onto the road to the Green Machine.

The moonlight is bright and we can see clearly. The cart is heavy, and the dried ruts in the road slow us down. However, with Helen and the boys pulling on the wagon's tongue, and Louisa and I pushing, we are at the compost shredder in twenty minutes.

The four older redbirds are needed to turn the wheel. They pull Bond's body out of the garbage before they start and lay it out in front of the chute. Manuel and Francis have long knives from the kitchen, and they cut the body into pieces that can fit into the chute without jamming the mechanism.

It is quiet work except for separating the joints. Some sharp cracking noises are made when the shoulder and hip joints are separated.

With the wheel going around, deafening us with the whine of the blades, Louisa and I feed the garbage and the bloody bits of Citizen Bond to the Green Machine.

I think about the dead babies being fed into the hopper to make Baby Burgers. Blackshit Burgers. *Blackshit Burgers hit the spot, Six big ounces, that's a lot.*

It's funny to think that Citizens Lathrup, McDermit, Maison, and Bond will show up next year in the dining hall vegetables. I laugh as the redbirds on the wheel chant.

It's whining, it's roaring,
The blackshit is snoring,
He went to bed, we cut off his head
Now he won't get us in the morning.

Bondburgers.

I almost fall in the chute I am laughing so hard.

Bondburgers. Bondburgers, Maisonmelons, Lathrup—

—funny. I can't think of a vegetable that begins—leeks! Lathrupleeks!

I come up behind Louisa holding Bond's severed forearm by the wrist. I shake the fingers in front of Louisa's face. "Let me lend you a hand, little girl."

She giggles.

Come, Igor. It is time to build the monster.

Yeth, Mathter.

Horror.

I must make a friend of horror.

Wardate: 21:36-7AUG2033
Downlimit: 170931:26:03

78

Christmas. Ugly Doris beats me at chess, she says, for the thousandth time. I don't know why she plays with me, since I'm no challenge.

I play because how the pieces move and relate to each other is beginning to make sense. Also it fills my head, forbidding me to be aware of anything else while I'm playing.

The Christians sing some songs. I remember a couple of them from Mommy and Daddy singing them. I remember the music. The words are gone though.

Peace on Earth. Goodwill something.

Late in the night.

The guards call out all dorms to witness punishment. They want to prove to us that they are not afraid of us, which proves that they are.

We are taken downstairs. The redbirds form ranks by dorms in the big hall on the first floor. The ranks are backed against the walls, facing the center of the hall. The first floor guards and wardens stand at the center, where a thousand years ago I put two books and my childhood into a paper barrel.

I think of the titles: *Huckleberry Finn* and *Life on the Mississippi*. A gift from Daddy. Glorious fantasies about boys who exist in some sort of dimension warp. I don't believe the stories anymore. Far beyond my ability even to dream is being as happy as the slave Jim.

A redbird is standing with the guards and wardens in the

center of the hall. An older girl from downstairs. It is Elana, the girl who helped me tie my shoes in the shower room on my first day. Why did I have to know her name? I look down at my laces and see Ann looking back at me shaking her blond pigtails.

"Don't you even know how to tie your own shoes?"

"Yes!" I cry. A hand slaps me across the mouth, knocking me into the rank behind.

"Stand him up!"

The guard walks away and hands push me to my feet. I don't feel where the guard slapped me. My head is light. The hall hazy like a dream. I think.

Shoelaces. What is it with shoelaces? Touch Thomas Windom's shoelaces and die.

A male warden steps out from the blackshit gathered around Elana and faces the formation, his gaze passing around the sides of the open rectangle.

"This redshit," he points at Elana, "this redshit talked back to a guard. A very smart mouth on this one."

The warden walks slowly around the rectangle of redbirds. All of the guards carry guns. "Redshit casters don't talk back to guards. We are citizens. We belong here. You are nothing. Nothing at all. This caster has to learn that. You learn it too and save yourself some leather time."

He stops beside the girl and unsnaps the top of her reds. Taking her collar, he pulls her uniform top down to her waist and yanks her arms out of her sleeves. A guard behind her uncoils a long whip. Elana's lips are deathly pale.

"All of you learn what nothing means."

I am only a couple of meters away from the girl. I watch, helpless, as she trembles in shame and fear. The warden takes one of her tiny breasts in each hand and fondles them. Tears stream down Elana's face and the warden laughs. He squeezes her breasts violently.

Elana screams as an automatic growl of rage erupts from the formation. The ranks take a half step forward.

"Freeze, redshit!"

The guards have their guns out. They motion the redbirds

back into ranks. The warden releases the girl and she sinks to her knees, holding her battered breasts.

"I see you don't understand what nothing means. But you'll learn. You'll learn." He kicks Elana's thigh. She curls up into a ball, weeping uncontrollably.

The ranks stand motionless.

"Beginning to understand? You are nothing. Nothing!"

The warden turns to two of the guards. "Lay her out."

The two guards yank Elena forward to give the whip man more room and spread-eagle her on the floor, facedown. She screams and screams. I almost curse her I so want her to stop her screaming. It tears at me. I feel my heart bending with her pain.

Now that she is squirming on the concrete in front of me, I can see her back. She has been whipped before. One of the guards squatting down to hold her left arm turns to the whip man, "Now, don't you miss, Billings."

"Then move back, you fat fart."

The guard is squatting in front of me with his back toward my rank of the formation. The guard's gun is holstered to free his hands.

In my dream I step forward, take the gun, and pull it from its holster. It is very heavy.

I aim it at the back of the guard's head and pull on the trigger. The pull is too hard, and as the whip man yells and the guard turns around to look at me, I pull with both forefingers on the trigger. The guard's face disappears.

Around me the redbirds attack, screaming and clawing at the guards. Another redbird gets a gun away from a guard and begins shooting at anything wearing black. Another redbird takes the gun from my hand. The guards return fire at the advancing children and in seconds the hall is bloody chaos.

The quiet comes.

Eleven blackshit and sixteen redbirds are down. I know that what has happened is important, that I should feel something. But there is nothing to feel. I ought to examine that—

"To your dorms!" Helen and the other dormkeepers are pushing the stunned children into action.

The floor is all scuffed up. It'll need to be polished again.

"Go back to your dorms!"

Godfrey takes my arm and begins pulling me toward the stairwell. I suddenly pull back, digging in my heels.

"Tommy, we have to get out of here!"

"What about her?" I point at Elana, trapped beneath the body of the guard I killed.

She is still and has Hey You's familiar vacant look.

"What's your dorm?" Godfrey rolls the guard's body to one side and sits her up, shaking her bare shoulders.

"What's your dorm, girl?"

A boy runs into the hall from the main entrance. "Zip it! More blackshit coming!"

"What's her dorm?" Godfrey tries fitting her rubber arms into her reds.

" 'B' Dorm."

The boy jumps over a body, and he and Godfrey drag the half-dressed girl to the "B" Dorm door. Eager hands pull her in. The boy runs to the "C" Dorm door and it closes quietly behind him. Godfrey and I are the only ones left alive in the hall.

We both hear heavy boots running up the steps to the main entrance. I am paralyzed.

Lifting me, Godfrey runs over and around the red and black bodies, down the length of the big hall to the back stairwell. As the door closes behind us we hear the guards coming in the front.

Hardly touching the steps, Godfrey flys up the stairwell, through the second floor door, and up the hall to "E" Dorm. It is dark inside. Unseen hands strip me and put me into my rack.

—sirens coming down the road.

—screaming. I hear someone screaming.

—I feel a pillow closing over my face.

There is a different kind of darkness. It embraces me.

Wardate: 21:36-7AUG2033
Downlimit: 158547:02:07

77

Time.

Time is my ordeal.

Darkness.

Darkness is my weapon, my defense, my protector.

How little I recognize the passage of time is my measure of success. My skin is the wall of a fortress. The dragons are on the other side of my skin. I let nothing cross that barrier.

If I hear, I will hurt. There are voices around me, but I do not hear. If I see, I will hurt. There are faces around me, but I do not see. If I feel, I will hurt. There are words, touches, looks, taunts around me, but I do not feel.

The sun is warm, the tongue on my hand warm.

I see this light, this day. Am I back? There are children in dirty red uniforms feeding weeds into a green machine. What is the horror of that—

The warmth on my hand. I am sitting in the grass, in the sun. I remember Sun. Little black dog licking my hand. Little black dog loves me. Wants to play. He climbs on my lap, trying to lick my face. I laugh a little, but then remember the risks.

I get to my feet and pick up the animal. I get in line and I toss the little black dog into the Green Machine's chute.

If I feel, I will hurt.

I do not feel.

I will not hurt.

—there is a man in a black uniform standing over me. He is screaming at me, his face bright red, there are tears in his eyes.

I am lying on the grass holding my face. The man in black must have hit me. But I don't feel. If I don't feel, I won't hurt.

There is a metal drum in the center of the tiny, windowless room. The drum is on its side, and that side is sunk into the cement of the floor. Also set into the cement are pairs of steel loops, a pair on each side.

I don't hear the words or feel the slaps, but I can tell that rough hands are skinning me down.

That's a strange expression: skinning down. It means undressing. I don't know why I know that.

I see my wrists are tied to a pair of steel loops and feel hands pulling on my ankles. My penis is caught between my body and the thing—the drum—beneath me. I move a little and feel better.

The man in black. He is saying—his dog. I killed his dog.

"I'm sorry."

Sorry, he says. Sorry doesn't do it.

—They tie his wrists to the wooden grate and stand aside.

"Prisoner ready for punishment, sir!"

"Commence punishment!" orders bloody Scott-Padget.

"Start the roll!" orders Sergeant Kneebone.

"One!" orders the master-at-arms as the drums begin to roll.

And then the cat swings—

—holdit! Grip the rop—

One of Daddy's favorite old movi—

Damn the Defiant. *Damn the* Defiant. *Damn—*

—God it hurts'n'Ipraythat—

—this is for a dog! A dog!

My spine is showing! I swear my spine is coming through—

What if he finds out about Citizen Bond? Bond—

* * *

I know where I am.
Who.
Why.
Ann, Elana, Bond, McDermit—
If I let go, if I let myself fall to my dark center, I will stop thinking. If I can stop thinking, I cannot hurt.
Fall. Down, fall.

The fortress.
Inside my fortress the world is very simple. Full, empty, hot, cold.
One dragon is on the inside of my wall. The word *murderer* stands to one side, not connected to me, waiting. I curl up into the opposite corner of myself, refusing to recognize the word, refusing to remember why that word stands there.

I am beaten, and do nothing.
I am kissed, and do nothing.
I am embraced, and do nothing.
I am wept over, and do nothing.
I am left alone, and do nothing.

A million years, or a couple of seconds, pass. There is a light before me, my old window to the universe. It runs and I drink it in, for if it comes in through the window, it isn't real.
I see old friends: Marshal Cain and Marshal O'Niel, the Bladerunner, THX 1138, King Arthur, and El Cid. There's Captain Crawford! He has only one arm, though. But that means that bloody Scott-Padget is dead.
Great Frith, where is Watership Down?
I am again safe in my attic room. All they can do is to hurt my outside. If I do not go Outside, and if I do not allow my outside in, I am safe again in my attic room.
There are things that I feel, things that feel me, but I don't feel.
I don't feel.

Wardate: 21:36-7AUG2033
Downlimit: 126435:31:14

76

Here I am, sitting here, watching him watching me.

Hey You.

Another dragon slips into my fortress.

There is a voice and it says something. A thing in me rebels at what the voice says. I do not hear the voice. I do not understand what the voice says. I do not know why I rebel. The something fills me with rage, terror. It is inside my wall and I must recognize it if I am to catch it and put it in chains next to my word *murderer*.

I open my wall just a little. There is a face looking down at me. A redbird I don't recognize. He is calling me a name.

"Hey you."

Hey you? *Hey you?* Not Hey You. *Never* Hey You.

"Don't call me that."

His face looks surprised. Shocked. "You talked." He looks away and shouts. "Somebody! Hey You talks! C'mere!"

"Don't ever call me Hey You—" I'm weak. I try to kill him, but I can hardly move my arm.

The boy still is looking away. "Helen! Helen, come here! Hey You talked!"

I try to get up, my fingers aching to close upon the boy's throat. My legs shake and wobble. I fall back on the floor. "I said not to—"

"Tommy?"

Her voice. Helen's. Strange, this feeling. An ancient thirst. I miss her. For so long. My hands look clumsy, distorted, enlarged. My legs are too big. My feet are huge.

I'm filthy.

Helen is standing next to the boy. She is different. Her hair cut very short. Her face older. Her breasts much bigger. I almost laugh at the size of Helen's breasts.

Another voice calls me Hey You.

Icy fear turns into white hot anger.

I look at the boy. "Don't call me Hey You. Never—"

The boy squats and points a finger at me. "If you can talk, then you can listen, scrud. I don't care if you piss in your pants, you fucking vegetable. Just don't do it on my floor."

Helen taps the boy on his shoulder. "Back off, Jolly."

"You made me responsible for the—"

"I know. Back off. I'll take care of it."

The boy stands, glares at Helen for a moment, and walks off. I look down. I feel the wetness. The smell. My face grows hot with shame. There is a scar on the back of my left hand. I don't remember getting it. It is an old scar. My fingernails are long and dirty.

I look back at Helen's face as I begin to feel the edge of panic. Where is my safe fortress? What's happened?

She places her hand on my cheek and smiles. "You're back, Tommy. You were gone, but now you're back."

Gone? My lips form the words, but I have no voice. Her hand on my cheek feels very strange. I touch my cheek. It is covered with fine hair. It is hard. Thin.

What happened? What is going on?

"Tommy, what's the last thing you remember?"

"Remember?" Helen nods at me and I try and think. Helen touching me. The boy called Jolly calling me Hey You. A little dog licking my hand.

"Pillows. Pillows over my face. To keep me from screaming. The blackshit and redbirds fighting downstairs. All of those dead bodies. Elana—" My heart is pounding so hard I think it will burst.

"Do you remember anything after that?"

I close my eyes and shake my head.

Helen is quiet for a long time. I look at her. She bites her lower lip and looks down. "Six years ago, Tommy. That was the Christmas riot, six years ago." She looks up at me.

"Six?" My voice is strange. Rough. It hurts my throat. Six years? Almost half of my life passed without notice? *Six years?* I can't seem to add the numbers.

"How old am I?"

"Thirteen."

Thirteen?

A beautiful girl, her face excited, walks up and stops next to Helen. "Is it true?" She squats down and looks into my face. Her hand moves out and touches my cheek.

"Tommy?"

I stare back at her.

"Do you remember me?"

I continue staring.

"Louisa."

"Louisa," I repeat. I remember a little girl named Louisa. She used to watch the door while my brothers, sisters and I drove lumber up Citizen Bond's ass. Could this be the same little girl?

Behind her looms a tall man with a dark face. Godfrey. The man next to him is Manuel.

I cry. Helen holds my head against her breast, her arms around me.

I am so ashamed of my odor. So ashamed.

Wardate: 21:36-7AUG2033
Downlimit: 125883:36:29

75

The face in the mirror is a stranger. Thin, without expression. The eyes possess a kind of lifelessness that almost hides from others the nightmares that dance behind them.

In between the nightmares are these moments of hopeless despair; moments when it seems that my mind no longer functions. It is almost as though I am a huge baby, helpless and incapable of taking care of myself. I dissolve into tears with no warning, or burst out in anger at nothing.

Then I am an ancient, fragile thing, waiting in horror to be crushed, convinced that I have already lived too long. Then I become resigned to horror, placing myself beyond fear by expecting the worst that never comes.

I am comfortable with neither the baby or the ancient. Both of them remind me of Hey You.

This is not the year 2013.

This is 2019.

I cannot get it through my head. This is the year 2019.

Everything is different. The riot caused an investigation. The investigation led to public involvement. Things are better. I wonder how many will have to die to get attention the next time.

This body of mine, which embarrasses me with its size,

shape, and hair, is so different. My face, Helen, Godfrey, Manuel, Louisa.

The one I used to call Hey You has gotten bigger, older. The muscles of his arms and legs have atrophied. The newer redbirds call him the Potato. The first chicken I heard call him that I almost killed. I don't remember much about it.

I don't look at Hey You's eyes. I know what is behind them and I don't want to go back there.

Most of the guards are different, although Citizen Sayther is still here. She is older. Gentler. Her face seems softer. She is the deputy warden.

Citizen Sayther is married now. Her husband's name is Bob. She brings Bob out to the orphanage to show him around, and she introduces him to all of us at evening chow. He says some words about the soul being the part of God that God lets us borrow until we die, when God reclaims what is his. That is, unless we sell our piece of God to the Devil. If we do that, then we have to go to hell until we can work off the debt and get our souls back. According to Bob there are ways we can sell our souls that can never be paid back. He begins listing the ways and I stop listening after "murder."

Bob is some sort of clergy. My protein burger got cold while he was talking and now it tastes like shit.

Wardate: 21:36-7AUG2033
Downlimit: 124875:52:01

74

The others say that there have been no incidents since the Christmas riot. Everything—even the hate—has changed. But to me, to this face in the mirror, the Christmas Riot happened only days ago.

The bullet holes in the walls of the big hall have all been filled, sanded, stained, and finished. On the floor, just in front of where I stood that night, is a patch in the concrete floor. It is slightly lighter than the rest of the floor, even though I have waxed and polished it many times. When I blew that guard's face off, just a few days ago, the bullet passed through his head and gouged the floor. There is the mark.

If I look at that patch long enough, I think I see the stain of blood on the floor.

The trees and shrubs outside are much, much bigger. Everyone has changed so much that I do not know them. I find myself so alone.

I am thirteen years old, and I am expected to act as though I am thirteen. But only a few days ago I was seven.

The chief warden's office is no longer off the big hall on the first floor. Instead there is a new building behind the mess hall, where the CW's office is, and also that's where the new infirmary is. A real doctor comes to Outcasters five times a week and holds sick call.

In the CW's old office there is a television. We are allowed to watch it when we are not on details.

One of the new guards, Citizen Haskins, sometimes comes in to watch the television. One night between shows he asks me what I remember about the last three years.

"I don't know, Citizen Haskins."

He sits forward in his chair and nods toward the television. "Don't you remember watching shows in here?" He looks at me, his eyes studying.

"No, Citizen."

Again he nods at the television. "For the three years that I've been here, and for I don't know how long before that, you've been sitting all day in front of that tube. You don't remember any of it?"

"No, Citizen."

He nods and leans back in his chair. With his finger he points at the television. "The show's starting."

I look back at the set. Is it possible? These memories of seeing old friends? I remember that THX 1138 even talked to me. That's what I remember.

Tonight I watch an old movie called *Iceman*. Scientists find frozen in the ice a young Indian hunter from forty centuries ago. They call him Charly. Forty thousand years ago he set out on the ice alone on a dreamwalk to offer himself to his god. In exchange his god would return the animals and save Charly's people. But this only if Charly was worthy.

Instead of awakening in his god's world, he awakens in an ice station's operating room surrounded by scientists. The scientists want to keep Charly and study him to learn small things, petty things. Things about freezing, preserving life, language, history, where the human race came from. But Charly is trying to reach his god.

When the movie is over, my eyes are wet, and Citizen Haskins is gone.

Wardate: 21:36-7AUG2033
Downlimit: 124323:09:32

73

Death.

In a very important way, I am dead. The flesh is colorless, loose and smelly. I can sit here and grieve over my death, or I can accept it and go on from here.

There is something in me, however, that rebels at accepting my death. Someone should pay—

That's it.

Someone should pay. That is my feeling. I am owed.

I am owed.

Ugly Doris is studying the chessboard. We sit on opposite ends of my rack the way we used to do. She's been studying the board for a long time.

"Girl, don't drool on my rack."

"Shut up." Her gaze doesn't move from the board. Her fat fingers reach down, and she moves her remaining black knight. She looks at me, that stupid grin on her face. "Eat it, Dumbs. Eat it."

I move my rook. "Checkmate."

"Hah!" She looks at the board. "No. No you don't."

I watch her as she looks at the board searching for her victory. This is the first time I have ever beaten her and she doesn't believe it. For the first time I hammered her right into the dirt.

I won.

I won and I really don't care.

Ugly Doris begins setting up the pieces for another game. I lean back until my head is on my pillow. With my foot I sweep the board and pieces off my bed onto the floor.

"I want to play another game, Dumbs."

"I have a game."

She examines me, that drooly smile back on her face. "What game?"

"It's called Why."

"Already it sounds stupid, Dumbs."

I close my eyes, clasp my fingers behind my head, and nod. "It's stupid."

"Okay, Dumbs. How does it go?"

"You ask 'Why?'"

"Why what?"

"Why anything. Why am I here? Why are you trapped in that ugly body? Why is Hey You still trying to hide from a beating that ended seven or eight years ago? Why Outcasters?" I sit up and wrap my arms around my knees. "And you know why those are stupid questions?"

She grins at me. "I just bet my chance at becoming a fashion queen you're going to tell me."

"See, we ask 'Why' just hoping someone will try and answer so we can say 'That's not good enough' in the hopes that it might change something."

I close my eyes and rest my forehead against my knees. Ugly Doris moves and I hear her picking up the chess pieces. "Will you play another game?"

Another game. Can there be more to life than killing time or trying to survive? I nod. "Okay."

She sits on my rack and begins setting up the board. "You call me ugly again, boyturd, and I'll sneak up on you after lights out with something sharp and give you a face that'll make mine look good." Again the grin.

"Your move."

Wardate: 17:14-9AUG2033
Downlimit: 114819:39:40

72

There are classes.

The classes are a way to insulate myself from my thoughts. The first year I devour my lessons. I begin with the first form. By the end of the first trimester I am in the seventh form. By the end of the year I am fourteen and in the ninth form. The teachers are impressed.

The novelty of impressing the teachers wears off. The next year the classes are little more than endless, meaningless, repetitious tedium. It is something like: Here is what you should learn because. Why because? Because that's what children have always learned. Because someone from the last century said so. Because that's all we know. Just because.

Just because.

The teachers are shipped in from the city. They don't know much of anything about us. They don't know much of anything about how to teach what I want to know. They just don't know much of anything.

Why? Outcasters. *Why?*

At the beginning of each trimester I have read all of my class texts by the third week. The teachers don't want to discuss things or answer questions. They just talk at us from the book, give tests, and drink coffee. I have read the book. I want to learn more. But there is no more.

I am fifteen and have exhausted the knowledge available in my universe. The new ground is on the other side of the fence.

I feel as though I know with exact certainty what every remaining moment of my life will be like. From the morning whistle to lights out, I know what it will be.

Why Outcasters? And if the reason isn't good enough do I get issued a new reality? A new past?

New redbirds move into "E" Dorm. Before they settle down, Louisa gets permission from Helen to move into the cot next to mine.

That night she whispers a question. "Tommy. All of those years. Where were you?"

"Why?"

"I want to know. Sometimes I would sit and watch you, your eyes staring, hardly ever blinking. When things were bad, I used to dream that where you were was a beautiful, safe place."

"I don't know where I was. I think I was dead. That's safe, I guess."

She giggles. "Then at least you know where you go when you die."

I turn my back to her and close my eyes. She is right. I do know where I go when I die. I go to hell.

Wardate: 17:14-9AUG2033
Downlimit: 101955:21:22

71

Christmas Eve, 2021. "E" Dorm is dark. Eight years ago tonight I shot that guard in his face. I still don't know his name. All I know is what Citizen Billings called him: fat fart. I don't want to know his name.

Eight years ago tonight I killed the fat fart. I didn't kill a father, brother, husband, or man. I killed the fat fart, and his mark is still in the big hall floor, downstairs.

Strange, I think, to be able to say "eight years ago." My head is still in a place that hasn't yet reached my tenth birthday. Where will I be when I can say "twenty years ago"—"forty years ago?"

—birthday.

The shadows of my mother and father flicker in the corners of "E" Dorm.

It's time to think about something else.

I inhale the pine smell of the Christmas tree next to Helen's door. It has no lights, but we have a Christmas tree. The smell of it fills the dorm.

It's decorated with little paper and wooden objects, and some special little things: a bracelet, a chain, a paper rose, a pendant. In the reflection from the security fence I watch it and try to remember my home.

We never had a Christmas tree. Probably my father figured it would attract attention. You probably only bring one home if you have children, and the Windoms had no children at home.

Maybe there was some other reason—

I roll over, facing Louisa, my head treadmilling a hundred thoughts.

In another three months I will be sixteen. I am not yet used to not being seven. I close my eyes.

Sometimes I will stand quietly in the front stairwell and stare at the fence. In those moments I want to be on the other side of the fence. Imagining being on the other side, however, frightens me. Outside is freedom. The unknown—

Outside, the place of Sun, Sky, Moon, and bullshit—

—buzz, buzz, buzz—

Am I more comfortable with the horror I know? Can civvies be any worse than the monotony of Outcasters?

I want out.

My restlessness frightens me. I don't fear the guards anymore. I fear something worse. Killing was a way to strike back—an edge I could taste, feel, and smell. To go on day after day, doing nothing but school, working the fields, standing formations—

Do I like killing? Is that why I feel this fear?

Do I fear myself?

I shake the thought from my head and concentrate on losing myself in the light patterns on the ceiling.

It is still there.

This fear of again going insane.

The girl Feena haunts the dorms, telling anyone who will listen about God. No one really listens to her, but others talk of God. I listen to them a few times and think about what they say. I decide to stay away from the goddies. I don't think I am able to take on any additional burdens.

I sigh at the dark. How can the others sleep?

These questions!

Why are we being schooled if all we will ever do is work in the fields? Manuel says we will get our citizenships, but everyone says he's been saying that for years.

But why? Why?

I look again at the reflection of the security lights on the ceiling. History keeps me awake. History and the man the book calls "The Father of the Compact of Nations," Aubry Cummings. The book says that this pain, my dead parents,

Outcasters—all of it—are necessary to human survival. My guts writhe in rebellion against that. But I have no facts and can't argue with the book.

The book describes a machine, MAC III, that makes the decisions and issues the orders that govern half of Earth. And no one can argue with MAC III.

Yesterday keeps me awake. Ann, that guard's head stuck fast to that board, all those bodies in the big hall years ago, and Citizen Bond's skin glistening as I hammered that stake up into his guts.

There is the boy whose name I can't remember; the one who thought friends were too expensive. His escape and murder. What is it like to be beaten to death?

Back in the shadows I think I remember being stretched across the barrel in the Drum Room, tied to the loops, and beaten. But I don't remember any pain. I can still make out the scars in the crapper mirror, but I don't remember any pain.

What is it like to be beaten to death?

This place and history.

My father taught history. Did he use the same book when he and my mother decided to create me? But he taught a special kind of history: movies. Was my father a kind of Hey You, his head in a movie fantasyland? Is it possible that he just didn't know? Didn't believe? Didn't care—

I feel my eyes beginning to fill with tears as I realize that I can no longer remember what my father and mother looked like. Godfrey says that as long as you can see someone in your mind, that someone will never die. He once described his father and mother to me. He did it in such detail that I can remember them better than I can remember my own parents.

Of my own parents, there is the feel of my mother kissing my hair. I remember that. There are the tears in my father's beard—

Again I shake the thought from my mind. Think again about the fence. Freedom. It is all a fantasy, but harmless. Manuel doesn't think it's a fantasy, though.

Seven billion humans on Earth, and Manuel keeps saying that the redbirds will join them someday. I think again about all of those people beyond the fence.

Every cough or wheeze in the dorm annoys me, keeping me awake. Louisa is sound asleep. Throwing my covers aside, I get up and poke around in my shelf for something to eat. My home stash is exhausted. I'll have to steal more my next time on kitchen detail.

I sit back on my rack, looking down the length of the dorm. How can they sleep? How can they all sleep?

I remember the night before. I spent hours standing in the front stairwell looking out the window at the other side of the fence. The fields looked dead, but the few houses across the road had warm lights in their windows. I thought about those warm lights.

Who lives in those houses? What is being part of a family like? Do they ever think of Outcasters? We're right across the road from them. They must. What do they think?

Thanks to MAC III, the Compact government, and Aubry Cummings, the schoolbooks I read say that they *have* to hate us. They *have* to.

From the stairwell I can follow the road with my gaze for quite a distance past the Wardate sign. In class they say that the Wardate is the time of the beginning of the new world. But it is past that sign, toward the city lights, where the new world is.

Freedom.

I argue with myself, remembering some of the ones who tried to escape. Killed or captured. The ones killed turned out to be the lucky ones. I have no papers. I wouldn't last a week. Everybody knows that.

Everybody but my feet.

Every now and then a redbird escapes and is never heard from again. Every now and then someone makes it. Somehow.

Last night in the stairwell I noticed that the number on the red sign had changed. It now reads 17:14 9AUG2033. Before the Christmas riot Godfrey once told me that the sign advertised the end of the world.

"How will the world end, Godfrey?"

"It will burn."

"Why will it end?"

Godfrey never did answer that. He still treats me like I'm seven years old sometimes.

Louisa moves under her covers.

All of my tooth-grinding and hand-wringing must have disturbed her. I sit still, hoping she will go back to sleep. Her eyes open to sleepy slits.

"Tommy. Is something wrong?"

"No. Go back to sleep."

Her covers are pulled up to her chin, her eyes wide open. I'm sitting naked on my rack and for some reason it embarrasses me. I get under my covers.

My eyes close, I hear her moving. I should do my tooth-grinding out in the stairwell.

"Tommy?"

"What?" I keep my eyes closed.

"Lift up your covers." I turn toward her and see her standing naked between the racks, her long blond hair to one side over her shoulder. Dressing and in showers I must have seen her naked a thousand times before. But at that moment, in the bluish light from the fence, she becomes a dream.

There is a strange pain in my chest and even stranger stirrings in my body.

Always more things to be frightened of.

I lift my covers, slide over, and she slips in next to me, pulling the covers around us both. I am rigid, afraid, not knowing what to do, suddenly terrified of touching her. I've seen some of the other redbirds creeping around at night, climbing into each other's racks. It meant nothing to me before. Why don't I just tell her to—

Her hand touches my chest, slides up to my neck, and holds my head as she kisses me, first gently, then hard, the length of her body touching mine. Her skin burns while mine is like ice. As though by its own volition my hand moves to her waist. Her skin is soft. My hand glides down the curve of her hip to her thigh. Her skin is so smooth.

I've been naked in bed with Helen before, trying to keep warm. We touched, but that was a million years ago and—

Bringing my hand up the length of her body, putting my

other arm around her, I pull her toward me. Bright lights flash behind my closed eyelids, my heart pounding so hard it hurts. I grow hard. It touches her thigh and I move back, embarrassed. Her hand finds my hardness and drives everything from my mind but her touch. Once more my hand glides down her, the dip in the small of her back, the firm softness of her cheeks, caressing her. My hand moves around her thigh to find the hot wetness between her legs.

"Tommy."

"Louisa. I don't know—"

"It's all right, Tommy. I do."

Delirious fumbling; clumsy ecstasy. As she guides me inside her the pain of not crying out is almost unbearable. And when I am done I cry. I do not understand these tears.

She curls in the crook of my arm and we sleep.

Wardate: 17:14-9AUG2033
Downlimit: 101949:17:04

70

The next morning in the mess hall I listen to the words, hardly allowing myself to believe them. I whisper to no one in particular, "Manuel is right!"

"You are very lucky children and you should be very grateful. Preparatory to receiving your citizenships—"

We're getting our citizenships!

An old fat woman from the penal department explains it all to us. We will be graded by our regular teachers and given a series of tests. If we pass the tests we will be given citizenship status as soon as adoptions or school entrances can be arranged.

The fat woman smiles around at the redbirds. "Adoptions for those in good health and under sixteen years of age are almost certain. For those over sixteen, the chances are still very good."

I'm not sixteen yet. I'm fifteen! Adoption almost *certain!*

I imagine my new parents. What will they be like? Their look, their feel? In my mind I can see the home I want. Few walls, many windows and doors, and a room of my own with a real bed.

Doors seem to open in my mind. Instead of a narrow path to a dead end, the future becomes an infinite network of passages leading anywhere I want it to go.

What will I become? After school, what? A trans pilot, space explorer, sea farmer, anything. Anything I want.

Manuel is way too old to be adopted. He is over twenty, and he tells me that he wants to go to school and study electronics.

He never stops talking long enough for me to talk about my own plans. Godfrey is skeptical about the citizenships, but we don't want to hear that, which is just as well because Godfrey doesn't want to talk about it. Ugly Doris thinks that Godfrey is afraid to go outside the fence, but that sounds stupid, and I tell her so.

Outside and in the dorms even the guards and wardens are smiling. Citizen Sayther passes me in the big hall and wishes me a good morning. I feel shocked. Then I begin to see that the blackshit wants to see the end of Outcasters too. Their jobs are safe. Maybe they can see themselves doing real protection work now. They have been prisoners here too.

Wardate: 17:14-9AUG2033
Downlimit: 101253:11:42

69

Testing day. The smell of the new snow is sharp in the air.

For the first time in all of my years at Outcasters I see the chief warden. He speaks to us at morning chow, but I am so excited I can hardly eat, much less listen. The big blackshit talks very quietly, and I can't hear him anyway with all of the buzzing going on around me. He wishes us luck and we applaud.

When the trays are cleared three civilians distribute small black boxes, one per redbird. A fourth civvie sets up and adjusts a larger black box on the warden's table at the front of the room.

My box has a number keyboard with ten buttons, and below it another set of three black buttons, a silver "enter" button, and a toggle switch. Following the civilians, the wardens and guards hand out thick printed booklets. We are told not to touch either until instructed.

I look at the cover on my booklet. The paper cover is plain white, printed in blue with the misty compass-rose insignia of the Compact of Nations centered above the title. The title reads:

DOP-938 APTITUDE AND PERSONALITY PROFILE—
PART I

I feel as though my entire future rests behind that cover.

Another guard hands me a pen. There is a place on the cover for my name, class, and registration number, and we are told to fill these in. I write mine in as neatly as possible. It would be silly to deny me my citizenship for bad penmanship, but I've seen sillier things. I take no chances.

The short civvie wearing the brown suit coughs, coughs again, and waits for the hall to quiet down. Then he begins. "Some of the responses to the booklet questions are to be entered into your terminal. The instructions on how to do this precede each applicable section of the test. Read these instructions carefully. One of the things we will be looking for is how well you can understand and follow instructions. To the booklet questions there are no wrong answers. Enter your registration number into your terminal and begin."

I punch in my number, hit the "enter" button, open the booklet, and start. At first the questions are easy to understand and are answered with a yes/no/I don't know, true/false, or a choice from several answers to the same question. There are questions about my parents, friends, and how I feel about them. There are more questions about things I get angry at, things that make me feel good, what I think about, how I think about it, what I want, what I hope to achieve.

How do I see myself?

The questions move over into the confusing. I read them several times each, looking for the tricks, but I can't be sure what they want.

Sex?

The questions don't seem disapproving. I don't have to name anyone and I answer them.

Blobs and shapes need to be matched up with other blobs and shapes or with what I think the blobs and shapes look like or don't look like. Colors are to be arranged in an order of my own choosing; pictures to be matched up with little stories; an endless trail of numbers and letters.

Finally it is time for lunch. The boxes and booklets are gathered up by the guards.

I go outside and take several deep breaths. I can't understand why I suddenly feel exhausted. Dizzy.

After lunch there is another break then it is back to the tables. The guards and wardens redistribute the boxes and hand out new booklets:

DOP-2062B APTITUDE AND PERSONALITY PROFILE—PART II

Again I enter my registration number and begin. More questions, more blobs, more shapes, matches, colors, pictures, and stories. At the afternoon break my head is so tired I walk in a daze. Everyone looks ragged. I go to the crapper and wash my face.

After the break we return to the tables. The dining hall windows are covered, killing the outside light. There is just enough light to see the black boxes. The booklets have been gathered up during the break.

For the third time I enter my registration number into the little black box. Next to the large black box on the warden's table at the front of the room there is a screen. Pictures begin flashing from it accompanied by a recorded voice. The voice comes from the large black box. Scenes, faces, animals, machines, things, odd shapes, colored patterns.

The voice asks the questions and offers a selection of answers. Using the group of three buttons at the bottom of the box and the toggle switch I respond to the questions.

Some of the questions ask what the picture is or what it means, how I feel about it, how I think I ought to feel about it, do I want to do what the person in the picture is doing? The pictures come so fast I have to answer them without thinking. For two solid hours my eyes watch the picture, my ears listen to the question, my hand punches a button on the box; next picture, next question, next response, until my head aches. More pictures, more questions, more buttons punched in response.

At last we are finished. The black boxes are left behind, and the redbirds are dismissed. When I get outside I realize that it is almost time for dinner.

Wardate: 17:14-9AUG2033
Downlimit: 101241:41:01

68

After evening chow, stretched out on my rack, I am amazed at how tired I am. I lift my head and look at the rest of the dorm. It isn't just me. The entire dorm is dead. I let my head fall back upon my pillow.

My brain feels like it is made out of a million tiny muscles and that I had exercised all of them hard, and most of them for the first time. The feeling is pleasant and I close my eyes to enjoy it. To enjoy it and to dream about my new family.

"Hey, Tommyyyyyyyyy!"

Manuel jumps over my rack and lands on it hard. At twenty he has put on a lot of weight, and the poor rack groans. He slaps me on the arm.

"Hey, Tommyyyyyyyyy! Whaddaya know, man? We gonna be free!"

"God, Manuel. Go lie down and get some rest."

"Rest?"

"Aren't you tired?"

Manuel stands and looks around at the dorm. He snorts at the collapsed redbirds.

"Rest? I show you some rest, man!"

Reaching down, he grabs the edge of my rack and flips it over, dumping me on the floor.

"Hey! Everybody up! C'mon you redbirds, outta those racks! We gonna be free!"

He dances up the aisle, weaving in and out of the racks, screaming and laughing, pulling pillows out from under sleepy heads, flipping over racks. "Wake up! Wake up! Wake up! Don't wanna let the war catch ya."

Francis gets dumped, and after untangling himself from his bedding, he grabs his pillow and begins sneaking up behind Manuel. I grab my own pillow and join in, with Louisa shouting encouragement from her rack.

In seconds a small army of redbirds is chasing Manuel around the dorm, pounding him with pillows. Soon everyone in the dorm is pillow pounding anyone within range, screaming and laughing. Manuel trips and he is buried in squirming red bodies, all laughing uncontrollably.

We all hear the sound of the hall door opening.

"What's going on here?"

The noise level in the dorm instantly falls to death-silent. Citizen Sayther stands at the door. A young male guard stands next to her. We untangle ourselves and come to attention.

"Answer me, Manuel. What's going on here?"

"We wasn't doing nothing, Citizen Sayther. Just, well, celebrating a little—"

"What? Celebrating what?"

"Why, you know, Citizen Sayther. Our tests—citizenship."

She looks from Manuel to the rest of us, then to the torn up dorm. "You aren't citizens yet," she hisses. "None of you! What in the world has gotten into you all? You are still redshit and will obey the rules!"

The guard doesn't move. He stands beside Sayther, his thin lips pulled back into a tight little grin. The glossy visor of his uniform cap is pulled down so far I can't see his eyes.

He speaks very quietly. "I'll take over now, warden." She nods, looks around the dorm once more, and leaves.

The guard does not move for an eternity, arms folded, legs slightly apart, the redbirds sweating at attention. Unfolding his arms, he turns and closes the hall door. Turning back to face the dorm, he refolds his arms and begins rocking back and forth on his shiny black boots.

"I am Citizen Wing. This"—he unfolds an arm and sweeps the dorm with it,—"will never happen again."

He crooks a finger at Manuel. "Over here, redshit."

Manuel walks over and comes to attention before the guard. "Are you responsible for this?"

"Citizen?"

Manuel shrugs, but as quick as a striking snake, Wing sinks his fist into Manuel's stomach, doubling him over. Bringing up a knee, he smashes it into Manuel's face. Manuel falls on his back, spitting blood and teeth. Wing walks around him, kicking him in the shins. Manuel screams, and the guard keeps kicking him in the shins, ribs, and head until Manuel passes out.

Standing over Manuel's body, breathing hard, Wing puts his hands on his hips. "You redshit! *Citizens!* I have some news for you people, and for your sake I hope you copy!" Still puffing, Wing opens the door. "You are nothing! *Nothing!* That's the way you stay!"

He waves his arm around the dorm. "Clean up this shit. One zip from the day guard, and I'll come looking for all of you!"

Wardate: 17:14-9AUG2033
Downlimit: 101238:23:10

67

Late at night the "E" Dorm girls club meets.

Manuel's face is swollen and he can barely walk. I help him to the back stairwell and down to the meeting place. Helen and Godfrey weren't in the dorm when it happened, and Louisa explains it to them. I can see the worry on Helen's face. It has been years since the club met last.

Francis speaks. "I move that Wing dies." Helen looks around the table and I raise my hand. She nods at me.

"I second it."

"Discussion?" She looks from face to face, stopping on Louisa.

"Wing punished our brother beyond what was called for and for what all of us did."

"Tommy?"

"I agree. It's starting again. If we let this go, sooner or later a redbird dies."

"Francis?"

"It's our club's responsibility to set this thing right. We owe it to every redbird in here."

"Godfrey?"

"I want to hear what Manuel has to say."

Helen nods at Manuel.

Manuel's voice comes out strange and choked. "I want to kill him. I want to kill him so bad. With my own hands." He looks around at us. "But we are so close, see? Citizenship. Maybe when we are out, when we are citizens, I do something. If we kill him now, the investigations start all over again. Maybe we mess citizenship up for everybody."

He opens and closes his fists. "Now, we do nothing."

"What about the rest of us?" Francis looks at Manuel. "How long before we get our citizenships? What if the blackshit starts up again like before and we still aren't citizens?"

Manuel shakes his head. "I don't know, man. All I know is I been waiting for twenty years to walk free. I used to be locked in a cellar before Outcasters. I don't want to start nothing now, so close."

Helen looks around the quiet room and nods. "Vote."

I place my fist on the crate thumb down for the kill.

Francis does the same.

Godfrey puts his thumb up.

Louisa hesitates and puts up her thumb. As president, Helen has no vote. It is up to Manuel.

He puts out his fist, thumb up.

Later, in the dark of "E" Dorm with our racks pulled close together, Louisa and I hold hands. I roll over and whisper in her ear.

"What happens? What happens if we don't get our citizenships? What then?"

She pokes her left hand out from under her covers and makes a fist, thumb down.

Wardate: 17:14-9AUG2033
Downlimit: 100710:44:06

66

Each morning at inspection for the next three weeks, the day guard calls out names. Those called are told to gather up their things, including their bedding, and wait in the hall. Their citizenships have been assigned. We never know who will be called and have to say our good-byes with silent looks.

There are only nine left in "E" Dorm for inspection. The day guard, Citizen Haskins, calls out Helen's name, Godfrey's, and two others.

The four of them gather up their things and leave. On her way out, Helen touches my arm. I tell myself that I should be happy for her. I guess I am, but I will miss her so much. The clearest memory I have is of her holding me, kissing me, that first night in Outcasters. She was the one who was there when I came back from hell. My arm aches where she touched it.

Godfrey's eyes are wet, and he stares at Manuel for a long time before Citizen Haskins chases them all into the hall. Manuel, Francis, Louisa, Hey You, and I are all that remain.

I feel a little better thinking that my own citizenship is so close now. I listen to them walking down the hall. Citizen Haskins turns until he is facing the dorm, his hands clasped behind his back.

"The rest of you gather up your things and your bedding. You're being moved to 'A' Dorm on the first floor."

Manuel raises his hand. "Citizen Haskins?"

"Yes?"

"How long before we get our citizenships?"

The guard looks at the floor for a panic-filled second. He

shakes his head and looks up at us. "You have all been rejected for citizenship. I don't know why. Every dorm has a few. We're putting you all together in 'A' Dorm."

Manuel holds out his hands, his eyes wild. "Why? Man—I mean, Citizen Haskins, what happened? Why?"

Again the guard shakes his head. "I don't know. I guess they have their reasons. I'm sorry." He points toward the hall door. "Let's go. Gather up your things."

I stumble to my rack as if in a dream. A mistake, a horrible mistake has been made. My grades are the highest in my class. I'm no dummy like Hey You. A mistake has been made, I just know a mistake has been made.

I pull my extra reds and underwear off the shelf and throw them on my rack. Louisa squeezes my arm and I look at her eyes. They glisten with tears. I touch her face and nod. Together.

I turn back and pick up my bedding roll.

Together. Is being together going to be enough?

As we leave, none of us looks back. We say nothing as we walk down the hall to the stairwell. I find it difficult just to place one foot in front of the other. Manuel has a dark, uncomprehending stare. In front of me, guiding Hey You down the stairs, Louisa throws back her shoulders and holds up her head.

I nod as I realize something. She is stronger than I am. It is a new feeling I have for her. Respect. For the first time I give myself permission to love her.

On the first floor, Citizen Haskins holds the "A" Dorm door open for us and we walk in.

"Get settled. Your dorm guard will be by for inspection in half an hour." He looks at Manuel, drops his glance, and leaves.

There are twenty-four others in the dorm, standing sullenly in small groups or by themselves. We begin moving down the aisle to the empty cots at the back of the dorm. On the way a large boy in his late teens grabs Louisa by the arm. He is heavy and very ugly.

"Little redbird. You come nest next to Andy."

He pulls her around so that she is between him and the

wall. Without thinking I drop my stuff and jump on Andy's back, my arms around his neck. With a roar the boy swats me into the aisle. Turning back to Louisa, he takes her bedding from her and puts it on the empty rack next to his, spreading it out. He turns back to her and slips one of his meaty hands between her legs.

"You like Andy."

Louisa struggles, but the boy is one large muscle. I try to get up, but Manuel pushes me back down as he walks past me, coming up behind Andy.

Manuel puts his left arm around Andy's throat, grabs his left wrist with his right hand and squeezes hard. The fat redbird fights to get loose, but Manuel is very strong. Andy's face reddens, his body goes limp and Manuel lowers him to the floor. Andy is still breathing. Manuel stands and looks at the other redbirds in the dorm.

"Count 'em." He points with his finger. "Twenty-nine of us. The blackshit has over sixty. If we going to stay alive, we got to stick together."

He nudges Andy with his toe. "Somebody tell this porker when he wakes up." Taking his right thumb, Manuel draws it slowly down the right side of his jaw. Twelve answer the sign. "Tonight."

That night fifteen attend the girls club meeting. I notice that none of the old club dorm commanders are left. They have all gotten their citizenships. Paco, the new "A" dormkeeper, is elected commander. We discuss the case of Citizen Wing, but agree to do nothing until we can see our situation better.

Manuel is placed in charge of the escape committee. I am made a member.

Wardate: 17:14-9AUG2033
Downlimit: 100638:00:13

65

All classes are canceled. Convicts from the detention center help us work the fields. At the end of February, Outcasters is officially transferred from the Penal Department to the Department of Agricultural Resources and renamed Compact Farm No. 128.

Extra guards and wardens from Outcasters are assigned to institutions within the Penal Department, leaving behind twelve guards and Citizen Sayther as chief warden. Someone from Agricultural Resources is placed in charge, but we never see him. His name is Citizen Donatti.

Beech becomes the day guard, Wing is on night duty with Haskins, Kostner, Brown, Novak and Fauglia made detail, gate, and fence guards. There are more, but those are the only ones I ever see.

The detention center provides its own guards for CDC work crews, and we never mingle with the center inmates. With the guard force pared down we breathe easier, and the matter of Citizen Wing is tabled. The short-range concentration is on improving our situation. Long-range concentration is on escape.

"A" Dorm can easily house twice the number of redbirds that bunk there, and Paco suggests to Citizen Sayther that we put dividers between the racks for privacy. She has no objection as long as the redbirds do the work and the results look neat and clean.

Soon Louisa and I have a "room" of our own, while the other redbirds divide themselves up into one-, two-, and three-person cubicles. At night, Louisa and I hang an extra blanket across the aisle end of our dividers. Francis sleeps with a girl that used to be from "F" Dorm.

Manuel sleeps alone.

Wardate: 17:14-9AUG2033
Downlimit: -99990:31:20

64

Spring planting. The red number on the sign next to the road continues to read: 17:14 9AUG2033.

A bookmobile is allowed to visit Farm No. 128 once a week. "B" Dorm is converted into a recreation room with a few games and a Ping-Pong table. The television is moved there from the old chief warden's office. Citizen Sayther moves her quarters into the old chief warden's office. She is no longer married to Bob. Her door is cracked open slightly and I catch a glimpse of her crying.

I feel sorry for her but am not fool enough to tell her so.

The Potato, Andy, Elana, and some others are entered into a program at one of the city hospitals. After a few weeks they are moved permanently to the hospital facility. We get to keep Ugly Doris.

Late Tuesday afternoons, after details, the bookmobile comes by and I am always waiting for it. The driver, Merle Sawyer, jokes with me because I am always there. Merle is a retired schoolteacher.

I am allowed only three books at a time, and I spend the entire time the bookmobile is here agonizing over which three books to choose. My agonizing increases a hundredfold after Merle shows me the book index that enables me to order any book from any library in the system. The amount of knowledge in my universe has acquired stunning proportions.

My attendance at escape committee meetings falls off and then ceases.

Through spring and into summer I leap from one subject to the next, trying to drink in everything, only to get a tantalizing taste. On his visits I discuss the books I have read with Merle, frustrated that we can only spend an hour per week together.

Summer ends and Merle gives me a gift: a box of books. "They're some of my old high school and college texts. I don't need them anymore."

"Don't need them?"

"I guess not. It's been a bunch of years since I was a student."

"The books— Do you mean they're mine?"

"They're yours." Merle reaches into his pocket and pulls out a sheaf of papers folded into thirds.

"I requested a study plan from the library index and this is what the machine suggested for you, complete with assignments. The way the machine has it set up, I can check your assignments on my visits." He smiles as his eyebrows go up. "To tell you the truth, Thomas, that plan looks a little stiff to me. If you can't hack it, we can work up something a little less demanding."

He tosses the papers into the box. I just stand there holding the box, not knowing what to do or say. Merle pushes me out of the van door and starts up the vehicle's fans.

"Get to work."

That night I show Louisa the books and Merle's program. Together we begin working through the assignments. Through the harvest, winter, and into the next spring we read and teach each other. Both of us meet the van on Tuesday afternoons to discuss the assignments with Merle and have him answer our questions. One time Merle brings a study plan for Louisa. It is considerably different from my plan.

Wardate: 17:14-9AUG2033
Downlimit: -91230:26:33

63

The fog lifts from my existence. The more I learn, the better I become at fitting together the pieces of my reality. The high school and college human ecology texts paint in the broad outlines of human survival equations and how they made the citizenship acts necessary. I learn that even Outcasters was necessary at one point.

I spent my time at Outcasters in a mix of fear, confusion, and rage. The rehabilitation classes taught that the system was necessary and that necessity made justice. Doubt joined the mix. Studying at Merle's direction, the doubt is removed layer by layer. Perhaps the brutality of the system was unnecessary. The system itself had to be.

Past generations had made the choice for us. Past generations traded the future for present indulgence. They had met warnings with: "What difference will it make in a hundred years," "Something will turn up—it always has," and "In the long run, we're all dead." Humanity pandered to ideology, power, tradition, religion, wealth, popularity, and moral altruism, ignoring only the facts of reality and their bearing on human survival—the future of the human race.

I learn that population, energy, irreplaceable resources, arable land, pollution, rate of economic growth, and dozens of other things are functions of a complex, precariously balanced equation of human survival. Outcasters and the citizenship acts were created to balance the factor of population which threatened to bring Earth to a point of no return.

There was the horror of the unplanned future. Choked with

mouths to feed and nothing with which to ease their hunger; crawling with disease and no resources with which to make medicines or build hospitals; naked and shelterless and no hope save that others might die faster than oneself. Earth would return to a primitive culture. With the race's mines empty there would be no second industrial revolution to give the race another chance at the stars.

The Father of the Compact, Aubry Cummings, and other scientists, environmentalists, industrialists, and politicians in the 1980's and 1990's had initiated a series of events that had resulted in the formation of the Compact of Nations.

When I put it all together I am awed at the size of the threat and even more so by the sweep of the solution. Half the world committed to the preservation of civilization, and, in its way, Outcasters had served that purpose.

What, then, were my parents? Were they indulgent fools, traitors, what? I can't answer this. And what of me? When I look through my own eyes, I am important to myself. I begin to understand the view of those who have to look for the future of the human race.

I learn about the coming war.

Expressions like "Hurry up, the war'll be here before you're done" are such a fixture of my environment I never thought about what was meant. Otherworld will attack the Compact as their only hope of surviving the indulgences the Compact did without. The real name of the Wardate is the Optimum War Probability Projection Date. The time and date contained in that number is the Department of Projection's prediction of when the war will *have* to happen.

I am still confused. The war is such an important part of the future, but everyone seems to ignore it. They act like it is never going to happen. Even in the books, they talk about the war as though it might not even be a real war. I talk about it to Merle.

"I don't know, Tommy."

Merle scratches his ear. "The war is coming; there's no question about it. But it's a long way off. I guess we all just put it out of our minds until the time comes."

"Merle, in the human ecology text it refers to something

called disciplinary projections several times, and to a few books on it. Can you get them for me?"

Merle whistles and shakes his head. "I can get the books, Tommy, but do you really think you're ready for projections?"

"Why?"

"It's tough. I remember an introductory course I took in college," Merle laughs. "I guess what I'm trying to say is I don't remember it."

"There's a lot of things I want to understand, Merle, and from what I can see, projections is the only way I'm going to find out."

The van driver nods and turns to the book order index, activates the screen and punches in the desired field.

"There are over five hundred subcategories. Maybe we can find some introductory stuff." Punching in the appropriate code, a list of forty-six introductory works appear on the screen. At the bottom of the screen a prompt code begins flashing. 30-30.

I point at the flashing code. "What's that mean?"

"The big computer wants your registration number."

"Why?"

Merle shook his head. "Maybe to compare you against your test performance so it can recommend a work on a level you can handle? Okay?"

"Did the machine get my number to make up my study plan?"

"Yes. I got it from the warden's office. Is there a problem?"

There is something gnawing at the back of my head. An uneasiness that has no apparent source. "No. I don't think so."

Merle enters my registration number. The machine recommends Aubry Cummings's *Essays*. I recognize it from some of the footnotes in my texts.

Merle hit the reserve code. "You've got it. I'll bring it on my next visit."

Wardate: 17:14-9AUG2033
Downlimit: -89790:55:01

62

Cutting across the corner of a field, on the side of the farm opposite the Green Machine, is a tiny stream. Beyond the fence it flows into a pond, and the pond has ducks. When it is not raining, next to this stream is where I study the books Merle brings me.

I lie on my back, my arms folded over this one damned book, looking up at the clouds. *Essays*. I have read Aubry Cummings's *Essays*. I don't understand any of it.

A door is locked against me. It's frustrating because I don't know if I am searching for a key or if I have simply run out of ability. I have a very hollow feeling. It is like the time my father gave me a book printed entirely in Japanese. I remember looking through the columns of characters in the horror of believing that no matter what I did, I could never understand what was printed on those pages. This is the same feeling, but this time I can understand the words. I just can't make any sense out of what they mean.

I sit up, and a sparkle of light draws my notice. A clot of grass and dirt has fallen into the stream causing a tiny pond to form. The tiny pond reflects the light.

Placing the book on the grass, I dig a few more clumps from the bank and add them to the small dam. I find a dark-colored flat stone and insert it in the dam for the spillway bed. The pond widens. I look beyond the ripples on the surface and see a small dark thing in the pool. It looks like a miniature lobster. Every corner, every wall, the bottom of every upturned leaf, it explores with its claws. But it isn't trying to escape.

It's making its cage as large as it can.
I look inside myself, trying to remember where—

—In *Mirage*: Gregory Peck and Diane Baker watch a black panther pacing around in its cage. The woman asks: "*Have you noticed how they use every inch of space in the cage? She's making it as large as she can.*"

He says, "*She's looking for a way out.*"

"*No.*" answers Diane Baker. "*Not anymore.*"

Is that what I'm doing?.

I look down at the book on the grass. Is that what I'm doing? Making my cage as large as I can? What was it Citizen Haskins called movies? A magic carpet that can fly over and far beyond the barbed wire. It can fly past time and far beyond reality. And is the book telling me that I have run into the prison walls of my mind? Maybe I can ask Haskins about it.

Haskins is okay. We've had some pretty good talks about movies and things. He's from Lancaster, State District of Pennsylvania. He once had his mother cook up something called shoofly pie and he brought me some. Shoofly pie is the most incredibly wonderful thing that I have ever tasted.

Haskins doesn't like the new movies either. He says that everything released after '95 was written and produced by the Department of Projections. Not officially; by indirection. Citizen Haskins is down on the discipline of projections. I found this out the day I brought my copy of *Essays* into the TV room.

He paged through the copy, his face becoming redder and more angry with each page he turned. Then he slammed the book shut, handed it back to me, and said something very strange to me, or to himself:

"I suppose it's like being angry at God. There's plenty of cause; there's just not much point."

At times Citizen Haskins seems like a regular person. At other times he is moody and withdrawn or full of fun and laughter. I like talking to him about movies and things. He knows a lot and he's the only guard that ever told me it's okay to call him by his first name. One day soon I will try it, although calling Citizen Haskins by the name Bill seems awfully like asking for the Drum Room.

My father once told me that all I needed to do to understand the book printed in Japanese was to learn how to read Japanese. I still remember finding a word, *tomasu*, that was so close to my own name I learned how to write it, but I have forgotten how. *Tomasu* means to enrich or make wealthy.

I clean off my hands and pick up *Essays* for another try.

Wardate: 17:14-9AUG2033
Downlimit: -89142:03:12

61

Three weeks later I am sitting in the TV room, *Essays* on my lap, watching the projection segment of the evening news. I had to ask Merle for a month's extension on the book. I've read the thing four times and had my mind stretched in eleven different directions. But I still don't understand what Cummings is trying to say.

On a monitor screen to the commentator's left, the Wardate appears in red against a blue background.

17:14 9AUG2033.

"—the expected fall in the war projection date, due to the Soviet incursion on the border of the Compact nation of Turkey, did not take place. The immediate dispatch of Rapid Strike Forces to the area, in addition to DOP intervention on the diplomatic front, seem to have been sufficient to hold the Wardate. Despite this, the border conflict is very volatile and in the opinion of Representative Morio Tokuda, Assembly Minority Leader, this is further evidence that the Wardate reported by DOP is fraudulent."

The image cuts to a smiling, pleasant-looking man sitting behind a cloud of audio pickups.

"The Soviet Union has actually attacked a nation of the Compact, yet the war projection number didn't shift as much as a minute. I don't think any further proof is needed that the reported number is nothing but a propaganda tool. I have every intention of initiating an investigation into the DOP's policies in this and other matters."

Cut back to the commentator, who mentions that Secretary

of Projections, Aubry Cummings, on his way to spend a few days at his home in Webster, New Hampshire, was unavailable for comment.

"The spokesperson for the DOP, however, assured reporters . . ."

I rub my eyes and look again at the screen. It is an itch I can't scratch. A lock without the proper key.

On the screen the projection person smiles at the anchor person, makes a joke, and begins with the agriprojections. Weather, soils, resources, prices, value of the credit, interest rates, processing and distribution factors, labor, current regulations and so on are quickly entered into the visual display, producing crop yields, future prices, availability of goods.

I shake my head. I still don't understand the difference between that and plain old statistical forecasting. Maybe it's just beyond my ability to comprehend.

The projections person reads off the Department of Projections orders and recommendations, and then moves on to the weather.

". . . and it's too bad the Department can't come up with an adjustment for this weekend, 'cause it looks like nothing but cloudy skies and showers. Like the man says, everybody talks about the bleedin' weather, but nobody ever does anything about it—"

—and it hits me!

Taking the data base set up through statistical forecasting, along with an additional data base considered irrevelant in forecasting, the actual factors can be altered to achieve a desired goal. That's what the Department of Projections does: it issues the orders that alter present factors to achieve various goals. Even the government is subject to the orders of the DOP. The future is being planned and the human actions in regard to that future are planned. They are all functions in an enormous equation to achieve an immense number and variety of goals. Future reality is being machine-designed and manufactured.

The things I had read in *Essays* suddenly come into focus. The survival of civilization is one such goal, and Outcasters, the Compact of Nations, so many things, are factors under projected manipulations to achieve that goal.

The television breaks into my awareness. A familiar name.

"Aubry Cummings seen here coming from the Executive Office at the Steel Palace where he met with President-General Drucker . . ."

On the television screen I see a bent old man climbing with difficulty into an air-limo. The glimpse I have of the man's face, before the back of some reporter fills the screen, shows that he is worried—perhaps only very tired. He's awfully old.

I suddenly realize that Aubry Cummings has become something of a hero to me. It is that old man's mind that has caused the current form of just about everything in the world.

"—our source indicates that Secretary Cummings will probably relent under the increasing Consolidationist pressure to resign—"

The screen goes blank.

I look up and Manuel is holding the cord to the TV set in his hand. His face is dark with anger.

"I was watching that, Manuel."

"Shut up!"

"What's going—"

"I said, shut up." He tosses the plug to the floor. "You sitting around reading books, watching TV with your blackshit boyfriend, playing stickyfinger with Louisa—"

"That's enough!"

"No, that's not enough. You shut up. I talk, you listen. Where you been for committee meetings?"

"I don't have to tell you a damned—"

"Chew it off! I tell you where you been, boy. Right here in 128 like the rest of us. And right here is where you going to stay. You want that?"

"No, but—"

"But, nothing, man!" He grips my collar, choking me. I swing my book and strike Manuel on the side of his head, making him let go. Manuel staggers back and I get to my feet, picking up one of the metal chairs.

"Don't push me, Manuel."

"I tear you apart—"

"No. Now you listen."

"Shit! What you got to say? You like it here?"

"No. You wouldn't understand. It would be wrong."

"Escaping?"

"I said you wouldn't understand."

"You damn right I don't understand! Wrong? You call this right? You call this right, boy?"

"Manuel, this is all part of . . . I guess you'd call it a plan. I don't understand it all myself, but we won't know what we'll be doing if we escape."

"What's going on?"

Louisa stands in the door looking at us both. I lower the chair as Manuel walks toward her. He stops at the door and looks back at me.

"You forget Ann? You forget what happened to me? What happened to you, man? I know what I'll be doing when I escape. I'll be outside, working every minute to kill the blackshit. We don't owe nobody, man! Nobody! They owe us!"

"Manuel, what is it?" Louisa places her hand on Manuel's arm. Slapping it away, he storms from the room. Hurt, she looks at me.

"Tommy?"

"I don't want to talk about it."

I take her hand and walk into the hallway. A guard near the main entrance is holding a redbird by the arm. Seeing us, he releases the girl and she runs into "A" Dorm. The guard swaggers out of the main entrance.

It's Citizen Wing.

On the tiny pond near where I study, a black branch floats. I watch it on a Sunday afternoon as it moves toward the spillway. A startlingly-red spider is on the branch spinning a web. It will die soon, yet it continues spinning its web.

Why?

Maybe it can't see the spillway? Maybe it doesn't understand what meaning the spillway has to its future? Maybe the spider sees it, understands what is going to happen, and just doesn't care?

Perhaps the spider just doesn't appreciate the wicked turns the universe can make. I am going over the spillway, says the spider, attempting to accept the worst possible case. But reality may have other plans—worse turns than that.

Wardate: 17:14-9AUG2033
Downlimit: -89094:27:58

60

In the TV room we are waiting to watch an old movie called *An Officer and a Gentleman*, Citizen Haskins—Bill—and I. We have been looking forward to seeing it for a long time. Paco and Manuel walk into the room and sit down. Paco whispers something to Manuel and they both snicker. I look at Bill but he is staring at the TV screen.

As I try to keep ahead of what is happening, I miss the beginning of the movie. The boy Zack has what the moviemakers think is a terrible childhood in the Philippine Islands. Zack joins what used to be the U.S. Navy to fly jet airplanes.

Manuel whispers something to Paco and they both snicker again. Zack shows up for training, and Lou Gossett, Jr. is waiting for him. He plays a training officer, and he walks up and down the row of trainees, degrading them about how they used to listen to Mick Jagger music and badmouth their country.

Paco and Manuel whisper and laugh some more and Bill stands up. "Is there something you two want to say out loud?"

Paco shakes his head and Manuel just looks back. Lou Gossett grins at one of the trainees and says, "*You want to fuck me up the ass?*" Both Manuel and Paco burst out laughing. I look at Bill and his face is bright red.

Bill climbs out of his chair. He's trembling. "Get out! Both of you, *get out!*"

Manuel and Paco walk from the room, still laughing. Bill

turns and looks down at me, his face pleading. "It isn't the way they make it look, Tommy."

"Make what look?"

"You needed someone. Where would you be now if it wasn't for me? You needed me, and I was there."

I am an idiot. A fool. A blind man—

"You want to fuck me up the ass?"

My mouth feels very dry. "What did you do? When I was sick, what did you do to me? When I didn't know—"

"Tommy, it's not the way—"

"Tommy? *Tommy?*"

I remember the lightheaded, warped feeling when I killed McDermit. I have it again. But there is no slow motion this time. This time it is all blank until I feel rough hands grab my arms.

Wing and Fauglia are holding me.

Haskins is getting up from the floor. Blood is flowing from his nose.

"What the hell's going on?" demands Fauglia.

Haskins shakes his head. "Nothing. I fell and hit my head on the table. That's all. Let go of him."

"Bullshit." Wing turns me and looks at my face. "What about it, redshit?"

"What about what?"

Wing straightens up. "Don't get cute with me, you—"

"I said, let him go!" Haskins waves a blood-covered hand. "Go on! Let him go and you two get the hell out of here!"

"Okay, okay." The two guards release me and walk from the room, closing the door behind them.

Haskins and I are alone in the room. There is something about a box factory on the television screen. Haskins has a wad of tissues in his hand, holding them to his nose. There are tears in his eyes. All he does is shake his head. He doesn't have anything to say.

I turn and run from the room.

I go to the place where there is a tiny stream and a tiny pond, where a tiny red spider is spinning its tiny web while contemplating its death by drowning. I pick up a huge flat rock and throw it down upon the spider with all of my might. I tear the tiny dam apart and drain the pond.

I will never come here again.

Wardate: 17:14-9AUG2033
Downlimit: -83670:12:08

59

The winter comes; the beginning of spring. I refuse to recognize, to own, any of it. I have nothing to do with Haskins. Nothing.

Tuesday afternoon and Merle is late.

I have to talk with him about Manuel. About Louisa. About Haskins. About what I should do. I'm certain that he won't report me, but it doesn't make any difference. The books tell me one thing, and everyone and everything around me tells me something different. Manuel and the other club members avoid me. Even Louisa is acting sullen and won't talk to me. I am so confused.

Where is Merle?

I pace in front of the gate where the van must enter. The guard, a new man named Joyce, looks up from his paper and offers me a smoke. I refuse, thanking him. He is young. Not much older than I am. In minutes we exhaust all topics of mutual interest, he goes back to his paper, and I resume my pacing.

The gate closes for the night at six, and the guard says it is already after five.

Where *is* he?

I hear the fans of the bookmobile. After a moment the van pulls up at the gate. Merle isn't driving. Just some old woman. The guard opens the gate and the van enters, stopping near where I am standing.

"Good afternoon, young man."

I just stare at her, a familiar horror knotting my insides. "Would you care for a book, or a magazine? Maybe a comic?" She shakes her head, stands and opens the van doors. "Don't be shy. Come on in."

"Where's Merle?"

"Merle?"

"Merle Sawyer."

"I'm sorry, young man, but I don't know any Merle Sawyer." She frowns then holds up a finger. "Oh, do you mean the driver who used to run this route?"

"Yes."

"Oh, I see. I see."

The old woman steps out of the van and sits on the doorsill. "Are you a friend of his?"

"Yes. Why isn't he driving the van?"

"I'm sorry, but he passed away. That's how I got the route. It's a retirement post. It's nice the government sets aside these jobs—"

"He's dead."

"Yes. I'm sorry. Are you sure I can't get you a comic or something?"

"What?"

"Can I get you something?"

"No. No, I don't want anything."

I walk away, my feelings numb. After evening chow I take Louisa into the woods past the Green Machine. I tell her about Merle. She doesn't cry. She kneels in the grass for a moment, her face without expression. She gets up and takes the road back to the dorm, leaving me alone.

By myself among the trees I demand answers. How should I feel? What is left in the great world plan for me? What should I do? Louisa is deciding to go. Manuel. Helen and Godfrey are gone. Ann. My parents—

—This thing, this boiling dark thing I refuse to feel about Haskins.

I look up at the treetops and watch the leaves against the cloudy sky. Their sharp outlines blur. "All this? For opening a window? Just for opening a window?"

The few tears stop. Louisa and Manuel haven't left me.

They're waiting for me—waiting for me to smarten up. I push myself to my feet. As I dry my eyes on the sleeve of my reds, I look at the tiny clearing. As I turn and head for the road I know that I will never see that clearing again.

That evening Manuel walks by our cots. I call out, "Manuel." He stops and looks back without changing expression. "When's the next meeting?"

He smiles. Louisa sits up on her rack, leans over, and squeezes my arm.

"Tomorrow night, Tommy," Manuel answers. "See you then?"

"I'll be there." Manuel continues down the aisle.

Louisa moves over and sits on the edge of my rack. "Why, Tommy?"

"I don't know."

"What about all those things you said?"

"I don't know anything. I don't know anything at all." I take her hand in both of mine and try to explain. "Merle. He was like a window out of here. I don't even remember much about the past year except movies, Merle, and studying. I don't think I really cared that I was in 128. Understand?"

Louisa nods. "And now the window's shut. All you see is the fence."

"I just can't stay here any longer, knowing what tomorrow is going to be like, and the day after, and the day after that." Louisa touches her fingers to my lips and begins unsnapping her reds.

"Put up the curtain."

I get up and begin stringing up the blanket between the aisle ends of the dividers. Citizen Wing walks slowly down the aisle and stops by our cubicle.

As I raise the blanket, Wing lowers it with his short whip, looks across the top of the blanket at Louisa and smirks. I push the whip aside and hang the curtain, cutting off the guard's view. As I climb into my rack I hear Wing walking away.

Wardate: 17:14-9AUG2033
Downlimit: -83646:00:03

58

The next night the entire club is packed into the meeting room to hear the escape committee. Even though everyone seems friendly, I am nervous. I nod at Paco as I enter and turn to Manuel who is sitting at the crate.

"Louisa's held up on a detail."

"Okay." Manuel points at a vacant box next to the wall. "You fill her in later."

Paco looks around the room and nods at Manuel. "Okay, Sam," says Manuel, looking toward a heavy brown-haired kid, "you go first."

The boy called Sam shakes his head. "There hasn't been any change with credentials. We got hold of two warrants from the blackshit, but they're no good."

Paco waves his hand. "What's wrong?"

"They aren't regular citizenship warrants like the civvies have. They're for Penal Department employees of the Compact Forces. You, Manuel, and a couple of the girls are old enough to pass as blackshit, but this leaves the rest of us without papers."

"You try altering them?"

"We don't know what a civvie warrant looks like. But, yes, we tried altering them. Screwed up both of them. If you try and do anything with that paper it turns dark purple. Anyway, we'd never get enough warrants to go around without the blackshit getting on to us." Sam leans back against the wall. "That's it, Paco."

Manuel shrugs. "There wasn't much of a chance with the

papers, but we had to check it out. Papers would've been a big help. So we stay with the original plan." Manuel nods at a stern-looking girl my age. "Tessie?"

She looks around the room. "I'm in the kitchen, and food is no problem. We worked out a plan to get to an Otherworld nation. We can't shop along the way, so we have to bring our own with us. Back in the Outcaster days, the guards were part of the Compact Force Reserves. I checked out the rations left in the storeroom, and they're still good."

"Good."

"The instructions say ten kilos per person will last us about eight weeks."

Someone behind Manuel speaks. "Isn't that stuff checked every day?"

"Yes. We have to lift it just before we go. There won't be any trouble with that." Tessie holds up two keys on a string. "We can get in after the kitchen guard closes down for the night."

"Did you try them out?"

"Yes. The one for the storeroom is a little rough, but if you work it around it'll open the lock. The one for the kitchen door is perfect."

Manuel turns toward Ugly Doris. "Doris is on security."

I laugh, and Doris smiles back. Doris looks too stupid to find her own face in a mirror. She wanders wherever she wants, and the blackshit never suspects a thing.

"As good energy conservationists, some time ago the blackshit stopped the electricity in the fence. I tested it myself. My guess is the juice was turned off when we became farmers instead of Outcasters. We can get through at night with no trouble. I picked a spot in the woods near the Green Machine where I'll cut through. It's pretty overgrown and it can't be seen from the main building or the road."

I wave my hand and Paco nods at me. "Question?"

"Yes." I look at Doris. "What if they turn on the juice before we go?"

"I wired the fence over the insulators to the fence post." She grins. "If they turn on the juice, all they'll get is a lot of smoke." She faces Manuel. "The only watch on the fence at night is a guard that rides around outside on a bicycle. He comes and goes approximately every hour and twenty minutes."

Manuel nods and looks at me. "Everybody knows where we going except you. Argentina. We steal a boat and take it down the coast, traveling at night and hiding during daylight. We steal the fuel we need along the way."

"Argentina? Why not try Eastern Europe or East Africa?"

"We talked about this a lot, Tommy. We figure a boat that would have that kind of range would be too well guarded. Anyway, none of us knows how to navigate. All we got to do to get to Argentina is turn right and follow the dirt all the way down."

"Not to mention missing a patrol or two," says a voice from the rear. A quiet chuckle moved through the room.

Manuel holds up his hand for quiet. "There's something else all of you should know. Paco, you tell them."

"In Argentina is an organization that will help us once we get there. They already got fifty or so redbirds in it who escaped before. Stokes, a boy from old "F" Dorm, told me about it before he got his papers. He's down there now, and he got word back to me."

"Paco?"

"Yes, Tommy?"

"For their help, what do we have to do for them?"

"I don't think anyone will object. We help them accomplish their mission: to tear down the Compact of Nations; to kill the blackshit."

Before the buzzing has a chance to get started, Manuel holds up his hand for quiet.

"Just before we go, we tell the others. Anybody wants to can come along. We don't have to wait on the papers anymore, so we go tomorrow night."

Wardate: 17:18-9AUG2033
Downlimit: -83643:02:44

57

After the meeting I work with Tessie on how to fix up the stuff from the storeroom. The others work out other details. I'm not comfortable about that organization's help and what we'll have to do in return for it. I put it in the back of my mind. The important thing is to get safely away and to get to where we are going.

After the meeting, returning to my cubicle, I feel Louisa's cot in the dark and find it empty. I'm a little angry. There are so many things I want to talk about with her. Manuel must have cornered her to fill her in.

Lying down, I force myself to concentrate on the escape and Argentina. The hard part is getting from 128 to the marina Manuel picked in Ossining without being discovered too soon. Cop blackshit is all over the streets.

Paco is worried about the boat trip. The only maps we have are leftovers from rehabilitation classes. They contain hardly any detail at all. Paco suspects that there is more to taking a small boat almost halfway around the world than turning right and following the dirt to our destination. Only two of the redbirds at 128 know how to swim. It's not something one learns while hiding in an attic or cellar.

There is Argentina itself. Otherworld. It and the other three Latin American nations that refused to join the Compact are armed police states, government-heavy, bankrupt, and crawling with poverty and revolutionaries. All predicted. All necessary consequences of prior decisions.

But what is Argentina like? It has large cities. Manuel said they speak Spanish there. Manuel speaks Spanish. He says it isn't hard to learn. He can teach us Spanish on the boat trip. There doesn't seem to be much point in learning, however. From Argentina I will make it to Eastern Europe and then to one of the Pacific island nations that won't be obliterated in the war.

I get up from my bed, walk down the dark aisle and quietly enter the brightly lit hall. I climb up the stairwell and look again at the Doomdate. It is up four minutes.

17:18 9AUG2033.

The war will begin four minutes later than before. I wonder at the magnitude of the thing that must have happened to cause the shift. Perhaps that thing on the Turkish border is going badly. Perhaps it is going well. After all, that's four more minutes without war.

I catch myself and nod. *Essays* is very clear on that point. The war has to be. And it has to happen at the proper moment. It bothers me not knowing what the significance is of the four minute shift. I return to my rack.

As circumstances change, the Wardate changes. The Downlimit must change, too. The Downlimit is the point in time after which the survival equation is permanently out of balance. What would the world be like past the Downlimit? Would it be like Mad Max's world, or like in *Soylent Green*, with the human race going crackers? I always think it will look, for a time, like the Bladerunner's world: dirty, dark, shabby, and crumbling.

Sometimes pictures of Otherworld cities are on the television. Dirty, dark, shabby, crumbling, and choked with large, sad, hungry eyes.

Lying in the dark I think about the deal Paco wants to make in Argentina. There isn't any point in joining that organization down there or trying to help it. The Compact isn't something that can be torn down by a few terrorists, even with Otherworld governments supporting them. Even if I can't be a part of it, I still understand why the Compact has to be.

Also there is MAC III. There is no way that an unsophisticated bunch of revolutionaries can keep pace with DOP's projection facility. If I understand *Essays* accurately, it's probable that every move made by the group in Argentina is influenced, if not planned, by the Big Computer—

For a moment I think I might have an insight. Is MAC III to the Compact of Nations what the Green Machine is to Outcasters? Both are designed for a job. Both of them do their jobs very well. However, I have seen some of the additional jobs picked for the Green Machine. My hands still never feel clean.

I wonder if MAC III does any side jobs. There was something Cummings wrote about one of the results of establishing the Compact of Nations under the control of the MAC system. Something about there being nothing human that would be capable of judging the machine's decisions or controlling its actions. Could the damned machine be picking its own side jobs?

Is Outcasters—my life—nothing but a machine-generated program error? I had seen plenty of those in my computer classes. Even worse: has everything in my life been dictated by that unfeeling machine for a reason? Deadly, cold, logical moves in a game too complicated for a human to understand?

Back when we had computer classes, I would get angry when I lost at chess to the machine. But I would get even more angry when I would win. The machine doesn't feel good when it wins; it doesn't get angry when it loses. Win, lose; it's all the same to a machine. The machine doesn't care.

There is something more horrible than that: has it all been for nothing? Is this thing that controls reality simply indifferent to this sorry scrap of flesh that is caught up in its mechanism? Dead or alive I make no difference to MAC III, the Compact, or to anything else?

I sigh and close my eyes against the dark. Past; future. Too much thinking. Always a bad idea at Outcasters. Concentrate on the now, Helen would tell me.

I miss Helen very much. Again I put off the feeling, concentrating instead on one of the stories she used to tell me. The story about the Now Road.

"The redbird looked to the wall of monsters on his right. They stank and growled and dripped horrible slime.

"'Who are you?' the redbird asked.

"'We are the future,' answered the monsters. 'We are all of the terrible things that you will do and that will happen to you. We are injustice, cruelty, pain, old age, disease, revenge, death, and worry. You cannot escape us if you walk here.'

"The redbird then looked to the wall of monsters to his left. They also stank and growled and dripped horrible slime.

"'And who are you?' the redbird asked.

"'We are the past,' answered the monsters. 'We are all of the terrible things that you have done and that have happened to you. We are injustice, cruelty, pain, youth, disease, resentment, birth, and guilt. You cannot escape us if you walk here.'

"Between the walls of monsters was the road called Now. The road was clean, straight, and bare. The redbird knew that anything good or bad that he would find on that road he would have to put there himself. He walked there, on the Now Road, and although they called him many times, neither the monsters of the past nor the monsters of the future could touch him—"

"Tommy."

A voice swims into my dreams. "Tommy, wake up." Manuel is shaking me.

"What?" His hand covers my mouth.

"It's Louisa. She's dead."

I look into Manuel's eyes. And scream.

Wardate: 17:18-9AUG2033
Downlimit: -83619:34:07

56

The next night we are behind schedule.
It is still dark.
I concentrate on stuffing little brown boxes into little white sacks. The Now. I hand the stuffed sacks to Tessie who hands them to another redbird outside the storeroom window. I think about the boat trip, Argentina, the war, Cummings's *Essays*, anything that can crowd from my mind that monster of the past—that last look at Louisa—naked, bruised, and bloody, facedown on the crapper floor—
The Now.
Eight little brown boxes into each little white sack. Two little white sacks for each little redbird—
—that milky gob on the back of her left leg. Her knees torn up from the crapper's tiled floor. Her left arm broken. He took her kneeling from the rear, like a damned animal—
Eight little brown boxes into each little white sack—
One of the redbirds on her detail fingered Citizen Wing.
Wing.
The Now. The Now. The Now—
"One more will do it, Tommy."
I tie up the last sack and hand it to Tessie. She climbs out the window with it. I pick up my own food sacks and follow her, pulling the window down behind me.
I can still hear the two blackshit in front of the guards' quarters laughing in full view of the kitchen door. Because of them we had to force the kitchen window and are behind schedule. The saw-edged breadknife I lifted in the kitchen jabs

me in the leg and I slip it into one of my food sacks. The others are already gone, and Tessie and I wait in the shadows to make sure no one follows.

Tessie puts her lips very close to my ear and cups her hands around her mouth. "Tommy."

"What?"

"I'm sorry. About Louisa—"

I push her from me. "Shut up. Just shut up and keep your eyes open."

The night sky is cloudy. The two guards stumble into their quarters and we move at a crouch around the dining hall and run straight into the woods. We follow the path and come out on the Green Machine road.

Cautiously we move down the road, the trees to the left and the trees to the right looming over us like top-heavy, monolegged giants, knobby arms and thorny claws. As we near the Green machine, hissing stops us cold.

"Hurry up. The guard'll be here any minute." It is Doris squatting in the shadows.

We follow Doris off the road into the woods to a small clearing where the other redbirds are gathered. Eighteen are going to try it. I look for Manuel. Manuel has a promise to keep.

"Tommy."

Manuel's loud whisper comes from the other side of the clearing. I walk over, my eyes straining against the dark.

Very close I can see his face. "It's me."

Manuel nods. "We're ready." He turns into the woods and I follow. Manuel's hand slams into my chest.

"Get down!"

I press my cheek against the cool loam of the path and listen to the clatter of the approaching guard's bicycle. The fence lights don't penetrate far into the trees. Doris has already cut the fence and the guard is coming up on the hole. The bicycle clatters past without pausing to examine the bush growing through fence. Doris has uprooted the bush to plug the opening.

I feel a hand on my shoulder. "Let's go."

I get to my feet and follow Manuel for a few more steps until I see several black shapes in the shadows. One of the shapes moves a lantern shield giving us a crack of light. It is Paco.

The shape on the ground is Citizen Wing.

"Is he alive?"

"He's alive."

"Is he awake?"

Paco holds the lamp up to the guard's face. Above his gagged mouth, Wing's eyes are wild with fear.

"Good." I motion to the others. "Take off his trousers."

"Tommy, we're late—"

"Take them off."

Manuel jabs another black shape. It is Francis, and between them they pull Wing's trousers down over his boots. The guard struggles, but another redbird tightens a strap around the guard's neck and he quiets down.

"Hold his knees apart."

Manuel and Francis each grab a knee and pull it down to the ground, the guard's heels still together, tangled in his trousers. I stand on Wing's ankles, squat and unsnap the guard's drawers, exposing his genitals.

Wing squirms. Gently I cup the guard's testicles with my left hand and squeeze them together.

"*Nnnngh!*"

"Hold him."

"Hurry up, Tommy."

I look up at the redbird holding the strap around Wing's neck. "Sit him up. I want him to see this."

The guard is lifted into more of a sitting position by the strap around his neck. His head is forced down. Sweat from his face mixes with spittle from his gag, soaking his shirt. His eyes beg me. I laugh.

I grab the head of Wing's flaccid penis and pull it tight. The guard struggles but cannot move. I reach back into my food sack, withdraw the toothed breadknife, and hold it in the light in front of the guard's eyes. I release Wing's penis and search the ground with my left hand. I pick up a stone and begin slowly drawing the knife's teeth over the stone, dulling them.

"Get moving, Tommy. We're late."

"Shut up." I smile at my dark companions. "If this knife is too sharp, I just might hurt someone." The edge of the blade tested, I drop the stone and say to Wing, "Watch. Watch this, blackshit."

Again I pull taut his penis and lower the knife, Wing's eyes following the blade. He begins screaming like a duck with a mouthful of socks.

I saw very slowly. Back and forth. Back and forth. I borrow God for a moment and pray that it will take a very long time. That Wing will stay awake and scream for the thousand years it will take. Back and forth. Back—

The flesh parts, surprising me.

The guard is still awake as I hold it up in front of his eyes, then tuck it into his shirt pocket.

I take the lamp from Paco's hand and examine my work. Wing's blood is pumping out onto the forest floor. I look back at the guard's eyes. Still conscious. Good.

"I don't want you to die just now, blackshit. That's too quick. Too quick for you."

I spit on the lantern's shield and the spittle bounces off with a hiss. "I guess that's hot enough." I hold the lantern by its handle and base and say to Wing, "Bye-bye, blackshit."

I shove the searing hot lantern shield between his legs, into his crotch, hard against that bleeding stump, the smell of burning flesh heavy on the air.

It is dark.

Quiet.

The guard is still.

I leave the lantern burning in his crotch.

It is time to go.

Wardate: 17:18-9AUG2033
Downlimit: -83617:12:10

55

Manuel and Francis argue with me for a moment, then give up. I watch them move off into the night. I cannot go with them. I stay in the woods, near the fence.

Freedom.

Freedumb.

Damn freedom.

I can't tear myself away from the damned place.

Why?

I start off to see if I can catch up with Manuel, but I come back to the fence. I look from the shadows at the main building almost with longing. I curse myself.

I can't stay in the woods. I'll get nabbed by the blackshit. But my life happened here.

God, what is it?

God?

I find myself across the cleared road from where we left Wing. Late in the morning a guard finds him. Moments later an ambulance fans up and takes him away.

My work is discovered, and the chief witness is still alive. What is this thing I feel?

Is it shame?

I can't drive Louisa out of my mind.

What I did to that guard.

Always in sight of that big gray building, almost wishing to be back inside.

Homesick?

I laugh at that.

And laugh.

Cry.

For a moment I feel myself slipping into that nothingness that hid me for six years. I beat my head against the ground in rage at Outcasters, at Wing, at the image of Louisa, at my own sick weakness.

Days after I run out of food I am there, haunting the fence around Outcasters.

Wardate: 17:18-9AUG2033
Downlimit: -83449:04:01

54

". . . we are the past," answered the monsters. "We are all of the terrible things that you have done—"

Water dripping on my face.

Icy cold water. I open my eyes.

It is raining.

I push with my arms until I am sitting up, my back against the trunk of a tree.

Muscles sore and weak.

It is very quiet. Peaceful. Only the tap of the raindrops on the leaves. The hole in the fence, I remember, has been repaired.

I feel terribly cold, but I'm not shaking.

Teams came out for a few days. Did I want them to catch me; punish me?

The charred remains of that dog I found a thousand years ago. The electricity is back in the fence. Across the orphanage grounds the Wardate sign glows. No change. It is still at 17:18 9AUG2033.

I am alive. Hungry.

Hunger. It whips me like one of the guards.

I struggle to my feet and stumble off into the woods, away from the fence, to find food. I don't look back. There is nothing left for me at Outcasters.

My dreams lurk in the shadows. Faces, scenes. Dogs barking. I run, not knowing why or where my aching legs carry me.

Away.
Away from the dogs.
Away from the blackshit.
Away from the nightmare.
As my toe catches a gnarled root, it looms black before me. There is no way to avoid it. I meet it, feeling nothing.

"Hey, Tommyyyyyyyyy! Whaddaya know, man? We gonna be free!"

The pain. It wakes me. The pain in my head. The limbs and leaves swim against the blue above me.
There is no more rain.
I gingerly touch my forehead and find a lump crusted with dried blood. A tree. I laugh. I ran into a tree.
Hunger reaches up and clears my thoughts. Clears them long enough to curse myself as a fool a thousand times.
Why didn't I go with Manuel and the others? Without papers I have almost no chance at all. Weak and hungry—
Some redbirds have made it outside, but I don't know who to contact—didn't even think of it. Didn't think of anything.
If they get me back at Outcasters . . .
Daniel.
That was his name. The one who thought friends were too expensive. Captured alive. Tortured to death.
I sway to my feet and look around. I can't remember which way I came from. Which way had I been going?
Food. Find food.
I walk, letting my feet pick the direction.

I remember *Midnight Express,* where the boy escaped from the Turkish prison. But what happened to him after that? Once he escaped, how did he survive?
He was a human being, though, not an outcaster.
Bill and I saw *Midnight Express* together. It was a powerful experience.
—yes, there again I am an idiot.
There was the scene where the boy and the other prisoner are exercising together to dreamy music. And they are facing

each other. And the prisoner reaches out his hand and begins caressing the boy's arm. The hand slides up the boy's shoulder to his neck, the way I touch Louisa—used to touch Louisa.

The boy pushes back the prisoner, shaking his head. He didn't do it angrily, but with understanding. Compassion.

—And I notice Bill looking at me. When he sees me looking back, he quickly returns his gaze to the screen. But I remember his entire body trembling.

Idiot.

Any fool could have seen it coming. Any fool—

A fence. A field behind it.

Just a split rail fence, old and rotten. I climb through the rails and crawl through the tall weeds to the top of a rise. On my knees I cautiously lift my head.

Buildings? A village!

Even before I get to my feet I am running, tripping, rolling down the small hill, my sight fixed on those buildings.

A garbage can, cycler, or garden. I damn myself for every scrap of anything I had ever left upon a plate or scraped into a garbage can.

Another fence, through a yard.

I see a pale blue garbage can at the back door of a large white house.

Moving toward it my eyes blur. I dream of all of the garbage that I had ever thrown into the Green Machine. Peelings, bones, rinds—the smells make my mouth slaver—

The back door opens.

Someone coming out, running toward me. A man. I hold out my hands and cry, "Please—"

I pull my face out of the dirt, my mouth full of something gritty, the taste of blood. The mixture tastes good.

I look in time to see a foot swing into my ribs.

Don't mind. Can't feel it. Doesn't hurt.

Fists, shouts, more kicks.

Strange how good the blood tastes.

I'm very tired. I think I'll take a little nap.

Wardate: 17:18-9AUG2033
Downlimit: -83435:22:07

53

It shows me that it wants me, this misty shadow. It bargains with me, proving that it offers a deal better than life. A land without threats, without fear, without feeling.

I remember you—from before. You are this suffocating death; this friend—

There is a piece of memory left from when I hid behind the walls of my mind. It is a small black dog licking my hand. I am sitting in the dust of the road. I reach out to pet the dog—

Even in this hall of horrors called my dreams, there are nightmares I can refuse to see.

Swimming in and under an ocean of ink, I grope for a handhold.

Something cold, solid, unmovable.

I open my right eye. The left eye is swollen shut. In my hand is a metal bar, its surface pitted and greasy. I look up, see what it is, and close my eye as I rest my temple against the coolness. The wall is made of bars. The men in black have me.

I laugh a little, thinking of my father telling me, "Never open a window." "Sink me," I whisper, "but I'll certainly listen the next time."

Sink me. That's what the Scarlet Pimpernel says. After we saw the old movie, Daddy and I went around for days looking through a circle made from thumb and forefinger like a monocle, saying, "Sink me."

Sink me, but it's time to do the dishes.

Sink me, but I think I'll hie me to the bathroom.

Sink me, but I'll remember next time not to open the bleeding window.

The giggles hurt so, but all I can remember about my father is this disembodied brown beard, which makes me giggle more.

It's hard not to laugh when you are in a place where laughter is forbidden.

"He's crying in there, Wally. Have a look."

The voice sounds very far away, but I freeze. I slowly lower myself back onto the rack. A sharp pain in my chest makes me gasp.

I move my fingers over my chest. Bandages. They are so tight I can hardly breathe. My reds are gone. I have new underwear.

The familiar sound of boots.

I look at the cell door as a man in black swings open the door. I curl up, my back pushed against the bars.

Whoever it is, I can still bite. My fingers aren't broken. I can go for his eyes. Ugly Doris says, "Go for the eyes. Go for the nuts if you can't reach the eyes, but if you can reach them, go for the eyes—"

"Here."

The guard holds out a small basket. I take the basket but don't look in it until the guard backs away. I look.

Breadrolls! Five golden breadrolls! A treasure! Holding the basket between me and the bars, I begin gulping them down.

"Slow down, or you'll puke it all up."

I can't hear anything. My only command: eat. My only sensation: the taste and feel of the soft, sweet bread in my mouth.

In seconds the basket is empty.

I vomit.

"You listen real good, you do."

Shaking his head, the guard goes out the door. A little later a gray-headed prisoner comes in with a mop and pail and cleans up the mess. He talks. The prisoner's name is Jack. Jack is an illegal parent awaiting trial. His two illegal sons were killed during his arrest. Jack is terrified of dying. Jack looks at me as though he blames me for it all. I look at Jack as though I blame him for my nightmare.

When the guard returns he has two more rolls in his hand. I eat them slowly, keeping the guard in sight.

More footsteps. Another face appears outside the bars. More blackshit.

"That's him, huh?"

"Yessir."

"You got his number entered?"

"Yessir."

"I'm going past there tonight on my way home. I could drop him off."

"Doc says not to move him until tomorrow. He's weak, and he's got two busted ribs."

The second guard laughs. "Little shit'll get worse'n that when they get him back up at the orphanage. You hear about what they did to that guard up there?"

"Yeah, everybody's heard about it."

"Cut his pecker off. Man, they whacked it *clean* off! The poor bastard's still alive, too."

"From what I heard it wouldn't have happened if he had kept it in his shorts in the first place."

"Is that what this little reddie said?"

"He hasn't said anything."

"Well, you can't believe everything you hear." The second guard leans against the bars. He has lieutenant stripes on his sleeves. "Hey, kid. Yeah, you. Are you the one who snatched off that guy's joystick?"

I just look at him, frozen.

"Sure glad I never pulled orphanage duty. Little redshits. After they hacked off his dick they stuck it in his *pocket*. You ever hear of anything like that? In his pocket?"

He shakes his head. "I'll be damned if I know what makes you kids tick. Jesus, cut off a man's dick. Stick it in his pocket."

"I'll drop him off tomorrow after my watch."

The lieutenant pushes away from the bars. "Be glad to get him out of here. People in town are gettin' ugly. You sure I can't take him off your hands? I'm goin' that way."

"Thanks anyway. I'll get him out of here first thing in the morning."

"See you tomorrow night then. Keep an eye out; things are stirrin' on the street."

"Yessir. Goodnight."

The other guard goes away. The one in the cell watches me until he hears a door close outside the cell area.

"What's your name, redbird?"

"Thomas. Thomas Windom."

"I'll get some more food to you in the morning. Those rolls were all I could scare up on short notice."

"Thank you. Citizen . . ."

"My name's Wally. You get some sleep. I'll turn off the lights."

The guard turns and leaves the cell, closing the door behind him. The light bars dim and go black. I lie down and close me eyes. All I can think about is the feel of the bread in my stomach.

I sleep in a land without dreams.

Wardate: 17:18-9AUG2033
Downlimit: -83432:18:11

52

Voices.

From the cell window.

It is still dark. I wipe the sleep from my eyes, wincing as I forget and touch my left eye. Sitting up, I put my bare feet on the cold floor and try to keep my head from spinning.

More voices joining the first.

Angry voices.

My knees wobble as I try standing. I have to use the bars for support. Hand over hand I pull myself along the bars until I am beneath the window.

I reach out and pull a wooden stool close to the wall. Clawing up the rough surface, I stand straight on the stool and look through the heavy metal grill at the street below.

Six civvies are standing in front of the building, gathered around Wally the guard.

"There's more of us'n you can handle, Wally."

"Go home, Mike. All of you, go home."

"That caster. You know how he mutilated that guard. He was one of your own. Come on."

"I don't know anything of the sort. Go home."

"Everybody knows about it 'cept you. God, Wally, it's been on the news for weeks."

"C'mon, you live in this town, Wally. You going to shoot us, your own friends and neighbors?"

"Yeah, and over a caster?"

"If I have to shoot you old farts, I will. And not over a caster. I'll do it just for the target practice. Now, I said go home—"

—Dizzily I begin giggling again. Sink me, but it's a lynch mob! Oh where have I seen this before? Is Atticus down there keeping the rednecks away from my cell? I never did understand why you shouldn't kill mockingbirds—

The one called Mike steps forward, and Wally catches him under his chin with a fist swung from the sidewalk. Mike falls backward and lands hard. Another steps forward and Wally draws his gun.

"Do you really want to tangle assholes with me, Bert?"

"Now, easy, Wally. Easy." Bert moves back quickly, holding up his hands.

"All of you go home before someone gets hurt. Take Mike with you."

"All right, Wally, just watch that thing before you hurt somebody by accident."

"If I hurt someone, it'll be no accident."

"Jeez, give a guy a black cap and a little bit of authority and he acts like he owns the damned town."

"Prick."

"Jeez."

The five men drag Mike to an aircar and drop him in. Two others get in with him. The other three get into another car, and both vehicles fan out in a hurry.

Wally steps off the curb into the right-of-way, looks up and down the dark street, and goes back into the building.

Why is the blackshit cop doing anything for me? Why? I'm confused. Maybe I'm a mockingbird.

Dizzy.

Head spinning.

I slide down the wall, just making it back to my rack. Strange how soft, dark, and painless death is, sleep is—

Wardate: 17:18-9AUG2033
Downlimit: -83425:22:02

51

My eyes open.

It is morning. Through the window the sky looks gray. Outside in the guard room there is talking.

Wally enters the cell area stretching and yawning as he buttons up his black uniform blouse. "Hit the concrete, redbird."

He unlocks the cell door. "Let's go."

I get to my feet. They seem steady enough, but everything hurts. "Uh, Citizen—Wally?"

"Yeah?"

"Last night. Those men."

"What about them?"

"Why did they want me? What did I do to them?"

"You survived, kid. You stayed alive." He cocks his head toward the guard room. "Let's go."

"Thank you. For what you did out there. Thank you."

The guard nods once and walks through the door. I follow him out of the cell area into the brightness of the guard room. Wally points to a pile of civvies on the corner of a desk. "Go ahead. Put 'em on."

"Where are my reds?"

"Phew!" Wally holds his nose. "I threw 'em out. Go on and get dressed. You can't go around naked."

I put on the civvies. A heavy plaid shirt and brown denim trousers. It's the first time I can remember not wearing a one-piecer. They almost fit. I think I would feel better except for where Wally is to take me. I try not to think about it.

The guard points out some socks and old leather shoes on the floor. I begin putting them on. Sitting on the floor tying the shoes, I hear a toilet flush. In a few seconds another guard comes into the room wiping his hands on a paper towel. He looks down at me.

"Shit, Wally. This caster a relative of yours?"

"I can't bring him back naked, Frank."

"Don't see why not. Those duds aren't going to do that little pecker-chopper any good when they get him back to Casters."

"You don't know he's the one who did it."

"Think that'll make any difference to those guys at 128?"

"Anyway, he's cut up some. I don't want him to bleed all over the cruiser."

"I suppose."

Frank lowers himself behind a desk, pushes a few papers around, then reaches to a coffee pot and pours himself a cup. The coffee smells good.

"Wally, did you ever pull orphanage duty?"

"No."

Wally shows me a tray with cold eggs and toast on it. Even with my stomach in knots, I wolf down the food.

"I don't think I'd care for it much—will you just look at that little dork-snatcher shovel it down— Orphanage duty." He sighs. "I guess I don't care all that much for police duty either." Frank rattles a paper as he slurps his coffee. "You had some trouble here last night, huh?"

"It's all in the night duty report."

"Mmmm."

The other guard looks over the paper on his desk, still sipping his coffee. "Big Mike Patterson again. Bert Carpowitz. We ought to shoot those two assholes." Throwing the paper aside, he puts his boots up on the desk, yawns, and leans his chair against the wall. "You know, for a half-note I'd put in for transfer back to the Forces."

"Catch me payday, Frank."

"Ho, ho."

* * *

The police cruiser fans out from the village station. I sit next to Wally, up front. We travel the main street right-of-way until we get to a connection which brings us to the main express line. As Wally switches to external power, I recognize the line to Outcasters.

It was so long ago. I was only seven years old. But I still remember.

The turnoff is only a minute away. I can see the Wardate sign poking above the tops of the trees. There are flashes of the main building's black roof between the trees.

The guard's holstered gun is on his right side facing me. I wait for Wally to have both of his hands occupied with the controls. As he moves to pass another car, he switches the battery to "charge" while holding the wheel with his other hand. I reach for the gun, but the pain in my ribs makes me cry out.

Wally's hand closes over the handgrip.

"I can't go back, Wally! You don't understand what's going to happen to me! Please! Please—"

"Sit back and enjoy the ride, Tommy. You're not going back." As we fan past the farm turnoff, Wally grins at me. Slowly he draws his right thumb down the right side of his jaw.

I sit for a moment, stunned. Then I lift my own hand and answer the sign.

I crawl painfully to the crest of the hill, staying low in the tall grass, to look back at the place where Wally told me to get out of the police cruiser. I look down the hill, but all that remains of the cruiser is a fine haze suspended above the dirt road.

It didn't feel odd. Hugging the man in the black uniform.

I stand and begin walking in the direction Wally gave me.

Wardate: 17:18-9AUG2033
Downlimit: -83417:41:21

50

I stand in the shadows of the trees, looking down at the small farmhouse surrounded by young evergreens at the foot of the hill. The house is at the bottom of a bowl of tree-covered hills, safe from prying eyes. The red metal roof is rust-stained. The walls carry a gray, weathered patina. A broken upstairs window pane is stuffed with a wad of something pink.

In front of the porch's sagging roof, beneath the fir trees, are the rusting remains of an old car. The car's shape is not the modern elongated dish of the aircars or even the angular flatness of the older wheeled electrics. It seems to stand much taller, with lines carved by a wind that no longer blows.

Holding a hand to my taped ribs, I move out of the shadows and walk warily down the slope, my eyes constantly searching. As I come abreast of the car I pause and study the front of the house. The windows have drawn white curtains. One of the curtains moves slightly aside and drops back into place. A moment later the front door opens and a skinny old woman with short gray hair steps out onto the porch. She wears patched denims and a tan work shirt. Her feet are bare.

I step away from the car. The old woman jerks her head toward the open door.

"Inside." She turns and enters the door without looking back.

I walk the overgrown path, step up on the porch, and enter the darkness of a tiny vestibule, the smell of cooking filling my nostrils. Directly in front of me is a staircase going up. To my left is a small living room. It is a strange combination of neat, clean, sparse, and shabby. There are noises coming from the right. I push open the swinging door and enter the kitchen. The old woman is bent over a sink facing the window. The sink is full of vegetables.

"Sit down."

She points a dripping hand toward the center of the kitchen. "There."

I pull out a chair and sit down at the small table. In front of me is a plate and on the plate are cut carrots, tomatoes, and celery.

"Eat."

As I eat, the woman picks up a towel, turns from the sink, and faces me, drying her hands. "How are the ribs?"

I frown at the carrot stick I am holding and look back at the woman. "Ribs?"

"I was told you broke a few."

"Oh. They're okay. Sore."

She slings the towel over her right shoulder and leans against the sink. "My name is Rhona. You'll stay here until we can boil up some papers for you."

"I don't understand."

"We have to forge you a set of citizenship papers. It will take two weeks. While you're here, stay inside and stay out of sight. Don't offer any information and don't ask for any. The less we know about each other the less we can spill to the blackshit."

I pick up another carrot stick. "What about numbers? On the citizenship papers. How do we get me a number that won't be a big arrow pointed right at my back?"

Rhona smiles. "What do you know about citizenship numbers?"

"I've done some studying. I know you get a number with your citizenship birth warrant and when you die the number gets retired. I know that if the number on your warrant doesn't agree with the blackshit computer you're dead."

She nods and steps away from the sink. "Very true." Pulling out the chair across from me, she sits down and leans her elbows on the table.

"What's your first name?"

"Thomas."

"Okay, Thomas. Don't get the idea that the papers you are going to get will be your key to the right and bright life as a free citizen. You will have to stay out of situations where your number will be run. No property purchases, no loans, no jobs requiring bonding, no jobs that are eligible for taxation, welfare, or unemployment benefits. Never cross a national district line. Stay away from marriage, adoption, college, positions requiring a security clearance—anything that involves a written contract. Above all, never get arrested."

Her eyebrows go up. "Why are you sulking?"

"I'm not." I feel my face getting hot. "It's just that this is beginning to sound like Outcasters with a bigger yard."

"How old are you, kid? Sixteen?"

"Seventeen. Eighteen tomorrow."

Rhona sits back in her chair. "Thomas, for the past seventeen years the absolute intelligence, technology, and power of half the world has been dedicated to killing you. You are still alive. If there is ever going to be any point in you staying alive you had best stop thinking about all of the things you don't have and begin being grateful for the things you do have."

An edge of sarcasm creeps into my reply. "All the things I have, like no parents, no family, no home, no future—"

She reaches across the table and grabs my hands. "Life! That's what you have, boy! *Life!* And every second you keep on breathing is another victory!"

Rhona releases my hands and stands. "The papers we will get you won't be able to bear too close an examination. With them, however, you will be able to secure class twelve employment. Class twelves aren't taxed and aren't eligible for any benefits. It's seasonal stuff with the government, but it will get you a government employee's citizenship warrant. The government warrant is a legitimate set of papers that can stand up under any kind of examination, except for running your number. Speaking of numbers, have you had your Outcasters registration number removed yet?"

"No."

"I can take care of that. It's a bit painful, but necessary. Any questions?"

With a piece of celery I trace a circle on my plate. "I guess not. Except, why. Who are you? Why are you doing this?"

"Don't start on me, boy. The less you know, the better off both of us will be."

"It's important to me. I've spent my whole life not knowing why the people around me did what they did. Not knowing, but having to pay the price for it. It's not hard to figure out that Wally was a redbird. But what about you?"

She is motionless, a hard glitter in her eyes. She looks down for a moment and turns back to the sink. "I told you. The less we know about each other the better."

I watch as she resumes vigorously scrubbing the vegetables in the sink. Rhona is too old to have been in Outcasters. Maybe she has a younger brother or sister in. First Sets. The legal children whose younger brothers and sisters were taken away to be put into the red suits. There is another answer, but it never occurred to me before that there are some illegal parents who had escaped the blackshit. A parent. A mother.

Old woman alone.

The husband probably twitched dead, hung on some blackshit wire. The children, swallowed by the system—

I get to my feet, walk around the table, and come to a halt behind her. I place a hand on her shoulder and turn her around. The hard lines of her face are softened by tears.

I feel my own tears brimming, not knowing what feeling moves me. I wrap my arms around her and bury my face in her neck. The chains on my feelings dissolve into sobs.

"No." She places her hands on my shoulders to push me back. "No." She hesitates. Her arms go around me and she whispers as she kisses my hair.

"No. Dear God, no."

Wardate: 17:18-9AUG2033
Downlimit: -83408:03:55

49

Late that night, in the glow from the open door of the wood stove in the living room, there is a son resting his head upon his mother's lap. There is a mother stroking her child's face and hair.

Both of us know it is wrong. Stupid. Opening old wounds to participate in a futile fantasy. Still we say the words that we imagine mothers and sons exchange. A tender glowing moment to throw into a universe of lonely nothing. A little something to carry into the empty terror of the future.

—You've been away so long. So long.

—I didn't want to go. Mommy, they hurt me. They hurt me so.

—Here. Let me put my arms around you and make the hurt go away.

—I love you.

—I love you.

For a long time we are silent.

"Why can't I stay here?"

"*Shhh.*"

"Why?"

"Be still."

If I stay I endanger her. The farm would become a new prison, the frustrations driving us apart into resentment and hate. Room has to be made for the next refugee from the system. Sooner or later I would be noticed by those on the outside.

—The old woman on the farm. She has a boy living with her now?

—Yeah. I seen him.

—Who is he, now? Her son?

—Could be. I don't want to make any hasty accusations, understand, but could be.

—She always was a loner, that one. I mean, it's not like she ever acted like she was part of this community. I wonder what she's got to hide.

—We better call in the blackies.

—You're right. If she doesn't have anything to hide, she shouldn't mind. We better check it out.

Eventually we would kill each other. I know all that. But why? Why does it have to be?

"Why?"

"*Shhh.*"

Wardate: 17:18-9AUG2033
Downlimit: -83121:33:26

48

In the early morning dark, eleven days later, I stand on the front porch holding the paper-wrapped package containing my clothing while Rhona fusses with my buttons.

"What's your name?"

"Thomas Mills."

"Middle name?"

"No middle name."

"How old?"

"Eighteen."

"When were you born?"

"January 3rd, 2006."

"Place of birth?"

"Pittsfield, New Hampshire."

"Residence of record?"

"Box 2117B, Elton Station, Monroe Junior College, Ashland, Mass."

"Citizenship number?"

"US forty-four, three oh nine six, two sixty-seven."

Finished fussing with the buttons, she brushes imaginary lint from my coat and places her hands upon my shoulders. "And if the man goes off to check any of this?"

"Run like hell, find a telephone near a good hiding place, cover the camera lens, dial nine nine two seven three, leave the phone off the hook and hide until the telephone rings. Then, if no one is around, I answer the phone and do what I am told."

She looks up at the sky. The last of the stars are fading in the west. "It's clear and it shouldn't be too cold today. Do you have your papers?"

I pat my jacket pocket. "Yes. And the money."

"How's your shoulder?"

"The itching stopped. The number's gone."

"Your ribs?"

"Okay."

"I guess that's everything."

"Yes."

She slowly lowers her gaze until she is looking into my eyes. She touches my cheek with her hand. "What should I tell you? Have a good life? Keep out of drafts? Brush your teeth every day?" She laughs, the beginnings of tears in her eyes. She places her hand around my neck and pulls me toward her until our foreheads touch.

"I never got to see my boy, Thomas. I never even got to see him. I want you to know that whenever I think of my son, of what he could have been, in my mind he will be carrying your face."

—he will be carrying your face.

As I reach the crest of the hill I pause and look back at the house. It is dark, and the porch is empty. I move my package from beneath my left arm to beneath my right arm. The sky to the east is very bright. If I don't hurry I will miss the trans and have to wait an extra two hours—two dangerous hours in public.

I turn and begin walking down the road to town, trying to remember my mother's face. Rhona is who I see.

Wardate: 17:18-9AUG2033
Downlimit: -83117:21:00

47

I am an island, dark and desolate.

See them around me—others—brightly lit ships, signaling to each other, sailing reality's ocean to their individual destinations, celebrating the existence of each other, passing me by without notice.

The ticket agent at the trans station, the other passengers, the woman with the hostile brat, the soldier with the missing arm. The car conductor with his blue box, coding tickets. The man across the aisle, balancing the case and papers upon his knees, working furiously, attempting somehow to accomplish something before somewhen reaches somewhere.

I could be a monster in their midst, a bomb about to explode, a thing suffering incredible pain, and it all happens without them noticing a thing. Without them noticing me.

Shadow puppets.

There was the one movie Ugly Doris would watch every time it was on. *The Year of Living Dangerously.* The little woman in the movie explained the Indonesian shadow puppets. Look at the shadows, not at the puppets. The shadows mean so many things; but shadows can be ignored. If you ignore the shadow, the puppet becomes invisible.

There was another movie Doris would watch. It was a funny western called *Silverado*. The little woman with the shadow puppets played a saloon girl in *Silverado*. That was the one time Ugly Doris cried. She said out loud, "I love Linda Hunt."

I laughed at her. "Why? You're not a dwarf."

"Neither is she!" Then the tears appeared in her eyes. Just as quickly the tears were wiped off and that ugly grin was back on her face. "You are a cripple, Dumbs. You are so locked up in your own head. You're not the only one on this planet. Check it out, Dumbs."

I didn't laugh at her to be cruel. I only did it because she was always laughing at me. I care about others. I notice them more than they notice me.

I sit next to the window, the soldier across from me, the man with the case and papers to my right. As the trans speeds north, I become morbidly fascinated by the man with the case and papers. His concentration upon his work is so intense. He is oblivious to his surroundings. The trans, the conversations in the car, the passing landscape, MAC III's tentacles upon his every moment, the starvation in Otherworld, the conflict in Turkey, the coming war—the universe beyond the limits of his case and papers does not exist.

He bites his lower lip as the pen in his right hand scribbles notes, the fingers of his left hand paging through more notes and punching buttons on his calculator, the direction of his gaze rapidly alternating between the calculator, his printed notes, and his writing. The urgency of his effort almost makes me want to offer my help.

I lean to my right, attempting to glean a clue concerning his work from his papers. It must be terribly important. I look. I see. I sit back, my head against my seat's backrest, my eyes closed, amazed again at the real world. Amazed again at the things considered of all-consuming importance.

The man with the papers sells cocktail onions.

What is the thing that determines what and where we are at any given moment? The Big Machine? God? Who is it that decides that this one will lose an arm, that one will have a baby, the other one will sell cocktail onions, and the one asking all of the stupid questions will be an escaped Outcaster? Feena, the goddie freak, used to say that everyone is exactly where he or she chooses to be. I told her that I sure didn't choose to be at Outcasters. She said that I did choose to be there; otherwise I'd be over the wire or in a grave.

Some choice.

I think about another old movie I saw on television called *Charly*. Charly was retarded and was the experimental subject in a surgical attempt to increase his intelligence. Charly went from being a funny-looking janitor in a bakery who couldn't manage to learn to spell "work" to a level of brilliance that shadowed his teachers. But the effects were temporary. He slid back, becoming again that funny-looking baby in an adult's body.

I remember not being certain what the point of the story was. That was because Charly the brain-damaged moron was a very happy person. Charly the genius was a very unhappy person. Charly the born-again moron was, again, happy. Charly the genius didn't belong; Charly the moron did. Why, then, did the genius fight so hard against going back to being a moron?

It's a dumb movie.

Wardate: 17:18-9AUG2033
Downlimit: -83115:14:13

46

Louisa lay on her stomach, naked, the blanket protecting her from the grass stubble in the clearing. Her skin is warm from the sun, the dip of her back, the arched climb to her buttocks, traced by my fingers.

"Tommy?"

"What?"

"Why is your face so strange?"

"I don't know what you mean."

"Don't you enjoy making love?"

"Of course I do."

"Then why do you always look like you're in such pain? Like right now."

"I don't know what you mean." I stand and shout at her, "I do not know what you mean!"

I run into the woods, coming to rest against a tree, my eyes staring through the forest at the hulk of the Green Machine standing watch upon its precious rotting mountain.

—Four-and-twenty blackshit baked in a pie—

That vague memory of the little black dog licking my hand races by my closed eyes. I honestly cannot remember that or any other dog at Outcasters. Pets were dangerous. But there was a beating, wasn't there? And for killing a dog? Was it a guard's dog? In that unfeeling nightmare of mine, did I kill—

Think about something else.

Ugly Doris had a pet swallow for a few weeks until a guard, Citizen Misner, took it and wrung its neck, killing it. Two months later there was a sudden fire in the guards' quarters, and Citizen Misner was the only casualty. Everyone, guards and redbirds included, was surprised when Ugly Doris requested permission to attend Citizen Misner's funeral. His family had no objection, so Doris attended, accompanied by Citizen Sayther.

After the ceremony Citizen Sayther made a point out of telling us how touched the deceased guard's family had been by the tiny wreath Doris had placed on the coffin. The wreath was made of white, yellow, and blue wildflowers. In the center of the wreath, its wings spread in flight, were the mummified remains of a barn swallow. At the graveside, Misner's mother stood with her arm around Ugly Doris's shoulders.

The girls club didn't hit Misner; not just for killing a bird. I figure Doris torched him all on her own. Even so, it didn't make up for the death of her pet. Not to Doris.

Would beating me senseless make up to that guard for killing his pet dog? The monsters in my head argue among themselves. Anything bad you can do to a guard is okay. But then anything a guard does to a redbird is okay. But they did it to us first. But if it was *my* little black dog that some caster threw into the Green Machine, I would have killed the—

—Voices.

A bump in the rail. Voices.

I open my eyes and rub the sand from them. In the seats facing mine are the soldier with one arm and next to him a woman cradling a baby.

"She's almost seven months."

"Nice." The soldier nods. He looks uncomfortable. His eyes are glazed with emotion. I get the feeling that if the conversation before me goes on much longer, the soldier will strangle the woman with the baby. "Very cute. Congratulations."

The woman smiles at the soldier, her face warm and soft. "Thank you." She places a hand on his shoulder. "It will be all right. You'll see."

The soldier looks out of the window as the woman gets up

and takes her baby to another seat to share her good fortune with another passenger.

"Do you believe that?"

The soldier is talking to me. "I just woke up. I didn't—"

"She just got her kid back from the hospital. An operation to correct a birth defect. She's been running up and down the aisle bragging." The soldier shakes his head. "It must be wonderful going through life like that."

I don't know what to say. He looks at me for a long moment. "How old are you, boy?"

"Eighteen."

He again turns and looks out of the window. "When your turn comes, stay out of the Force. Stick an icepick in your ear, rape the draft officer, whatever you have to do when they come at you with that duty and the salvation of humanity shit. Until this world blows itself to hell, take what you can. Take it and damn the rest."

He continues looking out of the window, the conversation ended. There are four red stripes on the empty sleeve of his black uniform blouse. He is a sergeant. I glance to my right. The man who sells cocktail onions is still hard at work. He also sells olives and gourmet pickles.

Wardate: 17:18-9AUG2033
Downlimit: -83113:02:01

45

I get off the trans at Rutland, State District of Vermont. There are many near my age applying for summer work with Forestry Resources. I am issued temporary papers and assigned to the base camp at Bloodroot. At Bloodroot I am given a cot in an all-male barracks, issued work uniforms, boots, and hardhat, and am assigned to a crew, John Allen, chief.

The barracks reminds me of "E" Dorm.

There are ghosts in the night. Ghosts of the living and ghosts of the dead. Louisa, Ann, Manuel, Helen, Rhona.

As I look at the reflections of the dim lights on the barracks ceiling I feel a knot of anxiety in the pit of my stomach. As I have done so many times before, I am waiting in fear for the lights to go on; for the new day to begin.

To dread the night, to dread the morning. The world is working through an equation of circumstances, each particle of humanity serving the equation in some capacity—except for me and the few others like me. We are being left behind. However the equation eventually resolves, the warrantless will share no part of it. It should not bother me, not belonging. But it is there. When I let it, it tears out my heart. I want so to belong.

I think of holding Louisa. Her touch, her breath in my ear, the feel of her driving all existence from my mind. Her strength when I had none.

I surprise myself because I realize that I miss Outcasters. The surprise doesn't last for long. At Outcasters I had brothers and sisters. Here in Bloodroot I have no one. I can let no one know me. Intimacy is death. I am so very lonely.

Loneliness.

It will take some time to make certain, but eventually I must reach a decision. Is this life worth living?

Louisa.

I realize I have an erection. Shame fills me. In anger and pain I empty it.

Wardate: 17:18-9AUG2033
Downlimit: -82753:17:11

44

Mornings are cold. Days are hot. The work hard and monotonous.

I look at them as the truck bounces along the fire lane, the Green Mountains surrounding us.

There is Eva Messer, a projections major at the University of Nations. She is all business, knows where she is going and just how to get there. Every morning at four she wakes up and runs ten miles around our Bloodroot base camp. For all practical purposes she chiefs our brush clearing crew.

Gaff and Dice, loud and scrufty, are brothers. In between the patches of immature facial hair, they are white. They are spending the summer in the Forestry Resources Service working to pay off their fines for defacing Compact property. They call themselves revolutionaries, but they look like something unstable from the last century. At the end of the summer they will return to Boston University and resume their studies in business administration. If they ever outgrow the barricades, they will inherit their father's stock brokerage firm.

Paul Malcolm is serious, quiet, and black. Next fall he enters the U of N's Canton, Ohio campus to begin preastronautics. There has been no one in space since the Mars Station project closed down at the turn of the century. The program at Canton and a few other campuses says that we are again reaching for the stars. The crew calls him Spaceman.

They all have destinations. Futures. I arrived at mine the

day I saw Outcasters. Too clearly I remember riding the wagon with Ann and the others, Citizen Brown driving the ancient horse, on our way to the field to gather weeds to feed to the Green Machine. Today we ride a truck, crew chief Allen driving, through the fire lanes to clear brush to feed to the chippers. Instead of redbirds we call ourselves woodies.

It is grotesque, this running joke called reality.

John Allen is our crew chief of record. When we arrive at the uncleared portion of the fire lane, he will remain in the truck, leaving it now and then to relieve his bladder. At the end of our shift it will be necessary to shove him to the other side of the cab to allow Eva to drive us back to Bloodroot. Allen is addicted to alcohol. The crew calls him Ether Allen and they call themselves the Green Mountain Boys.

Days I operate the electric knife. Nights I watch my barracks ceiling. There is this constant knot of fear in me that I might slip and be discovered. Even more, I fear that I will never be discovered; that this will go on forever. I hide in myself, allowing no one to get near me. There is my existence as a Hey You to consider. It was hell. But the time did pass.

I feel a strange brotherhood with Ether Allen. He is a corpse waiting for sufficient reason to fall down. He has reached his destination, too.

It is the beginning of April. The birthday of someone called Windom happened last month and he forgot to notice.

Wardate: 17:18-9AUG2033
Downlimit: -80401:31:33

43

July.

The night in Bloodroot is hot and heavy.

Most of the woodies in camp are down at the lake swimming. I am driven by boredom into the rec shack. The only one there from my crew is Spaceman. He is sitting at one of the letter desks reading a book. I look at the cover. It was written by one Frederick Bellenger.

"What's it about?"

The Spaceman comes back from his personal galaxy and frowns at me. It takes him a moment to focus on me. "What?"

"The book. What's it about?"

"About?" He looks at the cover almost as though he didn't know himself what he's reading. "Bellenger. It describes his theory for a practical SL drive."

"What's that?"

"Supralight? Faster-than-light? For space travel?" He shakes his head and turns back to his book. "Forget it."

There are a few faces from other crews in the hall. Some writing letters, reading, playing cards. Most are watching the TV.

The one called Nelson is bitching because the movie he wanted to watch will be delayed. I ask what the movie is and am told that it is a first-run called *The Othello Error.* I find the listings and read the release date: 1997. Too recent. Too much MAC in it for me.

My father used to say it that way: too much MAC in it.

That's why he stuck with the old movies. Citizen Haskins used to say it that way, too.

I'm about to return to the barracks.

On the TV screen is the break sign of CPBN, and I remember. Secretary of Projections Cummings is to make a statement tonight to the press about his resignation.

The rest of the camp has been rumbling with rumors for days, opinion on the consequences of the old man being given the boot divided between those who think it will herald in a new age of freedom and those who think it will end life as we know it.

A million years ago Cummings wrote that the system—the Compact—the Big Plan, depends upon no individual. If he stays or goes it makes no difference. MAC III simply takes the new circumstances into account and adjusts accordingly. Probably before Cummings himself knew he was going to resign, the circumstances regarding his resignation had already been adjusted. What does the old man hope to accomplish by making a parting explanation?

It does not serve a function in the Big Equation.

There is iced tea, and I pour myself a glass and sip it as the commentators hurl speculations at each other in the name of journalistic objectivity.

Before my debate about whether to watch or not is resolved, the screen shows a dark blue lectern in front of the lighter blue and gold of the Compact flag.

There is a hushed voice.

". . . *department press officer, Mel Patterson, informed the reporters that Secretary Cummings will deliver a brief statement concerning the reasons for his resignation. He will take no questions afterwards. Speculation concerning Secretary Cum—*

"*Ladies and gentlemen, the Secretary of Projections.*"

Nervous coughing.

A low buzz of voices.

Silence.

That frail old man walks onscreen behind the lectern, stops and looks at the reporters. He wears a gray suit and vest. I cannot read his face. It has no expression.

He removes his old-fashioned glasses, tucks them into his breast pocket and stands to the left of the lectern, his hands in his trouser pockets. He looks up for a moment, then brings his gaze down, a tiny smile on his face.

He begins speaking.

"Once upon a time there was a student of mathematics who arrived at the wrong answer to a problem. The student wanted to know what was wrong with his answer.

"The instructor replied that the student's assumptions had been in error. 'You see,' said the instructor pointing at the paper, 'here you have two plus two equaling eight. Two plus two equals four.'"

He pauses.

"What is this shit?" A boy seated in a chair toward the front gets up to change the channel.

The words jump from my mouth. "Leave it."

The boy looks back at me. His face carries one of those stunned scowls used by thugs to signal that they are not used to having their wishes disputed.

"Say what?"

"You heard me." Another woodie tells the boy to sit down and shut up. After some obligatory blustering, the boy sits down.

Cummings rocks back and forth upon his toes for a moment.

"Well, the student was stunned at this statement. He asked the instructor 'Does two plus two always equal four?'

"'Yes,' replied the instructor. 'Always.'

"'Why, that's terrible,' cried the student. 'Isn't there something we can do about that?'"

Chuckles from the reporters.

"The student was quietly led away and placed under close observation at a maximum security mental institution."

More chuckles from the reporters.

Coughing.

Silence.

Cumming's face fills the screen. There is not a hint of humor in his expression.

"Some time later a prominent citizen publicly demanded to

know why we execute illegal parents and lock up their children." The old man withdraws his left hand from his pocket and leans his elbow upon the lectern. *"This man demanded to know why government controls invade almost every aspect of his personal and business life and why the coming war with the Otherworld nations has to be. 'Why,' he asked, 'can't everybody just love everybody?'"*

Cummings pauses and smiles.

"It was carefully explained to the citizen that two plus two still equals four."

Silence.

"'Why, that's terrible,' replied the citizen. 'Isn't there something we can do about that?'

"The citizen was subsequently elected President-General of the Compact of Nations."

Cummings removes his elbow from the lectern, waits a moment, then turns and walks offscreen.

For a stunned moment the screen is filled with the empty lectern, switching suddenly to a confused-looking woman's face that becomes unconfused-looking the instant she realizes she is on.

I laugh as the woman makes a feeble attempt to subject Cummings's statement to broadcast analysis.

"What's so funny?"

I don't know who asked me. I can't stop laughing.

Faces looking at me.

Can't explain.

I stumble from the hall and go down to the lake to share my laughter with the loons.

Wardate: 17:18-9AUG2033
Downlimit: -80397:06:29

42

Later that night, in the dark of the barracks, I think about the old man. Aubry Cummings. Kicked out. Humiliated. Half the planet damning the air he breathes.

It is nonsense, but it is as though I share a great secret with this man. Out of the world's billions, only he and I know what is really going on; what will happen; what will have to happen.

It is a foolish fantasy. The information has been published, taught and debated for decades. It is there for anyone who wants it. But no one wants it.

I have taken up my studies again, obtaining books through the base's branch library. My mind is again filled with the tools and the promises of disciplinary projections. There will be a new world. Not paradise, but a wonderful place compared to now.

More than any other person in human history, Cummings is the savior of the human race. And how do I feel now that the savior has been nailed to his bureaucratic cross?

Angry.

Frustrated.

Impatient.

And absolutely delighted.

Wardate: 17:18-9AUG2033
Downlimit: -79197:12:20

41

The end of August.

I sit on the forest floor, leaning with my back against a tree, eating my lunch, concentrating on my book as some of the other members of the crew piss and moan about the food, the job, the day, and the state of the world. Spaceman is still cracking his head on Bellenger.

"Spaceman, you gonna eat that babyburger?"

He looks up from the book. "Gaff, if you're still hungry hit the roach wagon again. Eva, pass over the tea."

"Here. Hey, Space, what'd you think about the Orzaya Bill? Did that shut off Cummings's water, or what?"

"Don't mean a thing. I leave that crap to you worldsavers. I'm on my way to the stars." He closes the book. "How about it, Gaff? Happy now that MAC III can't send you off to war without the President-General's blessings?"

"Shit. The way that old fucker Cummings worked it you can count on it that it all fits into the Big Plan somehow. How do we know that the PeeGee isn't wired into the big machine?"

Dice takes up the theme. "For all we know the PeeGee is a robot, or maybe a bunch of electrons—"

Guffaws from the others.

"—now wait! Look, you ever see the PeeGee except on the tube? Computer generated images aren't anything new. Shit, for all we know the Orzaya Bill and the whole damned government might be nothing but dots on a screen. I know I never seen any of 'em in person."

"You're paranoid."

"Hey, Space, paranoia's the definition of getting in touch with reality in a world that's spent the last thirty years sitting on its ass waiting to wipe itself out."

Eva laughs and turns toward me. "Thomas?"

"Yes?"

"What's the book?"

I pause, then push myself to my feet and come over to where the others are sitting. I take another bite out of my sandwich and face the cover of the book toward her. It is Engle's *Aubry Cummings: An Unauthorized Biography.*

"At last! One I've read." She winks at the Spaceman. "This kid's been reading shit I don't even want to think about until grad school."

I ignore the wink and sit down between Spaceman and Eva, crossing my legs. I place the book on the carpet of dead leaves and tap it with my finger.

"This man, Engle. He doesn't know what he's talking about."

Gaff and Dice whistle and elbow each other.

Eva's face reddens. "That's your opinion."

More whistling and grabass from the agitators. Dice dumps his tea in Gaff's lap and takes off into the woods running.

"You—" Gaff scrambles to his feet and runs after his brother.

I pick up the book and flip back a few pages. "As Gaff would say, Engle couldn't find his own ass with both hands and a mirror. Here he says that the whole motivation for the outcaster system was Cummings's own childhood. Because Aubry Cummings was a orphan."

"He was, wasn't he?"

I grimace at Eva. "That's shit. The orphanage system was a synthesis produced by the necessity for population control and the Compact Assembly's refusal to enact the infanticide provisions of the 1998 Citizenship Act draft. MAC II designed the orphanage system as a circumstance adjustment alternative."

Spaceman raises his eyebrows at Eva. "Mah, mah but don' he tawk dat shit good?"

She sticks out her tongue at Spaceman and looks back at

me. "Engle also points out that Cummings designed all three MAC computer complexes as well as the discipline that made them possible. A computer only does what a human tells it to do. And the way Cummings designed the Compact, the government also only does what it's told to do. In this case it only does what it's told to do by Aubry Cummings."

I shake my head, smiling in exasperation. There's no point, but I continue. It's the only chance I ever get to talk about anything but girls, drugging, and clearing brush. "Eva, it's the other way around. MAC III is way beyond a pocket calculator. Everybody, including Cummings, gets his orders from the machine. Do you think he wanted himself fired?"

"Who built the machine? Who designed it? Who came up with the goals the machine is trying to achieve?"

"Several different companies did the initial construction, MAC III was designed by MAC II, and the goal limits were defined by the original projection run done on the first MAC facility."

"You're being silly, Thomas. MAC III hands out the orders now, but way back before the computers that designed MAC I were plugged in, there was Aubry Cummings telling the computers what to design."

I hold up the book and look at Spaceman. "Do you agree with this man? He has no training in projections at all. He's a sociologist."

Spaceman gathers up his trash and pushes himself to his feet. "Ancient saying, Thomas. To know a rotten egg, I don't have to be able to lay a fresh one." He looks down at me, for a moment, a question half-formed in his mind.

"What?"

"Nothing. Look, once Bellenger gets his drive working all of this will be just so much jaw exercise. The universe is a big place." He shakes his head and turns toward the portable toilets. "Fuck it."

I look back at Eva. "What's with him?"

"Maybe he's wondering how qualified an eighteen-year-old brushcutter is to criticize Engle. For me, mostly I agree with Engle. He goes overboard here and there and is a little sloppy in his arguments, but I agree with him that Cummings made up his mind that a war was the only solution to all of the world's problems, and that the man has spent the rest of his life inventing computers, goverments, and laws arranging to have that war."

I place the book facedown upon one knee and take another bite of my sandwich as I look up at the treetops.

"What are you thinking about?"

"Eva, have you ever read Cummings's *Essays*?"

"Just quotes in class texts. That's not exactly the kind of stuff I climb into bed with when I want to cuddle up with something interesting."

"Using the MAC I facility Cummings predicted the existence, the form, and the line of argument of the Consolidationists. When and how they would appear on the political scene, as well as the strength the movement would have at various stages."

"Kid, in projections you never know what was predicted and what was selected and created through circumstance adjustment. MAC III is the original self-fulfilling prophecy extrapolated to infinity."

I tap the book. "Cummings predicted this book. Even this guy Engle." I nod toward Eva. "Even you. What he called the anti-student of projections. Everything but your name. And MAC I was pretty crude compared to what DOP has now."

"Are you saying I am what I have to be? That I didn't have any choices along the way?"

I take another bite of my sandwich. "No. You had plenty of choices. It's just that they, and you, were and are very predictable."

Eva's face flushes dark with anger. "Look, kid, there aren't any wires on me, and I don't care what old man Cummings put down."

I try to explain my way out of it. I don't want her angry at me. "It doesn't mean that you're simpleminded, Eva. It just means that you're human." I frown as a familiar thought gnaws at me. "If you hate Cummings so much, why are you studying projections?"

"Look, stupid, projections properly used can be a fantastic sociological tool to end human suffering. And as much as

Cummings disgusts me, he contributed a lot to forming the discipline. But now he has twisted the whole thing until he has locked the human race into starvation, poverty, and war—all the things we could have cured by now if it wasn't for his influence and his damned computer."

"No." I shake my head. "Don't you see that what you study, the job you're working at right now, are all parts of an enormous whole that MAC III—"

Eva grabs her hard hat and gets to her feet. "As I said, that's your opinion. MAC III doesn't have any wires on me." She turns and walks back toward the roach wagon, calling back over her shoulder. "Wrap it up. Break's almost over."

I watch her for a moment and close the book. Leaning back on my elbows, I stretch out my legs and look up at the blue between the treetops.

The MAC III complex contains continually updated situation/choice profiles of every citizen of the Compact over the age of twelve, including Eva Messer whether she wants to believe it or not. Civilian government, military, business, labor, students, the poor, the crippled, the insane—everybody.

Presented with choice situation such-and-such, human so-and-so will probably act in such-and-such a manner. Even the key figures of the Otherworld nations are entered and what MAC III considers a key figure includes everyone in politics, all those in any kind of production down to and including lower management, all those in the military down to and including platoon officers. MAC continually increases the depth of the human race's profile as it increases its capacity. The book I read that in was copyrighted in 2011. For all I know MAC has a wire on everyone by now. Everyone in the world except the few of us that fell in between the cracks.

I roll to my left and page through the book until I come to the quote from Cummings's essay: "Social Reality."

> If a thorough base profile is performed upon a subject, and if the projectionist places all subsequent events, reactions to events and individual initiatives in relation to how they alter the subject, his reaction to a given

stimulus or event can be predicted. The reliability of the prediction is directly proportional to the projectionist's knowledge of the subject. If everything about the subject is known, the prediction can be absolutely reliable.

Thus the behavior of the politician, the bureaucrat, the journalist, the dissenter, can be predicted, and through the manipulation of the events surrounding and affecting them, they can be manipulated to aid in achieving vast social goals without ever being aware that they are doing anything more than what they think serves their individual interests. Indeed, they may honestly think that they are working to defeat goals that they are in fact making possible to achieve.

Engle uses the quote to support his case that Cummings is the essence of the mad scientist pushing around his human pawns in Machiavellian glee. Rather than credit Cummings with having a goal for the betterment of anything, Engle seems to think that the scientist is addicted to the pushing around itself. Perhaps the author is only projecting what he would do if such power were placed in his hands.

I look again at the treetops. Whatever the moral issues, the wiring is there. When the war comes, strengths, weaknesses, experience, courage, capabilities, tactics, weather, time, terrain, equipment—everything possible will move through the computer like lightning. And from the computer will come orders that will throw every Compact strength against every Otherworld weakness.

Everybody is wired.

Everybody but me.

MAC knows I exist, but doesn't know where I am or anything else about me. My personality profile is in the machine, but Thomas Windom is a phantom. His number doesn't apply to anyone. I am Thomas Mills.

There are labor force and population totals that can't possibly match exactly with the citizenship totals. Perhaps the computer decided that a certain number slipping through its electronic fingers would have no adverse effects on its ultimate goals. Perhaps I am just too insignificant to bother with.

The screams and laughs of Gaff and Dice grabassing among the trees confirm my thoughts. Their fines and sentences had been determined by MAC III. Perhaps even their crime. How would their crime serve the computer's goals?

Because of the values the pair had acquired through a computer dictated education, they go out of their way to be unappealing, unsympathetic, rejectable. Perhaps in rejecting them a portion of the population places just that much more distance between themselves and the pair's anti-Compact sentiments.

Perhaps the computer led the pair along their particular path to make certain that their stockbroker father was at less than peak form at a crucial moment. A hasty, thoughtless decision causing a sufficient scandal in a major brokerage house at the right moment would have highly predictable ripples throughout the Compact economy, affecting—

Or perhaps MAC III's conception of the quality of life doesn't include obscenities painted on government buildings, and it figures that a fine and a summer of hard labor will adjust Gaff's and Dice's circumstances. Whatever it is, it's consistent with what Gaff calls the Big Plan.

Everyone is wired.

I think again about the personality profile test I took at Outcasters. Whatever it was that caused the computer to refuse me my citizenship must have been contained in the profile. What had been revealed?

MAC knows a lot about me. More than I know about myself.

I hear Eva blowing her whistle, signaling the end of the lunch break. I get to my feet, place the book into my hip pocket, and begin walking past the roach wagon to secure my electric knife. There are other things to think about. Summer will end and I must find a place to hole up for the winter.

There is a town I found forty kilometers north of the service base camp in Bloodroot. The town is tucked away in the mountains and is called West Ellen.

West Ellen is at the end of a road. No one goes through West Ellen to get to some other place. The town is within hiking distance from Bloodroot. It has a steady population of under two hundred. The ski resorts are far away on the other side of the mountains. No one who doesn't live there comes to West Ellen in the winter. In the summer the population increases slightly because of the campers. In winter all the campers are gone. By next summer I will be gone too, back with the service, clearing brush.

In my breast pocket is the postcard from Avon Weeks. Weeks operates a string of summer camps and agreed to rent me a cabin for the winter in exchange for doing odd jobs. No pay, no taxes, no number run.

There are no uniformed police in West Ellen, that function being performed by a town constable who also runs the post office from the back of his tiny grocery and variety store. I'll be able to continue my studies. The town of West Ellen has a tiny public library with a central library system access terminal. I should be safe there. There are never any guarantees, but the probabilities favor West Ellen.

As I pull my knife from the tracked carryall my thoughts stand beside me like a presence. There should be more to life than just being safe. There is a world of places I can never see. A world of persons I can never allow to know me. A world of futures I can never experience.

The human race is moving inevitably toward an unyielding reality, and the future will see if the suffering is civilization's price tag or is simply all waste. But I cannot be a part of it. I am standing off to one side, insignificant and uninvolved, as the human race takes its most demanding test.

I put the knife's strap over my shoulder, walk to the edge of the cleared area, and position the knife close to the ground. I begin cutting, the hiss and crackle of the electric element filling my nostrils with the smell of ozone and charred wood.

The amount I cut easily keeps the rest of the crew occupied piling my slash. Carelessness on their part could cost a leg or an arm. When I cut, everyone takes care to stay well to my rear. None of them ever see my face when I cut. Now and then I wonder what it looks like as I visualize the ranks of blackshit that I am cutting down.

Wardate: 17:18-9AUG2033
Downlimit: -77037:15:11

40

The beginning of winter.

I stand on the south side of Main Street, West Ellen, a strange silence in my ears. The chill and gray sky of the morning that tickled my face with fluffy flakes of snow as I climbed the road into the mountains is now white, the snow beginning to gather on the ground.

There are large white frame houses with barns attached. They are ancient and fly in the teeth of every principle of heat conservation the Compact has tried to instill for the past thirty years. The street is dominated by the trunks and soaring heights of huge naked maple trees.

There is the smell of wood smoke on the street, and the chimneys on the houses issue steamy columns that climb into the sky until they disappear into the whiteness of the snowfall.

I am standing in front of one of the large houses. Bolted to the right of the door is a white sign with green lettering: West Ellen Public Library.

Farther down the street, just past the crossroads, one of the large houses has an illuminated sign hanging above the porch: Dyar's Variety. That will be the town constable. Somewhere in the tiny store will be another terminal, wiring in West Ellen's law enforcement to the rest of the Compact police system. There are lights on inside the ground floor of Dyar's. There are no lights on inside the library.

From across the wide street comes the sound of a door closing. On her porch stands an old woman in a bright yellow cape and hood. Placing her hand on the railing, she eases her way down the four steps to her walkway and marches across the street toward me. She comes to a halt in front of me and looks at my face over the tops of her wire-rimmed glasses.

"Are you waiting for the library to open?"

"No."

"I open the library promptly at nine o'clock every morning except Sunday. I was simply a little late this morning." She moves her face closer. Although she is frowning, her face is soft, kind.

"You're new."

"I'm looking for Citizen Avon Weeks. I'm renting a cabin from him for the winter."

Her eyebrows go up. "Citizen? You mind me, young man. Call Avon Weeks either Mister or Avon. He don't like to be called Citizen." Her eyebrows lower. "We're like that here in West Ellen. It's no reflection on the government. What's your name?"

"Thomas Mills."

Up go her eyebrows again. "Any relation to the Millses over to Monkton?"

"No."

"Didn't think so. I'm Meghan French. I'm the librarian." She turns and points in the direction of Dyar's Variety. "Down past Dyar's, keep on Main Street until you reach a fork. Take the left one. That's the Stark Mountain Road. The left one, now. Keep on that for about a mile until you see a really ugly sign on the left. That's Avon's place. You can't miss it."

"Thank you."

She looks back at me as she pulls the cape tightly about her frail shoulders. "I can't imagine what you'll be doing here. We don't usually get folks here for the winter."

"I'll be doing some odd jobs for Cit—Mr. Weeks."

"Do you read much, Thomas?"

"Yes."

"I'll expect you, then. Good day." She turns to her left, walks up the steps to the library, opens the door and enters. The door hadn't been locked.

I move the strap on my bag from my right shoulder to my left and begin walking slowly in the direction of Dyar's Variety.

Just beyond the store is a larger structure with a black-shingled spire rising out of its roof. A church. Across from the church is a run-down red-painted barn with faded letters above the large double doors. The letters identify the building as the home of the West Ellen Volunteer Fire Company. The former home, judging by the doors being nailed shut and sealed. A paper poster tacked to one of the doors gives the details concerning a bean supper to be held at the church some days ago.

From in front of the old firehouse I can look down the remainder of the road they called Main Street. There are three more of the large white houses before the fork to the Stark Mountain road.

I continue walking, trying to examine my feelings. It is almost as though I have dropped through a slot in time to some stable point in the past. Ever since I turned onto the West Ellen road there have been no vehicles zipping by. The town has no black uniforms. There is no red Wardate sign oppressing everyone's future. It is as though reality had been nothing but a bad dream and finally I have awakened.

I know it is a stupid feeling; the kind of feeling that can make me careless, that can get me killed. Still the feeling is there. It is so quiet, so peaceful.

In a window in one of the houses I think I see a curtain move. My footsteps hasten as I remind myself what I am and what I cannot risk trying to become. To be part of a family is fantasy. To be part of a community is hallucination.

Why would I want to? I know nothing of the people here; nothing save that the citizens here don't like to be called Citizen. I begin to regret ever having come to West Ellen. Something here is pulling at my hidden self. Something dangerous. That insidious desire to be counted among the normal. To belong.

At times I lose reality and the present moment as my brain spins with things, issues, matters—eternal who am I, where am I, why am I? Where is it all going?

Again I reach for Helen's redbird road. Stay on the Now. Stay safe from the monsters of the past; stay safe from the monsters of the future. West Ellen is just a place to spend the winter, perhaps to earn a few credits, to study. Nothing more unless I make it something more. If I make it something more it will become a death trap.

I reach the fork in the road and pause to look back at Main Street, West Ellen. It is just a place to spend the winter. I turn and begin the climb up the Stark Mountain road.

Wardate: 17:18-9AUG2033
Downlimit: -77036:12:01

39

The sign, its large letters carved into weathered natural wood, says Crystal Pond Camps. From the sign it is a five minute walk along a twisting gravel road lined with tall evergreens to a large log house with a wood-shingled roof. There is a note and a key hanging from a nail hammered into the log wall of Avon Weeks's cabin. The note is written on an old brochure advertising Crystal Pond Camps. I pick the key off of the nail, remove the faded brochure, and read the note.

Tom,

Sorry I can't be there to greet you. I had to go into Bristol. The snow wasn't supposed to start until next week and the belts on my thrower are all shot. I put a few things in your cabin you might need. We'll talk about your chores when I get back.

Avon Weeks

There is a map printed at the bottom of the page. It shows a network of twisting paths that connect twenty-two cabins surrounding a small pond. One of the cabins is circled in red.

I walk around the house and let my gaze search the shallow draw and the rising mountainside beyond for the cabins. I can't see any of them. A thin column of white smoke comes from beyond some trees, but no house is visible.

I find the end of the path indicated on the brochure's map and begin walking. As I work my way along the narrow paths it takes me a while to realize that the terrain is carefully sculpted.

Every cabin has a clear view of the pond, but no cabin's view includes another cabin. The paths and rises are crowded with tall, lush hemlocks, the dark green contrasting with the white trunks of birch trees. I can smell the hemlocks, the wood smoke, the snow, the increasing cold.

It is quiet here.

The cabin marked on the map for me is almost invisible from the path. When I take the side path to my cabin, it is through a wall of hemlocks and down to a small log structure perched between two large rock formations above a forested ravine. The smoke is coming from there, issuing from a silver metal pipe on the roof.

I climb the three stairs until I am on the porch, standing in front of the heavy plank door. I lift the latch and the door swings inward. It hadn't been locked. I place the key in my pocket.

Inside the cabin it is small and warm, the heat provided by the dying coals in a tiny, round wood stove. Stacked against the log wall is split wood for the stove. Facing the stove are two easy chairs made from leather-strapped rough logs finished with cushions. Behind the chairs is the counter of a tiny kitchen. A box is on the counter and in the box are some foodstuffs. There is even a small refrigerator. Without looking I know that there will be more food in there.

I move from behind the counter, drop my bag on one of the chairs before the stove, and enter the open door to the bedroom. The double bed is unmade, but piled on the mattress are sheets, blankets, pillowcases, and towels. Also upon the bed is a puffy quilt.

A strange feeling comes over me. A fearful sadness. A desire to call this part of reality home? I turn and go outside, closing the front door behind me. On the porch are two collapsed folding chairs leaning against the wall. I set one of them up and sit in it facing the view. I can see the ravine, and beyond it, the snow-dusted peaks of two mountains. It is very quiet, the snow falling gently through a windless sky.

There is something about the place. I pull the brochure from my pocket and open it. Swimming, fishing, tennis, backpacking. There is a small history of the camp. The site had been purchased in 2003 by land developer Nathan Gove of Burlington. Using landscaping designs purchased from the Department of Lands, the camp opened for business in 2005. Weeks purchased the enterprise two years later. Every site secluded, has a "spectacular view," water—

The Department of Lands.

I fold the brochure and stuff it back into my pocket. MAC II did the site selection and orientation, and designed the landscaping. How does Crystal Pond Camps fit into the Big Plan? MAC's fingers are everywhere. I think on it, but I can't tell whether I have slipped through those fingers or am unknowingly sitting in the middle of a tightly closed fist.

I shake my head. Someone had to come up with a design for the camp. It might as well be the Department of Lands. They're the ones who are *supposed* to do that. As far as the MAC II system doing the actual work, all government agencies use MAC.

The sky is thick with clouds and snow, obscuring the view from whatever orbiters MAC might be tied into. I'm not important enough for this kind of preparation. MAC III isn't waiting for me. Even if for some unknown reason someone back at the service base camp at Bloodroot had run my number, no one there knows where I am.

Childish grandiosity.

Paranoia.

MAC did a good job of designing the camp.

The winter. The snow. The quiet.

I begin seeing faces in the swirls of descending diamond dust. Helen, Godfrey, Manuel, Francis.

I wish they were here with me in the center of all this peace. Have Manuel, Francis, and the others made it to Argentina? Are they even alive?

Is it snowing where Rhona lives?

What is she thinking?

Does she miss me?

Has the blackshit caught up with her?

Is she alive?

For an instant I see Louisa's face. I chase the image from my mind. I lean forward, my face in my hands. "I can't afford to think about these things. I can't."

My hands come down, and I feel the coolness of the tears streaked on my face. I wipe them away, lean back in the chair, and look again at the mountain peaks. What does the world look like from up there? Before the winter is over, I will climb up there and find out.

A sound.

Again.

A moment later I can see the dark figure of a tall man walking the path. The man walks with steady, certain footsteps. His hands are thrust into the pockets of his woodsman's jacket. I begin getting to my feet as the man approaches the steps. He waves a hand.

"Sit back down, son. I'm not the kind to disturb somebody when he's watching snow. You're Tom and I'm Avon. That's about all the conversation we need right now."

I stay seated as the man climbs the steps and sets up the other folding chair. His face is narrow, stern, a hard look in his eyes. He sits next to me, crosses his legs, replaces his hands into his pockets and looks toward the mountains. His face is deeply lined, his hair pale gray and cut short. He is an old man.

I settle back and look at the mountains, the peaks now almost obscured by the descending whiteness. After a moment an edge of peace creeps into my soul.

There is no meaning, no purpose in the falling snow. And that is its meaning and its purpose.

I hear the old man speak. "It takes special people to watch snow fall the right way."

Wardate: 17:18-9AUG2033
Downlimit: -76844:03:00

38

In a few days I have learned my duties, there is almost a meter of snow on the ground, and Avon Weeks is in Florida. I use the thrower to keep the road clear and use snowshoes to circuit the property checking for human tracks. Camps in the winter attract vandals.

I am alone, but am at peace. I have the woods, the winter, and my studies. Late every afternoon I am at the library.

When I choose to interrupt my aloneness, there are the inhabitants of West Ellen. Once each week I go in to Dyar's for groceries. Herbie Dyar is a large man, outgoing and about as friendly to a stranger as anyone from West Ellen can be.

"So you're the fella Avon took on to watch his place."

"Yes."

"Down to Florida by now, is he?"

"Yes."

"Avon Weeks don't like the cold much. His people have thin blood, coming from Ohio."

"Mr. Weeks said he was born here, Mr. Dyar."

"*He* was, which don't make him native. Call me Herbie, son. My father was Mister Dyar. And about Avon, it takes maybe five or six generations to work up the blood necessary for this climate. His grandfather came from Connecticut, which is a bit south. I believe his grandmother came from Florida or Texas. That's some pretty runny blood. Where'd you say you're from?"

"New Hampshire. Pittsfield. But my people came from Canada."

"Canada? Well, I bet this weather's just a little too tropical for you."

"It's just right."

"Well, this is awfully warm for a Green Mountain winter. I remember back in . . ."

It frightened me at first, but it's not a means of exchanging information, this talk. It's like cats touching noses: a way two individuals have of establishing that all is well between them.

Rhona told me that making friends would kill me. I hold myself in because of that, but it is hard.

In a room in the back of Dyar's is the terminal that integrates the West Ellen constabulary with the rest of the Compact Police. It hasn't been repaired since Herbie accidentally allowed a two-liter container of raspberry ice cream to melt into the works. Herbie's pride and joy is his brand-new aircar.

His wife, Dottie, spends her mornings helping at the store. She has undertaken the burden of suffering humanity for a role, and the bane of her existence is Herbie's new aircar.

"Can you believe that man goes around daring folks to race with him? You'd think he would've outgrown that stuff back when he was your age, Tom. He must've dried up half the dairy herd on the Sayward place making Ross race with him."

"Now, Dot, Ross wouldn't've raced with me if he didn't want. And it was only once—"

"A grown man. Town constable. We're going to have to take on another constable just so we have someone who can arrest this over-the-hill teenager—"

"Lookit that mouth run. Well, I suppose it keeps the flies from settling on her."

"What're you laughing at, you old—"

"Excuse me, folks, but I have to be going."

Herbie and Dottie are deep into their peculiar form of lovemaking. Without losing a beat, Dottie issues me two pair of her hand-knitted wool socks on my way out of the door.

It is hard to hold myself back. Hard.

Wardate: 17:18-9AUG2033
Downlimit: -75812:32:12

37

On Main Street the district school bus is dropping off some of its passengers. It's the same kind of bus that took me to Outcasters. Inside there are faces in the windows. One of the boys waves at me and I wave back. His name is David. It bothers me how many of those faces have names. Kenny, Tania, May, Ricky, Paul.

Too close, I hear Rhona say in my ear. Too close.

Billy, Kathy, Heather, Joey. The bus pulls out, and I climb the library steps.

Too close.

Meghan French is sitting at a table near the door. She sees who I am. "Good afternoon, Thomas."

"Good afternoon, Miss French."

She taps the corner of her desk. The books I ordered from the main library are there.

"Thank you."

She turns back to her work, updating her ancient card catalog. Opposite her place is an expensive index terminal that already has everything possible cataloged and available at the push of a button.

I once asked why. The answer was predictable. The folks in West Ellen prefer the card catalog to the terminal. No reflection on the government.

I pick up the books, seat myself at the terminal, and begin scanning the headlines. A truce of sorts has taken place in Turkey; the Consolidationist Party is demanding an investigation to assure that MAC III cannot initiate a war on its own;

Aubry Cummings has been appointed to a minor post within the Department of Projections; the Wardate stands at 17:18-9AUG2033.

I index to the Cummings story. President-General Diaz has appointed Aubry Cummings to assume the duties of the Director of Special Adjustments, Department of Projections. The exact functions of both his office and his branch of the department are unclear.

"Thomas?"

I look over the terminal to Meghan French's desk. "Yes?"

She doesn't look up from her cards. "Those books you ordered?"

"Yes?"

"Do you really understand that gibberish?"

"Yes."

"Is that what you plan to work in? Projections?"

I sit back in my chair and look at the books resting upon the edge of the terminal. How does one with no valid papers get a job in projections? He doesn't. "I guess I don't know. I haven't made up my mind yet."

"Then, that's an ambitious hobby you have there." She sorts three more cards and looks up at me. "There. All the way to 'M' all done. I swear my eyes feel like they're ready to fall clean out of my head. Will you be working here again tonight?"

"If it's all right."

"It's always all right. Just remember to turn down the heat and turn off the lights when you go."

"I will."

She stands and begins wrapping herself in winter insulation. "Good night, then. I'm going home for supper."

"Good night."

"Don't forget about Sunday dinner after church. One o'clock."

"I won't forget."

Too close, Thomas. Too close.

After she is gone I sit looking at the terminal screen for a long time. Why am I doing this? My curiosity regarding the role projections played in my existence was satisfied some time ago. Where can I use this knowledge I am acquiring? Doing what?

Those are the kinds of questions I could ask this terminal if I was a citizen. MAC III would take my personality profile, educational performance and direction, potential, and compare it with the totality of assimilated experience. It would then present me with my options. But the machine needs my number to produce the answers I want. The temptation to enter that number teases at my head.

Thoughts like that can kill me.

I cancel the information I have on the screen, pause for a moment, and hit the silver on/off button, deenergizing the terminal.

Yes, I want to work in projections. I'm going to have to figure out my own way through the maze of possibilities to see if any of them are possibilities for me.

I pick up the top book and look at the cover.

APTITUDE AND PERSONALITY:
Construction, Testing, Maintenance and Evaluation
of the
938 and 2062B Personality Profile Series

As good a place to start as any. Who am I? What am I? And who and what does MAC III think I am?

I look to my right. Across the street, in front of her house, Meghan French is talking to a young woman. The woman is blond and the hood of her cape is off, leaving the evening sun to wash her hair with gold.

I can see her laughing. Her name is Colleen Marshall. She is a high school senior. As certain as the coming war, Meghan French will have a surprise for me at Sunday dinner. The surprise will be her niece, Colleen.

Colleen is very pretty, and she has a nice laugh.

I turn back to my book. For the one named Thomas Windom, the one named Colleen Marshall might as well be from another dimension.

It's a nice thought on Miss French's part.

But, too close. Too close.

Wardate: 17:18-9AUG2033
Downlimit: -74900:44:20

36

I look and see that I am near the peak of the mountain.

The thin, icy air is raw in my lungs, my nostrils closing and sticking in the cold, my legs wobbling from exhaustion. The only sounds are of myself. My harsh breathing, the blood pounding in my ears, the whisper of the snowshoes. Inside the too-large insulated parka I feel as though I am burning up.

Again snow begins coming from the overcast sky. It is just beginning, the wind beginning to rise. I think I can make the peak before it gets too thick to see.

After finally making the decision I began the climb, feeling excited at the prospect of seeing the world from the peak of Stark Mountain. As the cold and pain crept through my body I laughed at myself.

Even I know that such a climb alone and in winter, without telling anyone, is foolish. Still I continued up. Now there is no excitement, no self-condemnation, nothing but cold fingers, sweat running down my back, and pain.

Pain.

Pain in my legs, my back, my chest, my eyes, my head.

It pleases me.

I can think of nothing except the pain, the climb, going up. I do not ask myself why. I just continue. Concentrating on the present moment. That is the secret of my pleasure. It is impossible for me to dwell on the past, fear the future, or worry about what I am not and what I can never be.

Now.

This moment.

It is a glorious time in which to live.

I hover over this edge that divides death from life, the human from the savage, the real from the fantastic. In this instant there are no wars save my war with cold and gravity. There is no dimension save this inclined plane of white death. There is no time but now.

I listen to my muscles cry to me. There is no fear here, no hiding, nothing false. That which might kill me is impersonal. I climb naked before myself. If I can reach but a handsbreadth higher perhaps I can touch immortality.

There is a different taste to the air.

I stop.

I weave in place, the barren trees below me black and shadowless against the snow. The clouds move slowly over me toward the southeast, the tiny flakes stinging my skin. Another few steps and I see a valley on the other side of the mountain. I made it. I climbed the mountain. It is a secret piece of victory. A thing I can tuck away in my memory next to my moments with Louisa, my moment with Rhona.

Dare I think it? My moment with the guard, Wing?

—No. The moments I want to save are clean. Revenge leaves a dirty feel.

Even through the snow, I can see all the way to the Northfield Mountains. On this side of Stark Mountain there are supposed to be the remains of a ski area. On Avon Weeks's map it's called Mad River Glen. I can't see it.

I turn around and look down at West Ellen. A rise in the mountain's slope obscures the view. Below me there are only trees and snow. Surrounding me are the vague outlines of mountains. The snow is getting heavier.

I can see no sign that the human race has ever existed. Even the shallow trail left by the snowshoes has been almost completely covered by the blowing snow. Mostly it is just endless sky. An infinite number of whites, blues, greens, and grays.

I squat down and rest my legs, looking down at the uninhabited planet below me. This is the place to build a tiny shelter. By myself, with nothing but the animals and the sky. This is the place to be. I ache for it.

My mind drifts into the details of building my burrow as my eyes seek out a site. Perhaps down by that grove of hemlocks. Over there among those huge rocks. What about water?

There must be springs on the mountain. I could hunt for food, or grow my own. Maybe I could just live off the land.

Wouldn't it be fun? If Louisa were only here to share it. If Louisa were here.

I slowly shake my head, thinking of the Sunday dinner last week with Miss French and her niece Colleen. Gently they both bullied me into taking Colleen to a movie in Bristol. Colleen had to drive her aunt's wheeled electric, both of them very amused that I did not drive.

In the dark of the theater her hand stole into mine. From that moment until we kissed goodnight, the anger that boiled in my soul fought to get through my exterior calm. To her I must have seemed stiff, cold, dead. Even with the kiss goodnight that was expected of me. It must have been like kissing a store dummy.

But this girl doesn't *know!* She cannot be a part of me! We cannot connect. I sleep with a ghost.

Colleen Marshall hasn't paid dues enough to replace that ghost.

I stand and look up at the sky. "Are you there? Watching me squirm? Are you?"

The words are out of my mouth before I even know their meaning. God? Is this Thomas Windom talking to God? Maybe I'm talking to one of MAC III's orbiting ears?

At Outcasters, Jeth used to say that he needed to believe in a god because it gave him someone to be angry at for everything. Someone he could blame. And Jeth blamed. He cursed his god with words that frightened me.

Jeth caught his reds in some farm machinery and was dragged in and mangled before the machinery could be stopped. He died three days later at a hospital in town. "When I die," Jeth used to say, "I'm ready to go. Death is the price of my ticket to face the Great Scrud and begin collecting some of the things He owes me."

Could there be some kind of creature out there that is really responsible for it all?

I think of myself removing all of my clothing and lying down in the snow. I have survived so many things. Perhaps that would drive the god out of hiding.

They say freezing to death is just like falling asleep. Herbie did point out that no one who is in a position to know for certain is also in any kind of condition to tell us what freezing to death is like.

At times Herbie Dyar seems very wise. Once when I was waiting for him I looked at the police terminal in the back of his store. I could see no evidence of the Great Raspberry Ice Cream Disaster. The terminal looked new and was operating. It's not hard to understand. It just makes everyone in West Ellen more comfortable to believe that the terminal is down. No reflection on the government, of course.

When they discover my thawing body next spring, Herbie, Meghan, Colleen, and the others—

I begin shaking with chills.

Resting is no good. My mind wanders into dangerous places when it's free to roam on its own. I turn toward West Ellen and sigh. It's time to head back down.

Far below me the churchbell begins ringing. It is a danger signal. A fire, a call for assembly. A sudden rush of guilt sweeps over me. Are they starting a search for me because I refused to tell anyone where I was going or that I was going?

I begin working my way down the mountain, the falling snow growing thicker. In the west the light is beginning to fade.

Climbing the mountain was a real dumb idea.

Wardate: 17:18-9AUG2033
Downlimit: -75894:43:02

35

Dumb, dumb, dumb.

I repeat the word, the steam from my breath racing into the distance ahead of me, disappearing into the darkness. The ground is level, and I've lost my direction.

Before I could always head down. Down would be in the right direction from a mountain. But now I can't even see my own tracks. The pain from the cold in my fingers is unbearable.

Ross Sayward told me that when the pain stops, that's the time to worry. I try to remember every scrap that I can about keeping warm. Get out of the wind. Some trees are good, thick growing evergreens. Dig in. I can sense the trees easier than I can see them. After digging out a shallow depression in the snow with one of my snowshoes, I climb into it out of the wind.

I take off my gloves and pull my arms out of the sleeves of my parka, wrapping them around my chest, my hands in my armpits. The pain in my hands grows more intense for a moment, then eases. In a moment more I am rested, only chilly, and very hungry. Moving my arms, I stick my hands into the inside entrances to my parka pockets, looking for the things I absentmindedly picked up in my cabin before beginning my climb.

I feel a piece of sausage. Moving it in front of my face, I rip off a piece with my teeth and chew the spicy dry fibers in an ecstasy of taste and smell. As it warms I can feel the smoked goodness of the grease squishing between my teeth.

Back into the pocket goes the piece of sausage. My fingers find the bag of dried apricots. As I gnaw on one of the leathery fruits, I try to remember the things Herbie and his friends would talk about when they were calling up their hunting experiences.

Water.

The cold, said Ozzie Hildreth, dries you out like nothing else. You need the water to keep going. But you can die trying to eat the snow if you're cold. Shock to the system, or something.

The dried fruit is in a plastic bag. I empty the fruit into the pocket and take the empty bag. Moving it out below the string tie at the bottom of my parka, I fill the bag with snow. I pull the bag inside my coat and hold it with my other hand as I shake the snow off the hand that had been outside.

I discover that the coat is large enough to pull over my knees, almost down to my ankles. I pull the drawstring and am getting warmer and warmer, the bag of melting snow on my lap.

My head clears. Exhaustion, cold, and panic have run their courses. As I wait for the bagged snow to melt I listen and look. The wind has died down. The silence is complete, but the night is not totally black. I can make out the whiteness of the snow on the ground, the blackness of close trees against it.

I hear a rifle shot. Another.

"Hey! Hey! I'm here!"

The snow is good insulation. My words seem swallowed almost before they leave my mouth.

"Hey!"

I cannot even guess from which direction the shots came.

My legs are beginning to cramp. Half of the bag has melted and I move it up through the neck opening and take a sip. I seal the bag and put it in my pocket on top of the dried fruit.

I stand and shout again, "Fire once more if you hear me!" I wait, straining my ears. I think that if they are firing guns, they must be shouting, too. I cannot hear their voices. There is no reason to think that they can hear mine.

I shiver. That will help me keep warm.

It's frightening to think just how close primitive reality is.

But a few minutes' walk from where I am freezing to death, the tropical flowers on Dotty Dyar's windowsill are being monitored and controlled by tiny, inexpensive computers that come built into the flowerpots. Temperature, moisture, light, nutrition.

In Herbie's store he sells meats that are absolutely perfect: taste, texture, nutritional content, and very inexpensive. Still, the man would be thrilled to distraction to grab a gun and work all day to track down and kill some gamey wild animal, then gut and clean it, cook it and eat it in a state of rapture, each stringy mouthful having cost him four times as much as the product in his display case.

There was the motion picture classic Colleen and I saw. All of that wealth, art, and science spent to tell the story of prehumans in caves fighting the creatures of the day and night, fighting the weather, fighting each other for survival.

I smile as I wonder if MAC III had anything to do with writing the script for that motion picture. The story there is the same one that the Big Computer has been trying to teach all my life.

Survival.

Quest for Fire was the name of the movie. Funny.

Being still has stiffened me and cooled me to such a degree that I am alarmed. I must move. But where? Still there is no direction to follow. But, if I start moving, eventually I will either be going up or down. If down, I am heading in the right direction. If up, then I can turn around and be heading in the right direction. In any event, I have to move. I have to move if I want to live.

My legs move with difficulty at first. I try to be very careful. With my arms inside my parka and wrapped around me, I have no way of breaking a fall.

Lean to the right, pull the left foot forward, lean to the left, pull the right foot forward. Right, left, forever and ever.

I pause, thinking that there was something that I should remember. I hate that: going someplace to do something, then, halfway there, forgetting what it was that I wanted to do. Standing there feeling like a fool.

I take another step. It is very hard. Up. It is an up step. I am climbing. I remember. I should turn around and go the other way.

But what if this is only a little rise within a descending path? I look and see only the dim whiteness against the night. I should check it out just to make certain. It could just be a bump in the terrain. I should investigate. But I arn so tired. I don't think I have the energy to spare if this is indeed a path going up.

But, what if? What if?

I try to take a step forward. My right snowshoe catches on something and I pitch face first into the snow.

Dark.

Cold.

Warm.

Helen would take me naked into her bed to keep warm when I was seven and convinced I was freezing to death. She would be naked too, her skin warm, her hands warm, the calves of her legs over my icy feet, warming them. We cried and complained at how cold the blackshit kept the dorms at night, but they were good times. Close times.

I was warm, but not yet sleepy. My blanket and sheets were spread on top of Helen's. I pressed my cheek against Helen's breast and inhaled her smell. I loved her smell. Earthy. Almost a spice. My left arm was around her waist, as her right arm was around my shoulders, her hand stroking my back.

I began stroking her. She nuzzled my head deeper into her breasts and began making longer strokes on my back. I brought my hand around to cuddle up and go to sleep, but I touched something. Where her legs joined, below her naval, was a thatch of thick, soft hair.

So smooth.

I petted it, moved my fingers through it. Helen made a quiet moan and kissed my hair. Instead of stroking me, her hand held me close. Her hips moved.

"Do you like this, Helen?"

"Yes." She giggled. "Oh, yes."

I wanted to please her. And it felt so good. Good enough to be forbidden. I rubbed harder, my fingers kneading the moistening mound of flesh between her legs.

Accidentally a finger slipped into a hot wet place. I jerked back, but Helen whispered in my ear. "It's okay."

I put my hand back on that mound and probed it with my finger. I found the opening and my finger glided in. "Gently," Helen whispered. Her hips moved until my finger felt a button of flesh moving beneath it. I rubbed it harder and Helen moaned again. I used two fingers.

Helen stroked my back again with her right hand. Her left hand moved down, touched my leg, moved up and caressed my penis. It was hard. Her hand moved against me, rubbing, her hips moving in a steady, powerful rhythm, her breath hot in my ear.

I slid my fingers deeper into the channel, her legs opened, and I found a silken-lined opening. I put my two fingers into it as far as they could go, pulled them back and rubbed the little button, slid back to the opening, back to the button—

Helen's right hand took my elbow and moved my arm against the rhythm of her hips. Faster and faster, her strength surprising me, the feelings produced by her hand on my penis amazing me.

She went rigid, her legs closing tightly upon my hand, her hand on my elbow forcing my hand almost painfully into her. I gushed something into her hand. It felt as though I had been emptied. Wonderful.

"Helen, did you like that?"

"Yes." Her voice sounded strange.

"I liked that. Can we do it again?"

She was quiet for a long, long time. "Go to sleep, Tommy."

"Can we, Helen? Can we do it again?"

"No," She released my penis and turned her back to me. "It's not good. We shouldn't. You're so young. I don't know what I was thinking of." Again she was quiet until I heard her crying. "I'm so sorry."

I'm so confused. Why is Helen so unhappy? I hug her close and stroke the cheek of her buttocks. She turns over on her back. "Tommy, I don't want—"

Again I place my hand upon that mound of flesh between her legs and rub. It seems to make her happy, and she is so sad.

Wardate: 17:18-9AUG2033
Downlimit: -75892:51:14

34

Cold.

It has a taste to it. My face is in the snow.

My face is in the snow, I'm freezing and suffocating, and I have an erection.

I move my hands around until they find my sleeves. Once inside of them, I push out my arms and lift my face from the snow. The coldness burns on my skin and I wipe it off. My hands are wet. Pulling my arms back inside my coat, I sit back on my ankles and look behind me. There is something in the snow.

With difficulty I lift my feet and pivot until I face the object. I bend over, trying to see, but I can't see anything. I can hear a whimper though.

"Hello?" I am reluctant to put my hands out again, but I do. Once they are out I put my gloves on and begin clearing the snow from the object. From the feel of it, it is a person. A child of maybe ten or twelve. "Can you hear me?"

That sound. That sound of a kitten in pain.

In an instant I am back in Outcasters, Manuel and Godfrey bringing Ann to her rack all beaten and bloody, that sound of a tortured kitten coming from her—

At times today is a difficult time to find.

I pull off my right glove with my teeth and try to find the child's face with my hand. I find it, but it is dry and so very cold. Moving closer I try to lift the child and shake it awake. The child screams, then is silent.

It finally dawns on me that this is the one that caused the churchbell to ring. She is why they are searching.

"Can you hear me? Can you hear me? You have to answer!"

I get to my feet and squat next to the child, trying to sit it up. The child's snowsuit is bulky, the fabric stiff with ice. If I can't get the kid warmed up soon, it will be dead.

I pull off the glove on my left hand and begin opening the snowsuit and removing the child's gloves and boots. The clothing inside the suit is wet. I open and remove that as well. The child is female. As soon as I have her clothing off, I brace myself and open my parka. The cold immediately robs me of my warmth. I open my shirt, pull the tail out of my trousers, and grab the girls ankles. I open her legs, put them around my waist, and lie down on top of her, the iciness of her skin making me cry out. I lift her, and sitting back on my ankles I seal the parka around her. Her hair is wet and frozen at the tips.

It seems to take forever, her feet keep slipping out of the bottom of my parka, but I manage to tie the drawstring with her feet inside. Her head is against my chest and she is still whimpering.

The cold.

She is sucking every particle of warmth from my body.

"God," I cry, "I can't stand it!"

I pull my arms into my parka and begin rubbing her back, her arms, her hands, her thighs. Soon the effort warms me, thereby warming us both. I swing her to one side and begin rubbing her feet. After an eternity, they begin to feel warm.

I pause, exhausted, my legs cramping.

And what now? She must weight fifty kilograms. Can I carry her, or should I wait for the search party? I place my hands beneath her buttocks to try and hold her. She still has her underpants on, and they are soaking wet. When I was taking off her clothes I meant to get them, but the legs of her trousers were caught on her foot, and by the time I had those off, I had forgotten.

Stupid, stupid.

I cry. The tears warming my face.

After a moment I hear her breathing, feel her breath on my

chest. She is sleeping. I pull at her underpants, find where the band has been sewn together, and tear them down the side to the leg opening. I pull the remainder of the torn garment down and off her leg. "What did you do? Go swimming?" I reach down and push the soaked underpants past the parka's drawstring.

Her hands move and she shivers, jerking violently.

"Are you awake? Can you hear me?"

Again I place my hands beneath her buttocks and lift, lurching and stumbling to my feet. I try to tie my shirttails beneath her to help hold her in place, but they aren't long enough.

Her snowsuit wrapped around my shoulders might give us a little more warmth, but if I go down there to retrieve it, I might never get up again.

The suit is wet, frozen. Won't do us any good. That's why I took it off of her.

Stupid. Stupid.

I look again to what is up, what is down, and turn toward the down. One of her icy hands steals into my left armpit and I scream with the shock.

Move. That is our only hope. Move.

My legs are weighted with iron bars, my feet numb. They don't hurt, which means I should worry about that. But I don't worry about that. I am so grateful. Even if they should have to take both my feet, it is good to have something that doesn't hurt. If I can only find someone.

She shivers again and begins sobbing. Holding her with my left hand I try rubbing her with my right. Then holding her with my right, I rub her with my left. It is warm inside my parka. If I can just keep moving, we will be warm. We will have a chance.

—that night I sat shivering after putting the ointment on Ann's cuts. I remember it so clearly. I was so cold, so sore. Her face was so beautiful as she slept. When she died something black and cold crawled into my heart. Feeding Lathrup to the Green Machine didn't make up for it. Couldn't—

"No. *No!*"

—can't think of that now. I can't afford it. *We* can't afford it.

Think, instead, of them finding us. The girl will be *alive*. Not dead. Dead like Ann. Dead like Elana. Dead like Louisa.

I can feel the girl's skin, moist, against mine. She is warm. Alive.

"Alive," I whisper. Alive.

Merle Sawyer is dead. What of the others? Did they ever make it to Argentina? Is it warm in Argentina?

I sing, "Is it warm in Argentina?" I giggle. Warm. Yes, if it isn't warm now, it will get warm. The war is coming. Funny, profound; the first three letters of warm is war.

—seemed profound for a second there—

Rhona told me that life is victory.

Look at you, Thomas, she would say.

Alive. You have already won. Keep on winning.

"Keep on winning, girl. Alive now. Keep on winning."

Alive—

—I drift, my mind detaching from my body. See, I am up in the falling snow counting the snowflakes.

I find two snowflakes that are exactly alike in all respects, but one of them melts before I can show anyone. This great law of reality that no two snowflakes are identical is bullshit. I had the proof right there, but now it's gone.

"It isn't fair."

And yes, world, here is Thomas Windom: Seeker of Justice. It isn't fair.

Sucker.

I look to see Thomas Windom pull those enormous snowshoes through the snow.

"Don't drag them! *Lift* them!"

That's what Herbie says. It makes sense.

I call to the boy in the snow, but he doesn't listen. His mouth is moving, talking to the great lump inside his parka. It would take much less effort if he would lift the snowshoes.

Lift them?

I begin laughing; me and the guy walking next to me. Lift them! What a joke! It is the funniest joke. Lift them!

I stop.

Silence. All is quiet.

I stopped for a reason. What was it? I remember.

I have to urinate. It is a problem that seems to be far beyond the capabilities of disciplinary projections.

I can't put down the girl. I'll never get her up again. They will find our skeletons next spring locked in this embrace.

What will they ever think of me? With her bones wrapped around mine, they might think we died making love.

The poor little girl. Raped to death in a blizzard by Thomas No-name, the Ice Lover.

That one winter.

What was it that we used to call Citizen Kennedy?

The redbird was only seven or eight; frozen to death outside. After detail he couldn't be found, and the guard brought the detail in without him. They found him the next day in the snow at the bottom of the west drainage cut.

He was naked, his reds wrapped around his ankles.

The blackshit said Billy must have slipped trying to take a crap when he was on detail.

But the redbirds know that the detail guard, Citizen Kennedy, likes to fuck little boys.

We never fed Citizen Kennedy to the Green Machine. He was just found naked and frozen to death in a field, fucking a snowman in the ass. Citizen Kennedy's first name was Fred, and that's what we used to call his memory: Freddy the Frozen Frost Fucker.

I laugh.

I was the one who put the grin on the snowman's face.

"Oh, my god!" Laughing. "Freddie the Frozen Frost Fucker!" God, those were good times. That was just before the Christmas riot.

Good times?

My brain is really bending. Good times. Almost as much fun as pulling the arms off of live babies.

Hey, let's tickle up a great time and drown a couple of puppies.

Decision.

The pressure on my bladder is severe. Painful.

What if I just did it in my trousers? It would be warm. Lush warmness coursing down my leg. Warm.

But the wetness. It would soon become cold. Robbing me of my heat, my life.

It seems almost too much to make any kind of decision.

I switch her buttocks to my left hand and reach down past the drawstring with my right. I fumble for what seems to be hours trying to unseal my trousers. Beneath them are the thermals. Then my own underpants. I damn near rip off my penis yanking it through the layers.

Finally I release the flood, the steam rising, the sharp odor awakening me. A black hole appears in the snow, more steam rising from it.

Black hole.

It is funny again. Peeing holes in the snow.

Citizen Wing pees no holes in the snow. Not anymore. Freddy the Frozen Frost Fucker and No Pee Wing.

That's No Pee-Pee Wing!

God, these jokes—and pissing on my boots. Laughing. Laughing is so much like crying.

So tired.

When I am finished it is all I can do to pull my appendage in out of the weather. Even though my precious warmth escapes from the opening, the seal on my trousers is much too complicated to understand.

What now?

The legs move again. Down, down, forever down the mountain.

She cries, she whimpers, she screams, she shivers, and screams again.

"Shut up, kid. Shut up. I can't think."

Louisa would say, if she was cold, she would put her mind in a warm place. If it was loud, she would put her mind in a quiet place.

Where should I put my mind?

Think of something. Anything.

I talk through the little girl's cries and screams. "We will be all right. Both of us. I'll come skipping into West Ellen with my bundle, someone's precious child; that's you. You're the precious child. Your father and mother will slobber all over us. So happy. I'll earn the gratitude of the entire town. A hero—"

Hero.

I stop as my head clears and my eyes open. The tender weight in my arms has become a monster. If I bring her back, that's exactly what will happen. I'll be a hero. Then some well-meaning fool will celebrate my deed to the point where my number gets run.

Run my number. Back in 128. I wonder if No-Pee Wing is still on the payroll at 128.

I feel the girl in my arms. Flesh. Human flesh. Her breath is on my chest, relaxed and regular. I don't even know what she looks like or whose child she is.

I encircle her with my arms and hug her close to me. She has no breasts. Who would blame me if I just let her die in the snow? What would she think?

Well, what she would think is that illegal children have brought the planet to the brink of destruction, and that Thomas Windom should go off and do the decent thing and evaporate himself, returning his valuable minerals and organic compounds to the soil.

Project Two Thousand. That's what they called the worldwide brainwash designed to implant worldwide values. This little girl would kill me if she had the chance. If—

—I feel a new warmth on me as a smell comes from the neck of my parka.

She is pissing on me.

She *is* pissing on me!

"Little girl? Oh, little girl? You are not helping your case at all. It's not nice to piss on Thomas—"

Light!

In the distance is a light! It is bobbing, turning this way and that. A search party.

They could have waited long enough for me to make up my mind. Now that I have no choice, I want to know if I would have killed her or saved her.

"Hey! Hey!" I notice that it is my voice calling.

"Hallo!" comes the reply. There's another light joining the first.

"Up here!"

They gather down there, a dozen fireflies, lazily moving up toward me. They smear and fade in my vision, then disappear below me.

I am lying on my back in the snow. The girl, on top of me, her mouth shoved next to my ear, is crying.

I cannot breathe I am laughing so hard. "Darling," I say. "We must stop meeting like this!"

I hope I can remember all of these terrific jokes. They tell a lot of jokes in West Ellen. I usually just sit and listen. But now I have some great material.

Terrific jokes.

You ever hear the one about Freddy the Frozen Frost Fucker? Stop me if you've heard this one—

—How about the one called the Now Road? Stay out of yesterday; stay out of tomorrow; walk the Now Road.

Tell it to No Pee-Pee Wing.

Just you *try* and stay out of yesterday.

What a joke.

One of the fireflies is now a sun, burning into my eyes. "Tom?"

It's Herbie. The town constable. Up there somewhere the Big Machine is laughing. I believe computers have a sense of humor. God does. He invented it. Humor, not computers.

The Cosmic Comedian. Take my sins, please.

Wardate: 17:18-9AUG2033
Downlimit: -75896:44:41

33

Tap, tap, tap, tap.

Tap, tap, tap, tap.

I smell sheets, feel a bed.

Before I open my eyes I feel my hands and feet; count my fingers and toes.

Everything is still there. All of them have feeling in them. The bed is warm and hard; my mouth very dry.

Tap, tap, tap, tap.

I open my eyes.

The room is dark.

Near the door there is a dim light. I can only see the folded arms and crossed legs of a man sitting in a chair. His foot is twitching nervously. In time with the twitching, the back of the chair taps against the wall. A band of fear encircles my chest.

Tap, tap, tap, tap.

His clothes are rough civilian. "Who is that?" I whisper.

The twitching foot freezes. "Tom?"

Herbie. It's Herbie Dyar. The fear drains from me. "Can I have some water?"

He pushes himself to his feet and walks to the side of my bed. In a moment a flexible tube is inserted between my lips. Tepid liquid flows into my mouth. It is water, but strangely unsatisfying. I move my face away and the tube is withdrawn.

"Thank you."

Herbie's shadow stands between me and the light. I sense he

wants to say something, but I speak first. "What about the girl?"

"She's okay. Just exhaustion, same as you. Both of you are luckier than hell."

"Lucky."

That's me, Herbie: luckier than hell. I nod. "That's good. Who is she?"

"The girl? You don't know?"

"It was too dark to see."

The shadow reaches back into the light and grabs the back of the chair, moving it next to my bed. Herbie sits down and from the light reflected from the floor I can just make out his face. "John Pittman's little girl, May. You know, he has the sugarbush east of Week's camps. You remember May."

"I remember."

Black hair, brown eyes, a happy laugh. I'd see her on the Stark Mountain Road sometimes when the school bus picked her up or dropped her off. May is Susan's best friend, the pair of them always together.

"Is anyone else missing? Susan—"

"Everybody's accounted for. The pair of them had a spat and May got lost in the storm coming home. John Pittman's outside right now waiting to thank you."

I focus more clearly. The walls are light colored, the mattress beneath my knees raised. Above me on the ceiling are silver-colored fixtures.

I lift my head a bit. I have a nightstand. Behind it, built into the wall, is a panel with lights, valves, buttons, and plugs. "I'm in a hospital?"

"That's right. In Bristol."

He waits like he expects me to say something else. "May."

"What about her?"

"Why was she wet?"

"She fell through the ice crossing the mill stream below the dam. You saved her life, boy." I say nothing, and Herbie leans back in the chair.

"Tom, when we got to the two of you, you were talking some very weird stuff. Is there something I should know? Something you want to tell me?"

"Tell you?" A million things leap to my throat, but I hold them back. "What did I say? What weird stuff?"

"You were saying things about blackshit, redbirds, someone called Helen, somebody else called Freddy. About the only thing that made any sense was that you didn't want your number run. You kept repeating it." He sits silently for a moment.

"Tom, is there something I should know? Are you in any trouble?"

I am simply numb. Defeated. Empty. No matter how you want to look at it, Herbie Dyar is blackshit. Blackshit in civvies; but blackshit all the same.

"They ran my number when I was admitted, didn't they?"

"Nope. Doc Cordwell took care of that. They used to run a number on everyone to get the medical records and stuff like that, but they only need to run your number now for the government insurance. The doc told them that you aren't covered."

The Cosmic Comedian works His magic. "I'm not."

"Then nobody's telling any lies." He pauses and leans forward. "Are they?"

I close my eyes, my face warm with embarrassment. "What do you want me to say?"

"I don't want you to say anything more'n you want to. It's just that me and six other men have our necks stuck out right now keeping what you did quiet. I should have reported all this the minute we came in off the mountain. Is it worth it? That's what I want to know, son. If the whistle blows and it all comes out, will it have been worth it?"

"I don't know— Look, Herbie, as soon as I can get up I swear I'll be gone and out of your lives forever. You'll never see me ag—"

"If we wanted to get rid of you, Tom, we would've let them run your number. We certainly wouldn't be paying for your stay here at the hospital."

"The seven of you?"

"That's right. Me, John, Doc Cordwell, Ross Sayward, Don McCafferty, Darrell Nason, and Woody Rollins."

"Why?"

"*Why?* Now, that's about the dumbest question I ever heard in my life. Boy, you just saved May Pittman's life. We're grateful. Understand?"

Understand? Grateful? Do I understand? No, I don't understand anything. Not anything at all. "I shouldn't stay, Herbie. It's dangerous for all of us."

Herbie laughs and places his hand on my shoulder. "You are going no place for quite awhile. Doc says that once you get out of here, you should take it easy for a couple of weeks, anyway. Now, nobody knows what you did except for the seven of us, and we aren't talking. As far as anyone knows, our search team found the Pittman girl."

He squeezes my shoulder. "Now, remember that. And remember that you were on that search team with us and collapsed. Can you remember that?"

I shake my head, still unable to accept this help. Herbie pats my shoulder and removes his hand. "Son, West Ellen takes care of her own."

"No reflection on the government, huh?"

"Maybe you're catching on, Tom." Herbie gets up to leave. "I'll check in with you tomorrow afternoon."

"Herbie?"

He stops and faces me. "Yes?"

"When I can, I'll tell you about me. I can't right now."

A single nod of his head. "Get some sleep. I'll chase the rest of these guys home. You should see John, though. Just for a minute."

He leaves the room, and I feel the tears burning my eyes. I'm glad it's dark. I can't even sort out the way I feel. I can't analyze this. It's too real; too close; too now.

Maybe this is the Now Road.

John Pittman's face appears around the edge of the door. He looks very tired. His gaunt face has a white stubble on it. I didn't think he was that old. White hair in his beard. I didn't think he was that old.

He carries a large white and gold plastic bag by one hand. "Tom?"

"Hi, Mr. Pittman."

He comes all the way into the room and stops next to my

bed. "I just wanted to thank you." He is looking down, his head bowed before his feelings. I can see the tears coming down his left cheek. He drops the bag on my bed, takes my right hand in both of his, and holds it for a moment.

"I don't know what to say." The frown on his face deepens. "I got you something." Replacing my hand on the bed, he opens the bag and pulls out something bulky. He unfolds it and holds it in the light for me to see. It is a new coat, a parka. Bright red.

"This'll fit better'n that raggedy blue thing Herbie gave you. Besides, that one is just a little ripe, if you know what I mean. Never get the smell out—is red okay? Seems a little loud, maybe, but it looks real good. They have lots of other colors, though."

"Red is fine, Mr. Pittman. Thank you."

Damn the world. I am crying.

He hangs the new parka on the back of the chair. He stands for a moment, looking at it, rubbing at his eyes with his big-knuckled hands. Without looking at me, he speaks very quietly. "I can't ever pay you back for what you did, son." His voice becomes a whisper. "I don't care what you done. Count on me."

He turns, opens the door, and leaves the room. It closes silently behind him.

West Ellen.

I belong to West Ellen.

I belong to West Ellen and I must run. Somehow, to somewhere, I must run. I am valuable to too many who are valuable to me. There are these chains on me. I have to break them, get away—

But tomorrow. I'll think about escaping tomorrow. I'm too tired right now. And there are still these tears.

I look at my new red coat. I stare at it until a nurse comes in to monitor the medication and nutrition patches. When she is finished she begins picking up the coat from the chair to hang it in the closet.

"Please."

"Yes?"

"Could you leave the coat—my new coat—on the chair?

Please?" The nurse shrugs and hangs the coat back on the chair.

"Is that better?"

"Yes, thank you."

She turns out the light and leaves the room. After a few moments my eyes adjust and I can make out the red of my coat from the light coming through the window.

I don't understand feeling so good that it hurts; that it makes me cry. And it hurts so.

I close my eyes. There is something in my head that refuses to go to sleep; a thought; an unresolved problem.

With all of the medical facilities in the Compact tied into MAC III, a physician can call up a patient's entire medical history with the push of a few buttons. Everything would be at the doctor's fingertips: personality profile, physical development, a record of illnesses needing treatment, allergies, the use and the results of every medication the patient was on and had ever been on.

I am very thankful that my number wasn't run. But still it would have made sense for the hospital to have run my number. I can't think of any reason why they no longer routinely run patient numbers. A change like that could only have come from the computer itself.

There is the edge of an answer, but before it presents itself, I am asleep.

Wardate: 17:18-9AUG2033
Downlimit: -75844:32:00

32

Within two days I recover enough to move to a room with seven other patient beds. There are only three other patients in the room. An old man, Arthur Phinney, is here recovering from a hernia operation. Another old man, Claud Belisle, is here having some tests done. His doctor suspects cancer.

In the bed next to mine is the third patient, Mark Rowe. He is nineteen and keeps to himself. His left leg is in traction, bottles feed into his arm, and a tube drains from under the covers into a clear bag that hangs from his bed. The contents of the bag are dark yellow laced with red. He was in an aircar accident where two others were injured and a third killed. Mark Rowe does little except stare angrily at the ceiling. When he sleeps he has nightmares.

Miss French and Colleen Marshall visit me often. John Pittman comes one more time. He doesn't like others to be able to see his feelings. Herbie comes twice more, both times with others: Ross Sayward, Jim Bennings, Margaret Tinings, and Woody Rollins. The question is still in Herbie's eyes, but he never asks. That's good because I am all out of believable answers.

Late at night I wake up. Claud is bending over me, his face hidden by the dark.

"What?"

"Get up, boy. Come over to my bed. Hurry."

"What is it?"

Claud scurries to his own bed without answering. The

screen is up around his bed, and I can see light from his television reflecting off of the ceiling.

I push off my covers and gingerly climb into the slippers Colleen brought me. What could the old man want? I look but Mark and Arthur are still asleep.

I walk over to Claud's cubicle and enter. He sits at the head of his bed, his legs crossed beneath him, his gaze nailed to the television screen at the foot of his bed. The MGM lion growls, spooky music starts as a flying saucer races down the screen. The title, *Forbidden Planet*, appears.

"What is it, Claud?"

"*Shhh!* Watch." He shakes his head in wonder. "My god, I was ten years old when I saw this film the first time." He counts on his fingers and nods. "That's right, ten years old." He looks at me. "Sixty-nine years ago. You ever see *Forbidden Planet* before?"

"No."

He points at the chair next to his bed. "Sit down. You're in for a treat."

I look at the listing. The movie comes from 1956.

A good story. And the horror element is something that will tease my nightmares for the rest of my life. There is a huge machine designed by an alien race that allowed them complete release from instrumentality. Everything done by thought. This race, however, annihilated itself moments after its wonderful machine became operational. The machine tapped into the subconscious as well as the conscious minds and unleashed every individual's subconscious monsters upon the planet all at the same time.

What would happen if my monsters were set loose upon Earth? The hate, the revenge, the desperate needs—

When the movie is over, Claud and I talk. He comes from a strange time. When he first saw *Forbidden Planet* there was still a United States of America, a United Nations, immigration and trade with many of the nations now part of Otherworld.

In the narration that opens the movie, it says that it was not until the final decade of the twenty-first century that man landed on the moon. A year after the movie was released, the

Soviets put the first satellite into Earth orbit. Only thirteen years after the movie was released, and approximately one hundred and twenty years ahead of the movie's prediction, man walked on the moon.

I think of the incredibly huge machine the fictitious aliens—the Krell—constructed in the movie. The same day it was made operational it wiped out the aliens and every above ground sign of their civilization. Then it sat and maintained itself for two million years, waiting for the next race with subconscious monsters to release.

The images of the vast machine, the many mile-wide ventilation shafts with giant illuminated trolleys and spark gaps, weird lights and sounds, that go to the core of the planet, 7800 levels, and this shaft just one of 400 similar shafts. This is the image I have of MAC III. This is the image I have of Aubry Cummings's child.

Claud gets the news the next morning. It is cancer, indeed. Malignant. Inoperable. Terminal. Three months; maybe six. I wonder if MAC has been keeping a cancer cure from humanity. It makes sense if keeping the numbers down is your first priority.

After having the stretching-it-out-to-the-last-possible-moment option described to him, Claud packs up, says good-bye, and goes home. I ask him "Don't you want to live for as long as possible?"

"Twitching isn't living, Tom. Back in my high school biology we took frog legs and zapped 'em with electricity. They twitched. They were dead. That's not for me, Tom. When I'm dead, I want to stop twitching."

When he leaves he still has three weeks paid up on the use of his television, and he lets me have it.

I spend a lot of time thinking; trying to separate incidents of chance from incidents of planned manipulation by Cummings's big machine.

Back in Bloodroot, after his resignation, I saw a TV retrospective on Aubry Cummings, presented almost as though the old man had died rather than resigned. A brief portion of the program showed a TV debate from near the turn of the century.

A repeat of the interview is shown as a part of the *Turning Points* historical documentary series.

Aubry Cummings, his hair mostly dark brown, graying at the sides of his head, is arguing with a beautiful woman, Marta Escondella, chairperson of the Greenworld Committee.

At one point Marta Escondella drags out the Big Chill—the old nuclear winter argument against the eventual war with the Otherworld nations. With passion and conviction she rolls off the facts and figures that prove that any kind of nuclear war will be suicide for the entire human race. Very little nuclear weaponry needs to be employed to throw enough dust and smoke into the stratosphere to cut off the sunlight for months, ending the world as we know it.

Throughout the statement Cummings sits patiently, waiting for her to finish. When she finishes it is with a question:

"Knowing this, how can you possibly be in favor of a world nuclear holocaust?"

That enigmatic calm on the old man's face. Even then. "Are you addressing me?"

"Why, of course."

"I asked because I am not in favor of nuclear war, and I never have advocated the use of nuclear weapons."

"To the contrar—"

"My turn." His hand is up. He lowers it slowly. "Let me go on and see if I have a hope of clearing up any of these issues."

He inhales, then exhales. "My desires have nothing whatever to do with events. What I want, what I prefer, has absolutely nothing to do with what will be. It doesn't take much to figure out that the nations outside the Compact will attempt to gain by force our resources once their own are exhausted. The purpose of the Department of Projections is to arrange things such that the goals of the Compact will prevail, and in the most efficient manner. I can assure you that a nuclear winter is very inefficient and quite contrary to our goals."

"But, Dr. Cummings, the kind of war you are talking about

will kill off billions of men, women, and children and leave the Otherworld nations completely at the mercy of the Compact. Nuclear war is the only way—"

"Please, Mrs. Escondella, I wasn't finished. As far as we know, that kind of war serves no purpose. Other ways have to be found. For example, a nuclear weapon could wipe out a Soviet brigade, but it would also have devastating environmental consequences. MAC's purpose is the preservation of humanity's future. Killing off humanity, therefore, violates the program."

The woman's eyes say she hates Aubry Cummings. "Tell us your alternative."

"Again, it's not *my* program. However, there are alternatives." Cummings pauses and leans forward, his elbows resting upon his knees. "What if one of the soldiers in that Soviet brigade, Ivan, shoots another soldier, Vladimir? Igor, in turn, shoots Ivan, and Nikita shoots Igor, one-by-one through the entire brigade until the lone remaining soldier, depressed at the death of his comrades, commits suicide. The brigade is eliminated, and without the use of weapons."

The woman laughs, "Absurd. Do you believe that the Red Army will shoot itself to death? Do you believe that your department can manipulate them to that degree?"

Cummings looks up. "Do you believe that agents of ours could fabricate a love affair between Ivan's wife and Vladimir convincingly enough that the jealous Ivan would have a high probability of shooting Vladimir within a predictable time frame?"

"I suppose, but—"

"No buts about it. We can also adjust circumstances to influence Igor to shoot Ivan within a predic—"

"Dr. Cummings, you are beginning to sound silly. Dangerous, but very, very silly. I mean, do you have any conception of what it would take to manipulate just a hundred persons in the manner you suggest?"

"Yes. A quite accurate conception, actually. It is limited only by the capacity of the current MAC facility. The facility is self-expanding, and I can assure you that by the time we reach the Wardate, there will be sufficient capacity to do what needs to be done."

Manipulation.

Everyone is wired, I once told Eva Messer.

Probability, cause-and-effect—uncounted trillions of manipulated motions that, in turn, create predictable circumstance alterations that, in turn, influence still further motions along predictable paths. Have I really fallen in between the threads of this web?

Rhona told me that I must hold my own survival as my very first priority if I expect to live. It is getting difficult, however, to imagine life without the people of West Ellen.

Laying around in bed day after day is a good way to go crazy.

I look again at the cover of the book I refuse to read. I have read everything I could *about* Aubry Cummings. This book, however, *is* Aubry Cummings. I don't mean it is *by* Cummings. It *is* Cummings.

This book is the first of a new kind of biography. It is written by MAC III, and it tells the person's life, the way that person sees it, in that person's words, as it was seen. Three days ago I got it off the library cart. I open it again.

I see little Aubry Cummings, five years old, being ignored at his mother's funeral, and damning the universe with his most secret thoughts for the unfair way it is treating him.

I almost laugh, but I don't. I don't laugh because I know exactly how that little kid feels. And there is something else. The Big Machine's capacity to know any person this well is—

It's—

I was about to say that it is unfair.

I think I refuse to read any farther because the Big Machine frightens me. I know it's powerful; I'm afraid it's more powerful than I think it is. If it can pluck these feelings out of an old man's forgotten past, what could it—

How can it just unscrew a human mind, dumping experiences, feelings, thoughts—everything—on paper for just anyone to paw over and—

"Would you like to keep it for a few more days?"

"Huh?" Joanne, the woman who pushes the library cart, is standing in the doorway. I close the book and hold it out. "No, thank you."

"What do you think of it?" She comes into the room, her feet not making a sound. She does a quick scan looking for Mark Rowe, but my roommate is elsewhere being fitted with an artificial dick. Anyway, that's what he said before he was wheeled out.

I shrug. "I don't know. I didn't finish it."

Joanne reminds me a little of Citizen Sayther. Mostly around the eyes and the way she wears her hair. "Here, look at the last page."

I push myself up a bit and look. Joanne holds the open book in front of my face.

The last page says:

CUMMINGS, AUBRY
RUN COMPLETED

WARDATE: 17:18-9AUG2033
DOWNLIMIT: -80401:31:33

—READY
—READY

And so on with the word READY repeated in a column down the entire left side of the page.

"What does it mean?"

I shake my head. "I don't know."

"That Downlimit number was around when he resigned. I looked it up."

"I don't know."

Joanne closes the book. "Would you like to look at the cart? I've got all new books."

"No. Thank you."

She leaves, taking her damned book with her. I close my eyes and wait for sleep to come.

Run completed. What does that mean? Maybe it means that the Big Machine has used up and thrown away the husk of one Cummings, Aubry. Maybe it means that the theoretical machine-generated event called Cummings, Aubry has been put through the system and has too many bugs. Maybe Gaff and Dice are right. Maybe the whole thing—reality—is nothing but dots on a screen. Too many bugs. Does a machine generated image *know* that it's a machine-generated image? Does—

I turn on the TV and search for a movie. Laying around in bed all day is a great way to go crazy.

Sometimes Mark Rowe talks to me at night when he can't sleep. He only asks questions to which he wants no answers.

Wardate: 17:18-9AUG2033
Downlimit: -75172:20:03

31

Doc Cordwell sees me often, of course, and he picks me up when I am ready to leave the hospital.

In the parking lot, wearing my new red coat, I look up at this part of Bristol through the window on my side of the car, marveling at the bright sunshine, the melted snow filling the old gutters.

The doctor starts up the fans, then lets them whine down.

"What's the matter?"

The doctor opens his door. "I must be getting old," he says as he gets out. He reaches in and picks up several cards that had been sitting on top of the car's control panel. He leans in his head and speaks. "Tom, I have some business to take care of." He shakes his head as he glances at the cards. "Death notices. I don't know how many times I've been by here and forgot to post them. Do you feel well enough to come along, or do you want to wait here?"

"I'm okay. I'll come along." My hand trembles as I open the door and climb out. I follow Doc Cordwell back into the hospital building.

Death notices.

It's taken perhaps days for them to get filed.

As far as the computer knows, those people are still alive, still part of the Big Equation, their numbers still valid.

Inside the building we pass the lobby, continue down a hall, and turn left into a brightly-lit room. There are four persons working at terminals. The doctor walks up to the closest of them. The man at the nearest keyboard leans back and smiles up at the doctor. He looks very tired. "Hi, Doc. What can I do for you?"

The doctor extends his hand and holds out the cards. "Three death notices to file, Carl. I've been meaning to get them in for days, but one thing and another."

Carl points to a small pile of perhaps a hundred similar cards. "Stick 'em there, Doc, and don't worry about it. I'm so far behind right now I'll never catch up. Who's your friend?"

"Carl, this is Tom Mills. He was a patient here and I'm taking him home. Tom, this is Carl St. Laurent."

"Hi."

Carl nods and clasps his hands behind his head. The image on his terminal screen reads:

CITIZENSHIP WARRANT RETIREMENT
617-4434-922 SS, Davis, Harold Michael
Died: 04:51 21JAN2027

The 99-99 in progress code flashes at the bottom of the screen. The doc puts down the cards and motions for me to wait for him as he turns and walks from the room.

The image on the screen doesn't change and the operator, Carl, is attempting to fill his time with foot-tapping and sighing. I point at the screen.

"What's taking so long?"

Carl raises an eyebrow at me. "Know anything about projections?"

"A little."

"Big MAC has been chugging along the past six days on the assumption that one Harold Michael Davis was alive."

"So any projections or circumstances based on that assumption are in error."

Carl smiles. "Right. So what MAC is doing now is readjusting everything. Old Harold Michael must have been a real gob in the Big Picture. This has been going on for fifteen minutes."

The operator picks up a white card. "I don't know why. The guy was only a mech. He repaired fans and wheelies at a garage here in Bristol. You wouldn't think that would be enough to tie up DOP for fifteen minutes, would you?"

I think. A man who repairs cars might have devastating effects on the Big Picture. Depending on who was driving or riding in the vehicle in question, a late repair, or a poor repair, could result in important changes. If an important business person was late, or died in an "accident." What did Harold Michael Davis's father and mother do? His children, sisters, brothers? Each person touches so many others who in turn touch so many more, in ways that only MAC can fathom.

Ivan kills Vladimir, Igor kills Ivan, Nikita kills Igor, and so on until a billion soldiers are eliminated.

—but what if Ivan is already dead and DOP doesn't find out until six days later? Yes, there will be much humming among the appropriate circuits while MAC tries to convince Vladimir to commit suicide, or something else.

In this there might be a way for me to get a valid citizenship warrant. Not just a warrant; I can be a part of West Ellen, free and clear. With a number that can be run, I can make full use of the terminal in the library—

Miss French had asked me if I was related to the Millses of wherever. Rhona had picked a name that would be common in New England. Somewhere there is a Mills—a Thomas Mills—close to my age and near death. He will have to be an orphan, a stranger to those around him. If I can get to his warrant retirement notice before it's posted and substitute my own, I could take on—

Slow down.

Take it slow. I will have to study everything closely, making certain that I have left no loose ends. What appears to be a clear path to me could be nothing more than a trap, doing the big machine's work for it.

The Davis retirement concludes, and Carl begins posting the remainder. I carefully watch him post four of the warrant retirements before the doc returns and we head back to West Ellen.

* * *

That evening in my cabin, Colleen, Miss French, John and May Pittman, Herbie and Dottie Dyar as well as Doc Cordwell welcome me back. May Pittman is very quiet. I think she is embarrassed. Her being undressed when we were discovered is part of the embarrassment. Pissing in my coat is the other part. Knowing West Ellen, the story will outlive her.

Before the evening is over, she kisses my cheek.

Wardate: 17:18-9AUG2033
Downlimit: -74836:11:03

30

The research concluded, two weeks later there is a killing to do.

The words sound threateningly comfortable. Godfrey had said them to me when I was seven years old preparing to help the club put down Citizen Bond.

There is a killing to do.

From the terminal in the West Ellen Public Library, I have searched the communications indices for the New England districts and have located one thousand and twenty-four citizens named Thomas (no middle name) Mills. Using a sociological survey program, I collated them by age, occupation, relations, and physical infirmities. Out of the total there are fifty-two of them between the ages of seventeen and nineteen who have no living relatives. Nine of these, because of jail, drug addiction, insanity, and other illnesses, are neither employed or in school.

However, I cannot predict their deaths with enough accuracy to enable me to get to the location and switch warrants before the late Thomas Mills's warrant is retired.

I can't, unless I, myself, am the cause of death.

There is a killing to do.

Out of curiosity I check the communications directory for Thomas Windoms. There are almost six hundred Thomas Windoms in the New England districts. There are three of them living in Boston. All of them fit my requirements:

between seventeen and nineteen, and alone. I can even have my own name back if that is what I want.

What *do* I want? The name *Thomas Mills* is what I need to settle in at West Ellen, go to school, fall in love, get a job, buy a home, be a person. But before that, there is a killing to do.

Why not? It's not like no one ever did such a thing before. It's not like I never did such a thing before. But, what if—

There are questions that I do not think I need to ask about this killing. This will not be justice at the hands of the girls club. This killing will need a different name.

It should only take a day. I catch a ride with Herbie into Bristol, trying to stay as close to the truth as I can. Sightseeing. I tell him that I've never seen Boston.

He says to have fun, but to watch out. When he was a kid and made his first expedition into the City of Beans, he got drunk and wound up in jail with a fat head and a flat wallet.

He says that the weather projections are for rain in Boston.

As the car nears the trans station, one of Bristol's Wardate signs comes into view. I think about weather projections. Weather can't be a projection unless it is manipulated somehow by MAC. And MAC manipulates the weather.

Through its orders to the departments of agriculture and industry, it influences the contents of the gases making up the atmosphere, the temperature of the waters that surround us, and therefore the movements of the air masses, the frequency of the rains.

Perhaps there are even more things. An old article I read proposed a series of satellites that could fire dye capsules down into the stratosphere to control temperature in specified places. Dyes that could block light for a predetermined period, after which they would lose most of their light-blocking properties, were already in existence when the article was written.

I see something so clearly now. The Wardate does not describe a nuclear event with masked and lead-shrouded soldiers pulling their weapons and clawing their way through a biochemical nightmare. It probably won't even be a war in the way we mean that word.

Cummings had lked about Ivan shooting Vladimir, Igor shooting Ivan. MAC can also make it impossible for Ivan to grow food, to keep warm, and therefore, to keep order.

Four and one-half billion men, women, and children crammed into an impoverished space with no food, no warmth. They will tear down the Otherworld governments, then tear apart each other.

Compared to this, nuclear war is a holiday; a clean, sane ending.

Sanity. This is a word of hidden meanings.

No sane person could inflict this fate upon half the world—not and remain sane.

Of course.

That's why we built a machine to do it for us.

When it becomes necessary to kill illegal parents, to condemn illegal immigrants by birth to hell, to destroy half of the human race to preserve the other half, we will have clean hands.

A machine will do the killing.

The same machine will convince us that it was the machine that was responsible for the killing. Then we may all go to sleep and dream the dreams of the guiltless. And it was even the machine that told us to build the machine.

This is the thing I am trying to fool.

From Bristol I take the trans. Only patches of snow remain on the ground, and they seem to dwindle rapidly as the trans moves south and the rain begins.

I become lost in the water ribbons on the window.

Be cold.

Don't think about it. Don't feel. Just do it.

Instructions from Manuel on how to kill a guard.

Be cold.

The instruction could be from MAC. How else could humans contemplate the murder of billions? Build a machine;

let *it* take the responsibility for the execution. Let *it* do what needs to be done.

It would be nice. Still, I must do my own killing.

Passing through some town there are the red lights of a Wardate sign. I cannot read the numbers, but they have no meaning right now. Abstract principles, world events, futures of races have little to do with someone on his way to do murder.

Not just murder. When Thomas Windom murders he is close enough to smell his victims.

Wardate signs.

What a laugh.

I fall asleep watching the water on the window.

Wardate: 17:18-9AUG2033
Downlimit: -74830:04:00

29

It seems like only moments after leaving West Ellen I am in Boston walking this old street without a name, the smells of fish and rot in my nostrils. The broken pavement is gleaming from the rain. Even the rain smells dirty.

I wear a short, dark blue jacket and a black watch cap. My red parka is in a locker at the trans terminal.

There is a street sign. 1114G.

In the window of a shop there was an old map of Boston. On that map all of the streets had names, not numbers. Next to that map was another showing some of the streets with names, some with numbers. One of the streets on that map is named Peterborough. Is it named after where I was born?

Perhaps I will look at this street after I finish my murder. Perhaps not. Peterborough, both the street and the city, are far away.

Beware, Thomas Mills. Thomas Mills is coming for you.

Boston has five Thomas Millses. Two of them fit my requirements. One of them is in police custody. The remaining Thomas Mills, drug addict, should be in this neighborhood, in one of the two abandoned buildings at the end of this street, if the other addict at the Clean Beds rooming house was telling the truth.

With luck Thomas Mills will be stoned out of his mind, and I can switch papers on him and he won't even notice. Still I'd have to kill him. When he protests against the charges that his papers are no good, they will do a full ID check, part of which will be to find and apprehend whoever it is who is carrying Thomas Mills's warrant.

—Or maybe he'll already be dead. Can I search a rotting corpse for its papers? I've been in deeper than that. I can do it. If I can hammer lumber up Citizen Bond's ass, I can wrestle with maggots for a valid citizenship warrant.

There is lots of noise in the air, but coming from a great distance. Here on the street it is very quiet; the sound of my footsteps make me self-conscious. There are faces in the windows, dark and angry.

The buildings are small and old. Many of them abandoned; many have been demolished—decayed and missing teeth. The Thomas Mills I am looking for sleeps in one of these piles of rubble. When he can scrape together enough money, he rents some space at Clean Beds, where there is not a clean bed in sight.

There are eleven hopeless scraps of human leftovers at Clean Beds. How do they fit into the Big Equation, MAC? What part do they play in the Perfect World Plan?

Hoboburgers hit the spot?

Six big ounces, that's a lot?

In a manner, I feel superior to these things passing themselves off as humans. With valid warrants, all doors open to them, look at the way they live.

Wardate: 17:18-9AUG2033
Downlimit: -74828:00:07

28

The smell.

The smell is sickening.

It makes me grateful that it is still cold. Rainwater comes through the roof, trickles down the moldy walls, and soaks through the rotting floor. The stink comes from a bathroom and a closet on the same floor. The closet was used when the bathroom could hold no more.

God, the stink.

The walls are covered with grafitti.

The Electric Eel wants to know: Who killed Charley the tuna?

What this country needs is—

—enough shit to hold us over until the war.

God Bless You Aubry Cummings!

The Perfect World Plan: Turn the whole fucking thing into glass and start over!

Boom, Boom!

Bang!

Pow!

Zowie!

Dear Mother, How are you? I am so fine.

Did anybody get the number of that truck?

Just remember: wherever you go, there you are.

Drawings.

Thousands of drawings. Faces, hands, animals.

They are all twisted, distorted, in pain. From them I can pick out faces from my past. Ann is there. Citizen Sayther. Citizen Bond. Manuel. I even see my own face.

The eyes.

I know those eyes—

I stop looking at the drawings. There is a strange pain in my chest and I want to cry. This thing called Thomas Mills cries, and there is no one who hears. He sends written messages, and the world is blind because he mails his messages to hell.

To the side of the large room near the permanently open front door is a flight of stairs.

On the wall behind the stairs, painted in huge black letters, is the word "GOD" with an arrow pointing up. Painted in small letters next to the arrow is: "Hours by appointment."

The stairs are solid.

Quietly, slow step-by-step, I creep up into the darkness. A rat scurries by me as the second floor landing comes to eye level. Water drips from the ceiling and splashes on the slimy landing.

I lean against the wet bannister. There is the wetness around me, the dark, the filth, the cold, the odor.

What was it? What was my reason for coming here? What am I doing here?

I am here to steal someone's permission to live.

What kind of thing must live here? Do I want his papers that badly?

I *need* them!

Look at this.

Just look at this.

Such a thing deserves to die, doesn't he? Shouldn't I put him out of his misery? Who would care?

He probably wouldn't.

Up another step, and another.

The rooms on the second floor are littered with water-soaked trash. In relatively dry corners are piles of wrinkled newspapers. I can see where they have been used for sleeping. I kick my way through one of the piles, then another—

—to the window.

—breathe some clean air.

Whatever I kicked in that second pile fills the room with an odor that is unbearable. With my head a bit clearer and my stomach less queasy, I look down at my boot. Across the right toe wriggle a half-dozen maggots. I kick against the wall, knocking them off.

I have a headache, my stomach threatens any moment to empty itself. I breath the cold, rain-washed air.

Breathe.

I look across the street. There is a building similar to the one in which I am standing, except that it is not abandoned. There is glass in all the windows, light behind the glass. Curtains, painted trim.

So long ago, opening a window, revealing to the world that I existed. I wonder what happened to that woman who saw me?

"You."

I freeze. The voice came from behind me. I turn slowly, examining every corner and crack, finding no one.

Through the doorway, past the landing, a dark opening faces me. "What?"

Anything could be hiding in the darkness past that doorway. In which case, I think, it already has me.

I walk out of the room, onto the landing, and around the largest of the streams of rainwater coming from the roof. Standing in the doorway, my body is racked with chills as I wait for my eyes to adjust to the dark. Layers of newspaper cover the windows allowing only cracks of the dim light from outside to enter.

In the corner opposite the doorway is a shadow within the dark. Movement. A voice. "I don't have anything, man. You're wasting your time."

His hand reaches up and lifts a corner of the newspaper covering the window just above him. He is on the floor, covered with newspapers and old rags. He has more rags wrapped around his head and shoulders for warmth. His eyes are dark-circled and wide with terror.

The eyes stare at me for a long time, then go dull. In the space of a breath the fear leaves them, dies. He drops the newspaper curtain back into place, cutting off the light. He lowers himself back onto his bed of trash.

"Fuck it. Take what you want, man. I don't care."

The room is dry. I step inside the door and squat on the floor, my back against the wall, my gaze never leaving the shadow in the corner. There is no one else in the room.

There he is, all alone.

Everything taken from him except the one thing I need. It would take very little effort to kill him. The way he looks I could probably just wait a few hours for him to finish killing himself.

He revolts me. Disgusts me. I am so angry; so scared. I sit for a long time, letting the noise in my head subside.

"I mean it, man. I don't have anything. It's the truth."

"Your warrant." My voice startles me. "You have a citizenship warrant."

The shadow pulls himself up until his head and shoulders are propped against the wall behind him. "What's your name?"

"Thomas Mills, the same as yours."

"What good is my warrant to you?"

"It is."

The hand goes up again, lifting the newspaper curtain. The dark-circled eyes study me. "Why?"

I owe you something, Thomas Mills. "I'm an escaped outcaster. I need a number that can be run."

His eyes close and he shakes his head. "No, man, it's not that easy. Never that easy. They got that profile shit and everything logged against my number. Eyeballs, voice, fingerprints 'n' stuff. You can't fake that."

"I can adjust it. I know how."

"Huh." He seems to be thinking. "What about prints? Fingerprints, voiceprints—"

"They aren't used anymore."

He slides back down into his rags and papers. "Thought of everything, did you?"

"I don't know. You never know."

"Yeah." He laughs until he coughs. "Shit, yes, you never

know." When he finishes coughing he spits on the floor and settles back on his papers.

"So what now? Do you kill me and plant your bad papers on my mortal remains?"

"That was the plan."

He is silent. Thinking. He lifts a hand and scratches his face. "Do you have the guts? Can you kill someone?"

I push myself to my feet and stand looking down at the shadow. "It doesn't take courage. All it takes is fear."

"Did you ever kill anybody?"

"Yes."

"Bullshit." The shadow rolls over. Next to the trash bed is a shelf made from two concrete blocks and a length of board. On the shelf are a few papers, a couple of books, empty cans.

"Come over here, killer."

Is he reaching for a knife? Will he put up a fight? This will be so much easier if he fights; if he hurts me; if I can add my blood to his in the garbage on the floor.

I take a step. I take another. The shadow rolls back and pulls the newspaper from the window. His corner of the room is bathed in gray light.

"Come here."

I stand next to him, looking down at him. On top of his chest, clasped by his filthy fingers, is the bright blue and gold cover of a citizenship warrant. He lifts his hand and holds it out to me. I take it, and his hand is still out.

"Give me yours."

I reach into my hip pocket, pull out my temporary government employee warrant, and hand it down to him. He holds it up to the light and opens it. "You won't even have to change the picture."

As he places the phony warrant on his chest and clasps his hands over it, he turns his eyes toward the window and says, "Fucking rain. Fucking gray day. It figures."

His eyes close. "Okay, do it now."

"Now? Do what?"

His head nods. "C'mon, killer. Mutual exchange for mutual value. I give you what you want and you give me what I want. You want birth. I want never to have been born."

His eyes are still closed, his head turned toward the window. I take the shelf and its contents and dump it on the floor. Hooking my hand into one of the concrete blocks, I pick it up and hold it in both hands.

The sharpness of the edges.

The smell of it.

There was a lot of concrete back at Outcasters. The tears again, but these I understand.

He says something.

"What?"

"I said, 'God bless you.'"

I bring the block up. "Same to you."

Funny.

The sound it made.

Wardate: 17:18-9AUG2033
Downlimit: -74540:11:12

27

I am Thomas Mills.

My citizenship number is 2390141-408

With my number I can ask MAC what MAC knows about me. This I do.

I was born March 26th, 2006 in Kittery, State District of Maine. I am nineteen years old.

Shortly after I was born, I was abandoned by my parents but was ruled a legal immigrant by birth and put up for adoption.

I was not an attractive baby; I cried too much, and would not go to sleep easily. Three sets of parents took me on trial and returned me within days. Each time I found myself back at the Adoption Authority Home in Westbrook.

When I was nine I was taken on trial by a couple in Northampton, State District of Massachusetts. I ran away from them a year later, making my way to Boston. Almost two years later I was taken into custody for breaking and entering and was put into treatment as a drug addict.

Upon completion of treatment for addiction, three months later, I was returned to the Maine SD Adoption Authority.

At the age of fourteen I ran from the home and, again, went to Boston. For the next four years my life is something of a mystery. There are no records. During the fall of 2024, however, I move to West Ellen, State District of Vermont.

There I am reborn.

Back in Boston the body of a murdered wretch is cremated. His temporary government warrant in the name of Thomas

Mills is traced through the Forestry Resources Department in Rutland and compared against his filing papers, which turn out to be counterfeit.

The only record of his phony number is for a trans ticket to Rutland originating in Cold Springs, State District of New York, and a more recent ticket to Boston originating in Bristol, Vermont SD.

The date of the first ticket corresponds roughly with the escape of a number of inmates at Compact Farm No. 128 near Ossining. None of the inmates have been taken into custody.

Identity of victim unknown.

Case filed open.

Herbie and I are behind his store standing next to the stubble of Herbie's vegetable garden. He points at various places as he itemizes the things that are to be planted there, complete with instructions and handy tips.

"Herbie, do you remember when I was in the hospital; that I didn't want my number run?"

He laughs, turns red in the face, and nods as he looks at the ground. "Yeah, I guess I remember." His is an angry laugh.

"I'm sorry I took so long to clear it up, but, well, I'm a drug addict. I'm clean now, but I have a record. I'm trying to put my life back together, and I just didn't want anyone to find out."

Herbie puts his arm around my shoulders, gives me a squeeze, and never mentions it again.

The guilt I feel is beyond measuring.

Some things are just too big.

I sit in the library staring at the terminal's main screen. Now that I have entered the new profile and successfully completed my first number run, I must sort this out with care.

I touch the screen with my fingers.

This is a part of MAC. At the other end, through surface wires and satellite microwave relays, deep in the granite beneath the city of New York, is MAC's intelligence, its power to plan, correct, select, adjust.

This is an instrument that can detect and analyze the finest shades of personality and collate them with an entire planet's items of circumstance to manipulate seven billion humans into a special kind of war that everyone knows and no one believes is coming.

I am Thomas Windom, not quite nineteen.

Have I really fooled this machine?

If it knows the truth about me, the police should be on me like black on coal. The same holds true if the machine only knows that what it's getting from me is not the truth.

Have I done it? Have I fooled MAC?

The Department of Projections has been reducing the number of functions MAC performs. Just like for the hospital, no longer automatically providing medical histories.

Back in Bloodroot, Ether Allen used to complain about how more and more paperwork was being dumped on him. He had to make up his own work orders and schedules now. He had to supervise and keep track of his own equipment and maintenance. He had other computers for these, but he still considered having to go to more than one system an imposition.

The other day Herbie told me that West Ellen would be hiring someone to operate the police terminal. A lot of the paperwork items the computer used to handle on its own now must be handled by the local authorities.

MAC is freeing itself up for something.

Maybe, just maybe, this thing that is occupying MAC's attention has allowed me to slip through the computer's web and become Thomas Mills, human being.

At times I feel the wires all over me. Can I trust this moment? I must. Otherwise I would be running. I turn off the terminal, noticing that it is night and I forgot to turn on the lights.

The dark.

I sit, counting my ghosts, watching as Thomas Mills joins their ranks. I owe them, these spirits. Ann, Merle, Louisa. And Thomas Mills. I am not yet a human, but now I have the right. They bought me that right.

Meghan French gave me a lecture before she left the library for the night. I am a nice boy. Respectful. Polite. Studious.

Brave, if you can believe some of the people around here. But with a one-track mind. Every book I've ever read since coming to West Ellen has had to come from another library, and all on one subject. When I don't have my nose tucked between the pages of a book on disciplinary projections, my eyes are glued to that terminal screen.

She told me to follow her, and I did. We walked up and down the shelves of the tiny library. Meghan French continued the lecture as she pulled books from the shelves and handed them to me.

"There is an entire universe you're shutting out, Thomas. The way you're going, you might as well be in prison—here, this one, too." Another book added to my burden.

She sounded angry.

Books on painting, politics, religion. Novels. I have *Tom Sawyer* and *Huckleberry Finn* back, in addition to many more. Adventure, romance, science fiction, fantasy— "Here, this one, too. And this."

At the back of the library, the video room. A wall full of old tapes, a couple of comfortable chairs, and a television set with an old tape player unit.

"You've dusted back here, so I know that you know that this room is here. But you've never even watched one movie, have you?"

"I've watched some of the documen—"

"Oh!" Her eyes looked up in despair. "Help me, Hannah." Into the video room. She pulled red plastic tape cases off of the shelves and placed them on top of my wobbling pile.

"This one. This one. *El Cid*, Thomas. Do you know that story?"

"Yes." Another tape joins the pile.

Just before she left she wagged her finger in my face and told me to go through every single one of the items she had selected.

I look at the pile of books and tape cases on the chair near the door. It would take weeks, months, to go through it all. And why shouldn't I?

"Why shouldn't I?"

It's part of being a human, isn't it? When Colleen had asked me what I thought of Devastation, I made a complete fool of myself. I didn't know that Devastation was a musical group. Another part of my missing humanhood.

I look at the dark screen of the terminal. It's given me what I need to put Outcasters behind me. Nothing else is of consequence. My dues are paid. Instead of wars, murder, and hiding, now I can think of going to school, vegetable gardens, seeing a movie with a girl. Instead of circumstance selection, manufacture, and adjustment, I can explore love, a home, maybe even a child of my own.

College. I can go to college.

I am already collecting the barnacles of life. That's what Herbie calls them: licenses, insurance cards, and such. I have a library card. I have a licence and insurance certificate that authorizes me to operate Class "A" (non-commercial) vehicles.

I pull out the insurance certificate. I am now worth something. I am worth ten thousand credits dead. Right now the ten thousand credits would go to my estate, since I named no beneficiary. It has become very important to me to find a name I want to put on the beneficiary line in my policy form.

I get up and walk to the chair piled with books and tapes. It doesn't matter where I begin. I take the tape titled *El Cid* and go into the video room. In moments my head is filled with the familiar sounds and images of the purest knight of all.

"Hey, Cid, go to it."

Another time, another place, learning again these new values, new codes, new conceptions of love, courage, and honor.

Wardate: 17:18-9AUG2033
Downlimit: -74228:03:00

26

I sit in the chair, my feet on the sill of the open window. It's a chill spring night. From the library window I can still hear the music from the old firehouse. It is so awful it's wonderful. For fifty credits the West Ellen churchgoers obtained the services of a fiddle, a banjo, a guitar, and an accordian. They call themselves the Kent Corners Ramblers and are playing a raucous thing called "The Green Mountain Breakdown."

I danced my first dance tonight.

The room was hung with streamers and filled with sound and the smell of hot cider and cinnamon. There were over a hundred West Elleners there. Herbie and Dottie Dyar had invited me, but it was Colleen who dragged me out to dance.

It was a polka. After it was finished I wanted to dance all night. We danced a few. But Colleen would be leaving early Sunday morning to visit her sister in Presque Isle, state district of Maine. I took her home, and we kissed.

This is it. "Yes!" I say out loud, "this is it!"

This is love.

This is being a human.

This is belonging somewhere.

This morning Avon Weeks hired me full-time to help him ready his camps for summer. Last Friday I was accepted at the Barre campus of the University of Nations for their summer session. The week before that I borrowed Herbie's electric and took Roseann Whitley to Montpelier to see a play. The next day Colleen was angry. Outside of the library they argued over me.

Argued over *me*.

This is it, this is it, *this* is *it!*

The amplified voice of the lead Rambler announces that the next number is a polka called "Gator."

Herbie Dyar's new aircar fans down Main Street past the library. I laugh thinking about Dottie's exasperation at Herbie's love for his new machine, in addition to his regular violation of speed laws.

I get to my feet, pull the window closed against the icy night, and seat myself at the terminal. Except to do some filing for Miss French, I haven't touched the thing in over a month. My lesson plan and studies in disciplinary projections are ancient history.

I don't know what I will take when I go to Barre this summer. There are so many things, so many possibilities.

I look at my reflection in the de-energized screen. I hardly recognize my own face. I am alive, smiling, hopeful.

I look again, combing my hair down with my fingers. It is still hard to imagine: Colleen and Roseann arguing over me. But why not? I'm a citizen. I look—

—*Vale!*

It suddenly comes to me. *Vale*. Helen's last name. Helen Vale.

There's nothing classified about a citizen's address. Helen had gotten citizenship. I should be able to look her up in the address indices without giving anything away.

Many times the thought of seeing her again touches my mind. To see someone who knows me. I miss her so.

I turn on the terminal.

The screen is blank, but alive with a pale green glow.

For a moment I flash through a fantasy where this screen is but one of MAC's many eyes. Again I feel MAC's wires all over me. I shake off the feeling and go to the address index.

I enter the name: Helen Vale. I discover the Compact of Nations has many Helen Vales.

I shut down the terminal and look out of the window at the houses on Main Street. Beyond the trees there is a hint of turquoise left from the sunset. The temperature is falling rapidly, but the West Elleners are out in force, wearing light clothing, inviting illness, asserting their right to spring.

Back in my cabin is my gift for Colleen Marshall's birthday. It is a piece of rose quartz faceted into the shape of a heart, to be worn around her neck hung from a delicate gold chain.

Colleen Marshall, West Ellen, Thomas Mills, and college: That's now. That is the present.

I look at the dead screen of the terminal and from there to the papers and notes on the desk. That is the future. Reality twists and coils through the books and papers like some kind of foul serpent. The promise of the future is unspeakable horror. Bit by bit, somewhat more rapidly than predicted, the Consolidationists are whittling away at the Department of Projection's ability to control circumstances. To find out where it will lead means obtaining the kind of access to the MAC III facility that requires a security clearance.

I don't think I want to know where it is going. The world looks as though it is heading for random hell, but if my studies have shown me nothing else, I know that MAC is in control.

That is the future; Helen, Outcasters, and Thomas Windom is the past.

West Ellen is now. My home. It has weathered the best and the worst years of the Compact without changing much at all. I know better, but my gut feeling is that the world can blow itself to submicroscopic particles, yet things will stay the same in West Ellen.

The people.

The people are nosey, narrow-minded, suspicious, bursting with gossip and stingy with their friendships. But once extended, a West Ellen friendship is collateral. Thomas Mills loves the people of West Ellen. I am certain that several of them love Thomas Mills.

Rhona told me not to stay for too long in one spot. But now I have a number, and Rhona is part of yesterday. Today is John Pittman and I sitting in the stands of the Green Mountain Junior High Gym cheering May Pittman and the rest of the Green Mountain Panthers as they defeated the St. Johnsbury Hawks, winning the state district junior girls basketball finals. Today is dancing a polka with Colleen Marshall. Today is standing on a hilltop, looking down upon the lake, Avon Weeks's arm around my shoulders.

Headlights on the street.

I stretch up a bit and see Herbie's ancient wheeled electric slide to a stop in front of the library. The lights turn off and Herbie Dyar extricates his bulk from the tiny vehicle. I notice that the library's porch light is still off, and I turn it on and open the door. Herbie's face is in a frown, his hands thrust into the pockets of his jacket.

My fantasies about today and West Ellen turn into vapor and disappear. "Herbie?"

The big man waves without looking up. "Inside."

I back out of the way as he climbs the stairs and enters the door. I close it after him. "What're you driving that old thing for?"

Even though there is nothing burning in it, Herbie backs himself up to the wood stove. He raises a bushy brown eyebrow and glances at me. "Son, I got a problem."

I sit down on the edge of Miss French's desk and fold my arms. I can feel my jaw muscles about to part from the strain. "What is it?"

He looks down at the floor. "This business you gave me about being a drug addict?" He moistens his lips as he shakes his head, his gaze coming up to meet mine. "Is your real name Thomas Windom?"

All I want to do is shout: please don't do this to me. Not now. Please, just let me alone. Damn it. Damn these tears. "Yes. Yes, yes, yes."

To avoid seeing me cry, Herbie looks for a chair and sits in it. I take a deep breath and ask, "What now?"

Herbie holds up a hand. "Let me run out all the rope, son. Now, you know I'm town constable. Well, that clackety-clack in my office had a message for me today from the district. I'm supposed to arrest you."

In an instant I am both ready to run and resigned to the arrest. All that adrenaline and no place to go. I don't have a chance. Without food, transportation—it's still cold outside. I probably wouldn't survive more than a day or two in the mountains. Even if I could survive, it would be childishly simple to track me.

I look from the door back to Herbie. He is studying me. "They told me they're sending over a *squad* from Montpelier to pick you up. A *squad*. Tom, what in the hell did you do?"

I close my eyes. It's over. All over. "I'm an escaped outcaster."

"Outcaster," Herbie repeats. "Well, they want me to sit on you until they show."

"I understand."

Dyar snorts, "Well, I'll be damned if I do. But understand this, son. I'm a man of my word, and I'm sworn to uphold the damned stupid law. I was ordered to arrest you, and that's exactly what I'm going to do."

He pushes himself to his feet and looks around the book-lined room. "Just as soon as I take me a little pee."

He glowers down at me. "Now some smartass kid that has no respect for the law might want to take advantage of an old fat man like me, steal that Ellis Electric out there and head south to avoid the regiment of cops they're sending from the district." He drops a set of keys on Miss French's desk. "If he wasn't too disrespectful he might leave it someplace where a guy might be able to find it some day."

Herbie pulls a wrinkled letter-sized envelope from inside his coat and tosses it next to the keys.

"And some other smartass kid might steal what's in that envelope I want you to hold for me so I don't accidentally drop it in the toilet. So you wait right there, and as soon as I'm finished, I'll clamp you in irons and drag you over to the store to wait on the reinforcements from Montpelier."

I pick up the envelope and glance inside. Over three hundred credits in notes.

I get to my feet and see the glisten in the big man's eyes. I reach to embrace him but he grabs me by my shoulders. "Let me go pee, son. There's not much time."

He releases my shoulders, walks to the back of the room, and closes the restroom door behind him.

* * *

Rabbits.

Watership Down.

And the Great Frith said: All the world will be your enemy. And when they catch you they will kill you. But first they'll fuck over you some. First they'll make sure that you think you're free and clear. First they'll make certain that you have a reason for wanting to live.

It takes a million years to figure out how to start the Ellis.

Wardate: 17:18-9AUG2033
Downlimit: -74227:48:55

25

I drive in a fog.

South on Main, down the mountain.

I do not allow myself to think. Not about what Herbie had done; not about what I am leaving behind; and especially not about why it all has to be.

I must reach safety.

This need for safety is something on the outside of me. Inside I feel a numbness that makes it an effort to keep my outward panic alive. In this situation I *should* be running in panic, trying frantically to escape. This is what I should feel, so this is what I do. This is what Herbie wants me to do, so this is what I do.

Down the twisting mountain road, the lights carving a tunnel through the dark.

Does the blackshit know about the murder in Boston? They know Thomas Mills is Thomas Windom. They must know about the murder.

I burst out laughing, thinking of the others I have killed. What is one Thomas Mills on the pile, more or less?

A mountain of dead flesh. And the mountain feeds the world.

Baby Burgers hit the spot,
Six big ounces, that's a lot.

The laughter dies.

The murder of Thomas Mills is the only one I call murder. It is the only killing that shames me.

He *asked* for it.

He asked to have me kill him. Mutual exchange for mutual value, *he* said. I want to live and he wants—wanted—never to have been born. He did ask for it. He—

There was something about being not guilty before that made my life endurable; that made survival possible. I could blame, hate, aim the responsibility for it all at others. Now it is different.

I do not think I will be able to endure punishment if the right is on the side of the blackshit.

There is a strangeness I just notice. I think of myself as Thomas Mills. I don't think of myself as Thomas Windom using the name Thomas Mills; I think of myself as Thomas Mills.

And I have murdered Thomas Mills.

A strange feeling.

At the town limit of Lincoln.

I pull over to the side of the road and turn off the lights. I watch the moonlight on the budding trees. All winter I have been looking forward to seeing Stark Mountain wearing its green. I want to see the naked maples along Main Street with leaves.

Lights reflect from the rearview mirror into my eyes. I turn and look over my left shoulder. It's just another old electric. The blackshit rides air. I notice something in the back seat. I reach out my hand and bring it into the front seat. It's my shoulder bag packed with my belongings.

I unbuckle it and reach in. On top is the rose quartz heart. I don't remove it from the bag, but rest my hand on it.

My hand—

My hand feels very strange. It remembers something that I do not remember. What does it remember?

—Back at Outcasters.

The thing with the dog. That little time of light during the dark of my six dead years when I came back long enough—

My brain is boiling, my feelings darting through heights and depths I don't believe exist.

Alone.

I was at the Green Machine, sitting in the dust. Something about my hand. A dog licking my hand. No one around me except for this little black dog. It's built low to the ground with dark curly hair, more hair over its eyes.

It runs off, and I hold out my hand. The dog comes back. Almost I laugh as it jumps on my lap.

My hand—strokes it. I can feel the warmth of its body through its fur. I pause, and the dog looks up at me. Behind the hair are big brown eyes. Eyes that plead for approval, for love.

Whose dog are you, I want to ask. A name. I should give it a name.

But if I give it a name, I give the blackshit a handle to my heart. I saw what they did to Ugly Doris's pet swallow.

And the dog, I remember—

—I picked up the dog and held it in my arms as I stood.

I felt this thing in me: love.

This threat: love.

This handle on my feelings: love.

If there is something I love, there is something the blackshit will use to control me, to hurt me. This is what I thought before I threw the dog into the motionless blades of the compost shredder.

It cried. The dog cried until I moved the wheel. Now neither of us could feel.

My hand—oh, how I remember how that dog felt.

And the beating. I remember that. I remember the beating. The dog belonged to a guard, and I was strapped naked over the drum in the House of Pain.

What was the House of Pain? That's what the monsters used to call Charles Laughton's laboratory in *Island of Lost Souls*.

I remember wanting to be beaten. Begging God to let them beat me to death. I killed someone's dog and wanted to die for it—

Soon the whipping drove everything from my mind. Before that flaming pain was driven my guilt, my pain, my feelings, my awareness.

Blessed dark.

I push the bag into the passenger seat and face the front.

The Now Road. This minute I am in flight. This minute I am sitting in the town of Lincoln.

The other electric's tail lights vanish around the curve in the road. The blood is pounding in my head.

Rage. White hot rage.

"Aubry Cummings."

I spit out the name. It is a curse. There is a thread of memory. My father watching the television, saying "I just hope that bastard Cummings is watching."

Aubry Cummings.

My father hated Aubry Cummings.

The old man's image is in the darkest shadows of my mind. Aubry Cummings and his works have hovered over my existence like some nightmarish parasite, sucking the warmth and love from my life, feeding upon it like a cancer, leaving behind darkness, pain and despair.

My father hated Aubry Cummings.

Cummings killed him, killed his wife, made him rear his son in the dark like a miser hiding his coins.

Because of Cummings my father was denied the love of his own father.

In *El Cid* the king's champion lay bleeding to death on the floor, saying to his daughter, "Avenge me as my son would. Don't let me die unavenged."

Don't let me die unavenged.

I turn on the headlamps, grip the steering wheel, and ease the electric onto the road. The vehicle whines as it climbs up into the mountains toward the east and New Hampshire.

If I never accomplish anything else with my life, except to kill Aubry Cummings, I will be satisfied.

Wardate: 17:18-9AUG2033
Downlimit: -74223:39:22

24

I leave Herbie Dyar's electric in the trans station parking lot in Claremont. From there I hitch a ride on an empty long haul fan south to Brattleboro. In Brattleboro I pay a teenaged boy to purchase me a ticket to Boston with his number. I stay on the trans until the conductor registers the tickets.

At the station in Greenfield I leave the trans, hitch a ride east to Keene, and in Keene pay another citizen to purchase me a ticket with his number. Trans passage to Laconia, two stops beyond where I get off in Franklin.

I walk the distance from Franklin to Webster, State District of New Hampshire. Webster. The home of Aubry Cummings.

On the town line there is a sign claiming Webster as the home of Aubry Cummings. The sign has seen much abuse. I move off of the main road and hike through a field of dead weeds to a clearing on a hilltop overlooking the town.

Webster is a new town. One of the Compact's planned villages, MAC-designed for maximum production at minimum expenditure of energy and environmental impact.

In my studies I have absorbed the projection principles upon which such towns are designed, constructed, and governed. There are five facilities in Webster manufacturing electronic components, each facility serving as the center of a target composed of park and woodland greenbelts alternated with belts of residences. Each residence is small compared to the ancient houses in West Ellen. They are tailored to the temperature, the position of the sun, and to the minimum space and privacy needs of MAC-designed families of four.

The five targets are grouped around a complex that contains shopping, service, education, transportation, recreation, and town government facilities. There is nothing in town that is not within walking distance. Webster has very few cars. There are no chimneys; nothing being put into the air.

Webster, New Hampshire sucks.

What I wouldn't give to see just one of those rambling white frame houses with attached horse barns, brick chimneys belching white smoke into the sky. A West Ellen house. Houses you can call homes.

Webster really sucks.

Surrounding the five factory targets is a single, wide greenbelt that includes the hilltop upon which I am standing. Beyond it are MAC-designed and operated farms.

I squat, wrap my arms around my knees, and study the layout. The plan of the town doesn't seem to include housing a notorious government official and his security. The only vertical takeoff pad that I can see is part of the public transportation facilities in the center target.

Cummings needs his own facility. The only places available are the farms. I get to my feet and strain to see. Only the farms to the sides of the town are clearly visible. Those behind me and directly across the village from me are obscured. The farms on the sides seem to be nothing more than farms.

I turn around, leave the clearing, and walk into the shadows of an evergreen forest. There is the familiar odor of pine, but the trees bother me. They are too perfect, too well-spaced. I snicker at the thought of 2.7 birds per tree in a computer designed forest.

Minutes after leaving the clearing I see a metal mesh fence. Immediately I squat behind some brush. I study the fence. Signs every few meters warn that the property beyond is under the protection of the government of the Compact of Nations, and to keep out.

Beyond the first fence is a second. The second fence is clearly marked as being electrified. Beyond the electrified fence is a narrow road and more forest.

Between the two fences is a single row of green metal posts. Each post has a double row of dark spots aimed at the posts on either side of it. They are sensors of some sort. I look at the trees nearest the fence. All of the trees have been carefully limbed. On the ground between me and the fence, there are rocks, dead branches, the rotting trunks of fallen evergreens.

Almost two meters in front of me is a table-sized rock. It is not a particularly unusual rock. There is just something about the way it sticks out. Five meters to the left of the rock, equally distant from the fence, is a brown clump of weeds. Five meters to the right of the rock, equally distant with the weeds and the rock from the fence, is a rotted log. It is a very old log in a very young forest.

Quietly I move to my right until the log is between me and the fence. Five meters to the right of the log, in line with the weeds and the rock, is another rock. The spaces between the two logs, between the log and the rock, and between the rock and the weeds is clear. Another row of sensors.

There has to be some kind of threshold limit built into the sensors, otherwise they would trigger every time a leaf or a branch falls or when a squirrel runs past.

I close my eyes. Examine first the entire perimeter. And don't think in two dimensions. I smile thinking that it will be a pleasing irony if the man who finally managed to kill Aubry Cummings was able to do so because of his knowledge of disciplinary projections.

I begin backing away through the evergreens.

Wardate: 17:18-9AUG2033
Downlimit: -74220:17:11

23

Two hours later I stand on the walk across from the main gate. The electrified fence encloses most of the site, but only where trees hide it from casual view.

In the open parts the perimeter consists of a high fieldstone-and-wrought iron wall, the iron serving as ornate grids filling the openings in the stone. A tiny creek crosses the site. It enters and leaves the property through rows of small diameter pipes cemented into the wall.

It is still cold.

There are a few heavily-bundled tourists at the front gate, one or two taking pictures. A few dejected protesters wearily haul their signs, exhausted at trying to halt the inevitable with a slogan and a piece of cardboard on a stick.

At the tiny gatehouse there is a single brown-uniformed guard who pleasantly answers the tourists' questions. Far beyond the gatehouse is a modernistic structure that looks like a stack of flat planes, bristling with solar panels.

Next to the dwelling are parked three high-altitude aircars. Between the house and the gate the flag of the Compact of Nations hangs limply from a silver flagpole. There are no newspeople among the tourists.

This stinks. The whole thing stinks.

I turn my back on the front gate and walk down the drive toward the greenbelt street. The security around the site is a joke. It might be sufficient to hamper a burglar, if the burglar isn't very bright. But it can't protect against the kinds of enemies that would be brought against an official of the Compact.

There are any number of positions outside the perimeter that cover the grounds. One person with a rifle could put the entire site under siege. With something heavier a team could reduce the house to rubble within a few seconds.

There is no vertical takeoff pad.

If Aubry Cummings lives there, he is a fool. If Aubry Cummings lives there, MAC III is incompetent. Neither is true, and the old man does not live there.

I am murder with no victim to absorb my rage; death all dressed up and no place to go.

I am walking the greenbelt street to the main road, heading toward Franklin. Where I am going, and why, are mysteries.

A district police cruiser approaches from the opposite direction. My mind is loose from my body, and I am automatically paralyzed. The blackshit is here, Thomas Windom/Mills. What is our story? Why are we here? Walking?

No place to run; no time to run.

They see me.

The blackshit in the passenger seat grins and waves as the cruiser passes.

The wind washes over me. I turn and follow the cruiser with my gaze until it vanishes around the curve in the beltway. I notice that my right hand is in the air, waving.

My heart is pounding. I turn and continue walking toward Franklin. Beyond a group of designer trees and manicured shrubs I pass a vandalized roadside phone booth.

I can't kill him. His neck is out of my reach. The house—the town—decoys.

I see what I am doing for the first time. In broad daylight I'm walking down an open road with a pocket full of bad papers.

The blackshit has a description of me. Any kind of check and I'm nailed.

I look back at the telephone booth. What is the number Rhona gave me? "Nine nine two seven three." Cover the lens first; dial nine nine two seven three; leave the handset off the hook, hide until the phone rings, answer and do what I'm told.

Another police cruiser fans by. It passes and I go back to the booth. The camerea lens is shattered.

I feel dizzy. I lean against a corner of the booth, my shoulders against the shattered plastic windows. Random jabs of thought knife through my mind.

—If I wanted to arrest someone—someone who required an entire squad of blackshit to subdue—about the last thing I'd do is order Herbie Dyar to perform the arrest and to guard the suspect until the police arrive.

The phone booth.

A few pieces of a puzzle seem to hint at how they might go together. There is something between anger and humiliation in me.

And relief. The sense of a new threat.

I look at the phone. Someone has done a job on it. The door to the currency box, scarred and twisted upon its hinges, is still secure. The thief had obviously taken out his frustration at his failure to open the cash box upon the phone itself.

The screen is smashed, and all but two of the numeral buttons are missing their covers. The metal speaker grill is dented and the silver code entry button is dangling by a ribbon cable.

I drop two quarter-note pieces into the coin slot. The ready tone shows that the phone is still working. I speak into the grill, "Voice call."

A new ready tone comes on. I listen to the tone as I look at the dangling code entry button. I could give the number for Dyar's Variety. It's strange how I reach a conclusion before I can work out the paths leading to the conclusion. There is no arrest warrant. Or, if there was, it is no longer in effect.

—The silver code entry button is dangling from a ribbon cable.

A ribbon cable.

I hold the assembly in the palm of my hand. Even now the button is warm.

—The button is warm.

All of the silver buttons are warm. On every telephone, on

every terminal. Just like the silver plate they had me put my hand on at Outcasters. Just like the silver button on the coder when I took my personality profile. Just like the silver button on the telephones in the home of my mother and father.

—Daddy would supervise as I called Mommy on the other phone, the black buttons cold, the silver button warm.

I finger the dangling code entry button. The ribbon cable into the back of the assembly looks like it contains at least fifty color-coded conductors.

Everybody is wired. Even me.

I bounce the assembly with the silver button on my palm. I close my eyes tightly as I hold the assembly in my left hand and press the silver button with my right, cutting off the ready tone.

A single function switch doesn't need fifty wires running to it. Two wires operating a switching circuit is all it needs. Maybe a third if you're a safety fanatic and want a useless ground, and god the silver button—all of the silver buttons—are sensor plates.

Identification modems.

IDMs. Chemical composition of perspiration, body oil, electrical impulses—

The nonsense words the woman had me read while my hand was on the silver box. Voice print identification—

A monstrous web of signals, fields, and wires spreading over half of the planet, all leading to MAC III. *Everybody is wired.*

Even the stuff Merle Sawyer had given me. The books, the lesson plan—

MAC fed me the books I had studied. MAC kept me at Outcasters while the others received their citizenships. It kept the blackshit away from me as long as I did what it wanted, learned what it wanted me to learn.

Right now MAC knows where I am.

As long as I follow the path MAC wants, it stays in the background. When I strayed by wanting to settle in West Ellen, dropping my studies, it ran me out of town—sent a message to Herbie Dyar and goosed Thomas Windom back into the nightmare. One rogue circumstance smacked back within limits.

I yank the sensor assembly from the telephone and throw it out into the road. I walk to the little park beyond the booth. Shifting my bag from left shoulder to my right, I talk out loud as I look at the trees and flowers.

"What do you have planned for me, MAC? Where do I fit into the worldplan? What cog do I turn? What in the hell makes you think you can make me turn it?"

Edging the flower beds are real red bricks placed side to side on their ends. I swing my foot at one of the borders and loosen four of the bricks with the first blow. I kick again, then pull the four bricks out of the ground.

Three bricks are in the crook of my left arm, the fourth brick is in my right hand. I stand on the side of the road, waiting. A gray aircar fans by, the passenger frowning at me. A red aircar follows, two children shouting at me from a window as it passes. A bus. Two more passenger vehicles.

A black police cruiser fans toward me. The brick from my right hand flies into the air. It tumbles slowly as it traces its arc. When it reaches the proper height off of the road's surface, the police cruiser's windscreen smashes into it.

As the driver tries to regain control of his vehicle, I launch my second brick. The cruiser slows as it whirls around and runs up on the opposite embankment. The blackshit on the passenger side leaps out, rolls once, and comes to his feet holding a hand weapon pointed at me. I launch my third brick at him.

The brick seems to be frozen in the air in front of my eyes. Strange, the feeling in my chest.

Cold.

Not unpleasant. Just cold.

Out there is a voice, calling me names. Another calling an ambulance and the police garage.

Warm wind washes over me. A car fanning by.

A voice; loud; authoritative: "Asshole! Can't you see there's been an accident?"

Another voice; loud; defensive: "Don't call *me* asshole, asshole! You don't have any warnings up—visual, electronic, *nothin'*! Maybe I ought to take your number."

"You don't have the sense of a fuckin' eggplant, do you?

Didn't you see me bending over this man? My partner standing in the road flagging you down? That cruiser up the embankment?"

Fade.

Just let it fade.

Into endless bleached vistas. My eyes are closed and it is white. It seems as though that's the way it has always been when I close my eyes. I don't remember what dark looks like. I don't know if dark exists.

I can breathe, but I feel so weak that I might as well be paralyzed. I heard no shot; felt no slam. Interesting weapon. It seems made to answer so many requirements. It works, it doesn't hurt, it doesn't appear to pollute the environment. I wonder how MAC will use the larger versions.

Another warm wind.

Black figure in the white fog.

"Look at this. Remember that bad warrant that was put on the wire last night? This is the bird."

A second figure in black drifts in, reaches down, takes something from an outstretched hand. The black figure studies what it retrieved then tosses it down. "Yeah, but so what? That order was rescinded as soon as it was sent out."

"Well, now we have him with a whole new kettle of turds. Yessir."

A grinning face moves into my field of vision. It wags a finger at me, back and forth. "Little boy, it's not nice to throw bricks at the policeman. Policeman get cross and go thump, thump."

Inside I smile.

Adjust *this* circumstance, MAC.

Wardate: 17:18-9AUG2033
Downlimit: -74198:32:29

22

It is complete, this whiteness. No images, no sounds, no sensations, no feelings. I think of the whiteness of THX 1138's prison. But my prison is different. I have no furniture, no prison mates, not even a reason to leave.

This is a weapon of promise for the coming war. Very effective. Very sanitary.

There is the sound of a voice. It is angry, impatient, frustrated. It is a blackshit cop who wants to know why a kid can throw bricks at him, racking up a brand-new thirty-thousand credit police cruiser, and be bounced five minutes after charges are filed.

Another angry voice. It explains that orders are orders. "DOP." That's the reason: DOP.

Department of Projections orders, clown.

DOP.

"It isn't right," says the first voice.

"Are you one of those Seekers of Justice?" asks the second voice.

Tough shit, thinks Thomas Windom.

Angry footsteps leaving, a door hissing shut.

Is it possible for a citizen in the Compact of Nations to achieve the age of my arresting officer and not understand about the Department of Projections?

"Bring him up," orders a third voice.

A tone that I hadn't noticed before seems to lower in pitch. As it goes down the whiteness darkens, filling in with images, colors. I feel sick to my stomach. I don't know if it is a side effect of the arresting field being used on me, fear, or both.

There is a blackshit cop, a captain, sitting on the edge of a gray metal desk, his arms folded and resting on his potgut. He is looking at me. To his left and much nearer to me is a woman in civilian clothes. Peach colored suit and cape. White blouse. She wears a brimmed cap cocked over her right eye. Her hair is reddish blond. The brim of her hat—its shadow—hides her eyes.

She has peach color on her lips, too.

"How do you feel?"

Her lips didn't move. To my right there is a man—another blackshit. He has a stethoscope around his neck and an electronic instrument in his hands.

I can move. I sit up. Very sore, a headache. "My muscles hurt. My neck."

"Don't tense up against it. Just let it hurt for awhile, and it will go away."

That's the story of my life, blackshit. Just let it hurt awhile and it will go away.

The cop with the stethoscope gets to his feet and leaves the room, closing the door behind him.

I am sitting in a chair. The peach colored lips smile softly. "My name is Salena Booth."

She pauses, looking at me. She expects me to act like this is some sort of social gathering? Hello, I'm Thomas Windom, pleased to meet you? Do you come here often? The service sucks, but the food is really, really bad. Fuck you very much, Salena Booth.

I do a lot of editing before I speak. There is a large blackshit cop watching me. "You already know my name."

"Yes."

"What do you do, Salena Booth?"

"Do?" She grins. "What do you mean?"

"You know. For the greater glory of the Big Equation, the Big Picture, the Big Plan. Are you the one who tells me that this has all been a long test? Like some science-fiction funnybook, that I've been in training since I was born, and now the fate of the world hinges on my next move?"

She laughs. Her head slowly shakes back and forth. "I forgot. You're still a child, aren't you?" Her shoulders give a tiny shrug as she stands. "As for the fate of the world, don't overrate your importance. That has been a closed issue for a number of decades. As to what I do, I do as I'm told."

"Why?" I am about to explode. All of this—why? To me—why? "Why? I need to know why; if I've been led through it all, why? If everything I've done was manipulated into me by MAC, why?"

"No one really knows how much of your history was accident, the choice of others, your choice, or the results of manipulation through circumstance adjustment. No one knows why your life went the way it did, nor why its future will be what it will be."

"The *computer!*" I push myself to my feet. "MAC III knows."

"No. MAC III is a machine. It knows nothing."

"Somebody must know why things are done the way they are. *Some*body!"

"Perhaps one day you will be shown what the peejays—the projectionists—in DOP call The Shrine To Why. It is said that one look at The Shrine To Why is sufficient to cause the observer never again to ask that question."

"I was not joking, Citizen Booth."

"Neither was I, Citizen Windom."

"Citizen?"

She withdraws an orange envelope from her purse, opens it, and pulls out a small blue and gold booklet. She hands it to me and I open it. It is a citizenship warrant made out to Thomas Windom. Number 2077782680.

"You get to keep it if you do exactly as I say."

I look at the police captain. With a start I realize that I feel much closer to the blackshit than I do to the civilian. I am reluctant to follow Salena Booth.

The captain has thinning black hair, is overweight, and has a red face. He laughs as he stands up and walks around his desk to the other side and sits down. "Don't look at me, kid. I thought I was going to be an astronaut."

* * *

Where is right? Where is wrong? Is it true that the meaning of life is justice in a garbage grinder? If only assholes seek justice, why do we all feel the loss when injustice is committed?

Do we all feel the loss?

"What do you want, Thomas?" Salena Booth asks me this before the airplane leaves the ground. I look out of the window, not really seeing the other airships parked and moving around the taxiways. Above the field, Boston's sky is clear. What do I want?

"I don't know."

"I think you do."

I look at her, wanting to smash that smug expression on her face. "Then if I do know, I don't know how to put it into words—"

It is as though a giant, invisible hand is pushing me back into my seat. In an instant of panic, I realize that I have never been in an airplane before. It is taking off.

I watch through the window as the ground passes by in a blur. In moments we are far above Boston. It would be exciting to learn how to do this. To fly. The horizon is obscured by haze. The airship turns, blinding light fills the window, and we begin to head toward the ocean. The tightness in my chest climbs.

"Why are we going out over the ocean?"

"I suppose it's on the way to New York."

"But why over the ocean?"

Salena Booth's eyes are closed, her head resting against the back of her seat. Her lips move. "Are you capable of having faith that the pilot, the airline company, and the appropriate regulating agencies have good reasons for routing and flying this craft across the water?"

"I just wondered why."

"Is that an important word to you: why?"

"Wh—" My face becomes very hot. I turn away and look out of the window. "I don't know. It's just—" The words just aren't there. What do I attach to these wild angry feelings? "It's just that a lot of things would be easier to bear if I knew there were good reasons for them. That's all. What's wrong with that?"

"What's good enough to you, Thomas?"

"Good enough? Good enough for what?"

She smiles, her eyes still closed. "Good enough for it all. What reason could the universe give you that would make it easier for you to have been what you were where you were? Tell me the why that would make up for it all."

The why. What would make up for it all? I could kill Cummings, torture him to death and scrap his machine, but that wouldn't make up for even a little piece of my own hate. What must the whole world claim as a debt against Aubry Cummings?

The why. I know history. I've studied it and how it relates to the present until my head is a screaming cauldron of facts, figures, reasons, excuses, rationalizations, articles of faith, hope, charity, and fantasy.

The why. "There isn't any. Is that what you want to hear? There isn't any."

I look at her. The woman in peach is asleep or pretending to be asleep. For a second I am angry at her, but I let the anger pass. She is very beautiful with her face relaxed. Her cape is open. Salena is very attractive. I notice something for the first time. It is just a minor thing—a shade of tone difference in the skin of her left hand. It is a cosmetic cover for an artificial limb.

I study her face again. There is the hairline of a scar below the right corner of her mouth. Another on the bridge of her nose. The longer I stare at her face, the more scars I see. Hundreds and hundreds of almost invisible scars. It is as though her face had been skillfully reassembled after it had been first shoved through a meat grinder.

I look out of the window. There is a solid cover of clouds beneath us. I have this sense of riding on the hands of a clock that were set in motion a hundred billion years ago.

* * *

Strange things touch me. They are things I thought impossible, yet wished for. They are things I thought existed only in the darkest corners of my nightmares, yet wished for.

I have seen New York City from the air. From horizon to horizon there are streets and buildings divided by wide swaths of forest. The strips of forest almost remind me of the fire lanes in the forests of the Green Mountains.

How many humans must there be down there? It is fearful to be entering such a concentration of humanity.

The air is crisp, fresh, charged with the sounds of motion. The trans from the airfield is crowded. Salena points toward a stand of passing trees.

"Behind the trees. Do you know what that is?"

There is a building I can see. It is a raw-looking, ugly thing, made from truncated pyramids wearing their skeletons on the outside. I lose sight of it as we enter a tunnel. "No. What is it?"

"The Steel Palace."

"What's that?"

Salena studies me for a moment. The way she studies me makes me aware of every breath I take. "It's the residence and offices of the President-General."

I return my gaze to the window even though we are still in the tunnel.

"Where are we going?"

"To the heart of the Compact of Nations Government Complex, the Lowell Center. It houses the Department of Projections."

I stiffen. "The machine—MAC?"

"Yes. It's located deep underground. Do you want to see it?"

Tell me, Thomas Windom, how do you feel about meeting your maker? Do I want to see it? Do I?

"I don't know. Yes—no."

Out of the tunnel, light startling me. Salena points again to the right of and beyond the Steel Palace. "The silver-blue building. The one that looks like a knife blade?"

"Yes?"

"That's the Lowell Center."

I close my eyes and rest my forehead against the window,

the motion of the trans gently rocking my head against the coolness. For a moment I want nothing more than to wrap the simplicity of West Ellen around me. I almost panic, almost run, almost give in to the desire to fight my way free.

There is a desire to be free of something else, too. Fate? Destiny? Meghan French once said that teenagers tend to see their lives cast in dramas of intense experience. She laughed when she said that, and I had no desire to be included among those ignorant children who blanket their realities in melodrama. That's why I never told her how I felt about anything.

You want drama, Miss French? How about a seven-year-old boy standing in a puddle of piss hammering lumber up a man's ass? How about crushing a poor addict's head in order to steal his permission to live?

Can I understand the answers contained in the machine beneath that silver-blue knife blade?

Do I want to understand?

"Citizen Booth, I want to see The Shrine to Why."

She does not laugh."

Wardate: 17:18-9AUG2033
Downlimit: -74193:14:08

21

The Shrine to Why is in a huge space surrounding the emergency operations center on C Level three floors below ground level. The shrine takes up most of the level. From the floor to just below the overhead light panels the space is packed with film cabinets. I follow Salena Booth as she works her way through one of the narrow paths giving access to the cabinets. She stops and faces one of the walls of drawers. She opens one, reaches in, and pulls out a transparent sheet of film.

"There are fifteen layers of micromulsion that make up this card; each layer contains two thousand page-images of information, or thirty thousand pages per card. There are six thousand cards per drawer and roughly nine thousand drawers in these stacks, which comes to around one and a half trillion page-images of information. If you could absorb and retain a million pages per day, it would take you over four thousand years to do it all."

I walk past her to an intersection. I look and see nothing but stacks of drawers. I open one and it is filled with the pinkish transparent cards. Without looking back at her I ask, "What's it for?"

"Eleven years ago there was an order issued by the department. Carrying out the order resulted in the death of a high official in the Soviet government. Once this was discovered by the press, the Committee on Compact Security went berserk trying to find a villain to hang out to dry. All government employees and departments are bound by the

Compact Constitution to carry out properly processed orders from DOP, regardless of the nature of the order. But the committee demanded to know why the execution order had been issued. Instead of fighting or ignoring the order, Secretary Cummings ordered a hard copy made and delivered to the committee. He gave them just what they asked for. This is the copy."

Rows and rows of stacked drawers. The committee never asked why again. I bet that Cummings was there in the committee's hearing room as the copy was delivered. It's his kind of joke.

I let my fingers glide over the surfaces of the file drawers. Beneath my fingers is every aspect of known reality related to every other aspect of known reality in reference to a single circumstance adjustment. Given the goal of preserving human civilization, and given the limitations of possibility, humanity, technology, and efficiency, *this* is why Comrade So-and-So was deleted in a particular manner, and at a particular time, and location.

I have wasted my life trying to find out why. Why Outcasters, why the world, why me. Whatever made me suppose that I could absorb and understand the answers?

I lean back against one of the walls of drawers and look at Salena. She is resting with her right shoulder against the opposite wall, her arms folded.

"So what do I do now?" I fold my own arms. "Do I just take it all on faith?"

"No one's been able to come up with an alternative."

"What about fighting it?" Heat fills my face. Sometimes I cannot accept the amount of anger in me. "What about fighting it just for the hell of it!"

She leans her back against the opposite wall and looks up at the light panels. "You already know the answer to that. Every blow you strike will have been either planned or planned for. In fighting against the Compact, either your moves will be without effect or you will be helping the Compact."

I look at the floor. I know what she said. But now I know it deep in my gut instead of just around the fringes of my awareness. Now I can feel the wires. Bless you, Eva Messer, we are all wired.

"Are you aware, Thomas, that not needing to know why is one of the definitions of freedom?"

I add another bitter laugh to my collection. "Yeah." I push myself away from the wall of reasons for killing some Soviet official. "You expect me to treat MAC like some kind of god, doing *His* will like some kind of fanatic?"

"Until you meet the real thing, Thomas, MAC is the closest thing to God that you will ever see." Her eyebrows rise. "Are you familiar with the Book of Genesis in the *Old Testament*?"

"I read it. The Garden of Eden, Noah and the Ark, right?"

She pushes away from the wall of drawers and walks past me. I follow her out of the stacks to a heavily guarded bank of elevators. Salena points above the elevator doors. In crude, spray-painted, scarlet letters appears:

"The end of all creatures of flesh is in my mind;
the earth is full of violence because of them.
I will destroy them with the earth."

"A few Consolidationist terrorists managed to force their way in here about twelve years ago, back when Cummings was the Secretary of Projections. They were the ones who painted that."

It is an obscenity on the wall's pristine ivory and silver. "God talking to Noah. The story of the great flood, right? Why is it still there?"

Salena lowered her hand. "Secretary Cummings's orders. The way the story goes is that when Cummings saw it he said to leave it; that it would help those entering the elevators to remember that the Compact of Nations is our ark."

The elevators are the access to the remainder of the Lowell Center's underground levels—down to where God lives? If I remember the superstition correctly, isn't it Satan who lives underground?

Wardate: 17:18-9AUG2033
Downlimit: -72441:32:44

20

July.

From the window of my apartment in the Lowell Center I can clearly see four Wardate signs. Above them airships and fancars move from one side of the sky to the other. Below them wheelies, trans cars, and humans scramble and crawl across and through the city.

They are not aware.

My first summer at Outcasters I found a dead mouse on the road to the Green Machine. The flies dispersed as I approached. The flies were aware.

Their children, the maggots that filled the mouse's skin, did not notice as I picked up the mouse and tossed it into the hopper. They were not aware. They continued to eat until the blades chewed them into paste.

But the bacteria that fed upon the rotting flesh continued to do so through it all.

What is the significance of all this?

Am I looking for a miniature of the universe in a mouse's rotting corpse?

That is New York City down there. How many times at Outcasters had I tried to imagine this fantastic land? But look at all of the ants down there.

They are not aware.

I am afraid to leave my apartment in the Lowell Center.

I am aware.

* * *

My apartment. It is a large open room with areas devoted to preparing food, sleeping, recreation, and work. My apartment has a terminal. I ignore the terminal and watch old television movies for ten days.

Am I waiting to be told what to do?

Am I on strike?

I put off answers and wait.

Why do I feel so close to Captain Willard as he travels through a senseless nightmare on his mission up the river to kill Colonel Kurtz? Has it always been like this? Has it always been *Apocalypse Now*? Fighting, struggling against the unknowable toward goals without meaning within a universe that takes no notice of the contest. It makes no difference what we do?

From Captain Willard there is Willard and his pet rat, Ben. There is the rat that Victor Herman caught and ate in the ice of the Gulag. And the iceman, Charley, caught in the midst of his dreamwalk, finally meeting his god in the form of a helicopter. A cloud of the same helicopters rises above the palms of Nam as the Colonel tells them to put on the music. The Colonel is Robert Duvall, and I watch him as his men terrorize and kill the slopes. Then I watch him as THX 1138 as the world terrorizes him.

THX 1138 is still there. In the war movie Robert Duvall seems to be the only person who belongs there. For that reason he appears insane. In the underground world of the future, he seems to be the only one who is sane. For that reason he appears to be the only one who doesn't belong.

I see him in another movie. He is an astronaut who is angry and jealous because another astronaut will be the first person on the moon. It is all make-believe.

Make-believe too is the super-computer in *Colossus: The Forbin Project*. In many places it sounds as though the movie is talking about MAC. But it is not.

The movie computer is designed to do little more than to conduct the defense of one nation. Even so, it takes over the world to save it from itself. To rescue the world from fire, Colossus places the world in chains.

Collosus is too crude to be MAC. Collosus finds it necessary to threaten and blackmail to get the humans to do what it wants. MAC simply arranges circumstances until you want what it wants and you do what it wants you to do.

It is a good question, however: What will MAC finally do to save us from ourselves?

A few times I leave the apartment and wander the streets of the city. Twice I get on the trans. Once I travel all of the way to Bristol, but do not get out of the car.

I am free to go wherever I want, and free to do whatever I want. My problem is telling the difference between what I want and what MAC wants. The silent terminal squatting in my apartment knows the answer to that, but I will be damned if I will ask.

Of course, it knows that, too.

The movie I watch is a new one for me. It is a fantasy titled *Life With Father.* It is a comedy and I enjoy it. It is 1883 in New York; a time that never was in a place that never existed. The father, Mr. Day, I recognize as the butler in *My Man Godfrey,* another fantasy.

The mother is beautiful and very kind. Her big concern in life is to get her husband baptized. The oldest son in the movie, Clarence, is concerned with attracting the affections of a beautiful girl named Mary. He wants a new suit. The father and the two youngest sons are all concerned with the same thing: enjoying the family.

Mr. Day says to his son, "Clarence, there are things about women that I think you ought to know. Sit down—"

—I wake up on the floor.

The apartment is dark. The sky outside is the beginning gray of morning. My muscles are sore, there is a sharp pain in my left hand, and my head aches.

I push myself up on one arm. Dizzy; the taste of blood in my mouth.

The dim light from the window allows me to see the

devastation that is my apartment. It has all been ripped, broken, spilled, and smeared across the center of the floor.

I am frightened.

Where had I been? I don't know why I ask. I once spent six years there. I am insane. I was watching a movie—the one about the family—and here I am, sitting on the floor in the midst of my apartment's rubble.

I am insane.

I turn on a light. The wreckage appears worse with the light on. The television's wallscreen has been shattered. The terminal isn't damaged at all.

There is blood on the front of my shirt. In the bathroom I see the blood on my face. Somehow during my absence from reality I gave myself a bloody nose.

This headache is killing me.

There is a bruise on the right side of my forehead. I lean against the sink and spit blood into it. A mouthful of water to rinse out the taste. More water on my face.

I see him in the mirror. I see the child who lives for futile gestures; the illusion of struggle. Why is it so important for me to believe that I can believe that I am in control of this life of mine?

Look at me.

Look at me.

I set the chair upright before the terminal and sit down.

There is no point in again doing an inventory of my emotions or of my life's issues. I am tired. I reach out and hit the terminal's silver ID modem with my right fist. I lean back in the chair and watch the screen.

Tell me your will for me, machine.

Tell me what you want.

No more evasion, no more tricks with mirrors, no more bullshit.

Tell me what you want. Straight.

The screen comes alive.

There is no dramatic background music, no thundering voice. On the screen appears the introductory information concerning how humans can be modified to eliminate the need for terminals of any kind. The modification is called the Link. With it I can become a part of the machine.

In a way I am already a part of the machine. Ever since I was born I have been a part of it. With the Link, however, I can be an honest part of the machine.

No more bullshit.

Is that honesty worth anything to me?

Through the Link I will be issued orders and provided with whatever knowledge I will need to carry out those orders. Through the Link I can ask for knowledge and it will appear in my mind. The Link will be able to use every one of my senses, in addition to my conscious and unconscious minds, for its communications.

And for what purpose?

It is funny how I seem to go stupid at times.

I know the purpose, just like everyone in the Compact knows the purpose:

17:18-9AUG2033;

War;

Thinning out the herd;

Preserving a human future;

The deaths of four and a half billion men, women and children.

Wardate: 17:18-9AUG2033
Downlimit: -72397:01:40

19

The operation for the Link implant is like my nervous system giving birth without my body. A fluid is injected into a vein in my neck. In only moments I know that the fluid contains the Link—a microscopic robot made from some kind of vegetable matter. It lodges at the base of my brain and begins sending filaments to specific neural networks and branches.

As the filament contacts increase, I can see them.

I can see the filaments.

My sight is not with my eyes.

I can see inside myself.

I know the filaments are spreading, and I know they will reach their maximum influence in a few hours. I also know that it will not change me, it will not control me. I still control me. The Link is just what MAC said it is: a terminal.

It tells me there are things that need repairing.

Things about me; things in me.

Old business.

It tells me to get an air ticket for Peterborough, Ontario. A place sometimes called Petertown that I should not call Petertown because Mommy doesn't like the name.

I can refuse. I *know* I can refuse. But I also know there are a million tortures in the dark corners of my mind and that MAC can help me deal with them.

On my way out of the building, on my flight to Peterborough, I find that I automatically *know* who the other Links are. It is not something I can see; it is something I just *know*.

It is dangerous to talk to the other Links. That knowledge is in me as well.

That's it.

The white house at the end of Fowler street.

I stand on the sidewalk and examine the house, my faith in MAC's direction shaken. I do not recognize the house as the one in which I was born.

I turn about and look across the street. *That* house I recognize. Of course. I never got to see the outside of my own house. I wonder if the old woman who called in the blackshit on me still lives in the house across the street. It's a different color now: pale yellow with white trim.

There is a fantasy in my mind.

I knock on her white door and identify myself. "Greetings. I'm the little boy you turned in to the blackshit years ago."

She screams and drops dead from a heart attack.

While I play with the fantasy, the front door opens and a young woman ushers out a little girl in a party dress. They kiss, and the little girl runs down the steps and hurries down the street, her mother calling after her, reminding her not to run. The young woman looks at me for a second, turns and enters her house, closing the door behind her. I hear a dog barking. From far away I hear music playing. Birds singing.

This is all so unspecial. So ordinary.

I look back at the front door of what had once been my universe. It is such an ordinary front door—such an ordinary house. There are flat stones in the grass leading up to the front door. I walk them, my stomach knotted as I anticipate my mother and father still living in this house.

It's possible.

Maybe—

Before I can ring the bell, a strange man opens the door and looks down at me. He is skinny and has a large head. "Is there something you want?"

"Yes." My throat is so dry. "I used to live here. I suppose it would be too much—"

"Would you like to see the old place?" He steps back and holds out his hand. "Come on in. My name is Dave McCraken."

"Thomas Windom. Thank you." I am lightheaded as I walk past him into the hall.

The years strip away.

I look up the stairs. That was where I squatted and peered through the posts at Mommy and Daddy watching Aubry Cummings turn dead babies into burgers—

"Are you alright?"

"Alright?" I look at him. "Yes." I look past him into the living room. There is nothing in there that I recognize. It is so different with windows.

"Would you like to see the kitchen? Maybe the bedrooms upstairs?"

"The attic. Just the attic, please."

Dave McCraken looks embarrassed. He blushes and grins nervously. "I'd rather not take you to the attic. I'm sorry, but it's a terrible mess. My wife and I have spent months fixing up the rest of the house and the first visitor we get wants to look at the one place we haven't done over—"

"Please. I don't care how it looks. Please."

I follow him up, each step a reach into the past. We walk by the upstairs bedrooms to the end of the hall. He reaches up and pulls down the hidden staircase to the attic. The stairs are much smaller than I remember.

Dave gestures with his head. "There's really not enough room up there for both of us." He reaches out and flicks a switch, illuminating the stairs.

"Thanks." I climb the stairs into the oppressive heat of the attic. Boxes and junk have been crammed into the space. The windows are still painted black except for two small panes that have been replaced. The window I had opened is open now to allow the heat to escape. I see the woman's house across the street. I see—

—Can it be? The hole in the black paint? The hole through which I first saw Sky? Below it the crack between the wooden planks where the piece of paint hid.

A cobweb brushes my face and I use my hand to pull it away.

On the unpainted wall there is the corner of an old drawing tacked to the surface. On the brown paper is the top of a tree. The tree has flowers and a bird in it. I remember that the rest of the picture had a little boy standing in a field.

"We wanted a child."

I turn and see Mommy and Daddy standing next to my bed. I know they are ghosts—images created in me with the Link. But they are so dear to me. Can I touch them? Do they have substance?

The Link controls touch, as well. Mommy is sitting on the bed, my face buried in her lap, her hands stroking my hair. Daddy kneels beside me, his arms hugging me, his face buried in the back of my neck, kissing it.

"We love you. We love you so."

"I love you." Oh, there are so many things, so many blames, so many mistakes, so many harsh things I could say.

"I love you. I miss you so."

What is MAC that it would do this to me? What is MAC that it would do this *for* me?

Issues for another time.

This moment is for the smell, the sound, the sight, the feel of my mother and father.

Wardate: 17:18-9AUG2033
Downlimit: -72253:22:21

18

There is an airship at the military field east of Lindsay that takes me to the military field at Kingcome Inlet, Provincial District of British Columbia. I have never seen such mountains; such a lack of humans. There is a feeling like I had at the top of Stark Mountain, but it leaves me.

I am placed in the rear of a motor launch that takes me out into the ocean. There are three others in the launch, but they do not speak to me. After a few hours we approach a landmass. I know this is the southern end of the Queen Charlotte Islands. We will stop at Kunghit Island, and there I will pick up an underwater boat. No one will talk to me on that ship either.

I am an arrow that has been launched. Who talks to such a thing?

Death has finally found someplace to go.

It is partly a dream; partly a nightmare. I am participating in events of horrific consequence, yet I accept it. Does the Link suppress my self? Or is understanding all accepting all?

See the world in which I now stand? On this submarine there is only so much of anything. There is only so much air, food, water, energy, space. This world's population stands at one hundred and fifty-two men and women. They are trained to live in their world. They do not waste anything. Their world is designed to support one hundred and fifty-two at a specified level of life. If more than one hundred and fifty-two are in the world, a factor of stress is placed on the system. The equation must adjust. Either more must come from somewhere, everyone must get less, the civilization's time must be shortened, or someone must be eliminated.

It would be absurd to imagine half of the crew deciding their numbers were no longer relevant. The men and women in the forward half of the submarine use up their stores, have babies and more babies, and use up more stores. Things become more and more crowded. Soon there is no place left to go, nothing left to eat, no air left to breathe, no water left to drink, except in the aft end of the boat—the half that kept its numbers the same. But the equation can no longer adjust. There is no slack to take up, no sacrifice that can be managed. Humans need certain minimum things to live and to reproduce. If they become One Boat before the equation can be made to work, all of them die.

How would a sane person decide the problem? Here I am, a member of the aft end listening to the debate.

—You should see the pain in the eyes of those forward end babies. Just a couple of biscuits will fill those eyes with joy. What's a couple of biscuits to us?

—If we could each give up just a little space, the crowded conditions forward could be eased considerably. Who needs all of this space?

—You aren't choking are you? We have plenty of air. Well, they're choking at the other end of this boat! Do you want to be responsible for their deaths?

So clear.

On a submarine it seems so clear to me. If the aft end allowed the expansion, eventually the entire boat would die. Instead, when the aft end can assure itself victory, it attacks and eliminates the forward end crew in a manner that will not destroy the boat.

All we have in our larger universe is the thin film of our atmosphere. It surrounds a finite particle of mass. Within that film and on that mass, however, our billions are divided into the forward and aft ends. The Conservationists are planning the war that will reduce the numbers, making the equation of survival again a workable tool.

The Consolidationists want us to open our doors to the

hungry of the world, hoping that somehow someone somewhere will invent something that will save us all from reality.

It seems so clear on a submarine. There is a Link-supplied fact, however, that I turn over in my mind at least a thousand times a day during my voyage beneath the water. Sixty-seven percent of the boat's crew either belongs to or supports the Consolidationists.

I place my foot on China; Otherworld; the forward end of the boat. I see there a woman sitting in a lean-to by the ocean. The coast seems deserted, except for her. There are no birds, no insects. The vegetation is sparse and sickly.

The woman is looking in my direction with large dark eyes. She holds a baby in her arms. The expression on her face is a mixture of pain, betrayal, and anger. She does not move. Neither does her baby. They are both dead of starvation.

I head toward the smoky horizon. Beneath it is the job that needs doing.

Wardate: 17:18-9AUG2033
Downlimit: -71197:07:57

17

To kill not for revenge, not for hate, not for fear. To kill simply because that is the job that needs doing. There are no anguished whys screamed into the dark or at the sky. Every Link knows *why*.

I am standing in this dark little room in Ch'ao-an, Kwangtung province, People's Republic of China. I am waiting for a man. Our appointment was made decades ago.

Certainly the government recognized the population problem, and certainly the government instituted vigorous control methods. But they waited until there were over a billion Chinese before they began. China's equation was out of balance long before anyone knew that such equations existed.

The man's name is Leon Taksis. He is a chauffeur for the second deputy of the Soviet agricultural mission to the People's Republic of China. Leon is twenty-two years old and has no particular ambitions in life except for living well. His employment with the Soviet mission is a result of his mother's influence.

Leon's world is starving to death and is about to be consumed as mankind's payment for the past, but Leon only thinks about his vodka and the young Chinese woman he has sexual intercourse with twice a week on his day off. She is a secretary to a minor customs official. Her name is Contemplative Ice.

She is on the floor at my feet.

There is a beauty to this event.

Two nonentities, Leon Taksis and Thomas Windom, will

meet in the apartment of a third nonentity, Contemplative Ice. I will kill Leon and finish killing the woman. By so doing the aligned nations of the Eastern World Military Congress will become unaligned, the congress will become de-clawed, and the war to end the human race will be put off until 17:18-9AUG2033 at which time it becomes the war to save civilization.

Evidence showing that Contemplative Ice is a double agent has been carefully concealed in four different locations. Part of that evidence implicates Leon Taksis as a Chinese agent. The respective investigations of their deaths will create such an aroma that any attempt to launch a joint military effort will be doomed before it is begun.

But this is only the surface. The beauty is in the depth of detail. I bear a close physical resemblance to Leon Taksis. No one took notice of me entering the woman's apartment. By the time the woman realized that I was not Leon, she was unconscious.

Leon's mother is a clerk for the Soviet intelligence service's special unit that guards the integrity of their own computer systems. The unit's job is to make certain that MAC does not infiltrate Soviet computer systems. Since their computer systems, along with everyone else's, were infiltrated years ago by MAC, the object is to prevent this discovery of having any effect. Leon's shame will infect his mother, and in turn she will cast doubt upon the special unit's report outlining the extent of Compact control of Soviet military and civilian structures. The report will be discredited and the threat ignored.

Leon's employer, Mira Kopelov, has been trying for more than six months to sell the Chinese on a cooperative effort to increase agricultural production. Her plan, if put into operation, would almost double grain production utilizing virtually no more resources than are presently employed.

The mistrust caused by the spy scandal will end the agricultural talks, killing any possibility of the new methods being employed by the Chinese. The failure of the mission will discredit the use of the improved method in the Soviet

Union. MAC III has already adapted Mira Kopelov's proposal for use by the Compact of Nations.

The failure of the agriculturual mission will cause the Chinese delegation's leader to fall from grace, bringing shame upon his brother. His brother is a computer scientist. Years ago this computer genius attracted the attention of the government to the prospect of creating their own MAC system. For reasons that are unclear the government decided against continuation of the project. At present he once again has the attention of the government. Once again he is attempting to establish a MAC facility in the People's Republic of China. Due to the cloud of suspicion surrounding his brother because of the failed agricultural negotiations, the computer genius again will be ignored.

I follow out event chains, trying to guess which chain of events makes my mission a necessary one. It is more than just a hobby. It is a fascination. It's the same fascination I used to get as a child watching the ancient Sherlock Holmes movies as Sherlock reveals all of the items of observation from which he deduces that the noise just made outside his door was the footstep of a twenty-nine year old humpbacked Lutheran from Cairo, Egypt who is a cashiered general in the Salvation Army.

Given such-and-such set of circumstances, so-and-so will probably act in such-and-such manner.

The war must happen on time. Everyone who must die must do so on time and in the proper order. A Chinese computer scientist and a Soviet agricultural specialist will spend a great deal of time sadly shaking their heads, wondering why everything wrong seems to happen to them.

But I have seen them.

On the street, on the television, throughout history: I have seen the starving children.

The People give themselves an insane government with insane policies.

The People then starve.

Instead of demanding the removal of the insane government and policies, good hearts around the world chip in to subsidize the government and policies, entrenching them, helping to make starvation in that nation a permanent institution.

Forty years ago the center of starvation receiving the most publicity was Ethiopia. While gaunt babies stared with lifeless eyes at the fly-covered corpses of their mothers, the new government spent the equivalent of half a million credits on a party to celebrate their recent installation.

By the thousands the Ethiopians starved to death as the world wallowed in an altruistic orgy of hyped-up song-and-psalm singing, the profits piped into Ethiopia to ease the burden, and at the same time making clear that should they overthrow the government that is causing the starvation, the aid stops.

According to the documentaries, the Western hemisphere was buried in the din raised by a song called "We Are The World," the profits of which were to be turned over to African relief.

While the famous singers did their part to make starvation a permanent institution in Africa, the serene expressions of self-righteousness upon their faces seemed like something from a horror movie.

Not long after, Aubry Cummings delivered a speech before the assembly of the Congress of Environmental Sciences in Philadelphia. His speech was titled: "We Are The World: Save a Baby—Kill a Planet." A third of the way through his speech he was attacked by several members of the audience.

And the world watched as the relief food piled up and rotted on the docks while the Ethiopians starved to death in the middle of the desert.

I can look out of the window of the woman called Contemplative Ice and see them still: the starving children.

But I don't look anymore.

When I see those huge eyes in a tiny face looking back at me, I feel outrageously fat and sleek. I feel a need to explain to those eyes why—

Why.

But I have no courage when it comes to explaining projections, survival equations, and the necessities of the future to a baby's starving belly.

—A sound.

Feet on the landing.

That is Leon Taksis. Would he be proud to know how much his death will serve the future of the human race?

—The grating of a key in the lock.

I can see his heat through the door. I can hear and see his breath. The Link amplifies my senses.

The door handle turns, the door opens, and a pleasant-looking face looks around the edge of the door. The man has dark hair and very white teeth.

The Link is transmitting and receiving visible light comparisons.

"*Who are you,*" he asks me in Russian.

In this situation, if I respond by talking, Leon will talk. If he talks he will have time to think.

Voiceprint comparison completed, he is, without a doubt, Leon Taksis.

If I remain silent, Leon will act.

We depend upon Leon acting, not speaking.

I stare at him.

He opens the door all of the way and sees Contemplative Ice quiet on the floor. Although he carries a knife in his left hip pocket and is quite skilled in its use, in this situation he will charge blindly with absolutely no thought of how to go about it, or of the possible consequences.

As he screams, I duck below his outstretched hands, lean forward and spring at him, driving the heel of my hand into his heart. He crumples on the floor, stunned, but alive.

Contemplative Ice moans at the noise. I take Leon's knife from his pocket, open it, and thrust it into Contemplative Ice's heart. Checking to make certain that Leon is still alive, I open his mouth and let fall a clear drop of DF-61 stimulant. Leon gasps, and his eyes open. He looks like he is running out of oxygen. When he is at last still, I place the knife in his hand. In the lining of his hat I slip in a thumbnail-sized piece of microemulsion containing over three-hundred page images of what the Soviet Government considers highly-classified information. On the floor, already pressed with the woman's fingerprints, I drop a wad of ruble notes.

Lifting the woman's right hand, I grasp her fingers firmly and scratch them across Leon's left cheek, letting the projected image before my eyes guide the proper depth and angle. Letting her hand fall, I stand and tip over a chair, move a table, and crack the shade on a table lamp.

At the door I run the images of the fictitious struggle before my eyes, stopping to adjust the evidence against the image of the evidence as needed.

Leon came to deliver more information, but this time he had something special. It would require more money. A lot more money.

Contemplative Ice refused. She reminded Leon of their arrangement, not to mention the nocturnal fringe benefits, and urged him not to spoil a good thing. Stick to the agreement.

No. More money.

She pulled out the envelope—

—I take the envelope from my pocket, seal it, tear it open, and drop it on the floor—

—opened it, and withdrew the money, holding it out to Leon. Don't be a fool. Greedy ones do not get very far in the world.

Look who is calling me greedy. I'll tell you what. Give me the money, and when you come up with this much again, call me and I will turn over the information to you. Otherwise—

She took a pistol from a drawer, but before she could aim, Leon's knife was in her heart. She dropped the pistol and died, raking her fingernails down Leon's cheek. But the excitement was simply too much for Leon's weak heart.

I arrange her legs, check once more, and leave the room, closing the door behind me.

Wardate: 17:18-9AUG2033
Downlimit: -70909:10:00

16

Being a Link is like having a shield between myself and others. In a way it's like the movie, *The Invisible Man*. But my power is knowledge, not an ability to bend light. They see me, but who and what I am—who and what I might be—do not register. To my mind's eye the walls security officers place against me are nothing but holes. Their systems are nothing but collections of flaws. Their nets of regulations and procedures are ripped and tattered.

High in the Himalaya range in the pass north of Katmandu that crosses the Compact border into China, there is a forest of watchtowers. The Compact garrison guarding the pass consists of eight hundred soldiers stationed at Kodari. The Chinese garrison consists of forty-six hundred soldiers stationed at Nyenyam.

As I observe from the Chinese side, the feelings, the knowledge, the voices within me urge me to climb one of the watchtowers on the Compact side.

With modern weapons it takes only a small force to hold such a pass. Whatever transpires here, neither side will make a successful crossing into the other's territory. I cross to the Compact side without incident.

As I mount a watchtower on the Compact side of the border, I can guess this before it takes place. In the first watchtower across the border a Chinese soldier is standing guard. He or she is probably bored. Nothing ever happens here.

Perhaps he spends a moment asking his spirits why he was

the one chosen to be stationed in such an inhuman place. Maybe he will let his mind drift back to wherever it is that he calls home. He might be thinking of a girl when I shoot him. It doesn't matter. The shot will draw automatic fire from the Chinese side. The Compact guards will return the fire, and a border incident will be born.

Is it so that the Chinese can blow off some steam, easing the tension until the right moment? Is some situation in another area cooling down too fast? Is the soldier I am going to kill a significant figure in someone's life? When I kill him will his death cripple a scientist, drive a critical general insane, or—

Or is the key one of the other soldiers who will be killed in the incident? Myself, perhaps?

Perhaps all of our deaths serve the incident. Perhaps the incident itself is the key. Perhaps some critical components in the hectares of MAC's judgement have crisped and I am following the orders of a bum circuit.

It is only a joke. Admitting such a possibility would allow the slightest of cracks in my faith, and the vessel of my faith cannot afford a flaw.

Guessing at the event chains is beginning to appear grotesque to me. I allow the knowledge to meet my awareness. The answer comes. It is a military problem. The individuals are not important. Because neither side can either take or cross the pass quickly, the incident will rapidly become buried in protests, notices, threats, and diplomatic crotch cheese.

But the Compact soldiers at the pass are not prepared for an attack. There are too few of them and they are not standing a careful watch. As I make my way to the south and east, heading toward the Bay of Bengal and my subsurface transportation back to the DOP, many of the Compact soldiers will be killed. The incident will show the Chinese just how poorly prepared the Compact forces are. This information will flow upward and new tactics will seep down.

When the Wardate arrives, the incident will figure significantly in Chinese military planning. The Chinese will be prepared to fight a phantom enemy; one quite different than the one they will face. The Chinese army will underestimate the Compact Forces to the point of mass suicide.

What if Ivan, Vladimir, and Igor simply jump into a meat grinder?

They have a god they pray to in Katmandu. Its sole responsibility is the end of the world. Just an observation.

I ask and MAC informs me:
Her name is Spring Garden—the soldier I am about to kill.

Wardate: 17:18-9AUG2033
Downlimit: -66541:33:43

15

At night I sometimes flex my mental fingers. I can look through any lens, listen to any conversation, monitor any terminal. The only limit is MAC's knowledge of me and the degree of trust based on that knowledge. It is a perspective I have that seems to sort out entirely different sets of priorities for everything.

There is an absurd little man in Asia, a Soviet general, who has a plan. The plan seems so obvious to him, he cannot understand why he is unable to implement it.

For decades the doomsday machine has been a practical reality. The Soviet Union by itself has had the power to say: Give us what we want or we will end life on this planet for everyone.

A few hundred standard nuclear devices detonated any place on the planet will shroud Earth in dust, soot, and smoke for months. The lack of light will kill the oceans and crops and drop temperatures below freezing. What the nuclear winter will leave of the planet and the human race is too grisly to contemplate.

It is the Big Chill.

A few hundred nuclear devices make such a threat possible, and the Soviet general knows that his government has had many thousands of such warheads for decades. But the leaders laugh at his arguments. Even though a thousand Soviet citizens starve to death every day, they still laugh at the general.

There are a few, however, who do not laugh. For years the

general has carefully cultivated relationships that can aid him in accomplishing his purpose. Independent of his government and the association of non-Compact nations, he and his fellow conspirators can gain control of the weapons necessary. Then they can blackmail the Compact into opening trade and relaxing immigration restrictions.

The general and his friends know about MAC, and they know how to get around the use of MAC-infiltrated systems. With the same methods they can circumvent Soviet security.

That is why Link Salena Booth administered to the general a chemical vapor that burned out certain of the general's neural centers. Not only is it impossible for the general to control his conspiracy, it is almost as difficult for him to control his own bladder or put on his own socks. Three of the general's associates—the only three capable of taking over command of the conspiracy—have been neutralized. One has been arrested by the Soviet authorities, another committed suicide, and the third was killed in a Moscow mugging.

There are a few others whose attraction to the plan might have made them dangerous sometime in the future, but nowadays they see the images of the general, traitor that he is, the drool on his chin dribbling onto his chest, and wonder what ever had possessed them to entertain thoughts of such an insanity. This is why the prescription for the general was a fried brain instead of a tombstone.

And just look at this! The general was a good father and husband. Two children, both girls. He was a brilliant engineer and a beloved commander in the Red Army. His men still call him the Russian equivalent of "Daddy."

Drool on, Daddy, drool on.

Old joke:

FRICK: It's unfair!

FRACK: I think you have just discovered the meaning of life.

In an evening club for college students in Novosibirsk, an intellectual puts down his vodka long enough to say how disgusted he is. "Everyone is afraid to fight the Compact! Afraid!"

A few of the other students laugh nervously, and all of them turn away to become intensely engaged in vitally important conversations about nothing in particular.

It makes sense.

It's not something you can put your finger on, but everyone knows one or two persons who were radical in their views against the Compact and in how to fight the Compact.

Things happen to them. Automobile accidents, sudden insanity, death from a thousand dark corners. They change their views, or scandal brings them to the attention of the authorities, or they become swallowed by some new Jesus cult, or they become drug addicts, or—well, *things*. It's only a feeling, though.

Again the intellectual spits out his charge: "Afraid! Shit, you are *all* afraid! *All* of you!"

Some get up and leave.

"He's drunk."

"A raving paranoid."

"What kind of a dump is this?"

"Maybe a nice girl can marry him and straighten him out."

"He doesn't need a girl. He needs a poke in the nose."

—I see this thing sitting alone at the table: this intellectual/alcoholic; this rude, caustic, roaring anti-Compact agitator who is so frustrated with the content of his knowledge and the extent of his impotence that he will soon end his own life.

There is an event chain to peruse if I want to bother. Nineteen years ago, when it was determined that this fetus had the genetic loading to become addicted to mood-altering drugs, the baby was slated to follow the banner of extremist anti-Compact politics and was vested with a life-plan that fed off of both insanities, making him what he is today: a lurching advertisement against certain sentiments. His current nightmare was plotted for him long before he had his first bowel movement.

I need no sensors to understand what he is muttering beneath his breath as he sits there alone in the middle of a crowded room. I have been there so many times myself.

—This I know: this *thing* is coming.
—But you ignore it, ignore me, laugh at me!
—But it's *coming!*
—And you won't even listen.
—It's *so* unfair.
And Frack said to Frick, I think you have just discovered the meaning of life.

Did you know that one of our Links is a clergyman? He is an Episcopal priest. God talks to him. He says it is a different voice than MAC's. On his face he carries an expression of eternal serenity. Everyone can just tell that the priest sleeps at night like the safe and innocent.

During his career as a Link he has made eleven circumstance adjustments requiring the termination of selected individuals.

That's what I said: he murdered eleven men, women, and children.

He says he is saving lives. He says there are no conflicts in his soul.

I think he's crazier than hell.

Between assignments I work for Salena Booth as part of the operations security unit at the Lowell Center. We guard the electrical integrity of the computer system. I look at lights, read meters, and flip switches according to instructions. I have also been placed in an off-hours educational program where I study projections. The adjustment problems I am studying are all things that the computer does automatically.

There is no real point in my study of such problems, although it does fill my mind between assignments. They are huge, complex puzzles. It is a challenge to pit myself against these puzzles, imagining the fate of humanity hanging in the balance.

It fills my mind, and since the machine must work such problems, there is no responsibility left over for me. The best of all possible worlds.

Wardate: 17:18-9AUG2033
Downlimit: -64453:23:32

14

The orders.

I can keep them out of my mind if I choose. I am very good at that. There is always the screen, always the movies.

There is a 2019 remake of *Ship of Fools* starring Neal Pohltik as the dwarf. It is a pitiful attempt to update the story. The ocean-going ship becomes a vacuum shuttle between inhabited planets in a universe dependent upon improbable physics. The element of stress is an impending war with alien creatures heavy with slime-ed tentacle and tooth-ed jowel.

I watch the original movie *Ship of Fools*.

It is projected without color. Michael Dunn plays the dwarf, Karl. It is Karl who calls it a ship of fools. He is a smug, uninvolved, I-know-something-you-don't-know observer. It is 1933 and the passengers on the ship are wrapped in petty concerns, hand-me-down prejudices, and the politics of the path of least resistance.

I like to watch this film.

I do think of myself as a passenger on this ship called Earth. I see the petty concerns of my fellow passengers as we sail toward the stress factor of the Wardate. To them their concerns are not small. To me my concerns are not petty. Yet there is this feeling. I feel as though I have my own dwarf, observing me, commenting smugly upon my moves and feelings, laughing at me.

I punch up something at random.

"*—given a small blue and white button that said simply, 'I have seen the future.'*"

The colored picture is fuzzy, blotchy, strangely unreal. I punch for the beginning of the piece. It is a documentary called *The World of Tomorrow*.

I watch it. It is about the New York World's Fair of 1939—eighty-seven years ago. The theme of the fair is the future.

The future.

The ancients once took their sharpened sticks, gutted an animal, and read in its entrails this vision of tomorrow. The shabbiness, the hunger, the crowded despair of their present could be eliminated. A future pieced together by an all-seeing, benevolent prosperity would solve all problems.

There would be forests of skyscrapers, planned greenbelt villages, millions of vehicles moving the contented citizens along grooved paths of concrete and through the air in huge dirigibles. All would be clean, well-fed, modernistic, and wonderful. All it would take would be "informed democratic assent to central planning and a willingness to shake off the past."

The documentary follows the adventures of Mom and Dad and their two children, Babs and Bud, as they witness the promise central planning makes to tomorrow.

It is laughable, this child's view of the tomorrows that have become my yesterdays. Before the fair is half over a nation called Czechoslovakia is fed to a dictator named Hitler. Another nation called Lithuania is fed to a dictator called Stalin. The war that follows lays waste to continents and kills forty-five million humans.

Neither that war nor the series of subsequent wars make even the slightest dip in the population totals. Before forty years passes the world has more than twice as many mouths to feed. Within another ten years disciplinary projections, the MAC system, and the Compact of Nations has selected survival for human civilization.

The 1939 predictions were outrageous fantasy.

But they got their central planning.

A time capsule is buried at the fair. It contains "the brains of the world done up in a small package." It's meant to be opened in the year 6939. It's meant to be a message to those who inhabit the golden future from those in the hopeful past.

Five thousand years.

Five thousand years, less than ninety of which have passed. It makes me angry, this time capsule. Is it still there, buried in the ash dump sarcasm called Flushing Meadow?

Five thousand years.

It is such a presumption.

Those men in their baggy suits assumed that five thousand years from their day would see a United States of America. They assumed that there would still be a human race in five thousand years to paw over the artifacts of 1939. They assumed that in five thousand years there would still exist this continent in which their damned capsule rests.

Carnival of Fools. That's what I name the 1939 New York World's Fair. The Carnival of Fools.

Perhaps I am the dwarf.

I do have orders.

The world depends on me carrying them out.

I really ought to do something about them.

I punch up another movie. The Nazi publisher sailing the German ship *Vera* from Veracruz to Bremerhaven becomes the soldier/poet Cyrano de Bergerac—

—*you pug, you nob, you buttonhead!*

This actor, José Ferrer, is such a wonder.

—then he defends the accused mutineers of the *Caine* who eventually learn that right is wrong, that the obvious is not the true, and that the villain is the good guy after all and that they should feel like shit about what they did, and—

It can't all be for nothing.

It can't all be for nothing.

It can't all be for nothing!

My orders—

These—

My orders are to go to Argentina and to kill Manuel Ortega.

Wardate: 17:18-9AUG2033
Downlimit: -64381:00:09

13

Where do I hide from this? In my mind, where do I hide?

It is raining.

It is not within me to say that I just won't do it. There is too much at stake. But every step, every breath, is panic.

I do not get on the trans. Instead I walk the streets of New York. I find pieces of ancient sidewalk peering out from between the gleaming layers of nonskid plastic.

What burdens did they carry, the ones who walked these old blocks? This day, in between the office workers, visitors, and shoppers trying to stay dry as they hurry from someplace to someplace else, the ancient blocks of crumbling concrete hold a few soaked demonstrators. Their shoulders hunched against the rain, their signs demand that the authorities avert their plans to destroy this historical landmark.

I bend my neck back and look up into the dirty rain. There are some buildings in the city that I recognize from the 1939 World's Fair documentary. This is one of them. The Empire State Building was brand new when the documentary was made. Now it stands, abused and neglected, surrounded by shiny knives of plastic, glass, and metal. Workers are preparing to demolish the structure.

The demonstrators are few, wet, and short-tempered. The demolition workers and the blackshit cops ignore them, as does everyone else who passes by. If MAC wants the building demolished, it will be demolished. The protestors are there to make certain that it is demolished.

If I were dead, what would be the importance of anything?

It would all be over. The pain, the doubt, the fear, the sense of unbelonging, the murdering would all be over.

Say, for example, that I am dead when human civilization destroys itself. What would it be to me then? What is that to a dead man? Nothing.

Yes, but what if everyone who has an unpleasant part in saving human civilization begs off through suicide? In that case suicide would also be murder. That knowledge would sit behind my eyes in that last remaining moment of my life.

I think back to that movie, *Ghandi.*

I had been hiding in my apartment, trying to bury my present. I began watching the movie at the point where Gandhi returned to India from South Africa. I understood little of the passions that corrupted the India of that day. I did know that I fell in love with this funny little man. More than anything else in the world, even when the movie ended in Gandhi's death, I wanted to meet him. I wanted to live my life in a way he would approve.

I could not meet him, but I could see more of the movie. There was still the beginning.

I punched for the beginning and saw Ghandi as a young lawyer in South Africa fighting against racial injustice. But there was a speech he gave in a hall.

I damn the day my soul, greedy for belonging and rightness, craved more of this man. In his speech he said, "In this cause I, too, am prepared to die. But, my friends, there is no cause for which I am prepared to kill."

Line up your dead, Thomas Windom. Count the bodies. Look at what covers your hands.

"Would you like to sign the petition?"

I bring down my gaze until a woman with thick glasses and stringy wet hair is blowing foul breath into my face. "What?"

She holds up a board with a lined form on it. There are four signatures. "We're trying to save the Empire State Building. The city is planning on tearing it down, and we're trying to stop this tragedy."

"Tragedy?" Everything in the world becomes tinged with red. "Tragedy? A fucking building? Tragedy?"

I can't place the billion images of pain behind my eyes into words. Tragedy?

My god, a tragedy.

When I can see again the woman is getting up off of the sidewalk holding her throat. Two men are holding my arms. One of the men is saying, "Man, the damn building isn't worth going to jail."

The other man wears a lot of black. Cop. Another cop stands in front of me. His face looks very confused. He stabs a finger into my chest. "Look, asshole. I called you in and was told to cut you loose. I don't know why. Maybe your old man is the mayor or a Force general. Maybe you got pictures of the PeeGee playing pocket pool. I don't care. This time I'll cut you loose, but you fuck up on my beat again and I'll smoke you out of your socks first and *then* call it in. You understand me, asshole?"

"Yes."

There are tears of shame in my eyes; my face burns. "I'm sorry," I say to the blackshit. "I'm sorry," I say to the woman with the sore neck. The two men let me go and I turn and walk away, too ashamed to look back.

Wardate: 17:18-9AUG2033
Downlimit: -64380:00:00

12

Kill Manuel Ortega.

I see him, laughing, jumping over the racks in "E" Dorm, flipping over my rack, dumping me onto the floor.

"Hey! Everybody up! C'mon you redbirds, outta those racks! We gonna be free!"

Kill Manuel Ortega.

I need a place in which to find peace.

I am sitting in a church.

There is the smell of mildew and incense in the air.

It is quiet.

There are four others there, each one keeping to himself. I watch them, trying to guess why they are there. After all, this is my computer image.

Is that one sick?

Is the next one praying for a loved one?

Is the third trying to get some sleep before getting thrown out. Is the fourth one look—

—the fourth one is on his feet, walking toward me. His suit is all black, but like the clergy, not like the blackshit. His face carries every feature that a face must carry for me to trust it. It, of course, is an image generated by MAC.

A priest.

He sits next to me. I look at his steady brown eyes. "Should I call you Father Byte?"

The left side of his face pulls back into a slight smile. "You may call me whatever pleases you."

"I know you're a generated image."

Father Byte's expression doesn't change. "Then you also know that I know that you know. What's bothering you?"

"This—" I slump back in the pew and fold my arms. "You *know* what your orders are doing to me."

"Yes. I know."

"I can't do it."

"You can get close to him. No one else."

"There has to be another way."

"There are numerous other ways, Thomas. None of them are as efficient."

"I need to know why!"

"You have seen The Shrine to Why."

"Yes. And, Father?"

"Yes, my son?"

"Go fuck yourself."

I demand it and the image fades.

The church fades.

I stand facing The Shrine to Why. Hundreds of billions of bits of information. In theory the human mind can hold much, much more than that.

What is it that I want?

Why am I here?

The Big Plan doesn't depend on any individual. Why me? Why Manuel?

Can I hold an entire projection sequence in my mind? If I can, will I be able to understand it and work my way through the event chains? If I find a mistake or an alternate path, can I change the orders? And why would I be able to see an alternate when MAC can't?

I am absurd, but I am out of acceptable alternatives.

Why?

I want to know why.

||°°°| |°|°°|||°| °°°°° |||| |°|||| |°

|°|°||||| |°| °|||°° |°|°|°| |°|°|||

This is it, then: the universe of why; the lengths, widths, depths, angles, speeds, dimensions, times, sequences, quantities.

|||||| | ||°||°||°°° °°° ||°°| °° |||°

| °°°°|°° |°°°°°|| ||| °|| °|°|°|°||°

I know as much as God, and that is to know that I can never know as much as God. But there it is before the eyes of my mind: the Big Picture.

°°°°°|| ° |°°|°°|° ||||°|| °°||||||°||

°°°°|||||°°|°°| |°°°|||||°|°°|° |||°|

At the bottom of the Big Picture—significant but not absolute—is the death of my brother, Manuel.

And I ask the question: Why?

|||||| ||° || °°°°||°°° ||||° || °°°|

:: ::: ...::: .::: ....:: ::. :::.

|||||||| ||||||||| |||°°|

°°||°° °°||°

°°°°°||°°°° ||

°°|| |||||||

|°°| °°°°|

||||||||°|

They made it, then.

All of them made it to Argentina and joined the Free World Legion, an international Otherworld terrorist organization headquartered in Albania.

They are a magic combination: Manuel, Francis, and Ugly Doris. Manuel is handsome, charismatic, a natural leader. In these few years he has become the Latin American leader of the organization.

Francis is absolutely loyal to Manuel and has murdered several times to protect his leader. It turns out that Francis is very good at murder. In addition the act doesn't affect him the way that it affects Thomas Windom. If a murder is necessary, Francis accepts that fact and performs the act, never giving it another thought.

The key is Ugly Doris. I am impressed at how impressed MAC is with Ugly Doris. She is Manuel's brains. What I have had to struggle for years to learn about projections, she seems to know by instinct. That and much, much more. She has instincts for the right moment, for the jugular, for the sensitive.

With Ugly Doris working strategy, Charismatic Manuel providing leadership, and Graveyard Francis protecting their backs and removing the competition, the trio captured the Latin American leadership of the organization.

°||||||| °°||° °°°°| °°°°|| °° |||||||

Ugly Doris is about to implement her plan to split the Latin American faction of the Free World Legion away from its European parent.

Why do you want to do that, Doris?

||°°° ||||° || °°°|

:: ::: ...::: .::: ...

|||||°| ||||°°°|

Many years ago MAC created the Free World Legion to paralyze anti-Compact movements in Europe, Asia, and South America. The movement makes a great deal of noise, makes grand pronouncements, and gives revolutionaries social functions at which they can blow wind.

It consumes less energy to manipulate a sitting enemy, particularly if what you want him to do is to continue sitting.

Doris figured out all of that before she was thirteen years old, and she doesn't want to sit. She wants to help Manuel accomplish what he wants, and what Manuel wants is to destroy the Compact of Nations.

A splintered Free World Legion will disrupt the Big Equation, and killing Manuel will take the heart out of Doris, as well as neutralizing the movement to split the legion.

The event chains are complex, but it is only a matter of moral efficiency.

||||°°|| || |||° | |||°°°|

Alternative sequence: There are eleven persons, five men and a woman in South America and two men and three women in Europe, I can kill to achieve the same results.

What are the murders of eleven men and women against the murder of a brother? The murders require—

°°°°°|| °°| °°|

The injection of misinformation on a massive scale in such a manner that Otherworld anti-misinformation protections would be circumvented. This would require an enormous expenditure of scarce—

|||°° |||°° °°°°°°
||||°°° °°| °°| °°|
°°°°° °°||||° |||| °°

This chain and that chain, this sequence and that. My mind processes the chains, the alternatives to Manuel's death are either impossible, impractical, or terribly wasteful.

|||°° °°||°°

—But Doris never loses. In her mind is that she *cannot* lose. Her personality profile shows her vulnerable here. Let her lose, and keep losing, and she will curl up and die.

—die.

—die. Damn, double damn.

Not to Doris.

Not me. Somebody else.

Get somebody else to do this one.

||||||||| ||||°°

Doris has done her work well.

No other individual can get close to Manuel. As for teams, it would take a division-sized assault to successfully get in and eliminate Manuel. Besides the approximately two thousand casualties resulting from the assault, the event would bring up the Wardate by almost a full year, resulting in an additional three million deaths.

Well, what if I just say to hell with the job? What if no one does it?

°°°||| °°°||°| ||||||||

The Latin American faction of the Free World Legion will break off and become a separate organization under Manuel's leadership, which means under Doris's influence.

°|||||| °|°|°|°|°°||| °°°|

Under Doris's direction, a combination of terrorist and education groups infiltrate the Compact, circumventing MAC-directed security.

°°°|| °°°|| |||°°| |°|°|°

The groups will help organize Consolidationist sympathies behind the move to reopen the Compact to immigration and trade. Between Manuel's smile and Doris's manipulations, it will eventually happen.

|||||||||| ||||°||°°°|| |||°

The cost: human civilization's future.

I come back from my personal Shrine to Why.

As I said before, I have my orders.

It is time that I got on with them.

Wardate: 17:18-9AUG2033
Downlimit: -63924:21:11

11

I must get close.

The horror, the blackness of my dreams, rushes down upon me, and I must get close to something.

With or without a comma.

There is a special joke among the Links. See, the order is: go kill, Thomas Windom. But that's with the comma. See, without the comma it's: go kill Thomas Windom. Get it?

I guess you have to be there.

I am Captain Willard moving up the river to kill Colonel Kurtz. I am the Bladerunner seeking to retire the last replicant. I am the German soldier Steiner working my way through the guards to kill Winston Churchill. I am—

—the smoke.

The constant smell of smoke.

Ecuador, Peru, Bolivia.

It's a black, greasy, sweet smell. Burning fuel mixed with burning crops, burning homes, burning flesh. And this mark left on walls, sidewalks, the cheeks of the dead. The blood-red imprint of a left hand.

There is a war here, but we do not call it a war. Without the word, we make it something else.

The mark of the left hand. It is the legion. Manuel.

The war is on and it is too soon.

To stop it, Manuel must be stopped.

To stop Manuel—

* * *

They pass by me, these starving faces, these maggot-packed masks of the dead.

They pass by me, these weapons of steel, plastic, copper, gold and silver.

The food of the world hammered into weapons.

There in the dust is a boy of fifteen. His rifle rests on his legs, his back leans against the tread of a disabled self-propelled gun. His ragged shirt carries the mark of the left hand. He is one of Manuel's soldiers. The cost of the ruined weapon he is leaning against is enough to feed a town of a thousand for five years.

Junk.

The words come without effort; they are understood without effort. I wonder what language this is. I guess it's Spanish. Maybe some hill dialect.

"Who are you?"

"My name is Thomas Windom."

"And what is that to me? Why are you here?"

"Take me to Manuelo."

"Manuelo? Manuelo, no, Manuelo. Why are you here? Answer quickly, or maybe I cut out your tongue, see, Tomas, eh?"

How long, I wonder, has MAC bent our two lives toward this place, this moment? Look at this man. He looks so strong, so young, so healthy. His breath says that he has been drinking alcohol. The blood on his clothing says that he has been killing. He has had a very full day.

Look at his eyes. I think I can see it there a little.

No matter.

"Take me to Manuelo, or I will kill you with a look."

"Tomas! Ah, hah, Tomas! Kill me with a look! Are you God, then, pale one? Ah, hah, Tomas—"

He laughs and spits; laughs some more, his face growing very red.

I look at him.

His face grows ashen as he clutches at his left shoulder.

He gasps as he falls facedown into the dust.

He twitches for a bit, then is still.

I look at the next soldier.

"Take me to Manuelo."

The next soldier is a believer. He is reborn. He has seen the light. He has seen the Master, he has gotten religion, and he does his best to carry out the revealed will of his new god. In other words, he moves off like a motherfucker.

My name is handed to a sergeant, who gives it to a lieutenant, who moves off to hand it to someone else. Soon Doris will know. Soon Manuel will know. Soon—

The reborn soldier's companions stand and stare at me.

One of them whispers, *"Tomas. Who are you, Tomas? What are you?"*

In the armored air cruiser things clarify.

With no pain, nothing good is born.

That's why the Vow to the Sun must be taken. *A Man Called Horse*, Richard Harris, 1970. When I saw the movie, I was stunned at the power of the ritual of the Vow to the Sun. Stunned at the degree of pain. Stunned that the white man went through with it. Stunned at the reasoning.

With no pain, nothing good is born.

As I watch these beautiful mountains pass, as I smell the sweat of the driver and the lone soldier who dared to guard God, I see that my mission has different objectives. Perhaps foiling Doris and pulling the plug on the Free World Legion is useful; efficient. But never is there just one objective to be achieved by a circumstance adjustment.

Through this passage I will become different.

Part of why I am here is to achieve this difference.

With no pain, nothing good is born.

I shall feel pain.

With no pain, nothing good is born. MAC would assure a future for the human race. But there is a price. The price is pain.

Pain cleanses.

Pain crumbles old thinking, old defenses, old reasons.

Pain forges new resolves, new priorities, new willingness.

Pain is the great equalizer, the great humbler, the bringer of insight, tears, and the oneness with the human race.

Pain is the great teacher.

And, brother, pain hurts. Wakantanka, make me worthy.

The soldier in the cab watches me with terror in his eyes. He doesn't understand what is happening. That's why he is terrified.

I do understand what is happening. That's why I am terrified.

It would be so much easier if I could cast Manuel as the villain. If I could paint him evil.

There is not much left of this reality for me to hang onto.

Where—

—there. I can hide there.

And it is so much easier, now. I don't have to go insane to hide. The filaments simply alter neural discharge thresholds, bypassing this, keeping that from my awareness.

It can all happen without me.

But nothing good is born without pain.

To kill Manuel, they don't need me. They never did. To do the job they just needed my skin, and they have always owned that.

But if part of the purpose is for me to suffer, hiding and letting my skin do the job would be like taking the Vow to the Sun stoned out on drugs.

If I dive into the pain, however, it will pay off part of the debt. What debt? Owed to whom?

It will pay off part of the debt.

The cruiser lands, the pitch of the fans declines and dies. The cloud of red dust raised by the landing drifts slowly away. A heavily armed squad is waiting for me.

—And Ivan shoots Vladimir, Igor shoots Ivan, Nikita shoots Igor—

Well. I'll save that one for if I need it.

Above, on a road leading toward some forested hills, is Manuel dressed in an olive-colored uniform.

My hiding place is not nothing this time. As my body moves through the mist of the real, I see this image. It does not come from the machine. I am almost certain. It is too fuzzy, too indistinct, too real.

It is an arm, a strong arm, around my shoulders. All it does is hold me. I turn and look, but the image fades at the shoulder. Beyond I think there might be a face, but my mind plays tricks on me. The image of the face fades.

The image of the arm remains.

"It's a tough demand, the will of God. I'm a poor hand at it. And, look where I've got us now." Sahak, the Christian chained to Barabbas in the sulphur mines of Sicily, said that.

"And, look where I've got us now."

An arm. Is it possible that this shit is the will of God? Is it possible that I am doing the Good Work? Can it be that Crazy Feena back at Outcasters knew what she was talking about?

An arm.

A goddamned arm.

I remember what Anthony Quinn—Barabbas—said to the Christian: "God should make Himself plain, or leave me alone."

Preach it brother.

God should make Himself plain, or leave me alone.

But the arm is still there. It calms me, gives me power and strength to face the next minute, the next horror.

"What is this story I hear about you, brother? You have the Evil Eye?"

Manuel chuckles.

Francis chuckles.

The three guards chuckle.

I chuckle, because I know that he knows. And he knows that I know that he knows. And—

Ugly Doris only sits there like some judgemental maggot, studying me, her impressive brain running at top speed, trying to collate and evaluate the recent data.

Francis is behind me. I know that. And he will not hesitate to kill me, given current circumstances. Time to adjust the circumstances. I turn and look at Francis. Something puts a broad smile on my face and words into my mouth. "Hey, Francis!"

I stand and move next to him. My arms go around him in a hug. "Damn, but it's good to see you again!"

Another hug and I sit down, Francis's ability to perform split-second execution against me all fucked up. The arm is around me. With no pain, nothing good is born.

The pain will begin soon.

Wardate: 17:18-9AUG2033
Downlimit: -63899:02:00

10

Arriba.

Manuelo the bandit chieftain is in deep conference with his generals. The moment will soon come. The legion will be split, and Manuelo will carve into the north.

The Invasion of the Killer Tortillas!!

Mira, God, look at these characters. Check it out. Black and green berets, guitars, asshole songs from some drug-soaked remembrance of some failed cause.

Speedy Gonzales backed up by the Red Army Choir singing, "Don't Cry For Me Argentina."

Romance.

The romance of the lost cause. These creatures are in love with death.

On a porch in the shade I relax in a chair, allowing Ugly Doris to study me. The porch overlooks a courtyard filled with vehicles and revolutionaries busily packing up to move out.

"Do you still play chess, Tommy?"

Chess. That was a million years ago. "I've found more interesting games." I sit up and face her. "When you call me Tommy I wonder what you are hiding."

Doris laughs and shakes her ugly head. "Ah, Dumbs, you are back! And maybe not so dumb?" She clasps her pudgy hands over her lump of belly and looks at me with those steady beads of eyes, black and gleaming like wet olives.

"Then, Dumbs, what are these more interesting games you have found? Do you have another game of why?"

"No. No more why games."

"How are you going to attempt Manuel's murder?"

Doris might be asking about the weather or about the wheat rust problem in the south forty. Francis is inside the house, observing us through a screen. There are seven guards with weapons trained on me.

"What do you think you know, Doris?"

"You are here to kill Manuel."

"And?"

"You are part of that machine. We've been picking up your signal emissions. What makes you think you can do anything?"

I laugh. Every bitter moment of my life bleeds into that laugh. "Oh, Doris. What makes you think you can do anything to stop what is to be?"

"Do you mean other than all of the weapons I have aimed at you right now, Dumbs?"

It's no fun, this. Father Byte comes to me. He doesn't have to say anything. It's all been planned out in advance anyway. Shit, yes, go ahead.

There is the sound of a rifle shot. Another. Then many guns all going off at once.

See, one of Manuel's generals, Ramon Molino—

—What's the point of telling Ramon's story? Decades ago his insane attempt to take over the Free World Legion was planned. Circumstances were arranged, he did what he wanted to do, and now Manuel is dead. Unless Manuel's guards are really bad shots, Ramon is dead, too. Function served; Molino, Ramon; Run Completed.

I look at Doris.

The respect in her eyes. The respect for me.

Do not respect me, Doris. I did not defeat you. It takes no great amount of cleverness to kill a fox with a cobalt bomb.

"I see." That's all she says, and that says it all. Francis and his men are off to investigate the fighting noises coming from Manuel's headquarters. And Manuel never was the important mark, was he?

I reach out my hands and wrap them around Doris's throat, my thumbs digging in and collapsing her windpipe.

Still that look of respect in her eyes.

Look at Doris.

Her tongue is still too big for her mouth. She is no larger than on the night of the escape, except for two large breasts. Ugly Doris is a woman.

And this time, you lose the game, Doris.

Because I cheated, that's how.

You lose.

You all lose because you cannot do anything but lose.

As I try and stuff your tongue back into your mouth, Doris, as I close your dead eyes, did you get any before you died? Did you ever get a man in between those fat, crooked legs?

The arm goes around my shoulder; the peace enters me, calming the sickness. Another minute, another horror passes.

—But what if it is all for nothing?

Back at the end of the century, China had negative population growth as its national policy. The United States was at zero population growth. The air was getting clean. Every nation was looking at population, resources, pollution, war—

Too little, too late, too bad.

I look down at Manuel's bloody corpse.

Did you know?

Just before I closed your eyes, my brother, did you know?

Did you know what I was about? What we were about? What anything was about?

While you were down here working out your rage playing the bandit chieftain, did you ever—

The arm again comes and steals about my shoulders.

There is only one horror left to perform.

I will escape from this land with my life.

It knew that I would have me killed, this arm that is not a machine-generated image.

It would have me escape alive, this arm, and that is the horror.

The arm. "What are you?" I ask, but it doesn't answer. It doesn't answer, but it doesn't leave.

The arm.

Strange. This arm is always a left arm; never a right.

But, why not? There are places where God is a monkey, a rock, a rat, a wheel, a star. Why not a left arm?

I tell no one about this arm around my shoulders. I have laughed at God for so long, knowledge of this arm around my shoulders will cause them to say "I told you so."

Them. There is no "them" except Salena. I really know nothing about her, except that she values time too highly to waste it telling anyone "I told you so."

"Them" is in my head, and knows. "Them" has already said "I told you so" a million times.

I do not place much value upon time. I only pray for it to cease.

Salena says there are many kinds of insanity. The trick is to wind up with an acceptable variety. To do that simply grab one of the many sacks of bedbugs that the world has labeled "sane."

Koyaanisqatsi. It is a Hopi Indian word meaning out of balance, crazy, a way of life demanding change, all fucked up. It is the name of an old movie. The only movie that I watch.

Koyaanisqatsi has a message, which is the usual ecogram: technology: bad, bad, naughty, naughty—but I pay no attention. See, this movie has no characters, no dialogue, no plot, no tears, no laughter, nothing but images tied to an overwhelming musical score.

When the day is done, and I am alone, I can plug into this movie and drown out that crawling thing outside my door.

Ain't it awful, the movie is telling me. But all I see are the deserts, mountains, rivers, lakes, canyons, and cities. I fly, I bathe my eyes in the images, I numb my ears with the sounds. I put my awareness to sleep.

* * *

A New Year. Another. I am promoted to assistant watch chief, and again to watch chief.

The Nonaligned Nations' Alliance announces that it has achieved its goal of limiting deaths by starvation to under fifty million per annum.

Colleen Marshall is listed as having married Martin Stokes.

Time.

Time is chewing gum for the soul.

It is 2029. This year—

This year.

It is the ninetieth anniversary of the 1939 World's Fair. New York is getting geared up to celebrate the one hundredth anniversary by putting on an exact replica of the 1939 fair. Women will wear shoulder pads, large skirts, and heavy lip paint. Men will wear baggy suits and floppy hats. Every time I turn on the TV I find that documentary, *The World of Tomorrow*, playing.

There are now only four thousand nine hundred and ten years remaining before they open the time capsule.

This year, 2029, all of the Wardate signs are taken down. Compact Statute 882.1132, the Orzaya Bill, has been expanded. Not only is the President-General's approval required for the use of Compact military forces, but for a host of other things, as well.

This year the Consolidationists have achieved their first majority in the Compact Legislative Assembly.

A special unit of scientists and technicians has been created to isolate MAC from direct control of any government department.

This year the Compact has its first Consolidationist President-General, Emilio Paolini. You can still see the remains of his campaign: posters, bumper stickers, and buttons carrying the slogan "Never War."

Wardate: 17:18-9AUG2033
Downlimit: -39012:05:26

9

Salena Booth and I. Her outsides and my insides are machine-made. Added together we almost make a complete human. We make love and it is nothing more than shaft and bushing. Plug it in, a little oil, a little energy, and you get motion.

The things I remember about love were left back in West Ellen, back in Outcasters.

Funny that I can only get an orgasm by pretending that Salena is Ugly Doris. Poor Ugly Doris.

You win after all.

Just before Christmas.

The special unit of the Department of Intelligence is disbanded. There has been an investigation, and the Legislative Assembly doesn't want us to do that sort of thing any more. Salena takes full retirement and refuses to tell me where she is going.

I don't qualify for retirement and am transferred to Emergency Operations. My principal workplace is right in the center of The Shrine to Why. My job is to plot projection sequences, supervise the manning watch on the operations center on a rotating basis, and to supervise equipment calibration.

It is a routine job. It allows me to continue living in my Lowell Center apartment. It gives me something to do.

On one of my walks I pass the window of a tiny bookshop. There is a picture of a familiar face: Helen. Her hair is styled in a pile on top of her head, her eyelids and lips are painted, and her cheek no longer carries its scar. But it is Helen. Helen has written a book.

Redbird: The Story of the Outcast.

Somehow it fits into MAC's plan to have Helen be an author and to have her book be about the redbirds. I feel lightheaded as I place my hand on the shop's door.

I don't open the door. Instead I stare at the book's cover. It is black with a red title. In the lower left corner of the cover is a drawing of a little boy and a little girl. They are holding hands and are wearing reds. The little girl is blond and has pigtails. The boy—oh, God, the boy.

I'll be in there. In that book. Ann. Elana. Doris. Manuel. The blackshit: Haskins, Wing, Lathrup—

I take my hand away from the bookshop door. I walk away until I feel steady. Then I run. I run until the pain of running takes it all from my mind.

How could she? How could she spread it out on the pages of a book? How could she do it?

Two months after my assignment to Emergency Operations and I go on leave. I spend the leave in my apartment, flat on my back, my eyes closed, MAC numbing my mind. Perhaps, with enough time off from reality, my mind will heal.

But, a book!

In the pages of a book. Isn't it better just to sweep that foul stuff under the past and forget it? Does hanging it all out like Helen did make it easier to live with?

And where does it all fit into the Big Equation?

Would anyone reading Helen's book understand anything about the price some had to pay to save a future for humanity? Would they add two and two and get four? Or would the ones who need to read it shy away from the horror, while those who feed on horror complain that the story is too tame?

I could ask MAC, but I won't.

Near the end of my leave, I take the trans and go back to West Ellen. There isn't anything left for me there, but there is something I want to do. I want to tell it to Herbie. I want him to understand. From something, from somewhere, I want peace.

The street is deserted, the maples naked, the air crisp, the ice on the road old and rutted. Herbie's Ellis Electric is parked to the side of the store.

I enter Dyar's Variety, the familiar smells filling my nostrils. Coffee, chewing gum, onions, bread. I hear a television in the back. No one is behind the counter.

"Hello? Herbie?"

I hear a chair move in the back. A young man pushes the string beads aside and enters. His uniform is black. "Herbie and Dot are home watching the news. Can I help?"

Black. He looks so much like Godfrey I can't get it out of my mind. But he's too young to be Godfrey as old as Godfrey is right now, if he's alive and—

"Can I help you?"

"Wh—who are you?"

A big smile. "Well, I guess you could say that I am West Ellen's chief of police and sole beat cop. Harry. Harry Rolland."

"I don't understand. Herbie's the town constable. And isn't that his Ellis outside?"

"It was. He sold it to me. Herbie's retired as constable. It's a full-time job with the terminal gone, which leaves me as the current constabulary. He ought to be back in an hour or so, if you want to wait. Or you could go over to his house. Along with everyone else, he's home watching the news."

"What news?"

His eyebrows shoot up. "You're kidding."

"What news?"

"The Mars shot? You haven't heard about that?"

"No." I shake my head. "No. I didn't know anyone was planning on going to Mars." Well, Spaceman back on the brush-clearing gang was planning on going.

"Is the Mars station going to be opened again?"

Harry the cop shakes his head in wonder. "You really haven't heard. The drive experiment—you know, the Bellenger drive? It took less than twenty hours. On the way back they hope to cut it to under eight."

A billion years ago Spaceman was reading a text by a fellow named Bellenger. Just a theory. Faster-than-light. Spaceman figured that opening the stars would end the need for the Compact of Nations. Infinte space means infinite room. Infinite room means all of the food and babies possible to the imagination.

I ask MAC, but I suspect the answer even before I get it. Energy / resources / time / population. It simply takes too much of everything to ship the extra bodies off planet. Maybe in a hundred years, but not now, not soon enough, not in time. The stars are new business. Earth and I are part of the old business that needs clearing up.

I nod. "Interesting."

"Interesting? This is the most—"

I turn and walk toward the street. "I can't wait." I pause at the door. "Please tell Herbie that Tom stopped by. Tell him that I'm okay."

"Sure." I close the door behind me and inhale the smell of wood smoke. There will be more snow here soon. I can smell it in the air.

It takes special people to watch snow fall.

I walk. Past Colleen Marshall's home, past the library, past Doc Cordwell's.

I don't imagine that it would have made any difference, but I wish I had worn my red parka.

When I return home—for that is what I call my apartment in the Lowell Center—I initiate the procedure to have removed from my system the Link. I do not know what difference in my life, if any, removing the Link will make. Before they remove it, however, I will visit one last time with my ghosts. Especially Manuel. He has so many things left to say to me.

Wardate: 17:18-9AUG2033
Downlimit: -32628:10:00

8

A man named Schopenhauer wrote that every man takes the limits of his own field of vision for the limits of the world. Porky Pig said "That's all folks," and he wasn't telling the truth, either. I can choose the limits of my field of vision. I can reduce them to my apartment, to the little parks littered throughout the city, to the commissary, to the theater.

I do not watch television. I go to the theater to watch movies, and seeing them on a huge screen makes all of my old favorites brand-new experiences.

When I am watching I can forget so many things. The only way the Legislative Assembly can wrest any kind of control from MAC is if the act serves MAC's program. The world says that the madness of the Cummings Holocaust is over. Earth is off the hook.

Look at all of the improved ways we have of producing food and energy.

Look at the planet's population growth rate. It is at zero. Sure, that's because they are starving to death as fast as they are being replaced, but look to the stars. The Bellenger drive is everybody's answer to everything. The universe is a big place. We can put off the problem until we have to kill quadrillions instead of mere billions.

Look around you! Do you see any Wardate signs? It's all over. It's all over.

But there is still the procedure. See, if DOP calls down hell upon the planet, the President-General is to be notified. He is then required to give the orders initiating the appropriate sequence. The notification code word is Aceldama.

Aceldama means Field of Blood. It is the name of a graveyard for strangers in Jerusalem. It is written in Matthew, Chapter 3, Verse 8:

> Then Judas . . . brought back the thirty pieces of silver to the chief priests and the elders saying "I have sinned in betraying innocent blood." But they said, "What is that to us? See to it thyself." And he flung the pieces of silver into the temple, and withdrew; and went away and hanged himself with a halter.
>
> And the chief priests took the pieces of silver, and said, "It is not lawful to put them into the treasury, seeing that it is the price of blood." And after they had consulted together, they bought with them the potter's field, as a burial place for strangers. For this reason that field has been called to this day, Haceldama, that is, the Field of Blood.

The discrepancy between Haceldama and Aceldama has to do with which of several versions of *New Testament* eternal truth you want to pick.

Father Byte had his own word to initiate the Jay Sequence: Ormazd. It comes from the ancient Mithraic *Book of Resurrection*:

> "The Immortal will pray, and in answer Ormazd will cause to fall from the Heavens a Great Fire that will consume the wicked. The supreme defeat of the Prince of Darkness will be achieved, perishing Ahriman and his Devas in the flames of Justice.
>
> "The universe then will be happiness without end."

However, our President-General, Emilio Paolini, is sworn never to initiate the so-called war. "Never War," his slogan. I remember the crowds chanting that during Paolini's rallies. They do the same now for his public appearances.

Perhaps it is all over. The 1998 Citizenship Act is up for repeal. This will open the borders and allow each family to have as many children as it wishes.

Perhaps it is all over. Deep beneath the Lowell Center, however, the Wardate is still running.

Maybe we are spiders spinning our webs inside a box of high explosives. From all we can see, the world is a steady, predictable entity. Even though a timing fuse is moving us ever closer to the moment of ending, we don't see the fuse or hear it. Therefore we do not discuss the explosives or the timer. Instead we discuss the quality of our respective lives.

It seems almost as though I am the only one who sees this. And I really do ignore it. I go do my job, eat, sleep, walk in the park, watch an occasional movie.

I know what I do is very little. It doesn't move and shake the planet. It means I still don't belong to anything or belong anywhere. Perhaps it is even very, very dull.

But it doesn't hurt.

Wardate: 06:32-7AUG2033
Downlimit: -31246:56:22

7

It is the second night of an uneventful manning watch, and I am having a nightmare. It's strange how I can sit aside now, watching myself have nightmares. Usually I simply watch Windom twitch and sweat, perusing the performance and commenting upon the particulars. This time I dip into the dreampath. The edge is there: the excitement, the thrill and the adventure of having a living skeleton jump at me suddenly from the dark.

This dream.

This dream I am sitting high upon boulders of a naked mountaintop. It is the only mountain within sight, and surrounding me like the waters of a great ocean is the human race. My mountain is an island in a sea of living flesh.

What is horror? Not death, not torture. Not the infinite forms of dehumanizing degradation.

Horror is looking at those thousands of bodies being bulldozed into the pits at Auschwitz and realizing that each and every scrap of that flesh was a unique and valuable person. Horror is the desperately painful feeling of absolute loss that comes with such a realization.

Merle Sawyer showed me a book of pictures about concentration camps. Then he told me of an old friend of his. As an adult his friend repaired antique watches. But as a boy of five his friend and his friend's family had been sent to a concentration camp.

Merle cried as he leafed through the book, shaking his head. "Thomas, it has taken me a lifetime to appreciate this one little watchmaker, and I'm not really certain that I know all of him that can be known." His hand spread its fingers and covered a photograph of a mountain of naked dead. "It would take hundreds of lifetimes to know just these."

That is the horror of a mass murder: it is not a mass that is murdered. It is a number of unique individuals. We can never know them all; appreciate them all; love or hate them all. All we can do is call them a mass, thereby sucking the horror from the act, making it no longer horrible but, instead, something somewhat distasteful.

There is the human ocean surrounding me. But it is not an ocean, is it?

No.

It is billions of men, women, boys, girls, babies. As I watch the sharks swim among them, I know them.

The dead.

Every single individual the sharks kill I know. I know the victims, and the death of each one is unbearable to me, and they are dying by the millions, and I cannot escape my feelings.

They are all looking at me.

They are all looking at me.

The dead and the living.

They are all looking at me.

Perhaps I should step outside and return to watching myself have nightmares. But there is something strange here too. I am beginning to know Thomas Windom, and leaving him to fight his demons all alone gives me a dirty, guilty feeling.

But I know them.

All of those out there.

I know them all.

In the dark, my eyes open, a shadow above me, the smell of jasmine in my nostrils. I'm on a couch in the crew's recreation room. On the television screen THX 1138 is, once more, sitting in an absolution booth, vomiting on his god.

Strange that I didn't know *THX* was playing tonight—

"Citizen Windom?"

It is Teresa Aminez, assistant watch commander. I feel the

drool on my cheek and wipe it off with the back of my hand. "What?"

"I'm sorry to disturb you, but there's a problem."

I sit up and swing my feet to the floor. "What's wrong?"

"We're not sure. The Wardate is advancing. Fast. Is it—"

I'm up and running toward the door. With each step the door seems to become farther and farther away.

—and I know them.

I know them all.

Wardate: 00:00-00---0000
Downlimit: ----126:21:56

6

Haceldama / Aceldama / Ormazd. This is it.

"How in hell could the Wardate run up three years?" Tim Donegal, the Director of Intelligence, restudies the orders while Aminez supervises the confirmation and alternative sequence runs. Donegal lowers the reader. "I don't believe it."

"That is why you fail." It just slipped out.

"What was that, Windom?"

I shake my head. "Nothing. Just a line from an old movie."

"What movie?"

I rub my eyes and bite my lower lip as I try to control a giggle. "It was called . . . *The Empire, The Empire Strikes Back*."

"This is no time for humor."

"No sir."

He looks down at me. "Can't you locate Barnett?"

"No sir."

"Cantor?"

"No sir."

"Look, Windom, I'm not trying to give you a hard time. It's just that you're too young. You don't have enough experience. I'd just feel a lot easier with either Barnett or Cantor on the Kay Board."

"I understand."

Strange. Whatever will be will be. MAC is running the show, has always run the show. If being in front of the Kay Board serves the program, that's where I'll be. If not, I won't. Where does Donegal think a human ego can fit into that?

I look at the cover protecting the Kay Board. It is steel and is combination-locked in place. I look up at Donegal. "Sir, the procedure calls for removing the cover now."

He hesitates a moment, then nods abruptly. As I remove the cover, Aminez walks up to the director. "Sir, confirmation and alternative sequence runs completed. Aceldama confirmed."

"What's the Wardate?"

"Zero. We're in it now." The words land in cotton-lined silence. Now. Tonight. This is the moment the guard meant when he said, "Don't wait for the war," "Hurry up, the war'll be finished before you are," and "You waiting to carry casualties?"

Now.

Every second's delay costs something; something in time, lives, resources.

Now.

Aminez points to a screen, her long slender finger tracing the distance between a black line and a line dividing Wardate safe from Wardate defeat.

"With the current tolerances we have approximately five days before we hit the Downlimit and the equation is permanently out of balance."

"Five days?"

"Yes." Aminez stands there, waiting on Donegal. I watch Donegal. I think I am puzzled.

Here is a creature who has spent his adult life studying projections and working his way up in the DOP to where he is now the Director of Intelligence, second only to the Secretary of Projections. If there is anyone on the planet who ought to know what's going on, he's it. But he doesn't. He doesn't—can't—won't—believe it.

It takes him a moment too long, but he finally gives the orders to me. "Remove the safety interlocks, then stand down."

"Yes sir."

I twist and push in the locking tubes. As I push in the last of them, activating the board, the twin triggers rise from the panel. Spaced a half-meter apart, the triggers look like two pistol grips.

I sit back from the Kay Board. The other members of the manning crew are at their machines, trying to look busy. Other than getting the President-General's order to initiate the sequence, there's not much to do.

I make another attempt to locate the secretary, but he's still gone somewhere. Donegal has alerted the President-General. The signal Aceldama has been sent to all military units.

I feel lightheaded. When the President-General gives the order, I'm the one who'll pull the triggers.

I fold my arms and close my eyes.

Stand down.

Stand down, and do not think.

There is someone who should be notified. I turn to a terminal to put in a search. No one has notified him. I am amazed.

When I find the name and number, I call.

The buzzing sounds like an ancient bell system. The voice that answers is rough, strong. "Yes?"

"Secretary Cummings?"

"I'm not the secretary any longer. What can I do for you?"

"This is—" My mouth is very dry. "This is Thomas Windom." Where are the million and one things I want to say to this man?

"I'm sorry, Mr. Windom. I don't recognize the name."

"There's no reason you should, Mr. Secretary. I just called—" What do I say without violating a hundred regulations. "I work at DOP, Mr. Secretary."

"Yes?"

"This is it. I thought someone should tell you."

There is a silence at the other end, then a whisper, "When?"

"We're waiting on the PeeGee now."

"Thank you, young man. Thank you."

The line is dead.

I cut the circuit to my headset and stare at the triggers until my relief arrives.

A pain in my heart eases. I won't be the one after all.

Wardate: 00:00-00---0000
Downlimit: ----119:51:44

5

This minute? The next? God, when is the order coming?

"Well, boys, I reckon this is it. Nuclear combat toe-to-toe with the Rooskies."

The trumpets and drums play "When Johnny Comes Marching Home" as Major Kong climbs into the pilot seat and we pan back to see the ancient bomber flying against a backdrop of black-and-white mountains.

Dr. Strangelove or: How I Learned to Stop Worrying and Love the Bomb, a 1964 British film. It has a large cult following in certain anti-Compact circles. When I get off manning and collapse in my apartment, the old black-and-white satire is playing on the television.

Major Kong is giving his crew the pep talk. "*—Heck, I reckon you wouldn't even be human beans if you didn't have some purdy strong personal feelin's about nuclear combat.*"

Funny.

Still funny.

The CLN logo comes on the screen. I search the channels and everything has been interrupted for a special news conference from the Steel Palace.

This must be it.

The time grows long, the space behind the blue lectern empty.

There are no words with which to fill the screen, and this causes severe discomfort among some television persons.

WBN decides to recap the news.

—President-General Paolini is expected to issue a statement in response to the growing war rumors.

—more rumors and already protests from both Otherworld and Compact governments.

—no more details available on the mysterious death of former Secretary of Projections Aubry Cummings. The probable suicide—

No.

You don't sit where you were in my life for all of those years and then just leave, you miserable old bastard! Get—

—I race through the channels—

—unexplained death of Aub—oviet Union's protests are completely unfoun—don't think this is any sign of remorse or—dent-General's assurances that the Steel Palace, not the Department of Projections, that runs the Com—no sequence has been initiated, and no such sequence will be initiated—

I watch it on the news. It comes from Emilio Palini's own mouth. "There will be no war today."

Four different channels:

—No war today

—No war today.

—No war today.

And what of the future of the human race?

"There must be another way. There simply has to be another way. We must find it."

It's the comedy of the century!

Another way? Another way?

I don't believe how limited my vocabulary is. I mean, what words can I hurl at Emilio Paolini when I have already used up my assholes, motherfuckers, and meganerds?

I can't believe it, won't believe it.

I must calm down. Cummings wrote, and I know, that what serves the program exists. It doesn't matter how things appear. Things that appear *against* the program serve it—

I can't see how, unless there is some way for MAC to trigger the sequence by itself. But I've seen the reports on the isolation project. MAC has been isolated. There is no way to initiate the Kay Board sequence without—

Cummings wrote it again and again: no one person is indispensible. Or was it no one person's wishes could influence—

No.

I just don't know what's happening.

The Wardate has passed.

There are 118 hours left until there is no future for the human race.

Cummings.

How could he have killed himself?

Why, unless he knows.

But how *can* he know?

Or, look at me. How is it that a mentally doubtful, ex-killer, ex-outcaster is in a position to pull those triggers? How is it unless MAC stacked the deck?

But I *didn't* pull them! And I don't go back on manning for another forty-eight hours.

If we are all wired and rigged, what about the others on manning? Teresa Aminez once talked about coming from some hole in the New Jersey SD. As far as I know none of the others on manning were outcasters, special unit killers, or anything like it. But neither do they know anything about my past.

That's it.

It's so simple.

One of the manning Links, or someone else on manning, will yank the triggers before the time runs out.

We are all wired.

We are parts of the machine.

But it's all wrong. It just doesn't seem efficient. Human doubts, failings, scruples, a million things could foul it up. It would make a lot more sense for MAC to have reserved a way to initiate the sequence itself.

Unless—

Unless it serves the program for a human, rather than a machine, to do what needs to be done.

Unless it is necessary for the blood to be on human hands.

The terminal in my apartment cannot make contact with MAC. I try several times to activate the terminal's Link. I've been cut off. "Tell me, you piece of junk."

Tell me!

"Tell me what to do!"

Wardate: 00:00-00---0000
Downlimit: ----111:09:26

4

On the street there is a drizzle. The walkways are gleaming with moisture. The few persons on the street hide their necks and heads deep inside hoods, scarfs, and collars.

Walk. I walk until I am too tired to walk. I look for the subtrans but get on a surface fan. A bus.

I ride until I fall asleep. I sleep until a rough voice rips me from my sleep. "This is where you get off, fella. If you want to ride back, you have to buy another ticket."

I climb down off the bus and look around, the taste in my mouth something prehistoric. The place looks familiar, but—

Ossining.

I'm at the trans station in Ossining.

There was where the bus to Outcasters was parked. I climb the ramp and enter the station, almost expecting to see a familiar face. There are a few men, women, and children waiting for their runs. Everyone watches the terminal's huge screen.

There is no reason to listen. No one has said anything new since last night. But the viewers continue to view while handsome men and women continue rehashing old releases and polishing nuances, attempting to flog a ten pound story out of a two pound event, and all without giving a single line to the real story.

Flash: MAC is is not going to push the button. Unless someone takes up the slack, that is the end of everyone's story.

I sit on one of the benches in the station and rest back

against the warm metal. Those are the signs we use to tell us that things are getting better.

In the winter we are warmer.

In the summer we are cooler.

Progress.

There is a booth in the station renting personal transportation. I rent a new Ellis fan and fly down the roads of my memories. Past these neat little apartment houses and homes, past these manicured fields and well-trimmed forests, I will find the home of my ghosts.

It comes into sight and the limits of my universe shrink to fit the fence surrounding Compact Farm No. 128.

Outcasters.

I am back.

Wardate: 00:00-00---0000
Downlimit: ----106:00:02

3

Much of the barbed wire is gone, rusted away. Most of the security lights seem to be broken or missing. The gate is wide open and the guard shack deserted.

I walk through the gate and look up at the gray building. It is smaller than I remember. I see four windows that are broken. The lawn that I picked clean and trimmed so many times is mostly dead, full of weeds and spotted with litter.

Up the concrete stairs to the front doors. I pull one of the doors open and enter the big hall. Dark, musty smelling. The floor hasn't seen wax in a long time. Bags of fertilizer, chemicals, and feed are stacked against the west wall—the place where I blew the face off the fat fart.

The place is a mess, and it makes me angry. It is a silly anger, but it is there all the same. To spend your youth waxing a floor, then to see it like this—

"Hello?"

I turn at the sound of the voice. A woman wearing civilian clothes—old denims and a faded orange shirt—emerges from the old warden's office. I have to sort through a million faces, but finally hers registers. It was the civilian outfit that fooled me. That, and her face looks much older than I remember.

I swallow, my throat very dry. "Citizen Sayther?"

She nods. "Yes?"

All I can do is look at her. She studies me for a long time. "Tommy? Is it Tommy?"

"Yes." I can feel the tears welling in my eyes. What in the hell am I doing here? What—

Her face breaks into a broad grin as she rushes across the floor and puts her arms around me. She hugs me.

She hugs me.

I hug her back. She smells like lilac and cowshit. Her hand presses my head against her neck and she rocks me almost as though I am a baby. I cry so hard I am almost screaming.

This is madness.

This is absurd.

This is—

"Has it been so very hard for you out there, Tommy?"

I can't risk opening my mouth. God only knows what kind of foolishness would pour out of it. I nod. Finally I whisper, "Yes. Yes."

She leads me into the old rec room. Her quarters are there now. It looks very comfortable. She leads me to an overstuffed chair and pats my shoulder as I sit down. "I'll put some water on for tea."

There is music playing. Voices. Ancient Dixieland jazz. "*—You'll be fine after the brain treatment.*" I look toward the back of the room and find an old television set. There is a movie on, Woody Allen's *Sleeper*. I laugh. There is nothing else to do. Next to the television set there is a wall of shelves holding hundreds of video discs. Hundreds of movies.

I get up and walk over to the shelf. I never knew that Citizen Sayther could do human things like watch movies, or give out hugs. Look at all the movies.

The Day the Earth Stood Still, The Dirty Dozen, Dr. Strangelove, Dracula—

"Tommy, you were quite a movie buff, weren't you?"

"Yes. This is quite a collection."

"Do you remember Billy Haskins?"

A great emptiness opens in my center. The edges of it—sick to my stomach—sick to my heart—ashamed, and I miss him. "Yes. I remember him."

"This was his collection. He let me keep it for him when he was transferred to the Forces. He's dead, you know."

"Dead?"

"He was killed during that border incident with China a couple of years ago."

Ah, yes. The Thomas Windom kills Spring Garden affair. Spring Garden and how many others? Citizen Sayther's first name turns out to be Rose. We watch movies and talk late into the afternoon, Rose and I.

She tells me about the ones she knows about. Haskins, of course, is dead. A hero. Billy Haskins commanded the platoon that held its position, grinding the Chinese attack to a halt. When it was relieved, the platoon had only eleven left alive, all of them wounded. Billy Haskins didn't survive his wounds.

Once he recovered physically, Citizen Wing took a partial disability and retired from the Force. He then spent the next year suicidally depressed. After a succession of hospitals, he entered a treatment program for compulsive sex disorders. Upon completion of treatment he entered an anonymous program, took training in the treatment of child abusers, and became a counselor in the Teaneck Center, Teaneck, New Jersey SD. He received the Margaret Steenan Award for community service shortly before his fatal heart attack in 2028. At no time did he ever report the name of the escaped outcaster who had mutilated him. Wing: another hero.

Rose smiles at me. "And I've just been here, managing the farm. I have a degree in agriculture now."

"Really?"

"I went back to college and did it. I'm all farmer now. All the labor here is hired. No more convicts." Her eyebrows go up. "Do you remember Godfrey?"

"Yes."

"He works here now."

It seems that Godfrey stumbled back to 128 four years ago. He couldn't hold down a job, didn't know what he wanted, didn't know where to park it until he did know. Then Rose offered him a job.

No, I don't want to wait for him, thank you. And, no, I don't hear anything from Manuel, Francis, or the others.

I kiss her and say good-bye.

Wardate: 00:00-00---0000
Downlimit: -----94:04:27

2

I don't get into the Ellis. Instead I walk. I walk the fields and paths of Outcasters. Except that it's not Outcasters, nor Farm 128. Now it is just a farm.

When I at last look up I find myself facing the Green Machine. However, it is only green in patches now. MAC released power for consumption long ago. Now there are electric chippers and grinders to do the work. The Green Machine, clad in its rust, weeds, and dead leaves, squats next to the road, a monument to the past.

I look into the hopper. The blades look rusty, too. In there where I tossed the little black dog. In there where I tossed the pieces of Citizen Bond.

What was that little jingle we used to sing before Helen put a stop to it. A piece of it—

—Seven bits of Bond
Six lumps of Lathrup
Five motes of McIntyre—

—something like that. On the first day of Christmas my true love gave to me—

I look down at the spoked wheel set into the concrete. I can still see the circular path worn into the concrete beneath the wheel. How many feet had walked how far to carve that path?

I step down to the wheel and place my hands on one of the spokes. I push, then push harder. The wheel is frozen. I pull back, push forward, back and forth. Sliders free, old grease spreads to pitted bearings, half a turn, back, then the wheel makes a complete circuit.

Another, the speed picking up, the heavy flywheel beneath the concrete beginning to carry the load, the whine from the rusty blades rising in pitch. Around, around, seeing those other hands, those other faces.

Faster, faster—

It's whining, it's roaring,
The blackshit is snoring,
He went to bed, we cut off his head,
Now he won't get us in the morning.

The hands, the faces, I'm running, I trip—

—down I go, my hands gripping the spoke, the spoke dragging me around on my knees.

The circle slows and stops.

I get up and look at my torn trousers and bloody knees.

There is nothing for me here.

Nothing for me here.

Wardate: 00:00-00---0000
Downlimit: -----70:38:13

1

The seconds slowly eat away the time.

Maureen Rosner takes over the Kay Board, and my watch stands down. The triggers are still extended, but two armed guards are posted at the station. There is an open line to the Steel Palace, waiting on orders from the President-General.

Up or down, Emilio? Which is it going to be? According to the population projection boards, your indecision has already cost half a billion lives.

Maureen Rosner has brought a book with her. To read. So she won't get bored.

In the manning watch's recreation room, the off shift is killing time. We watch the Bad Movie Festival on the television. The on shift saw *The Attack of the Killer Tomatoes* and *Plan 9 From Outer Space*. They got to see the beginning of *The Greatest Story Ever Told*. We came in and picked up the story as the crucified Max Von Sydow expired and Rooster Cogburn dressed in Roman armor says, "Truly this man was the son of God."

During the break after *Greatest Story* the garishly dressed host, Captain Universe, makes several jokes about John Wayne as a Roman soldier. "Crucify him, pilgrim," and so on.

A recent addition to the bad movie lists is *Soylent Green*, a fifty-year-old overpopulation scare film where the government's solution is to encourage suicide and to process the human dead into crackers. "Maybe we are all going crackers," says Captain Universe.

"In a little under three days, that's going to be as good an answer as any we have." The speaker is Veronica Tillis, Dee Board monitor. She's a skinny girl with long straight hair.

Mark Lawton, program monitor, is frowning and staring at the far wall. "MAC's made some provision," he says.

A little under three days. I look at the Downlimit monitor. Fifty-one hours, twelve minutes, and some-odd seconds until there will be no point to anything.

Of course, that's if you believe MAC and Aubry Cummings. If you believe, instead, the rest of the human race, we'll find an answer somehow.

Somehow.

Somewhere.

Somewhen.

I always wonder why, when Max Von Sydow is nailed up on that cross, I wonder why he does the forgive them Father bit. For they know not what they do?

Why doesn't he look down and say something rational, like, "One of these days I'm going to get you assholes."

I don't know anything about these others on my crew. But I must accept that MAC put them here the same as it did me.

After a little talk, a little sitting around, a little eating, the rest of the crew wanders off to the bunk rooms. There is just me. Me and the television. I kick around the channels—

"*—What is coming for all of us?*"

"*Wars, death, and destruction. Blood and fire more terrible than has ever been seen by living man,*" responds the captured Moorish king to El Cid.

Alone, I settle in to watch again the story of Rodrigo, the Spanish knight who made a nation of his country and made a king out of his ruler. He had everything. However, for the sake of a little honor, a little mercy, and in recognition of the fact that murdering Moors didn't seem to be improving things, he was charged with treason.

Before I see him again fight his future wife's father, I remember when El Cid forced the new king to swear to his innocence regarding the death of his brother, King Sancho. For that El Cid was exiled.

Yet, when the crown again needed him, the Cid returned. Again to serve, again to earn the displeasure of his monarch.

El Cid, what do you serve? What gives you your courage? What gives you your strength? Your sense of mission? When you know you are dying, what drives you to order your body tied to a horse so that you might ride next to your King in the coming battle? I mean the king did nothing but shit on you! The country fed off your scarred carcass until there was nothing left of you but a legend. Is that what you wanted? To be remembered in a legend?

But you can see it in his face. All of his conflicts are outside of him. Inside he knows where right is. He knows where he is and why. He has no doubts. He has a strength that is—

At least Charlton Heston plays it as though he—El Cid—has this strength. In the movie.

It is a movie.

Hollywood bullshit.

Is that what it all is? Honor, truth, justice, courage, right? Bullshit? Eyeball candy?

How can it be nothing and—

"*—Let me now offer myself before the highest judge. If I am guilty, God will direct Don Martin's lance to my heart. If I am innocent, let Him be my shield.*"

Two kings claim a single city, and one challenges the other. Their champions will fight to the death, and the victor's king will rule the disputed city.

Rodrigo, still accused of treason, has slain King Ferdinand's champion. To clear his name, El Cid begs to be allowed to fill the place of Ferdinand's champion.

I put questions aside as Ferdinand orders El Cid to take up the gauntlet. "*And may God give you strength.*"

On his knee Rodrigo answers, "*May God give me strength.*"

I change the channel to WBS and find a movie in progress. I push the control and the title *The Tower Option* appears on the screen. I'm not familiar with it, but it looks like a recent release.

I put up my feet and attempt to zone out.

"*Madam Vice-President?*"

She opens her eyes and turns to face the entrance from the main hallway of the White House. A face peers out from behind one of the glossy wooden doors. "*Doctor Cummings is here.*"

I sit up and pay attention.

She nods and the face disappears. From the look on Katherine Tower's face, she is frightened.

She forces the feeling from her as the White House staff person opens the doors, revealing a tall middle-aged man wearing an unpressed gray tweed suit, a dark orange sweater beneath his coat, and an open shirt collar. He stands hunched over, his hands in his trouser pockets. On either side of him stands a large soldier in immaculate green uniform.

Cummings looks around the room at the ornate pressed velvet pattern of the deep scarlet wallpaper. His face has an expression of vaguely detached academic disgust. Vice-President Tower steps toward the door and holds out her hand.

"*I'm glad you're here, Doctor Cummings.*"

"*Yes?*" He pulls his right hand out of its pocket and points with his thumb over his right shoulder at the soldiers. "*Do I get to keep the jarheads or do you want them back?*"

"*Thank you,*" she says to the soldiers. "*That will be all.*"

The soldiers leave, the doors close, and Katherine Tower holds her hand out toward a chair. Cummings stands in the center of the room, his hands in his pockets. The actor playing Cummings is Robert Dell, and his impression of the old man is very good.

"*Why have I been dragged here?*"

Tower walks around an antique love seat and comes to a halt facing him, her right hand held out. "*Good morning, Doctor Cummings.*"

He hesitates a moment, assesses the expression on the Vice-President's face, and gives her extended hand a tepid shake. "*If you insist.*"

She releases his hand. "*You don't at all intend to make this easy, do you?*"

"*Mrs. Tower, in the midst of vital work you had me dragged bodily from my laboratory by a squad of armed grunts, and you expect amenities?*"

"*I would hardly call two men a squad, and they weren't armed. As to why, three times in as many days I have requested your presence here. Three times you saw fit to ignore my request.*"

Cummings frowns and looks at the red carpeting. "*My work simply couldn't be interrupted.*" He looks up at her. "*A matter, incidentally, that has not changed. To repeat, why am I here?*"

"*Sam Lowell was right, Cummings. You are a crusty old piece of shit.*" As I laugh, she turns and goes to a window.

There is an uncomfortably long silence until Cummings walks over and stands to her left, his gaze resting upon a distant line of demonstrators. "*What do you want?*"

She remains silent.

"*Mrs. Tower, I spend so much of my time in my own company and in the company of machines, I often forget how to behave. I apologize.*"

"*I accept your apology, Doctor. To be perfectly honest I'm not certain why you are here. I know that after Bill Russell talked to me four days ago, I felt compelled to see you, to talk to you.*" She unfolds her arms. "*I can't think of any other way to explain it. Please come with me. I want to show you something.*"

She turns and walks to the door to the right of the window. When she opens it she ushers Cummings into the ornate grandeur of the State Dining Room. She stands before the long table and nods toward the display of gold flatware, crystal, gold-rimmed plates. Voluptuous displays of orchids and carnations decorate three evenly spaced places on a line bisecting the table. "*It's for the Danish royal couple. This evening will probably be Bill Russell's last public function. As you know his health is rapidly failing. He's in bed right now resting up for the event.*"

She nods toward the head of the table. "*And after they have finished toasting eternal peace and friendship, Bill will talk of the Garden of Eden the United States and the rest of the world's nations will someday make of this planet. And he will be lying through his teeth.*"

"No." Cummings shakes his head. "*He will be telling the truth.*"

"*Not all of the truth, Doctor.*" Her voice lowers to a hiss. "*He won't be telling them the price of that garden.*"

"*Mrs. Tower, what was it that you wanted to show me?*"

She walks to a fireplace set between two large windows. As Cummings stops next to her she holds out her left hand and touches the raised gold lettering above the fireplace. "*This was written by the first president who lived in the White House. He wrote it the day after he moved in."* We move in to see the inscription:

I Pray Heaven to Bestow
The Best of Blessings on
THIS HOUSE
and on All that shall hereafter
Inhabit it. May none but Honest Nov. 2, 1800
and Wise Men ever rule under This Roof! John Adams

"The first time I ever saw this was almost forty years ago. It was on a tour. I was nine years old." Her fingers caress the letters. *"I saw this last line as the qualifications for the job of President of the United States. I was already honest. The women's movement took the gender out of the word 'Men.' I had to earn what wisdom I have."* Her hand drops to her side.

"As things now stand I will eventually preside over the virtual end of this government and of this nation, making possible the deaths of four to five billion human beings."

She cocks her head toward the fireplace. *"How are the history books going to record my fulfillment of this charge?"*

"The end we're talking about is the continued existence of human civilization. There is only one course of action open to us if we want to preserve it. Either we do it or we don't; either there will be a future or there won't. That's the choice."

"Could you be wrong, Doctor? Could there be some flaw in this plan of yours? Is it possible that we don't have to pay that grotesque price? Or if we do pay it, is it possible that what you want won't transpire?"

Cummings stares at her for a long moment. *"It is not my plan, Mrs. Tower. I am responsible for establishing the discipline and assembling the technology to detect and resolve a certain kind of problem. MAC-I asks for the information it needs and makes its own recommendations for action. That's whose plan it is. As to possible flaws in the plan, at this moment MAC-I is engaged in the process of designing its own replacement. The machine is already past any human's ability to judge whether or not it is flawed."*

He looks at the inscription above the fireplace. "*As to the history books, in a few short years you will be heralded as the greatest visionary ever to occupy the White House. Some time after that you will be looked upon as either this nation's biggest traitor or history's biggest fool. By then mothers will be using my name to frighten their children. After the conclusion of the process . . .*" He shrugs. "*I don't now how we will look. It's not important.*"

"*The war. When?*"

"*It hasn't changed since the most recent commission report. The Seventh of August, 2033.*"

"*Over forty years from now.*"

Cummings nods. "*There is an excellent chance that both of us will be dead by then.*"

A door opens. A staff person and two Secret Service agents stand in the doorway. She looks in their direction.

"*Excuse me, Madam Vice-President. The President asks that you come to the family quarters. Immediately. His physician—*" he continues in a hoarse half-whisper, "*his physician says that the President doesn't have long.*"

"*Thank you. I'll be right there.*" She faces Cummings. "*I guess why I really asked you here, Doctor, was for the answer to a question.*"

"*I'll answer it if I can.*"

"*How do you sleep nights?*"

He smiles. "*In a bed, Mrs. Tower. In a bed.*"

I just bet you sleep nights in a bed. Is that why you pulled your own plug, Aubry? Because your conscience was clean and serene?

I change the channel back to *El Cid*. Rodrigo is deep in battle with the enemy king's champion. The fight melds into my dreams.

How do you sleep nights?

In a bed, Mrs. Tower. In a bed.

Bullshit. Hollywood. Bullshit.

Rodrigo wins the combat. The city of Calahorra goes to Ferdinand. Ferdinand makes El Cid his new champion.

—But I am again on that mountaintop, that ocean of humans surrounding me.

I am serving in the place of the fallen champion, Aubry Cummings. And I, too, am responsible for killing the champion. Who has more right to take his place?

What now, though? If I win this contest, you will have Earth. If I lose, Earth will have none of you. But to win Earth for you, half of you must die.

May God give me strength.

In this dream that arm again steals around my shoulders. From it I draw strength, comfort, even love.

—hand shaking my shoulder.

Aminez. "Our turn."

"What?"

"It's our shift's turn on manning."

"Thanks." I sit up and rub my eyes. I am suddenly frightened. In panic I ask, and the feeling of this arm around my shoulders again comes.

On the television there is another endless debate about the war. The tone of the debate suggests that no one thinks it's really going to happen. And I know why they think that. What man could order half of the human race to death? Absurd.

I nod. You bet. Absurd.

I get up, and the interviewer, a man, speaks. "Still, remember what U.S. Senator Lowell is supposed to have said: 'I wonder how many of them out there suspect that the human race is probably going to fuck itself to death.'"

They laugh as I enter the hall toward operations. As I pass The Shrine to Why's endless stacks of cabinets, it suddenly dawns on me why the Lowell Center is named the Lowell Center. With the exception of Aubry Cummings, Samuel Lowell is the person most responsible for the implementation of the MAC system and the subsequent formation of the Compact of Nations.

The Lowell Center. When I get back to my post I'll look him up and give him a call. I think he's dead though.

Wardate: 00:00-00---0000
Downlimit: -----68:19:08

0

"President-General Paolini has ordered the Kay Board deactivated." Donegal is grinning so he looks like a refugee from some cartoon. He raises his eyebrows at me as though he expects me to argue with him or to protest the PeeGee's order. There's no point to either, so I do neither.

This watch is two hours old.

I am standing before the Kay Board.

I glance once at the armed guards and smile inwardly.

I am the only person on Earth who knows that he cannot die right now.

Perhaps I will be needed for the investigation.

There has to be an investigation, see? Every side of every reason for why I did what I did must be gone over to the point of exhaustion. There are only two things the human race must know: what I did was necessary. That, and a human—not a machine—did it.

How has MAC protected me for this moment? It takes only one person to pull the triggers. MAC designed that.

But what will keep me alive?

Maybe the blackshit guards are slow; maybe they just can't shoot worth a damn; maybe—

—well, it's time.

It's time.

It's time—

I reach out my hands, grab the twin triggers, and hold them down for the required 1.33 seconds.

I release the triggers and sit down, my hands folded in my lap.

Look at them.

Look at them all staring at me.

—the reports begin coming in: Ivan kills Vladimir, Igor kills Ivan—

They can't believe their eyes. The two guards are looking at each other, mouths open wide. I wonder which is the bigger horror for them: that four billion humans are now dead or dying, or that they are going to get yelled at for not stopping it. Sure, saving four billion lives is important, but you gotta cover your ass first.

The population table boards show something I hadn't figured on. It's so obvious, too.

Harry is also killing Tom, and Dick is killing Harry. Manny, Mo, and Jack, Frick and Frack.

The dying is taking place all over the world.

It makes sense.

The whole world has its population thinned, not just the Otherworld nations. Did I think the peoples of the Compact should be spared simply because we were put through hell to do the right thing?

After all, it would only be fair.

Am I one of those Seekers of Justice?

Silly boy.

This is the job that needed doing, and now it is done. And there is no world holocaust.

There're a few little wars heating up, ten or twelve revolutions kicking off, some floods, storms, an increase in the starvation rate, traffic accidents, disease, murder, suicide, carelessness.

Multiplied.

Most individuals probably won't notice that anything is happening, except that parking spaces will be easier to get.

Simple, really.

No war is necessary. Just increase the rate at which men, women, and children kill off each other and themselves. In the end, you still have your four and a half billion dead.

But I know them.

I know the names and the faces of every one of them.

Now it is done—

There is a place I must put myself.

"Monster! You fucking monster!"

It starts.

Something slams into the back of my head, I feel my face hitting the floor—strange taste in my mouth. There was that blackshit—McDermit—holding me by the hair, slapping me. That same taste in my mouth. A thousand years ago.

"Why? In God's name, why?"

That must be Donegal. How can I answer his question? Should I tell him: "It's a dirty job but some—"

—A knee in my back. Can't breathe. Foot kicking my head.

—Wouldn't it be a joke if none of this is happening? What if this is all a great computer run, all of us nothing but generated images undergoing generated situations? The Maker just wants to see what would happen if—

—a place I must put myself.

—the redbird looks to the wall of monsters on his right. They stink and growl and drip horrible slime.

"Who are you?" I ask.

"We are the future," answer the monsters. "We are all of the terrible things that you will do and that will happen to you. We are injustice, cruelty, pain, old age, disease, revenge, death, and worry. You cannot escape us if you walk here."

I look to the wall of monsters on my left. They also stink and growl and drip horrible slime.

"And who are you?" I ask.

"We are the past," answer the monsters. "We are all of the terrible things that you have done and that have happened to you. We are injustice, cruelty, pain, youth, disease, resentment, birth, and guilt. You cannot escape us if you walk here."

Between the walls of monsters is the road called Now. The road is clean, straight, and bare, but very, very narrow. I know that anything good or bad that I find on this road I will have to put there myself. I walk there, on the Now Road, and although they call me many times, neither the monsters of the past nor the monsters of the future can touch me.

This arm again steals about my shoulders.

I see a face.

Peace.

WINDOM, THOMAS
RUN COMPLETED
WARDATE: 00:00-00---0000
DOWNLIMIT: -------:--:--
---READY
---READY
---READY
---READY
---READY
---READY
---READY
---READY
---READY
---READY
---READY
---READY
---READY
---READY
---READY
---READY
---READY
---READY
---READY---------------------------------